THORAX

A Novel

THORAX

A Novel

Mark Katlic

atmosphere press

Published by Atmosphere Press

Cover design by Ronaldo Alves

Atmospherepress.com

For Katya

PROLOGUE

"God help her," said the nurse, crossing herself.

The girl, not yet four years old, lay on a simple wooden bed in the corner. Small for her age, she seemed dwarfed even by the narrow bunk, its rough planks rising above the mattress like the sides of a child's wagon. She had kicked off the layers of wool blankets in her fevered thrashing and now lay on her back, breathing rapidly. She was wearing a thin white gown which was bunched above her knees. She heard the click of the door as it closed and turned to face the nurse.

The nurse suppressed a gasp.

The child's skin was a deep red color, thick and smooth, her fingers like sausages about to split. Strands of hair clung in bas relief to the plum-colored face. Her lips were blistered and held apart as if it were painful for them to touch. A drop of thick, dark blood filled one nostril.

But it was the look of the eyes that held the nurse. *Oh*, she thought, *not the eyes.*

The child's eyes were solid, bottomless black.

"We must keep her in isolation," the Doctor had said two days earlier when the rash began. "Take her to my lake house and stay with her."

He had given directions and a key to Vasily, and somehow,

they had managed to tuck the girl into the back seat of the orphanage car—an old but well-maintained Jeep-like UAZ—and drive the hour to the eminent Doctor's property on the lake. Just south of the Arctic Circle in Russia, the roads were as frozen as the lake, but Vasily drove confidently, and the two nurses sat in back with the girl, mopping her forehead and offering sips of tea. They sailed through a sea of pine, the headlights casting pinpoint stars before them in the light crystalline snowfall. The day lightened some as they approached the lake, but since it was November, the sun would not rise yet for months.

The Doctor's dacha was isolated and they became lost, but eventually found the turn-off. Overhanging branches made a tunnel of the narrow lane, the virgin snow crunching beneath treaded tires. After several kilometers, they emerged near the big house itself.

Only a wealthy man could own this property, the nurse thought. The main house stood before them, facing the lake. Constructed of thick wooden beams, it was as imposing and elegant as the Doctor himself; it might once have been a nobleman's hunting lodge. The peaked roofs above the two floors and the decorative woodwork along the eaves took the nurse back to her schoolgirl days and folktales told by the kitchen fire. Immediately behind the house, the dark forest began, only willing to grant civilization a certain foothold.

The lane on which they drove passed to the right of the house as it faced the lake. They did not turn left into the courtyard at the back of the main residence but continued down along the edge of a field or lawn. The lawn sloped all the way to the lake itself, one hundred meters in front of them in its frozen whiteness, only distinguished from the land by lack of vegetation and by the lake house and dock on its shore.

The lake house emulated its larger neighbor up the hill but was much smaller, perhaps ten meters on each side. Its two stories were capped by a single peaked roof, and there was a narrow balcony on the lake side of the second floor. The wooden dock extended fifteen meters into the ice of the lake. In the failing light, only the unending pine forest was visible on the other shore three kilometers in the distance. A sudden wind from the lake filled the air with powdery snow as if a giant hand had turned a child's globe.

Vasily pushed on his fur cap and unlocked the garage door in front of them. The sound of the door being pulled aside woke the girl. The red spots, originally on her arms and face, had seemed to enlarge and move toward her neck and trunk. She was apprehensive. The nurse wrapped the girl in blankets and carried her into the garage, past the small raised boat, and up the wooden stairs next to a sauna room. As she entered the main room on the second floor, Vasily stepped from a doorway and motioned her forward. The main room contained two daybeds, a table and four chairs, a fireplace, and a small kitchen area. Two closed doors likely led to the water closet and the separate bath. Vasily stood in the lone bedroom, and he helped lower the girl onto the bunk in the corner. Out the window and the thin door were the balcony, the lake, and the distant shore.

After Vasily unloaded the food and bedding, he started the UAZ for the drive back to the orphanage. The nurses watched the car drive past the big house and enter the single opening in the forest, a fly engulfed by the imposing pines.

The next day the girl had been worse. The red spots had begun to merge, and her skin had taken on a puffy appearance, especially her face. Vermillion spots had also appeared in the whites of her eyes and it became difficult for the nurses to meet her worried gaze. Surprisingly, she still had an appetite and was able to eat some kasha and later some stew. The nurses had been inoculated by the Doctor months before but nevertheless wore masks and rubber gloves and vigorously washed anything that came in contact with the girl. They had seen disease, but never one so rapidly progressive, so blatantly visible in its virulence.

The two nurses worked in shifts, napping on the daybeds but seeming to get no rest. *Why had this happened to this girl?* A favorite at the orphanage since her addicted birthmother had given her up, she was due to be adopted by an American couple. Her eyes shone when she asked about "Momma" and "Poppa" who would be coming to get her.

The Doctor had gone to extra lengths with her to prevent infection, but something had happened, and here she was. He said there was no special medicine for this, no cure; she would either be strong enough or she would not. So far, she was not. And the worst of it was, in between periods of sweaty, fitful sleep, she was conscious and lucid, crying in pain as anything, even her light gown, touched her reddening skin.

That afternoon the whites of her eyes became as red as rubies, then swelled out around the central corneas as if ready to burst. The air in the room took on a foul, slightly sweet odor. She urinated blood.

Now she stared at the nurse with eyes black as ebony, an inhuman, snakelike black. A red tear slipped down one magenta cheek as she held out her arms for the nurse. With a mixture of revulsion and compassion, the nurse held her, carefully, for the skin felt loose enough to slide off the tiny bones.

A call to the Doctor indicated they were doing all that they could do.

"God sometimes seems capricious, but we must accept His plan," he said.

*

Later that day heavy snow blanketed the roof, the balcony, and the dock. It should have given a fairy tale appearance to the big house up the hill, but somehow to the nurse, the structure seemed imposing and threatening, as if it had something to do with the girl's suffering. Impossible, of course. The great Doctor had likely written one of his books in an upstairs study there, perhaps looking out one of those large front windows at some passing line of birds as he worked to improve surgical care.

She heard the other nurse call out and she ran back to the bedroom. Between the child's legs, the sheets were full of blood.

"From the rectum," her colleague said.

The little girl's respiration was shallow and rapid now, interspersed with occasional deep, sigh-like breaths. At least the eyes were closed, the terror they both manifested and evoked hidden. She seemed, finally, to be over the suffering. She would die this day.

And what suffering, thought the nurse. She turned toward the window and wept.

CHAPTER 1

"May I begin?" Nick asked the nurse anesthetist.

"Yes, Doctor." She looked over the sheet that isolated the head side of the operating table, the anesthesia machine and its colorful monitor on her right, surprised at his courtesy. Usually the young bucks, fresh from their surgical residency training, showed more swagger, full of juice. Perhaps Dr. Nicholas Turner was going to be different. "Thank you."

The patient, a twenty-three-year-old woman named Sarah Burley, lay left side up on the operating table, only her shoulder blade and ribs visible through a gap in the green drapes, her skin orange from the Betadine prep. She was not the patient Nick would have chosen as one of his first in private practice. She was young and healthy, a good operative risk, but this also meant that he could only make her worse if he did something wrong. Also, her father was a hospital board member, Harrison Burley—"Bull" Burley to those who watched him run the football at Glaston High in the sixties. He was still formidable now, in the first month of 2003, a big man accustomed to both accomplishment and attention.

True, Nick had not given her the two-inch mass that now rested near those important structures in her chest, structures such as the descending aorta. The mass had been found on x-rays taken during a recent ER visit for what proved to be a small but painful ovarian cyst. Confirmed by a CT scan, the mass now needed to be removed, chiefly to know what it was.

Removed without bleeding from the aorta, thought Nick, a vessel twice the diameter of her father's ubiquitous cigar.

"Knife, please," Nick said, and Gloria the scrub tech passed him a #15 scalpel. He made a three-quarter-inch cut several inches inferior to the tip of the scapula, the shoulder blade, and then used a curved clamp to spread the intercostal muscle fibers and pop through the parietal pleura into the chest cavity. He inserted an index finger, then removed it and placed the trocar, a hollow tube through which instruments could be passed.

"Scope, please."

White light coursed through a fiberoptic cable to the ten-millimeter round end of the eighteen-inch metal tube. Gloria had already attached a two-inch digital movie camera to the round eyepiece at the back end of the thoracoscope, so Nick looked across the operating table at the eye-level video monitor as he passed the scope with his left hand through the trocar. Nick, focused on the TV monitor, found himself zooming down a smooth gray tunnel and falling into the chest cavity. The colors on the TV screen now were predominantly reds and pinks and white: the sponge-like pink lung, the red intercostal and diaphragm muscles, and the inner surface of white ribs surrounding the cavernous space. *Like the belly of the whale in Pinocchio*, thought Nick, *or a spelunker's dream.*

Nick made two additional half-inch incisions, one anterior near Sarah's left breast and one near the back of the scapula, and he passed long blunt instruments through these sites. He grasped Sarah's deflated lung with the broad ring ends of the clamp in his left hand and retracted it forward toward her breastbone. There it was!

"Great," he let out. The mass appeared to be a benign cyst, thin-walled and full of fluid. But it was right on the aorta and seemingly inseparable from this vessel. The tubular, pale aorta bulged in time with Sarah's heartbeat, sending oxygenated blood directly from the heart to the lower half of her body. "It's just a blood vessel," Nick heard a senior resident say once, "like a water moccasin is just a snake."

"Endoscopic scissor and grasper, please." Nick took the long, fine-grasping instrument with his left hand and slipped it next to the ring clamp into the chest cavity; with his right hand, he passed the scissors through the posterior cut. He grasped the pleura covering the cyst and made a delicate cut with the scissors, his eyes fixed on the image on the screen. A few millimeters too deep and he could nick the aorta.

The pleura was a thin, nearly transparent tissue that covered the entire inner surface of the chest cavity; it was shiny and smooth and could be carefully peeled away from the inner surface of the ribs or other structures. It was much like plastic sandwich wrap. Sarah's pleura peeled away nicely from the visible surface of the cystic mass as the aorta pulsed nearby.

"Beautiful," Gloria said softly. Unlike open surgery, thoracoscopy or video-assisted thoracic surgery allowed everyone in the room to see the surgeon's technique.

Now comes the scary part, Nick thought. He had to dissect the cyst away from the aorta and the ribs on which both the cyst and aorta lay. If he grasped the cyst or pushed too hard it would rupture, but he had to see under it. He pushed it gently with the grasper and began carefully spreading the deep tissues with the scissors, cutting small bands of fibrous tissue as he went.

Suddenly a narrow stream of bright blood shot from the region of the aorta and struck the lens of the scope. A second squirt cast a red blanket over the screen. Nick could see nothing now, and he knew that with every beat of Sarah's heart arterial blood was filling the chest.

"Holy heck!" he cried. What had he done to cause the bleeding? He hadn't been cutting on the aortic wall. Clearly, though, this was bright red pulsating blood under arterial pressure.

He could not prevent the next thought: *this patient could*

die. This vital, perfectly healthy woman, Bull Burley's little girl, could bleed out during elective surgery for a benign cyst. His own life, the career he had worked for since junior high school—the college weekends studying while others partied, the twenty-hour medical school days, the eight marathon years of general and cardiothoracic surgery—would also effectively die on this table. He pictured himself squeezing Sarah's flaccid heart after he opened her chest, cross-clamping the aorta in a futile attempt to keep her brain perfused as her EKG tracing became erratic, then flat.

Settle down, he told himself. He had been in bad situations before, had dealt with bleeding from the heart itself. In fact, during residency he had a reputation as being an "Ice Man," a doctor who remained calm and deliberate while others in the room sprang into flustered and sometimes ill-advised action. If a nurse accidentally dropped a metal basin to the tile operating room floor everyone else in the room would jump six inches; Nick would keep operating, never missing a tie. To be honest, his whole life he had been an Ice Man, rarely showing emotion good or bad. He could tell you the twelve cranial nerves before he could tell you a good joke.

So, go back to surgical basics: first get good exposure, and then decide what to do. Most bleeding could be stopped, at least temporarily, by some form of direct pressure. The aorta, especially a young woman's healthy aorta, would hold sutures well if it came to that. The chest could be opened, and the ribs spread if other measures failed, though Nick even dreaded the thought of giving his patient a large scar during an operation for what turned out to be a small cyst. In anyone's priority list, however, life came first.

He pulled the scope out through the hollow trocar and handed it to Gloria. "Clean this quickly. Yankauer sucker, please."

Gloria handed him the slightly curved plastic sucker, and Nick inserted it through the posterior incision, blindly directing the tip to the area within the chest where the blood would pool. He then passed the clean scope slowly into the chest cavity so as not to get it soiled again. Now he could see a thin pulsating stream of bright red blood near the aorta. He pressed the blunt tip of the sucker against the area and called for a second sucker.

"Irrigation," he said and squirted saline through the anterior cut before passing the second sucker to clear out the saline-thinned blood. Now he could see. He pulled back the first sucker and saw the bleeding site clearly: it was not the aorta but an intercostal artery running beneath a rib. True, it was very near the aortic wall—from which it arose—but it should be possible to control.

"Maryland," he said to Gloria, and then passed the long thin Maryland grasper, with its fine curved tip, into the chest cavity, grasping the bleeding vessel as he pulled back the sucker. The bleeding stopped.

"Large endoscopic clipper." Nick passed the open end of the titanium clip beneath his Maryland grasper and squeezed the handle, closing the clip tightly across the intercostal artery stump. The clipper automatically loaded another clip and Nick placed it across the other side of the transected vessel, even though it was not bleeding now; it could be in spasm and, although only the diameter of a string, could bleed later.

"Not many surgeons would have remained so calm, Doctor," said Gloria. She had been a scrub tech for twenty years.

"It's both a blessing and a curse," said Nick. "Good in the OR, bad at a cocktail party or sporting event."

He finished dissecting the cyst from the surrounding tissues, then passed an endoscopic bag into the pleural cavity and put the cyst through the open mouth of the plastic bag; he pulled a string, and the neck of the bag cinched closed like the opening of a small purse. He slipped the bag out through the anterior cut and sent the cyst to the Pathology Lab for microscopic examination, though he was certain that it was benign. He placed a drain the size of his little finger through the middle incision, then closed the three cuts with absorbable sutures beneath the skin. Clear plastic dressings completed the procedure.

The entire operation had been performed as a video game might have been, Nick watching a video monitor while his hands manipulated the long thin instruments. This required a different kind of hand-eye coordination from that of the great chest surgeons of the past, not better but different. Not every surgeon was as comfortable or as good at this new minimally-invasive surgery, though this was becoming the standard for many operations.

Nick pulled off his paper gown, then with a snapping sound shot his gloves into the red trash bag as a child would shoot a rubber band. He picked up Sarah's chart and went to speak with her barrel-chested father, thankful that he had good news. And a live patient. He pulled down his mask and turned as he left the operating room.

"Thank you, everyone," Nick said, and the door closed behind him.

"Cool as a fucking cucumber," said Gloria.

"And a gentleman, too," said the anesthetist.

As Nick approached the waiting room doorway, Harrison Burley and his wife sprang to meet him. Bull Burley was Nick's height, about six feet, but surpassed Nick's skinny 160 pounds by an additional one hundred. He wore a dark suit, a blue shirt with white collar, and a red tie with a repeating pattern of some tiny blue logo; the tie was loose, the top shirt button undone. The prom king's ruddy good looks had survived the added weight, years, and scotch-and-soda business meetings for the family trucking business he now led. His petite wife, Marilyn, had lacquered blond hair and soft curves. She stood a step behind her husband.

"Sarah is doing fine," Nick said. He always began with this reassurance before getting into the operative findings. This was what loved ones most wanted to know. "Almost certainly, the mass will prove to be a benign cyst. It—"

"What do you mean 'almost certainly'?" Burley said, stepping closer. "After all this, you don't know?"

"The mass was completely removed and appears to be a benign cyst of some sort. The final pathology report will take several days."

"It *appears* to be a cyst *of some sort,*" Burley spoke each word slowly as if controlling an emotion. "Why don't you know?"

"I could have asked the pathologist to do a frozen section while Sarah was asleep, but it would not have changed anything that I did," Nick said. "The cyst was completely removed intact, and there was no need to prolong the operation." *And add expense for nothing*, he thought.

"How did she get this cyst in her chest?" Burley asked. "She's been healthy as a horse her whole life."

"I suspect that she was born with it," Nick said.

"But she never complained about her chest," Mrs. Burley said. There was a hint of a Southern accent in her voice.

"It might never have caused a problem. It only became apparent when she had a CT scan."

"So if it wasn't a problem, why put her through this operation?" Burley asked.

Nick swallowed. "As I told Sarah before the operation, the mass looked like a cyst on the CT scan but only a biopsy could prove it. And even a benign cyst can grow, can get infected. She knew that another option was to follow the mass with repeat CT scans. She made it quite clear that she wanted it out."

Burley stared silently for a moment, and then said, "I want to be called as soon as the report is back. And I may want another opinion." He turned to his wife. "Let's go, Momma. We'll wait in the room."

They walked away, but not before Nick heard, "I told you we should have taken her to Philadelphia."

They had given him no chance to tell about the small blood loss, Sarah's stable vital signs, or the fact that he'd done the operation through tiny punctures that would leave scant visible scar. He would not have told them anyway of the anatomic knowledge, dexterity, intraoperative judgment, and equanimity under stress that the care of their daughter had required, for these were expected. Nick himself expected these, too, and did not even think about them. But the satisfaction he had felt as he left the OR, the sense of a job well done, had been smothered.

Philadelphia, he thought, *give me a break.* He went back to the Recovery Room to write his orders.

CHAPTER 2

Nick needed to run.

He had always loved running. Probably, it was because he was so poor at every other sport as a child. He had been thin his whole life, physically weaker than his classmates, and certainly not built for football or wrestling. His attempts to climb the rope or throw the medicine ball in physical education class had been met with snickers or outright derisive laughter. His shoulders were slender, his neck long, and his muscles defined by their string-like visibility. Oh, but he could run.

In times of self-reflection—more frequent since Lynn's death—Nick also knew that running was a solitary activity and he was, in the end, a lone wolf. At age thirty-five, he had only his daughter and a few friends, most of them medical colleagues. True, he had been a student most of his life to date, and his lifestyle as a surgeon did not allow much time for socializing, but Nick was honest enough to admit that it was probably more his nature. And being both brighter and more compulsive than one's classmates did not always lead to warm friendships.

Nick pulled running shoes from the bottom of his OR locker and slipped them on. One of his patients had canceled her operation today, waking with nasal congestion and fever. He would still have time for afternoon rounds and paperwork after a run.

Nick stepped out the side door of the Glaston Memorial

Hospital and pulled on a black cap and light gloves. Late January in Northeastern Pennsylvania was brisk, but the day was clear and there was no snow. He stretched the cap over his ears and jogged down the drive.

His father, James Turner, had already retired and was living in Rehoboth Beach, Delaware, when Nick was born. He had been Chief Financial Officer of a specialty steel business in Baltimore, and he always maintained the picky perfectionism of the accountant he once was. One of Nick's early memories was of his father at the kitchen table, drawing precise ruled lines on paper to be used for listing Nick's chores. He always read the morning paper at precisely eight a.m., had a bowl of soup at noon and a balanced meal at 5:30 p.m., watched the CBS Evening News, and went to bed after Johnny Carson's monologue. He had married late.

Nick's mother, Joyce, worked in Human Resources at the same Baltimore office. A widower twenty years James' junior, she dreamed of a nice home and children, though time seemed to be running out for both. James, though, was captivated by her natural beauty and by the attention she lavished. They were married three years before he retired.

Joyce finally became pregnant, and Nick was born at the Beebe Hospital in Lewes, Delaware. He had his mother's straight black hair and dark eyes and his father's asthenic build. He would be their only child.

Nick ran past the modest, well-maintained homes near the hospital, then left the sidewalk behind as he turned left toward the center of Glaston. He could see the tops of a few office buildings about two miles ahead, none taller than eight or ten stories. Glaston's population, like much of eastern Pennsylvania, was stable but aging. The young left for the cities to find work, and the old returned because it was a nice place to live. There was little crime—people left their cars unlocked, often with keys in the ignition—and little traffic. A safe place to raise a daughter.

Nick had gone to college here, at Glaston University. Once Glaston State Teacher's College, the institution had added enough graduate-level degree programs to be called a university; it was basically, however, a small liberal arts college with a student body of less than two thousand. Nick might have gone to an Ivy League school, he knew. He got nearly straight A's in high school, lettered in cross-country, and had received solid recommendations ("extremely hard-working, diligent to a fault;" "unimaginative but very intelligent;" "not a risk-taker, always produced excellent work on time"). But Glaston U had a good pre-med reputation and, well, it just felt right. Maybe that was also why he ended up accepting a job offer in Glaston later; after the maelstrom year of Lynn's illness and his Chief Residency in Cardiothoracic Surgery, a small town just felt right.

Nick ran past the campus now, just to the east of the town proper. He had spent so much time in the chemistry and biology buildings and the library that even now, thirteen years later, he could mentally draw their floor plans. He had spent no time at the athletic field, just behind the fence to his left, since he had given up his high-school track activities in order to concentrate on his studies. He had not been much of a sprinter or even a miler, anyway, excelling more at the endurance distances of cross-country.

He did remember the open-air commencement on the field and his mother waving proudly from the bleachers as he received his bachelor's degree with honors. He remembered her blue dress, the incongruous square sunglasses on that bright day in late May, and her tears. His father had missed this graduation, too, having suffered a fatal myocardial infarction early in Nick's senior year of high school. Nick turned left to cut through the campus. He would take a different route back to the hospital, completing a five-mile circle.

Students dotted the sidewalks, many wearing only hooded sweatshirts, oblivious to the chill. Some wore caps like Nick's, though all with more fashionable logos, such as those of skateboarding companies. Everyone carried a backpack as if about to depart soon for the Appalachian Trail some miles to the south. He turned around the old Administration Building and, for a moment, stopped breathing.

A girl sat on a bench in front of the building, laughing at something another girl had just said. She had long black hair, twinkling blue eyes, and lines that suggested she laughed a lot. She wore a light blue turtleneck sweater and black pants. For a moment, Nick had thought she was Lynn.

Nick had first seen Lynn at the beginning of his third year in medical school. She was an ICU nurse and, as such, knew more than any medical student about actually caring for patients. Nick had just begun his basic surgical rotation and was quite aware that his life-long *modus operandi*—eye-watering reading, memorizing, preparing—would only go so far in caring for real human bodies, especially truly sick ones in the ICU. This was a set-up for surprise and embarrassment, and Nick liked neither.

The Chief Resident in Surgery had asked Nick to go to the ICU and put both a nasogastric tube and a Foley catheter in a man who was vomiting and becoming dehydrated. Nick had never done either procedure, but he knew where the tubes were supposed to go—how hard could it be? It did not, after all, involve scalpels or large-bore needles.

He entered the ICU and asked the unit secretary where he

could find Mr. Williams.

"Bed 10," she said without looking up.

Mr. Williams sat upright in bed, beads of sweat on his forehead and chest, a blue emesis basin in his hands. He was a black man in his seventies with salt-and-pepper hair and mustache. The sheet was down to his umbilicus and the healing incision and skin staples in the upper abdomen indicated likely gastric or biliary surgery.

"Perforated peptic ulcer," said the nurse entering the room.

Nick turned, then stared. The nurse was striking, with long black hair and large blue eyes. She was smiling, and the skin near her eyes crinkled. "I'm Lynn," she said, extending her hand.

"Nick Turner," he mumbled.

She waited, still smiling.

"Dr. Whitman wants me to put an NG tube and Foley into Mr. Williams. He looks pretty sick," he added.

"I'll get you what you need," she said and left for the supply closet.

While she was gone, Nick explained to Mr. Williams what he wanted to do. "Anything that'll make me feel better than this is awright, Doc," Mr. Williams said.

When Lynn returned, Nick peeled open the package holding the nasogastric tube and pulled on disposable gloves. Inserted through the nose and down the back of the throat into the stomach, the tube would keep the stomach empty, helping to relieve nausea. He lubricated the tip of the tube with water-soluble jelly and pushed it at a forty-five-degree angle up the patient's right nostril. It would not pass.

Across the bed from him, Lynn said, "Sometimes one nostril is easier than the other."

But the left side seemed blocked also. Tears came to Mr. Williams' eyes as Nick pushed the tube. How could both sides be blocked?

"Do you mind if I give it a try?" Lynn took the tube and,

holding it perpendicular to Mr. William's face, slipped it through the nostril and into the back of the throat. She told the patient to swallow, and in seconds, the tube was draining greenish brown fluid into a plastic bottle on the floor. "Sometimes it's best to put it straight in." Her eyes were alight, but she did not laugh.

Nick had dissected cadavers two years before but could not recall why the nose was long and pointing down if the passage was short and straight back.

He now needed to catheterize the bladder so that urine output could be measured each hour. With even more trepidation, he put the Foley catheter supplies on the bed between Mr. William's legs. Here, he was about to expose a man's privates in front of a beautiful nurse. He looked at Lynn, then the patient. "Just go ahead, Doc," said Mr. Williams, "she's been bathin' me every day anyway."

Nick pulled down the sheet, opened the supplies, and then put on sterile 7½ size gloves. He grasped the uncircumcised penis as he would a tennis racket, swabbed the tip with Betadine and, pointing it down between the patient's legs, inserted the lubricated yellow tube. *Oh no*, he thought as he met resistance. The catheter bent inside the penis as he applied more pressure. Mr. Williams moaned softly.

"May I show you a trick?" Lynn asked from across the bed.

"Please," said both Nick and Mr. Williams.

Lynn put on 6½ gloves and, with her index finger and thumb, securely grasped the loose skin on top of the penis, just behind the glans. She held the penis perpendicular to Mr. William's body, swabbed the tip, and slid the tube all the way in. Dark yellow urine dripped out. She asked Nick to inject five milliliters of saline into the small port to fill the balloon at the catheter's tip, thereby holding it in.

"Sometimes it's best to put it straight in," she said but turned before he could see her broad smile.

*

They began dating, mostly due to her taking the lead. *Heck, if she had waited for him*, Nick thought, *it might have taken months, or years.* He just wasn't good around girls.

Yes, he had gone to his Senior Prom with Rose Stanton, but that had not worked out too well. While their classmates were dancing closely, heads together, he had been trying to think of things to say to Rose as they sat near the wall. She did not seem very interested in his Biology project on the horseshoe crab. He felt awkward even holding her hand.

Most of his dates in college were in groups or foursomes with his roommate, a much more outgoing Psychology major named Jon LaPierre. They went to movies or out for pizza. Nick was certainly attracted to girls, but had not found one that he both felt comfortable with and willing to give up study time for. Even in medical school—and as embarrassed as he was to admit it—he knew more about women's bodies than most people on Earth, but was still a virgin.

Lynn Delaney, though, was different.

Somehow, she saw things in him that others did not. She perceived that he had emotions, strong ones, in fact, but just did not express them readily. She was always smiling and their instant rapport, present since that day in the ICU, resonated whenever he was near her. His sense of humor surfaced in her presence.

They started out talking in cafes after her evening shifts; heaven knows, he was awake anyway, memorizing biochemical pathways or drug pharmacokinetics. He made frequent rounds on ICU patients, even those of other students. Neither had much money, but Philadelphia begged to be explored. They spent hours together at the Zoo, Independence Park, and the Art Museum. They walked from Love Park past the fountain on Ben Franklin Parkway to the Rodin Museum, arms around each other. A Saturday afternoon on South Street was always fun, browsing the panoply of small shops. Inevitably, Nick's studies suffered, but to his surprise, he did well anyway. Instead of 100 percent prepared he was only 98 percent prepared.

She was his one true love; he knew it. He could not believe that she was with him. He had begun to assume that his life would be devoted to scholarship, to intellect, perhaps to medical research, but never that he might share it with a woman like this.

The first time that he went to her small apartment, about a month after their encounter in the ICU, they wasted little time in dropping their clothes. They made love passionately, then tenderly, then passionately the next morning. Before he went to class, they sat against her headboard, blanket wrapped around them in the cold room, caressing.

"I remembered what you told me in the ICU the first day we met," Nick said, smiling.

"What's that?"

"Sometimes it's best to put it straight in."

"Yes," Lynn said, "it sure is."

At his waist, Nick's pager vibrated, breaking his daydream. He had already run past the girl on the bench and through the campus onto the two-lane road back to the hospital. He looked at the pager window: extension 2000, the ER. He stopped, pulled his cell phone from the zippered jacket pocket, flipped it open, and punched the number.

"Hello, this is Dr. Turner," he said. "I was paged."

"Hold for Dr. Elias, please," said a woman's voice. In a moment, the Emergency Room physician came on.

"Nick, this is Ellen. We have a boy with a spontaneous pneumothorax. He's stable, though; just had some chest pain that wouldn't go away, so his parents brought him in. I'd say it's 20 to 30 percent on x-ray, but you wouldn't know it to look at him—he's breathing fine. No need to rush; just get here when you can."

Back to reality, Nick thought. He picked up his pace toward the hospital on the hill.

CHAPTER 3

Nick went straight to the Emergency Room without changing. Ellen Elias was a good ER doctor, but Nick wanted to assess the boy himself: another compulsion manifest. A few of the staff glanced at him as he moved to the x-ray viewbox, but in their line of work very little was surprising and the sight of this straitlaced surgeon in running clothes was worthy of little notice.

"What's the name of the boy with the pneumo?" he asked the secretary.

She told him and he pulled Alexander Corbett's radiology jacket from the slotted box near his knees. There were only two films, and he clipped them both to the lighted box at eye level. Both were x-rays of the boy's chest, one taken while he held his breath and one after he blew the air out. *They did not need to do both inspiration and expiration films*, Nick thought, *since the pneumothorax was clearly visible.*

Air appeared black on x-rays, the air in the lung being laced with fine white lines—the lung's blood vessels—and the air outside the body a featureless black. On the boy's right side, the lung markings went all the way to the ribcage, showing the lung fully and normally expanded. On the left, the lung markings went only two-thirds of the way to the ribs, then were stopped by a thin line—the pleural envelope of the lung—but the rest of the way to the ribs was only black, showing air outside the lung where there should be none. The lung did appear to be adherent medially at the very top of the chest cavity. There was no sign of excessive pressure or of the midline chest structures like the trachea being pushed to the right. *Yep*, Nick thought, *about 30 percent.*

Alexander Corbett sat up on the stretcher to the right of the door as Nick entered the small room. He was a slim, blond-headed boy with pale blue eyes; two clear prongs of oxygen tubing were lodged in his nostrils, and the extra tubing looped behind each ear. His anxious eyes darted to Nick, then to his parents. Nick extended his right hand to the boy.

"I'm Dr. Turner. I'm a chest surgeon. Are you Alexander?" Nick always liked to address the patient first, the most important person in the room, even if the patient was a child. The boy took his hand lightly, then looked to his parents again.

"Sam Corbett," said the man, standing, "and this is my wife, Megan." Nick shook their hands, then sat on the edge of the bed.

"Please excuse my appearance," Nick said. "I was out running when I got the call. How did this all begin?"

"Alex came and woke me up at about five in the morning," said Megan Corbett. "He said his chest hurt. Well, he's had a cold for two days anyway, and he didn't look bad, so we just kept him home from school. Does he really need a surgeon?"

"He probably does, Mrs. Corbett, but let's take it one step at a time. Then what happened?"

"The pain didn't go away, so after lunch, we went to the pediatrician. She listened to Alex's chest and sent him right to the ER for an x-ray."

"Can you tell me about any other medical problems, such as allergies, surgeries, daily medicines?" Nick asked. "Also, has this ever happened before?"

Sam Corbett leaned forward. "Alex was adopted from Russia when he was four, Dr. Turner. He knows all this, by the way. His birthparents are unknown, and the medical records in general are appallingly bad."

Sounds familiar, thought Nick, but he suppressed the urge to tell them about his own daughter. It was not his habit to release any personal information, certainly not to people he had just met.

"Apparently, Alex needed some sort of minor chest surgery just before adoption," Sam Corbett went on. "One of the orphanage staff indicated that he had a drain coming out for a day, but the procedure was done right in the orphanage, so it couldn't have been much. He does have a couple of scars. He's been absolutely fine for us, though. Until now." He looked at his wife, who nodded.

Nick reached for the stethoscope hanging near a blood pressure cuff on the wall and leaned toward Alexander. "I just want to look and listen," he said as he lifted the gown. "Okay?"

The boy did have three small scars overlying the left ribcage, each about a half-inch in length and barely visible; one of them was actually more in the back. *Kids heal so well*, Nick thought. He listened with the stethoscope, and the breath sounds were clearly diminished on the left. Alexander's heartbeat was strong and rapid. He looked back and forth between the boy and his parents as he spoke next.

"Alexander has a spontaneous pneumothorax. 'Pneumothorax' means air in the chest cavity outside the lung, and 'spontaneous' means that it was not caused by a puncture from the outside or an accident. Usually, in cases like this, there are weak areas in the lung, like little cysts full of air, that just rupture. That allows air to escape from the lung, and the lung partially collapses. This was not caused by anything that you or he did, though his cold may have contributed."

"So why does he need surgery?" Mrs. Corbett cut to what was most on her mind.

"There is only so much space within the chest cavity, so if some space is taken up by air outside the lung, there is that much less space for the lung to expand. Eventually, and once the small opening in the lung seals, the air would be reabsorbed. Your son is not particularly short of breath, so one option is keeping him in the hospital and waiting. Another option is putting a small chest tube or drain in to immediately let the air out. And the third is an operation, done with a scope under anesthesia, to remove the small cysts—the strange medical term is 'blebs'—and cause the lung to stick to the lining of the chest cavity so that it cannot collapse. Alexander is a little younger than most patients with this problem, and just putting the chest tube in would probably require anesthesia anyway."

"So why don't we just wait," said Mrs. Corbett, looking at her husband.

"One argument against waiting," Nick said, "is that there is a reasonable chance that this may happen again sometime in the future; the operation is about 95 percent effective in preventing this. Also, it may have happened once before, based on what you said about the drain in Russia, though I can't fathom exactly what they did with three cuts; maybe he required three tubes."

The Corbetts looked at each other and held hands. "What would you do, Doctor?" asked Mr. Corbett.

It was not the first time that Nick had been asked this question, but the patient in question had never been so similar to his own daughter. He knew very well that even routine surgery could have unpredictable complications, that even the healthiest patient could have a bad outcome despite a perfect operation. Heck, Sarah Burley's recent surgery had shocked Nick briefly.

"I would go with the operation, but it must be your decision. This is a very common procedure, but every operation has some risk of bleeding, infection, or problems with anesthesia. Alex is healthy, and children generally do very well, healing quickly."

Nick spent some time on the details and specific risks of the surgery, answered some questions, and they agreed. Alexander had a full stomach and there was no true emergency, since he was breathing well, so Nick scheduled the case for the next morning. This would also free his evening to spend with Anna. And after seeing this particular boy from Russia, she was on his mind.

Anna had not come along until he and Lynn had been married five years.

They had planned their wedding for the brief weeks between medical school graduation and the July 1 start of his surgical residency. The ceremony took place in a Roman Catholic church in the Philadelphia suburbs, one that Lynn had attended most of her life—until she moved to the city for nursing school—and where she had received First Holy Communion. The same priest in fact, Father D'Alessandro, married them. Nick's mother, having succumbed to a massive stroke three years before, never met the bride of her only son.

The previous March 15, Nick had "matched" to his first-choice surgical residency. The program across town was one of the most prestigious, with a long history of surgical firsts and well-known surgeons. In addition, Lynn could keep her job, and they liked Philadelphia. They moved into a slightly larger apartment, even bringing some of his parents' old furniture out of storage in Delaware.

Lynn wanted children, but they held off during his grueling internship. Nick slept at the hospital every other night, if he slept at all. He loved the surgery, though, and he still could not believe that he had a woman like Lynn to come home to. He added ten pounds to his gangly frame, but Lynn could still count his ribs. She remained trim, with small breasts and a waist that he could almost circle with his hands. She was gorgeous and so alive.

They stopped the birth control pills in his second year. Two years later, they saw a specialist in the Ob-Gyn Department and began the infertility evaluation: the sperm counts, tubal patency tests, and hormone levels. In the final year of his General Surgery training, they underwent a menu of the various *in vitro* fertilization procedures; all failed.

Nick had decided that he wanted to specialize in Thoracic Surgery and he was immediately accepted into the respected program at the same hospital. This was a two-year program, with the first year involving less-onerous research time in a laboratory: a perfect time to undertake the adoption they now sought.

Lynn had been researching this and working with an agency. Adoption of a Russian child seemed best for them, and they went ahead with the paperwork and social service home evaluation.

They waited months but eventually were told of a three-year-old girl in an orphanage north of Moscow. She looked cute in the grainy photograph faxed to them, her hair pulled up to the top of her head and held by a large bow, a pale ruffled collar at her neck. The accompanying two-page medical form was printed in Russian, and each open-lined space contained only a few handwritten words, also apparently in Russian. Nick found a translator through the Patient Liaison office of the hospital, but there was little useful information anyway, some notes about "mild developmental delay" and "treatment for intestinal infection." They stared at the picture a hundred times until the day of their flight to Moscow's Sheremetyevo Airport.

"Anna Banana," Nick yelled as he entered their house from the garage.

He had purchased the three-bedroom, two-story house a year and a half before, a month before he began practicing in Glaston. It was in an older neighborhood just to the west of downtown, as the University was just to the east. There was an attached garage for the Accord, a quarter-acre yard, mostly in the back, and a renovated kitchen. The realtor had called its style "Cape Cod." The two-lane street had trees, sidewalks, and little traffic. Nick had swallowed hard when he signed the mortgage, but the bank seemed willing to loan a new surgeon any amount of money.

Nick heard rapid footsteps on the stairs, and just as he turned, Anna leapt into his arms. She pressed her face into his shoulder, and he spun around the kitchen floor in two tight circles. He set her down.

Anna was a little small for her age but was perfectly healthy and always had been. Whereas Lynn had had visible cheekbones and lines when she smiled, Anna's face was broader, her nose a little rounder. Her dark brown hair and eyes were not too dissimilar from his own. She still wore the plaid uniform dress and white shirt of the parochial school where four months before she had started second grade.

"Shouldn't you get out of your school clothes?" he asked.

"Oh, we just got home. Mrs. Pennington and I went shopping after school."

He had been fortunate to find Mrs. Pennington. The widow of a career Army officer who had returned to Glaston after retirement, she was no-nonsense but caring. It was a fact of life that a single-parent surgeon would need help, and she was a godsend. She did not live in but did live nearby. Mostly, she stayed with Anna after school, but she was willing to be on-call for emergencies if he got called in. A wonderful, rare find and an arrangement far better than the collage of nannies and mother-in-law that had sufficed for the last year of his training.

"Well," Nick said, "if you went shopping, I guess I should anticipate a delicious dinner."

"What's 'anticipate'?" Anna asked.

Nick kissed her, then told her.

*

Nick had trouble falling asleep that night; something seemed to be troubling him. Certainly, Bull Burley had gotten to him with his suggestion that an academic surgeon in Philadelphia would have taken better care of his daughter. Well, Nick had trained with those surgeons, and he knew that, though less experienced, he was good. He had good judgment and hands, and he did not take chances. No resident had read more textbooks, practiced tying more knots on the bedpost, or volunteered to assist with more extra operations. This was the way he was: a little tightly wound, some would say, but not one to risk making a mistake. He was not what one would call 'adventurous,' but that was okay in a surgeon.

He had also been bothered by the black-haired girl on the bench. *Oh Lynn*, he thought for the millionth time, *why did you have to die? We could just about see the end of the residency and its twenty-hour days, and we finally had a little girl.* There was everything to look forward to. He had been in the medical field long enough to know that bad things did really happen to good people, but he had never had Lynn's religious faith that there was some higher reason for it.

And something about the boy Alexander Corbett bothered him. He was not worried about tomorrow's operation. It would be straightforward, one of the easiest chest operations, and one that he had performed many times. Maybe it was the fact that the boy was younger than most patients with this type of spontaneous pneumothorax, most of whom were late teens or early adulthood. Had Alexander experienced one in Russia at an even younger age?

Nick wanted the universe to be orderly and predictable, but it clearly was not. Two plus two should always equal four, but any time one dealt with humans, either human bodies or human minds, they might add up to three or five or even twenty-five. Nick did not like surprises, either. He had hated those fake cans of peanuts with the coiled spring snake inside, the jack-in-the-box that might pop out at any moment, and fun-house rides at the carnival.

He did not like unanswered questions. There would never be an answer for what befell Lynn, but he had a hard time letting go of the nagging little issues relating to his patients. He would care for Alexander Corbett tomorrow as if the boy were his own, his Anna.

He finally drifted off, thinking of his beautiful Anna, his bright star in the capricious void.

CHAPTER 4

Nick began Alexander Corbett's operation at 10:15 the next morning. One of the General Surgeons, Gerald McLeskey, had completed a laparoscopic cholecystectomy earlier, and the orthopedic block time did not begin until one p.m. Nick should have plenty of time.

He incised the faint middle scar and spread with the tip of a hemostat clamp between the ribs until he entered the chest cavity. Nick had decided to use the smaller scope for this child, so he asked for a five-millimeter trocar and scope. He passed the scope into the chest cavity through the hollow tube of the trocar and cut the two additional scars anteriorly and posteriorly. As always, he first inspected the pleural cavity. *Kids' anatomy is so pristine*, he thought as he retracted the pink, healthy lung, the lingular segment of the left upper lobe flopping like the tongue after which it was named. This was so unlike the anthracotic smokers' lungs that he usually saw.

Nick did see a few small blebs at the very apex of the left upper lobe. These thin-walled structures in the outer edge of the lung looked like cysts or balls full of air. Rupture of a bleb could result in air leaving the lung and staying in the chest cavity outside the lung, causing the spontaneous pneumothorax. These blebs would have to be removed.

"Why is the lung stuck like that, Dr. Turner?" Marge, the circulating nurse, asked. In fact, the lung was adherent to the very apex of the chest cavity over an area of about three or four centimeters.

"It's probably some scarring from a prior pneumothorax," he said. "Alexander also may have had a chest tube in the past." Such scarring was a good thing—and he was even going to remove the pleura in the chest apex to promote such adherence of the lung, a so-called apical pleurectomy—since it prevented the lung from collapsing in the future if he missed a small bleb. First, though, he needed to free the lung so that he could remove the blebs.

Using the long, thin endoscopic grasper in his left hand and the similar scissors in his right, he dissected the lung free. He then grasped the small portion of lung containing the blebs and, with a forty-five-millimeter endoscopic stapling device, removed this tissue. The stapler laid down four rows of fine, staggered staples and cut between them. The two rows remaining on the lung prevented bleeding or leakage of air.

Now it was time to remove the apical pleura, that plastic wrap-like sheet of tissue that covered the inner surface of the ribcage, in order to leave a raw, exposed area to promote adherence of the lung. He began near the area of prior scarring and cut the pleura with the scissors. He then peeled it away from the chest wall as he swept the closed scissors beneath it. It certainly seemed to be more scarred and adherent than usual.

"What's that?" Marge asked, pointing to the video monitor across the table from Nick.

The light of the thoracoscope glinted on a shiny surface that Nick had just exposed. He scraped around this area with the end of his grasper and exposed more of the material. It was about one-half-inch long and a quarter-inch wide. It looked like thick plastic. He insinuated the tip of the scissors behind the object and began pulling it away from the tissues at the apex of the chest, being careful to keep away from the subclavian artery and vein beneath his instrument. The object came away and fell down onto the aortic arch. Nick grasped it and carefully pulled it out through the posterior puncture site.

"Get me a blue towel, please," Nick said, then laid the small plastic wafer on it. He picked it up again and washed it with a wet sponge. He looked at it, bending his head close enough to risk breaking sterility. Incredible! How did a man-made object get into the chest cavity of a little boy? And it appeared to have been placed intentionally since it had been completely covered by the pleura. It was as if someone had made an opening in the pleura, constructed a pocket, inserted the wafer, and closed the pleural cut.

Nick focused the scope on the wafer and looked at the magnified image on the monitor. It was perfectly smooth around the perimeter, an opaque, colorless rectangle about three millimeters thick. In the center of the rectangle was a smaller rectangle that seemed to be depressed or sunken below the plane of the shinier plastic surrounding it. He turned it over. In the lower right corner was a tiny raised character. Nick brought the scope in closer and refocused. It looked like a backward capital R, a Cyrillic Я. He ran his gloved index finger over the letter, but it was too fine to feel until he gently scraped it with his fingernail.

Who would embed a piece of plastic in a young boy? And why?

"Put this in a sterile specimen jar," he told Marge. "I'll take it to the lab myself when we're done here."

The Pathology Laboratory was in the basement of the hospital. The pathologists spent most of their working day peering into a microscope, deciding if the cells they were seeing were or were not malignant and, if they were, what type of malignancy. Increasingly now there were biochemical, molecular, and even genetic tests that could help in this determination.

Once the type of cancer or sarcoma was known, how bad was it? Was it well-differentiated or poorly-differentiated? Was its mitotic index high or low? Was there evidence of blood vessel or lymphatic invasion?

Most of what they saw, of course, was benign: diseased gallbladders, colon polyps, ovarian cysts. They even performed a rare autopsy. Other labs were also in the basement, such as Microbiology, Chemistry, and Hematology, all single rooms in the same general area. For all these tasks windowed space was frivolous.

The Chief Pathologist, actually Glaston Memorial's only full-time Pathologist, was Dr. Ronald Smithwick. Smithwick had been raised on England's rocky southwestern coast near Mousehole ("pronounced 'Mowzul', hon") and had attended public school, University, and medical school in London. Following the Senior Registrar year of his Pathology training he had accepted a Cytology fellowship in New York City. There were no available consultantships with the National Health Service at the time, and a fellowship in Canada or the States was almost a prerequisite once one opened.

Smithwick liked the United States so much that he stayed. He particularly liked New York City and the gay subculture, but had moved to Glaston when his partner accepted a position in the English Department at Glaston U. He initially worked part-time at the hospital, then became Chief when the older Pathologist retired. The regular hours of his specialty did allow frequent trips to New York, Philadelphia, Baltimore, and, Nick had learned, a B & B in Rehoboth Beach.

"Nick, my Delmarva doppelganger," Smithwick exclaimed in his accent, spinning his chair around to look up at Nick as he entered the basement office. "What brings you to Dante's first level?"

"We do have a tenuous Delaware connection, Ronnie," Nick said with a smile, "but I am hardly your doppelganger." In fact, Smithwick was short and softly rounded, his blond hair thinning above an expressive face. He wore a long white lab coat over an open-collar shirt, khaki slacks, and—despite the weather—socks and sandals.

"I went for alliteration over accuracy, dearie. Probably Edward's influence."

"How is Edward?" asked Nick.

"Oh, he's trying to write a play. I told him he should do an opera since he's living with a Pirate from Penzance." Smithwick's whole body bounced as he chuckled. "Anyway, what's that little present you have in your hand? You know how I love surprises."

Nick handed him the clear jar containing the wafer he had removed from Alexander Corbett. The plastic rectangle rattled against the container's side as Smithwick held it up to the light.

"You're not going to believe this," said Nick, "but I removed this from the pleural cavity of an eight-year-old boy. I was operating for a spontaneous pneumothorax, and there it was."

Smithwick unscrewed the orange top of the jar, pulled on gloves, and removed the opalescent object. He held it between his index finger and thumb and brought it close to his eyes. "You mean this was just lying there in the pleural cavity?"

"No," Nick said. "It actually was buried beneath the parietal pleura at the apex, almost in its own little pocket. If I hadn't done an apical pleurectomy I never would have found it and it'd still be there."

"Well, obviously somebody put it there. I've been away from pediatric pathology for a while, but I don't believe that boys are being born with plastic chips. It could happen in the future, I suppose, particularly if the computer industry has its way, but not presently. The little lad must have had a prior operation."

"I'm certain now that he did," Nick said, "but that's part of the mystery, too. The boy was adopted from Russia when he was three or four. The parents were told that sometime before adoption, the child required a chest procedure. The medical records are so bad that no one seems to know the nature of the operation. One would think it was minor since it was done in the orphanage itself. It sounds as if the boy did end up with a chest tube."

"Well, there's your prior operation," said Smithwick.

"Yes, but the three small scars suggest a thoracoscopic operation. That's pretty sophisticated for an orphanage. And it probably required general anesthesia. In addition, making a pleural pocket like that in a small child shows a certain knowledge of chest anatomy, at least a modicum of technical facility, and some experience with minimally invasive thoracic surgery. A hundred years ago, surgeons would operate on their patient's kitchen table—I think Halsted removed a relative's gallbladder that way—but not in the twenty-first century."

"Let me take a closer look at this," Smithwick said, rolling his chair to another table holding the dissecting microscope. He peered through the binocular eyepiece and adjusted the wide lens. He said nothing until he had inspected both sides and all edges of the object, then turned it over and over again.

They must teach that in Pathology residency, thought Nick, impatient for Smithwick's thoughts and to get a magnified look himself. Surgeons always felt that Pathologists took forever before calling back into the OR with frozen section reports. Finally, Smithwick spoke.

"Most of it does seem to be a hard synthetic, plastic if you will. It's quite polished, almost reflective. The edges appear smooth, but under the microscope, there seems to be a fine line bisecting the edge all the way around. In other words, the object may have been formed by fusing or sealing together two separate thin rectangles."

"What purpose would that serve?" Nick asked. "If you're going to make a piece of plastic, you might as well make it as thick as you want right from the start."

"Not if you want to seal something inside. Haven't you seen those hollow chocolate Easter eggs with smaller chocolates inside? They didn't grow in there. Someone made two egg halves, put in the contents, then sealed the halves together."

"We're not dealing with candy here, Ronnie," said Nick. "And that thing's pretty small."

"True. And I can't really see through the plastic to tell whether there's any kind of chamber inside. The other thing that intrigues me, though, is the central rectangle on one side." He turned the wafer back over. "It's clearly made of a material different from the rest."

"I couldn't get a very good look at it in the OR, but it did seem less shiny."

"Yes, the material has a rougher texture, though still fine. A decorator friend of mine would say that it's like flat wall paint as opposed to glossy paint. I wish this microscope were a little more powerful, but that central rectangle seems to be pockmarked with very fine pits, actually smaller than pinpoints. And it's depressed below the level of the smoother plastic."

"May I have a look?" asked Nick. Smithwick rose and Nick folded his angular frame into the low chair. He adjusted the focus on the microscope.

"It's a white rectangle inside a white rectangle," Nick said, "like some abstract painting. Only the texture is really different. And the same texture is evident around the edges of the central rectangle, around the walls of the depressed area, if you want to call those thin edges 'walls.' I don't know what to make of that."

"What if the central material isn't as hard as the rest and is wearing away," Smithwick speculated. "Maybe it wasn't always depressed or pitted."

"All of this suggests some bizarre purpose that escapes me," said Nick. "Someone somewhere, perhaps on a kitchen table in a Russian orphanage, performed a sophisticated chest surgical procedure in order to implant a carefully constructed synthetic object in a little boy. For heaven's sake, why? The whole thing is ludicrous." The illogic of the situation offended his sense of order. It could not have happened, but it had. The wafer was right there; it could be touched. He had removed it himself during a routine operation on a healthy boy. He unconsciously flipped the plastic over.

"What do you make of this backward 'R' in the corner of the other side?" Nick asked. It was the only feature in the shiny expanse of hard material on this side, and it was slightly raised. This, too, had to be intentional; it had to be molded this way from the start.

The pathologist took his place again at the microscope. "Well, the boy came from Russia, and this has a Cyrillic look to it. I think it's a letter of the Russian alphabet." He looked over his shoulder at Nick. "Everything seems to point to Russia, doesn't it?"

It sure does, thought Nick.

Smithwick promised to cut into the object the next day when he had more time and would call Nick with any findings. Right now, Nick had to speak with the Corbetts, who were patiently waiting.

What was he going to tell them?

CHAPTER 5

Nick took the stairs to the second floor one by one, wanting time to think. Would it be better not to tell the Corbetts about the piece of plastic? After all, it had been completely removed now; it could do their son no harm. And it would certainly worry them, unnecessary worry at this point. Who wouldn't be concerned about a mysterious object embedded in their son's chest?

Nick had always been scrupulously honest, though, often to a fault. This had led to more than one tiff with Lynn. Why did he have to be absolutely truthful when she asked, "Is this outfit appropriate for the Department of Surgery dinner?" or "You would actually rather study than go to my parents' for Sunday dinner?" Why not tell a 'white lie'? The universe would not likely end if he bent the truth or just was silent once in a while.

He did not think that he could do it. He could never lie to patients, even when they had advanced cancer. He could be on the optimistic side rather than the pessimistic; he could present a plan of action; he could tell them that he would be with them as they "fought this thing together." But he could never hide the truth. Once a doctor did that, his patient would never know when the doctor was indeed being truthful. And despite what family members often expressed about their loved one, the patient was almost always strong enough to "take the bad news."

It would be much easier to tell the Corbetts if he knew more about the plastic wafer so he could answer their certain questions. He hated to be ignorant; he was supposed to be the expert about objects in the chest. Maybe they, too, would secretly wish that they had taken Alex to Philadelphia rather than subjecting him to this inexperienced young beginner. Why not leave out the part about the plastic when he spoke to them? The operation was clearly a success; he had accomplished exactly what he set out to do, and in a minimally invasive way. He could speak with them later about the wafer when Smithwick had given him more information about its nature. Then, at least, he could answer some of their questions, although he doubted that there was an easy answer to why the object was implanted there. Nick had never seen, heard, or read about anything like it.

He reached the landing and opened the door into the second-floor hallway. He had to tell the parents. Not only was it against his nature not to, but they had a right to know. Alex was their son, after all. If their questions made Nick look inexperienced, then so be it. It would not be the first time—not even the first time this week.

"Alex is doing fine," Nick told the Corbetts. "He's in the recovery room. You can see him in about half an hour."

Both sighed in relief, and Megan Corbett unconsciously grasped Nick's hand. Her eyes watered as she looked up. "I know that this was routine for you, Dr. Turner, but he's so little."

Always a little uncomfortable with displays of emotion, Nick went on. "I did exactly what we discussed yesterday. Removed the blebs, the weak areas at the top of the lung, then stripped away the pleura, the lining of the chest cavity, so that the lung will stick to the inner surface of the ribcage. He has one small chest tube. I used the same three small scars that were there already. I just checked the recovery room, and Alex is awake and doing great."

"Terrific," Sam Corbett said, pumping Nick's hand with both of his. "We really want to thank you, Dr. Turner."

"There was only one unusual finding." Nick chose his words carefully. Doctors used the word 'finding' frequently to describe an aberrant laboratory result or an abnormality on a physical examination, but in this case, it really was something found. Sam's pumping stopped, but he did not release Nick's hand.

"As I was peeling the pleura, that thin covering, away from the very upper part of Alex's chest cavity, I found a small piece of plastic."

Both Megan and Sam looked up questioningly.

Nick went on quickly. "I removed it completely, it's not there anymore. I sent it to the lab. Whatever it is, it's completely gone." Nick did not express the thought that just came to him: *what if there was more than one object hidden in the chest cavity*? A half dozen more pieces of plastic could be hidden there, under the inferior pleura, tucked into the mediastinum near the esophagus, under a lobe of the thymus gland.

"What do you mean 'whatever it is,' Doctor?" Sam asked. "You don't know what it is?"

Here it comes, thought Nick. It wasn't his fault that a bizarre chip just happened to be buried in his patient, but it would appear his failing for not knowing what it was.

"I can describe it to you, but we're going to have to do some tests to..."

"Wait," Sam interrupted. "It had to be left over from the operation in Russia, like when surgeons leave sponges and instruments in people."

Nick winced at the implication that surgeons were always leaving things behind. Heck, they even counted tiny needles now. But Sam was absolutely correct about the origins of the man-made object: the path led back to Russia and Alex's first operation. Since the subject had been raised, Nick asked some of the questions he had been planning to ask later.

"What do you know about that operation?"

"It must not have been much of anything, Dr. Turner," Megan said. "We were told that it was done right there in the orphanage and he does only have those three tiny scars. Alex has always been active, never any breathing problems. We assumed it must have been nothing much."

"And the records are practically worthless," Sam said. "We had the two pages translated, and only one scribbled line mentioned a 'minor chest procedure.' How big was this thing?"

"It was about a half-inch by one-quarter-inch rectangle of white or light gray plastic, about the thickness of a dozen pieces of paper. It was not something that I had ever seen before, not something that we ever use in surgery, though maybe it's used in other countries. I can't imagine why, though." Nick did not want to draw attention to the fact that it had been intentionally placed in a precisely constructed pocket by someone skilled in minimally invasive chest surgery. This would definitely concern them. Nick himself was very concerned.

"Can you get me the exact name and location of the orphanage?" he asked the Corbetts. "A phone number would be even better. I'd like to give them a call and see what I can learn."

"It was in Kirovsk, way north. There was a ski resort nearby," Sam said. "Although we were there, I don't remember the name. I can certainly picture it, and we even have pictures. It must be written down on some of the papers filed away at home."

"Maybe you could call me later or leave the information with my secretary," Nick said. "Call me even if it's after five."

"What could it possibly be?" Megan asked.

"I'll be honest," Nick said. "I don't know. But it's been removed, and Alex is doing fine. You'll be able to see him soon.

And for my own curiosity, I'm going to find out what it is."

For more than curiosity, Nick thought as he left the family waiting area. *There is more at stake here than curiosity.*

Nick was very well familiar with the fact that the human body could hide bad things silently, without causing a single symptom. Alex Corbett's plastic pellet may not be bad, but it certainly was silent. Many lung cancers that he had resected had been discovered on x-rays done for other reasons, perhaps a CT scan of the chest done to look for a pulmonary embolus, a blood clot to the lungs, in a patient with chest pain or shortness of breath. CT scans of the abdomens always showed the most inferior part of the lungs, so these radiographs performed for abdominal pain might show a lower lobe lung cancer. Abnormal findings in the liver or adrenal gland might be totally silent. In fact, it was often best to discover abnormalities this way before they caused a patient's problems.

Not all occult disorders were found in time, however. Nick knew this very well.

Lynn's mother had found her the day that Lynn's occult brain tumor spontaneously hemorrhaged and thereby became manifest. Even probing his memories after this happened, Nick could not remember Lynn ever complaining of headaches, nausea, balance problems, or anything. She ate well, worked and cared for Anna, and basically did the work of two or more since Nick was always at the hospital. She occasionally ran with Nick, although she was never the runner that he was.

Mrs. Delaney had let herself into their apartment in order to babysit Anna until Nick got home. It was about two p.m., and Lynn would need to leave soon in order to work the ICU evening shift, which started at three. Lynn's mother had knocked, come in, and called Lynn's name. No answer. She called again, then heard Anna crying from the region of the bedroom.

She found Lynn on the bedroom floor in front of the dresser, Anna on the floor next to Lynn, the infant holding Lynn's hairbrush and sobbing. Lynn had a dusky color and could not be aroused, but Mrs. Delaney thought that she saw slow, shallow breaths. She immediately called 911.

An experienced Emergency Medical Technician, to her credit, was able to intubate Lynn, and the team detected a thready, slow pulse, but both pupils were dilated and did not appear to respond to light from a penlight. There were no signs of trauma. They gave her IV fluid and drugs in the ambulance, and by the time they entered the ER, her heart rate and blood pressure had improved enough to allow a CT scan. They discovered a tumor in her cerebellum, one which appeared to have spontaneously hemorrhaged. There were no other abnormalities in the chest, abdomen, or pelvis, and blood tests, including clotting studies, were normal.

Nick later learned that sudden death from an undiagnosed brain tumor was a known, though rare, phenomenon, probably affecting a fraction of 1 percent of such tumors. He read of a University of Maryland psychology student who was found in her dormitory room by her identical twin sister in 1998; she had no prior symptoms of any kind. Cerebellar tumors were particularly dangerous if there was acute enlargement with hemorrhage, as there was limited capacity of the posterior fossa to compensate for the mass effect.

Nick had been scrubbed in the OR when Lynn arrived in the ER, but as a Fellow he was not the primary surgeon and could leave. He rushed to the ER, then to the CT area just as she exited the scanner. His heart sank when he saw her, and he was briefly light-headed. He had seen hundreds of patients with IVs and endotracheal tubes, but none had been Lynn. Her hand, when he took it, was warm, but there was no muscle tone whatsoever in her arm and no reaction from her. The

ER doctor, a man Nick had known for years, put his hand on Nick's shoulder and said quietly, "Nick, her heart and lungs are stable, but her pupils are fixed." All Nick could think was *No! No, no, no! It's a nightmare. This can't be happening.*

Lynn was admitted to the same ICU where she worked. The nurses allowed Nick to stay at her side, day and night, for the two days that were required to prove brain death with two EEGs. There were never any brain stem reflexes, spontaneous breathing, or other clinical signs of brain activity, but hospital policy at the time required the EEGs. Lynn had wanted to donate her organs if anything ever happened to her, and this was arranged. The limited autopsy that Nick requested confirmed a cerebellar astrocytoma.

Anna had known her beautiful mother for less than a year. She had stayed with Lynn's parents but was allowed into the ICU to see Lynn before she was declared brain dead. Anna wept, understanding nothing, and so did Nick.

The burial was at the small cemetery next to Lynn's church. Many doctors, nurses, and neighbors attended the funeral, but the burial was limited to family. Anna, wearing a black wool coat against the October wind, held Nick's hand tightly and bowed her head when she saw others doing so. Nick's profound sadness had not eased, and he could do nothing but hold Anna afterward and try not to show Anna how lost he was, to show her that somehow things would be all right while knowing in his heart that they would not be.

Although there were times during those days when Nick thought that he might quit surgery, maybe move back to Delaware and get a job with regular hours, a job which would allow him to be a more present father to his little girl, in the end, he stayed. He knew that he was a good surgeon and he doubted that he would be satisfied with anything less. He would try to control his schedule as much as possible to be there for Anna. This probably influenced his choice of the job in Glaston when his fellowship ended, for with his training and recommendations, he could have taken a more prestigious academic position at a big university hospital if he had wanted one.

Oh, Lynn, why? We had so much ahead of us.

At least Alex Corbett no longer had the asymptomatic object inside him. Even if it was not bad, how could it be good? And how did it get there? Nick hoped that Alex's dad would call that night.

CHAPTER 6

Sam Corbett called just after nine p.m., and the answering service put him through to Nick.

"I hope that I'm not calling too late, Doctor, but I stayed with Alex until visiting hours were over. Megan is going to spend the night there."

"No, Sam, I'm still up. How is Alex doing?"

"Some pain, of course, but mostly he's been sleeping."

"Kids generally recover faster than we would. Each day should be better. In fact, he'll probably be home in a day or two." Assuming that Sam called for a reason, Nick went on, "Were you able to find out anything?"

"It wasn't hard to find our 'Russia' file box," Sam said. "It's on the floor of our bedroom closet, pushed all the way to the left. We kept all the papers. Most of the ones in Russian we had translated by a student at Glaston U, including the sketchy medical records. You wanted to know the name of the orphanage, so let me..."

Nick heard papers rustling.

"Here it is," Sam said. "The City of Kirovsk Baby Orphanage. It was a pretty nice place. I mean, I'm sure that none of them are fancy or modern, but it was at least clean. Reminded us of pictures of American grade schools in the 1950s. Linoleum floors, painted walls. Bright inside, or maybe it seemed bright because it was always dark outside. Winter time inside the

Arctic Circle. Megan and I never saw the sun while we were there."

Nick was writing notes. "Do you have a phone number, Sam?"

"Let me see. Here it is," Sam said, and gave Nick a ten-digit number. "I think you have to dial a number for Russia first."

"Yes," Nick said. "I can look that up."

Nick thought for a moment, then went on. "While you and Megan were there, Sam, did you get a chance to look around the orphanage at all?"

"Oh yes," Sam said, "the Director was very proud of the place. He gave us a tour when we first arrived, even before they brought us to meet Alex. Of course, we weren't paying much attention since our thoughts were on our new son. I guess they had almost a hundred kids, so there were always little ones around, watched over by women wearing white uniforms and hats like nurses used to wear sometimes. Their sleeping rooms had many small beds in rows."

"Did you see any medical rooms?" Nick interrupted.

"We did look into one room that had a flat table like an examination table and one of those instruments on the wall to look into eyes."

"An ophthalmoscope," Nick said.

"Yes."

"Was there an operating room?" Nick asked.

"We just saw the one medical room that I mentioned. There was some other equipment in the corner, a cart with a TV screen or computer screen on top and some boxes that looked like stereo or radio equipment. There were a lot of cabinets and it smelled like disinfectant now that I think about it. But nothing we saw looked like an OR."

"Well, I really appreciate you digging out this information, Sam," Nick said. "Do you happen to remember the Director's name?"

"No, and I don't have it written down," Sam said. "There is

a scribbled signature that may be Boris something, or maybe that's just a last name."

"No problem," Nick said. "Is there anything else that stands out about the orphanage?"

"Not really," Sam said. "We were very tense and tired the whole time, but the staff or nurses or whoever they were, were great. As we walked out the door with Alex they were even crying and waving goodbye to him. It was really emotional."

"Again, Sam, I appreciate your calling. I will be in bright and early to see Alex."

The staff at Anna's orphanage had cried when she left, too, thought Nick.

Anna's building on the outskirts of Moscow had looked more like a factory than a 1950s school, set in a suburb—if any area of Moscow could be called a suburb—of nearly identical rectangular structures. Four stories tall and with a fenced concrete playground, it certainly lacked any warmth or appeal. Yet the staff had been caring, in a business-like, non-smiling way. They wore long white coats but not all were nurses. They led Nick and Lynn past the Director's office just inside the front door and they all climbed stairs to a small room with a low table and chairs and some toys. The walls were painted primary colors; there were fresh plants in pots in the corners.

Anna was brought in by a young aide with a soft, rounded figure and many gold teeth; she stayed. Anna was small and cute and, to their surprise, laughed readily. Her medium-length brown hour occasionally touched the mild rash on her cheeks that seemed to be common among the children. She played with stacking rings, and Nick coaxed her with a quarter hidden in his hand.

They had walked with Anna and the aide into a larger playroom. A half-dozen other children approached them, beautiful children, who might spend their lives to age eighteen in the orphanage. A sleeping room with a dozen low beds in two rows could be seen through a doorway, everything clean and neat. Anna had waved bye-bye as Nick and Lynn left that first day, but Nick's heart went out to the other children.

The orphanage had prepared a late lunch with a table set up in a speech therapy room. Soup, salad, beef, potatoes, apple flan, and tea were set out, but Nick had little appetite.

The next day, when they returned, Anna was shy with Nick but eventually let Lynn hold her. They were told that the children rarely see men other than the Director. Following a lunch of rice soup, beef ragout, mashed potatoes, and apple juice, the Director proudly completed the facility tour. The building housed ninety-eight children ages zero to six years, most in the middle of this range. The children were divided into groups of ten to twelve, each group with its own playroom, eating room, and group bedroom. Infants were in a separate group, disabled children in another. Nick and Lynn never heard a harsh word and there was much hugging of staff and children. The children went outside twice each day. Nick and Lynn were called "Anna's Momma and Poppa."

In the morning, Lynn dressed Anna in the new clothes they had brought while Nick distributed M&M's and Reese's peanut butter cups to the well-mannered children. Anna said *dosvidanya* to the children with whom she had spent her life so far. The Director made a small speech.

After donning their coats, they were told to sit down briefly, as a Russian custom demands that one sits before leaving on a trip. When Lynn forgot her purse and Nick returned for it, the staff was horrified, as it was considered bad luck to return once one has left; Nick had to look in a mirror to break the spell, which he of course did. Anna waved from Lynn's arms and the staff in the doorway all cried.

Nick remembered seeing a large medical room on the ground floor during the tour but no special OR light or equipment. A child would almost certainly have gone to a hospital for surgery despite the Corbetts's being told that their son's procedure had been done in Alex's orphanage itself. Nick hoped that he could learn more when he called that orphanage.

It was seven hours later in the western part of Russia. Nick set his alarm for three a.m.

Nick was accustomed to being awoken at night. As a Thoracic Surgery resident in Philadelphia, he had not been roused as often because he had not slept that often, frequently spending his nights in the hospital, every third night, working the entire time. There were operations for gunshot wounds to the chest and esophageal perforations. Although Nick had never intended to practice Cardiac Surgery, the training and certification were the same for all chest surgeons, so he was also involved in plenty of heart surgery at night. Nevertheless, he got up and splashed some cold water on his face before calling the number that Sam Corbett had given him.

He dialed 011, then the Russian country code seven, then the ten-digit number. It seemed as if nothing was happening, then he heard a number of clicks, then silence, then a repeated whirring sound. A louder click, then a woman's voice said what sounded like "flu-share."

"Hello," said Nick. "Good morning. Do you speak English?"

There was a long sentence or two in rapid Russian, then the sound of a receiver being put down. Nick waited.

"Hello," said a different female voice. The voice seemed younger, and the word sounded more like "allo."

"Yes," said Nick. "My name is Dr. Nicholas Turner. I am a doctor calling from the United States. I am taking care of a patient, a young boy, who was adopted from your orphanage."

"Da," she said. "Why do you call?"

"The boy required an urgent operation yesterday—I am

a surgeon—and I found something unusual. The boy had an operation while he was at your orphanage, and I would like to know—no, I need to know—what that operation was. It was a chest operation." Nick realized he was speaking rapidly.

"I do not know if we can help, but we do have records. What is the boy's name?"

Nick realized that he did not know Alex Corbett's Russian name. He had neglected to ask Sam. Nick and Lynn had changed Anna's name from Anastasia, and even 'Anastasia' might have been given to her by her orphanage rather than by her alcoholic birth mother. There was no requirement by either Russia or the United States that an adoptee keep the same name, and Nick suspected that many parents picked a more "American" name. 'Alexander,' however, was common in both countries.

"The only name that I know is Alexander," said Nick. "He was adopted when he was four years old, probably in 1998, and the operation was not too long before he was adopted. I doubt that there were too many Alexanders adopted that year."

"Allow us to check our files."

Nick heard the younger woman speak to the one who had originally answered the phone. There were footsteps on a wooden floor and the sound of a metal file drawer opening. Minutes passed, then more footsteps, then a conversation between the women.

"A boy named Alexander Kolossova was adopted by an American couple that year. Of course, he was called Sasha. The records show that he did have an operation that year by Doctor Nikolai Yatovsky. The operation was because of an abnormal blood vessel in the chest. I do not know how to say it in English, but the words written here are something like 'open tube or artery.' Something that he was born with."

"And the operation was performed right there at the orphanage?" Nick asked.

"I was not here then, but allow me to ask Raisa." The two women spoke back and forth.

"Raisa says that the eminent surgeon traveled to our facility a number of times every year, perhaps every few months. He would examine children selected for him by our doctor and would operate on some of them, often the next day. He would usually bring a nurse with him. They would check the children the next day and then leave."

Nick was intrigued. "Do you have an operating room there?" he asked.

"We have one room, what you might call a dispensary, where a nurse sees children with medical problems. A doctor comes once a week and more often if needed. It is not an operating room, but there is an examining table and a bright lamp that can be moved around on wheels. Wait..." She stopped as Raisa was speaking to her.

"Raisa says that the surgeon brought equipment with him in two large suitcases. He also left here a tall narrow table with a television screen at the top and a box that can emit a powerful light on a shelf below. She saw him plug two cords into the box one time when they left the door open."

Nick's thoughts were racing, but he did not think that the women could tell him much more about the surgery. "Is there anything else that you can tell me about the surgeon?" he asked.

They spoke to each other.

"Raisa says that he was not a nice man, even to his own nurse. How do you say...he had a big head, thought that he was always right and that the orphanage staff were beneath him. Even our doctor was beneath him." Raisa spoke more in the background. Nick heard the word 'kushka.' "Raisa saw him kick our cat, kick it hard, when it rubbed against his pantleg one day, then he bent to brush off his expensive wool pants."

"Do you have a phone number for the surgeon, or an office address?" Nick asked.

More talk in Russian. "Raisa says that he lives in Moscow. He was educated there at the prestigious Russian Scientific Centre for Surgery. She may be able to ask our doctor for a number or address. Can you call back tomorrow?"

"I will call back at this same time," Nick said. "You have been very kind. And I never asked for your name."

"Svetlana."

"Thank you again, Svetlana." Nick disconnected, but he doubted that he could sleep.

CHAPTER 7

After a fitful two hours of sleep, turning in bed, Nick got up and shaved. By the time Anna came down for breakfast, he had her glass of milk, bowl, spoon, and small box of Frosted Flakes cereal set out. She ran up and threw her thin arms around his waist, and pressed her head into his side. He kissed the top of her head.

Although a little picky, Anna had never had a problem eating. She loved sweet foods, and he had given up pushing her to eat oatmeal or fruit for breakfast. In fact, when she first arrived in their apartment in Philadelphia, Nick and Lynn would find small boxes of cereal under her bed. They supposed that it was some hoarding instinct instilled by her prior life in the orphanage.

Nick was happy to be relieved of the duty of selecting Anna's clothing, as she wore the same burgundy plaid skirt and buttoned white shirt every school day. This time of year, she also wore a long-sleeved, V-neck burgundy sweater. She finished her milk, pushed back from the square wooden table, and picked up her backpack. Nick helped her into her puffy winter coat and they headed for the garage and the Accord.

This was an office day rather than an OR day, so Nick had time to drive Anna to Our Lady of Charity himself. Mrs. Pennington would pick her up in the afternoon. There was a bus, but Nick was not ready to relax when it came to Anna. She was his life, his life without parents or Lynn, and he could not imagine what he would do if anything happened to her. He knew that he was considered over-protective by his partner and by other parents, but he could live with that. Nick was not even sure that he would have agreed to have Anna undergo surgery, as the Corbetts had done with Alex unless there was no alternative. He had already experienced the worst of a fickle, unfeeling universe when Lynn died, and all surgery carries some risk.

On an OR day, Nick would have been in the hospital by six or six thirty in the morning. He would see his first patient of the day and answer any final questions about the proposed operation. While the Anesthesiologist and operating room staff got the patient ready and took him or her to the OR, Nick would usually have time to round on his patients. He had no medical students or residents in this community hospital, so he would take out chest tubes himself and write his own orders. He would change into scrubs in the locker room and be in the OR to hold the patient's hand as she went to sleep. The patient would not remember this, but Nick, in some superstitious way, thought that it made a difference. Anyway, it seemed the right thing to do for a patient at a frightening time in his or her life.

There were patches of ice on the road, and Nick drove slowly, his mind wandering. The school was not far, and there was little traffic in Glaston, so the trip took minutes.

Anna gave him a kiss with her arms around his neck, got out of the car and ran up the concrete walk to the school doors.

Although he was anxious to talk with Ronnie Smithwick, Nick rounded on his patients first. Sarah Burley was doing great, and Nick would have discharged her, but her father acted so shocked when Nick called that Nick agreed to keep her in. Harrison Burley probably remembered some uncle who spent a week in the hospital on bedrest after an inguinal hernia repair decades before. Times had changed and minimally invasive surgery had been one of the true revolutions in surgical practice. Patients routinely went home in a couple of days, sometimes even the next day.

Alex Corbett also looked good less than a day after his surgery. Nick decided not to ask the boy's mother any additional questions about their time in Russia, as she was unlikely to know more than her husband and the orphanage staff did, and raising the subject would certainly upset her. When Nick asked Alex to cough, he saw a tiny bubble in the water chamber of the plastic receptacle attached to the boy's chest tube, so he did not remove the drain. He needed to be confident that there was no air leak whatsoever from the portion of the lung that he had stapled before he could remove the drain; there needed to be a way out of the chest cavity, or that air would build up, Alex's original problem. He would come back to check again after office hours. He hinted that Alex would be well cared for by the nurses if Megan Corbett wanted to go home for a couple of hours, but wondered if he himself would leave if it were Anna in the bed.

When Nick pushed open the door to the Pathology Lab, Smithwick looked up from his microscope. "I was just about to call you," he said.

"I couldn't wait. I can't get that bizarre piece of plastic out of my mind."

"Sounds like the refrain from a rock song," said Smithwick. "A very bad rock song."

"What can you tell me, Ronnie?"

"Well, you remember how the plastic had a thin line all the way around its middle, almost as if two pieces had been put together?"

"Yes."

"As if someone were making a sandwich of plastic," the Pathologist continued. "But why not just have a single solid piece? Why make a sandwich at all? Unless, of course, the sandwich needed to contain some filling."

"I have no idea what kind of filling that might be," said Nick.

"Neither did I," said Smithwick. "But this whole thing is unusual enough that I decided to take precautions before I cut into it."

"Now you're really worrying me. What could possibly be inside?" Nick asked.

"Nick, you trained at a time when if you stuck yourself while doing an operation and later found out that your patient had AIDS, then you wondered if you would die. So, surgeons used so-called Universal Precautions, assuming that every patient had the disease in case one actually did. Pathology is the same. We handle infected tissue every day, so we get a little paranoid."

"So, back to my question. What could be inside the plastic that would be so scary?"

"I put the dissecting microscope under the hood," Smithwick went on as if he had not heard the question, "and put on gloves and an N-95 mask. Then, I used a scalpel to carefully cut around that thin line and separate the two pieces of plastic. It looked as if they had been glued or fused together, but they came apart intact. Inside one of the pieces was a square-shaped hollow or bowl, and directly opposite this on the other piece was that depressed, granular square area that we noticed from the outside of the object."

"The object!" Nick exclaimed. "That object was inside a young boy. What the heck is going on?"

"Inside the hollow chamber was some tan, powdery material. I put the tiniest sample of it on a slide, stained it with H&E, and took a look. I looked under fifty power, then two hundred, then four hundred. There is some fibrous material, but what concerns me more are eosinophilic inclusions."

"What does that mean?" asked Nick.

"It often means the presence of a virus," Smithwick said.

"A virus! Can this get any wilder?" Nick stared at the Pathologist, thinking. "What purpose would there be in putting a virus inside plastic and then embedding it into a boy's pleural cavity? There could be no expectation that it would ever be found. Is it some sick practical joke? Like that story of the surgeon who burned his initials into the surface of a patient's liver, something which no one would ever see and which actually would cause no harm."

"Except that this might cause some harm," said Smithwick.

Nick looked at Smithwick's eyes, waiting for him to go on.

"Remember that depressed bumpy square area on one side of the object? What if it was once flush with the neighboring surface and smooth, but is slowly degrading?"

"You mean that one area could be dissolving?" Nick asked.

"The correct term may be hydrolyzing, but that's the idea," said Smithwick. "Let's say it was made of a different type of synthetic material compared to the rest of the object, a material that is meant to biodegrade, to go away over time. You know that there are 'dissolvable' surgical staples. Two of our Gynecologists use them when they perform a hysterectomy to come across and close the vaginal cuff. That way, Poppa does not have to feel metal staples against the bell-end of his erect tallywacker when he enters Momma."

"Tallywacker?" Nick asked.

"Would you prefer tadger? Or John Thomas? Anyway," Smithwick went on, "the staples become soft and start falling apart by four to six weeks and are totally gone by six months. They are made from some type of polyglycolic acid material."

"But that piece of plastic was inside Alex Corbett since just before he was adopted," said Nick. "That is, if we presume that it was put there during an operation that he had back then." He told Smithwick about his conversation with Sam Corbett and his call to Russia. "That was four years ago."

"I'm sure that a different plastic compound could be made that hydrolyzed more slowly if that was the intention," Smithwick continued. "But the depressed area on the plastic that you removed was already quite thin. It actually broke apart in one place when I separated the two halves of the plastic wafer."

"So whatever was inside that little chamber could theoretically get out," said Nick.

"Yes."

"Why didn't you call me yesterday about this?" Nick asked.

"I've been swamped, and I didn't have time to look at the object until last night. I didn't see the need to wake you. After all, the thing has been completely removed from your patient."

"So, if this was all done intentionally," Nick said, "then a surgeon put a piece of plastic into a four-year-old boy, one part of which would dissolve..."

"Hydrolyze."

"Hydrolyze," Nick continued. "One part of which would hydrolyze and release something from a tiny chamber into the boy's body. And they didn't want this to happen for several years."

"That about summarizes it."

"So, what is inside that could get out into a person's body?" Nick asked. "If it's some type of virus, then that could be really bad. Except that the virus would be dead after all that time in a plastic chamber."

"We really don't know if what I saw represents a virus," said Smithwick. "I would need an electron microscope, which Glaston Memorial does not own. Or perform polymerase chain reaction testing. What I saw was certainly suggestive, however."

"May I take a look?" asked Nick.

"Too late. I was so disturbed by what I saw that I sealed

the object and its contents in a glass tube, which I taped shut. Then I put the tube into a second container, which I sealed, then into this transporter." Smithwick held up a green metal cylinder that reminded Nick of his father's old Thermos.

"Ronnie, even if it was a virus, it's not viable now."

"You're correct that viruses need a host in which to live, like an animal or human. Some can be transmitted from an animal to a human, which is the way that AIDS was supposed to have started in humans. Some are just spread from human to human. But outside of a body, say just coughed or sneezed out onto a hard surface or clothing, the virus will not survive more than minutes or hours, or maybe a couple of days."

"So why did you seal the thing up as if it is nuclear?"

"There is one virus that has been shown to be viable, under certain conditions, for years. Theoretically, for tens of years."

"Don't keep me in suspense," said Nick. "What is it?"

"Variola," said Smithwick.

"Variola?"

Smithwick turned to look at Nick directly. "Smallpox."

CHAPTER 8

"Smallpox!" Nick sat down on a round metal stool. "I thought that was eradicated years ago."

"It was, and it wasn't," said Smithwick. He, too, sat down. "The history of smallpox is fascinating and colorful and could fill books. In fact, it has filled books. I was up into the early hours this morning reading after seeing what I saw under the microscope.

"Throughout history," he went on, "probably back before the Pharaohs, smallpox has been man's greatest nightmare. The virus only lives in humans and, in general, it either kills its host or moves on to a new one. There is no animal reservoir. But the way that it attacks the body is terrible, and it takes only a few viral particles. I read a report from Germany where a single patient with a cough, despite being isolated in a room, infected patients on three floors of a hospital."

"I remember pictures from medical school," said Nick. "The terrible rash."

"It usually begins with fever and a terrific headache, then the vesicular rash. The rash is painful and can cover the entire body. The lesions can even affect the throat, eyes, mouth, and anus. The rash can coalesce, blacken, and peel off the body. Apparently, there is a characteristic sweet stench. The patient convulses."

"You're painting an appealing picture."

"There are worse types than this typical presentation,"

Smithwick said. "The hemorrhagic type still has fever and head, back, and abdominal pain, but dusky erythema develops over the skin, then petechiae and then frank hemorrhage into the skin and mucous membranes. This is uniformly fatal. There are stories from ancient societies that parents would not name a child until he had both contracted and survived smallpox, since why waste a name if the child is reasonably likely to die."

"So, was it eradicated or not?" Nick asked.

"Well, I need to talk briefly about vaccination before I answer that one," Smithwick said. "We are all taught the story of Edward Jenner, a physician in Gloucestershire —which, by the way, is not very far from where I grew up, although really much closer to Wales and all that implies, if you know what I mean."

"I have no idea what that implies, nor do I care to," Nick said.

"In the late 1700s Jenner remembered a conversation he'd had with a milkmaid years earlier, who told him that she could never get smallpox because she had had cowpox. So Jenner scratched some matter from another milkmaid's coxpox blisters into the skin of an eight year old boy and two months later exposed him to smallpox."

"Exposing him to smallpox does not sound like *primum non nocere*," said Nick.

"Every child got smallpox anyway at some point, so it sounds more *nocere* than it really was. Plus, the boy did not get smallpox, and vaccination was born. Actually, the term 'vaccination' was later popularized by Pasteur. For centuries before this societies practiced variolation, which was introducing the actual smallpox organism into a person's body in order to induce a mild form of the disease. Well, usually, it was mild."

"And I presume sometimes it was not mild," said Nick.

"Apparently, the Chinese in the sixteenth century would dry out several smallpox scabs from an infected individual and puff the powder into the nostril of the one being variolated. You know, I don't think that is a word, and it sounds a lot like violated, which may be appropriate. Anyway, some would use a silver blowpipe, the business end of which was inserted into the right nostril for boys and the left for girls. In the Middle East and Africa, an infected cloth tied around a child's arm was the vector. All of this variolation business was eventually banned in many countries after vaccination, using a related but harmless virus like cowpox, was shown to work."

"You really did do some research," Nick said. "But do we really know that this is smallpox?"

"I always loved Microbiology, so I knew a lot of this." He looked at Nick. "Plus, I am a remarkably fast reader. Now, to your question: no, we do not know that this is smallpox but it is the one virus that both looks like this and might still be viable, be a threat." Smithwick leaned back in his chair. "Well, on to eradication."

"Finally," Nick said.

"Vaccination against smallpox became standard in many countries. Napoleon ordered it across France in the 1800s and it was routine soon after in the United States. I believe the last U.S. case of smallpox was sometime in the 1940s. In the late 1960s, the World Health Organization set out to eliminate it from the thirty-one countries in which smallpox was still considered to be endemic. They would balance the cost and the risk of vaccination side effects with the two to three million yearly deaths that were occurring and the severe facial scarring and blindness from those lucky enough to survive. And they did it."

"They got totally rid of it," Nick said.

"Yes and no. They first vaccinated entire populations and then just the small remaining populations at risk, so-called ring vaccination. Every outbreak was surrounded by a ring of vaccinated individuals. The last natural case in Somalia was in 1977. The WHO declared smallpox eradicated in 1980, the first human disease ever, or since, totally defeated."

"So it was eradicated," Nick said.

"Not so fast, my persistent friend." Smithwick leaned forward. "Stocks of variola virus still existed in laboratories around the world, a fact illustrated by a fatal case in my country in 1978, a case attributed to a lab accident. So a Global Commission of some sort in 1984 convinced all countries to destroy their stocks...except two."

"Why would they let anybody keep a stock?" Nick asked.

"It was really for research purposes. For instance, could a better vaccine be produced, one with fewer dangers, in case some outbreak popped up? Or to develop better diagnostic tests or even immune globulin to treat a case."

"So what countries still have it?"

"The United States, at the Centers for Disease Control in Atlanta," said Smithwick. He paused for effect. "And Russia, originally at the Institute of Virus Preparations in Moscow and now, let me see...." He picked up a paper. "The WHO Collaborating Centre for Orthopoxvirus Diagnosis and Repository for Variola Virus Strains and DNA, State Research Centre of Virology and Biotechnology in Koltsovo, Novosibirsk Region, Russian Federation. Commonly called VECTOR."

Nick brought both hands to his forehead. "Of course, Russia would be one."

"It's highly controversial whether these stocks should be maintained or destroyed," said Smithwick. "The WHO convened an Advisory Committee on Variola Virus Research composed of sixteen members from all WHO regions. In 1999, the committee recommended that under no circumstances should research using the two stocks be continued beyond the end of 2002."

"That's great. So, this is 2003. Have the stocks been destroyed?" Nick asked.

"Based on everything that I could find, the answer is 'No,'" Smithwick said. "Also, some advocates for destroying these remaining depositories openly express skepticism that Russia can be trusted, even if they say that they have destroyed theirs."

"Now I understand your equivocation," Nick said.

"Equivocation is better than no vocation." Smithwick raised his eyebrows. "Just as dyspareunia is better than no pareunia."

Nick stood up and walked a few steps. "This conversation is getting worse in more ways than one. You're talking about dyspareunia, and the Russians have a lab full of smallpox."

"Well, let me make it worse yet," Smithwick said. "Let me talk about bioterrorism." He turned to his right side and pulled a medical paper from his briefcase. "The man who led the campaign to eliminate smallpox around the world is Dr. Donald Henderson. He was at Johns Hopkins in Baltimore and still is, but now they actually call his unit...let me see... The Center for Civilian Biodefense Studies. He authored this paper..." He held it up. "...entitled 'Smallpox as a Biological Weapon.' Scientists have been writing about this for years, but he is certainly a world authority. This was published in JAMA in 1999."

"I have heard of Dr. Henderson," Nick said.

"He comes right out and says, 'The deliberate reintroduction of smallpox as an epidemic disease would be an international crime of unprecedented proportions, but it is now regarded as a possibility.'"

"Wait a minute," Nick said. "We have all been vaccinated against it."

"We have, but not everybody has," Smithwick said. "For years most children received it in their first year of life and certainly before school age, since most states required it for school. But routine vaccination in the U.S. stopped in 1972. No one under age thirty now has been vaccinated and that is a huge number of people, I am guessing nearly half of our population."

"Why was it stopped?"

"The risk of a person suffering a complication of the vaccination itself outweighed the risks of that person ever contracting smallpox, given that only humans could be a host to the virus and smallpox had been eradicated in humans. A rare person who received the vaccine could develop postvaccinial encephalitis, resulting in death or permanent neurological deficits. A rare person could get progressive vaccinia, which was almost always fatal. Usually these people were immunocompromised in some way, but we do not always know that until too late. Patients with eczema also seem to be at risk of a complication."

"So, everyone under thirty is at risk," Nick concluded. *And my daughter, Anna, gets eczema at times,* he thought, *so she would never get this particular vaccine.*

"Actually, everyone at any age is probably at risk," Smithwick said. "The duration of immunity after a standard single-dose vaccination is unknown but is probably five to ten years, not forever. We are almost totally exposed, begging to be invaded. One infected person can spread the disease to a dozen or more contacts. Smallpox spreads by droplets or aerosols expelled from an infected person or by direct contact, even with bed linens. In fact, one of the first uses as a bio-weapon was reputed to be during the French and Indian Wars in the 1700s when British soldiers distributed blankets that had been used by smallpox patients to American Indians, although that story may be apocryphal."

"So the entire country is vulnerable," said Nick. "I had no idea about any of this. Why should I, I suppose?"

"It gets worse," Smithwick said. "Our emergency stockpile of the vaccine is inadequate for an epidemic, and a new vaccine cannot be just produced with the snap of a finger. Vaccines were once made from the scarified flank of a calf, but that went away years ago, and production now requires the use of tissue cell culture. Dr. Henderson estimated that the establishment of a new vaccine production facility would take thirty-six months. And why would a company do this when there is no market for a vaccine? The government has not provided funds either. Apparently, researchers are developing an attenuated strain that causes fewer complications but I could not find any reference that this was completed. And in an unvaccinated population, the case fatality rate is 30 percent."

"Is there any other treatment?" Nick asked.

"There is vaccinia immune globulin, but it is difficult to make and to administer. And no one has yet come up with an antiviral."

"So, we would be in big, big trouble."

"Royally screwed, with a large espantoon."

"Dr. Henderson concluded in his paper," said Smithwick, " 'the discovery of a single suspected case of smallpox must be treated as an international health emergency.' He also said, 'Although smallpox has long been feared as the most devastating of all infectious diseases, its potential for devastation today is far greater than any previous time.'"

Nick paced between granite-topped tables. He felt as if he needed air, and there was no window in the basement lab.

"After all that, we really do not know if we are dealing with smallpox in that piece of plastic. And even if it was a virus, it would not be viable after four years."

"I agree totally," Smithwick said. "But first, recognize that we are dealing with something very out of the ordinary. Second, there were definite viral cytopathic effects, although those are admittedly quite non-specific. And most of all, smallpox is the one virus that might be viable after a long time. Those were the reasons that I focused on smallpox."

"What makes you think that any microorganism of any kind can survive that long outside some living host?" asked Nick. "It just defies logic."

"It may not be logical, but there is some empiric evidence," said Smithwick. "Even the world's smallpox experts would agree that it can survive for days and possibly months in scabs from the skin lesions and on cloth such as clothing and bed linens. Even some of the viral isolates at the CDC and at the VECTOR came from scabs. But listen to this: two researchers in the Netherlands collected a large number of variola minor scabs from three patients in 1954. The scabs from each patient were placed in an envelope and used for research studies but then were simply stored in a cupboard. Years later some scabs were put into a mortar and ground together with some broth and then inoculated into the chorioallantoic membrane of eggs. Two and one-half years after the scabs had been collected there were still fifty-six thousand viable particles per scab demonstrated."

"Two and one-half years!" Nick exclaimed.

"They continued to do this yearly. Each year the number of viable particles decreased, but at thirteen years, twenty-nine hundred remained. And an infectious dose is believed to be only a few virions."

"This is unbelievable. Thirteen years!"

"They could not say that this could cause an outbreak, but the virus could be subinoculated onto other membranes and this always gave rise to typical smallpox lesions, confirmed histologically and serologically. The authors pointed out that there have been rare outbreaks of smallpox among humans that could not be linked to infection introduced from endemic areas and they speculated that individuals might have come in contact with scabs present in old cloths or books.

"And remember when I said earlier that smallpox may have been around for thousands of years, from before the time of the Pharaohs?" Smithwick went on. "When the mummy of Ramses V was examined in 1979, he appeared to have had the classic rash, leading some in the infectious disease community to recommend vaccination of archeologists who excavated crypts. This led to a rash—excuse me—of letter writing to The Lancet. One letter confirmed by electron microscopy and immunostaining that a Neopolitan boy mummy had died of smallpox four centuries previously, and the actual viral particles persisted in the mummy. They sent material to the CDC, and I do not know what happened. This was 1986."

"You are not giving me much comfort," said Nick. "Admittedly, this is all wild speculation, but it was wild for someone to intentionally put this in an innocent boy."

"Here comes the *coupe de gras*," said Smithwick. "Dr. Henderson reported that a former deputy director of the Soviet Union's civilian bioweapons program described a successful program by the Soviet government, beginning in 1980, to produce smallpox virus in large quantities and adapt it for use in bombs and intercontinental missiles. The same former official described a research program dedicated to making strains of the virus that would be even more virulent and contagious."

"My god," said Nick. "This is insane."

"Well, obviously, nothing has been used yet, at least to our knowledge," Smithwick said. "But it does raise the possibility that they developed a strain which would remain viable for a long, long time under certain conditions, say a scab in a perfectly dry, sealed piece of plastic. They've had twenty years to work on this."

"What the heck are we going to do?" asked Nick.

"Well, there's no time pressure, since the object has been removed from your patient and it is totally sealed inside three containers," Smithwick said. "I am going to bypass the state lab and send it directly to the CDC."

"Good idea," Nick said. "We do not know that this is smallpox rather than some other virus, and whatever it is, whether it is still viable. I have to get to clinic, but please let me know the moment that you hear anything."

Nick decided not to share his greatest concern with his friend yet; maybe there was some time pressure. What if there were more children somewhere with a foreign piece of plastic in their chest, plastic that could release into them one of mankind's greatest demons?

CHAPTER 9

Nick's clinic took his mind off viruses and plastic for a few hours. He had inherited some long-standing patients of the seventy-eight-year-old Thoracic Surgeon, who had finally retired the prior summer, Dr. Anthony Lombardo. These were mostly lung and esophageal cancer patients who were seen every six months or every year as routine surveillance for cancer. These visits were usually straightforward and, frankly, usually enjoyable since the patients were almost always cancer-free, and it was nice to reassure them of that.

More problematic was one of the patients with newly diagnosed lung cancer, Mrs. Kirstein. A three-pack-per-day cigarette smoker, she had marginal lung function and might require a pneumonectomy (removal of the entire lung) due to the location of her cancer. But that operation would leave her short of breath and on oxygen for the rest of her life or worse, requiring tracheostomy and long-term ventilator support. Based upon the Pulmonologists's bronchoscopy report and the CT scan images, however, Nick thought that he might be able to do a sleeve right upper lobectomy and thereby spare a lot of good, functioning lung tissue. This involved cutting out a piece of the right main bronchus along with the right upper lobe and then sewing the right middle and lower lobes back on. He was not sure that much of this "bronchoplastic" surgery had been done at Glaston Memorial, but he had been trained to do it.

He would first need to accurately determine the stage of the cancer as well as perform his own bronchoscopy to see whether he could technically accomplish the procedure. He would need to see enough normal bronchus on either side of what he planned to remove, in order that he could safely sew things back together. If he could not totally remove the cancer, then there was no reason to submit Mrs. Kirstein to the risks of operation. He drew Mrs. Kirstein a picture describing the operation. He then asked his nurse to schedule a bronchoscopy and mediastinoscopy, the latter procedure to be done at the same time as the bronchoscopy, in order to sample local lymph nodes for possible cancer spread.

Two of his own postoperative patients were doing well. One sixty-six-year-old man, John Hulka, had completely recovered from an empyema, a bad infection in the pleural cavity, the result of pneumonia treated late. A forty-five-year-old woman named Chambers was still having some postoperative pain ten days after a lung resection, but that was to be expected. Her breath sounds, incision, and chest x-ray were all good.

Two patients had solitary pulmonary nodules, a common reason to see a Thoracic Surgeon. These small white densities, sometimes discrete and round and sometimes less distinct, were seen against the black background of air in the lung, typically on CT scans performed for other reasons, such as chest pain, shortness of breath, or even abdominal pain. Since such a density could be an early sign of lung cancer, it must be taken seriously, but many represented old scar tissue or even inflammation. One had been stable on a CT scan three months after the original one, so Nick ordered another CT scan at a longer interval, six months. If this were stable when he saw her in six months, then he would order a final scan for a year later, as one generally followed these for at least two years to ensure stability.

The second patient with a pulmonary nodule, Frank

Squire, was more worrisome. The density was larger, nearly three centimeters, and the patient was a heavy smoker. Nick ordered pulmonary function tests to determine if the patient would be a potential candidate for surgical resection if this proved to be lung cancer. Nick would see him back next week and, if the measured lung function was acceptable would schedule him for bronchoscopy and mediastinoscopy also. Nick remembered Dr. Lombardo telling him that if the patient could climb two flights of stairs without stopping to catch his breath, then he would tolerate removal of at least an entire lobe of the lung.

The final office patient, Gus Schmidt, had a newly diagnosed esophageal cancer. Although this cancer usually caused food to stick before it could get into the stomach and resultant weight loss, this one was discovered early when the patient underwent esophagogastroduodenoscopy because of severe heartburn. The patient required clearance from his cardiologist before scheduling the six-hour operation, but it appeared that he would be a candidate for esophagogastrectomy. This was one of Nick's favorite operations during his fellowship, but he had done only a half dozen in the months of his nascent practice. The procedure involved incisions in the chest and the abdomen, almost two operations in one, in order to remove the esophagus and bring the stomach into the chest to replace it.

Nick felt that he was fortunate to have entered an existing practice like this one, Thoracic Surgery Associates. One's reputation was everything in a small city like Glaston, and Dr. Lombardo had enjoyed a good one for decades. The younger partner who had joined him ten years before, Dr. Kenneth Olson, had an ego no larger than that of most surgeons and was willing to share new referrals equally with Nick. Although Nick could have joined an academic Department of Surgery at a big city hospital, he felt that Glaston and this practice were right for him and for Anna.

*

Nick had time for a run, and he needed to think.

He went to the male locker room next to the OR and changed into his running clothes and New Balance shoes. He pulled the cap over his ears and put thin black gloves into the pocket of his jacket until he got out of the hospital. He went down the back stairs so as not to encounter a patient's family.

He thought that he would go a different route today and he headed for Ballenger Park. Named for one of Glaston's anthracite coal barons, the park had a nice path that skirted a small lake, then wound through a woodsy picnic area, then circled back to the small bandstand. Nick got into a nice pace, about eight minutes per mile, and his breathing became regular.

The morning conversation with Ronnie Smithwick kept playing in his head. He worked through the facts logically, as he would in narrowing a diagnosis on a new consult. If he were asked to see a new patient, he would first establish the history of the patient's symptoms, then do a physical examination, then look at all laboratory results and personally look at all radiographic images. A differential diagnosis would be established, whether written down on paper or in his mind, and that list of possibilities would drive what tests to order next. Sometimes, these tests were procedures or biopsies that he would do himself. In fact, as much as possible, if there were something that he could do himself he would not punt it to another physician.

He passed another runner near the lake, his breath visible in the twenty-five-degree air. Some of the facts of Alex Corbett's case were indisputable, like laboratory results; some were speculative, like a possible diagnosis among several. It was clear that Alex had undergone a left chest operation in Russia, seemingly at the orphanage itself. He had the scars and the orphanage staff had records, however poor. It was clear that a piece of plastic had ended up beneath the pleura of his chest cavity since Nick himself had discovered and removed it. It was speculation that the Russian surgeon had put it there, but this was certainly the case; the boy had not been born with it, and how else would it have gotten there?

It was a fact that the small chamber in the plastic object contained something. It was highly speculative that it was a virus, specifically smallpox. But it was a fact that Russia contained a stock of smallpox virus and a fact that the cytopathic effects under light microscopy looked like a virus. It was highly speculative that a virus could remain viable after four years but a fact that smallpox had been proven to remain viable in scab material for as long as thirteen years and probably much more. It was speculative that the plastic object had been constructed with planned disintegration—hydrolysis—of a window into the chamber. But it was a fact that such material was used in surgery routinely and a fact that the plastic was disintegrating in that area.

Nick shortened his stride as the grade of the path steepened into the picnic grove. Most speculative of all was the Russian surgeon's motive. And did he intentionally select a child scheduled for adoption? It was speculation that this was bioterrorism but a fact that smallpox, whether modified by Russian scientists or not to be more virulent and more robust, was the perfect weapon for this: highly contagious, often fatal, the population susceptible, lack of enough vaccine, no effective treatment. Was this the idea of a rogue surgeon or, more likely, one backed by some organization within a country that is always, regardless of external niceties, inimical to the United States?

Finally, should he report this to somebody in authority? And, if so, to whom? Nick knew that the Central Intelligence Agency was involved in spying and overseas work and espionage, but how about the FBI? Did they do anything overseas? Nick remembered reading books about J. Edgar Hoover and "G-men" as a child, but he could only picture them fighting crime in the United States. What about Interpol, and what the heck did they do anyway? He decided that he really had nothing solid to report to anybody at this point. He would be patted on the head, figuratively, and told to come back when he had something real.

As he passed the bandstand and headed out of the park Nick experienced a profound longing to hug his little girl, and to never let go.

Nick did just that when he got home. He was still hugging Anna's slim frame as Mrs. Pennington let herself out the front door.

"Daddy, can we get a dog?" Anna asked, perhaps sensing Nick's mood. "I can take care of him. Or her."

"Let's wait until the weather is better," said Nick. "Also, I may have to take a trip for a few days."

Anna acted as if she did not hear him. "Rebecca has a black dog, and he never makes a mess inside. He sleeps in her room and protects her."

"I like dogs, but spring or summer is a much better time." Nick had already thought about fencing in the backyard, as this subject had come up before. Their street was not a busy one, but it would be much easier and safer to just open the back door to let a dog in or out. "Let's get you some dinner."

The alarm woke Nick at three again, and he called Alex Corbett's old orphanage. Svetlana answered after a dozen rings.

"Hello, Svetlana. Were you able to obtain any information for me?"

"I have an address in Moscow for the Doctor," she said. "But our Director refused to give me a telephone number. He did not want anyone to bother the surgeon. He seemed a little scared, maybe of the surgeon. He is not a nice man. I mean the surgeon."

Nick had her give him the address twice, the second time more slowly. "Is this his office or his home?" he asked.

"I do not know."

"Is there anything else that you can tell me about the surgeon?" Nick asked.

"No," said Svetlana. "He drove a very expensive car, a new black Range Rover, and he acted like the nurse that came with him was his servant. He would not even help her carry his cases of equipment into our building. Perhaps he will treat you with greater respect if you speak with him, because you are a surgeon also."

"Thank you, Svetlana. You have been very helpful."

Nick broke the connection, then stood up and walked to the window. He was using the spare bedroom as an office. He did not really need an office since he did not write or do research, but it was familiar to have a desk and a place to keep records. He looked out the front window. He could see the dark, empty street through the leafless branches of mature oak trees in the front yard. He bent down and picked up a filing box, setting it on his desk. This was the box of Russian material related to Anna's adoption.

Just before he and Lynn had left the orphanage with Anna the staff had given her a few gifts. One was a picture book about Moscow, since the orphanage lay on the outskirts of the city. There was the red bow that Anna wore in her hair every day and the small stuffed dog she sometimes carried. Maybe that was why she wanted a dog, Nick mused. He removed these, then opened a manila file folder beneath.

Nick dialed the number of Anna's old orphanage. It would be late morning in Moscow. He had been thinking about doing this as he ran through Ballenger Park and his curiosity had grown during his conversation with Svetlana. He wondered if the eminent—and apparently arrogant—Russian surgeon had driven his fancy car to more than one orphanage. He would not have had to drive far to reach one on the outskirts of the city in which he either lived or practiced. And it would be true in every country that the more sub-specialized a doctor became, the greater the territory, the 'referral area,' he or she must cover in order to treat the less frequent medical problems.

Another female voice answered with a Russian greeting. The connection was poor, and Nick had to repeat twice, "Do you speak English?"

Nick thought that he heard, "Nemnógo, a little."

Nick spoke slowly. "I am an American surgeon. I am trying to reach, I want to speak to, a surgeon, a doctor who may come to your facility." He thought that she might be more likely to help if there was some connection, so he went on, "My wife and I adopted a little girl from there a few years ago."

"I am new here. I will ask Tatiana." A phone receiver was set down. Nick watched a cat cross the street outside, its ears back as it trotted into a cold breeze. The cat crossed back as Nick still waited.

There was a rustling sound, and the woman spoke. "Tatiana says a doctor comes every week to see any sick children. She will also come if a child gets cut or hurt."

"Yes," said Nick. "She would be a family doctor or Pediatrician. Is there a surgeon who comes less often, who may do operations on your children?"

There was another pause and low speaking in the background.

"Tatiana says that there was a surgeon who came and did operations in the clinic. Children would be born with heart or lung problems, and he would fix them. But he has not been here for a number of months."

"Does she remember his name? Is it Dr. Yatovsky?" Nick asked.

More low speaking. "That is probably correct," the woman said.

"Do you have a telephone number or an address, please?"

Another pause. "The Director may have them, but he is away. Tatiana thinks that his office is on Tverskaya."

It was the same street name that Nick had heard earlier. The surgeon had been to Anna's orphanage. And to how many others?

CHAPTER 10

After a few hours' sleep, Nick drove to the hospital, parking in the doctors' lot in back. He had slept better, now that he had a plan.

Nick asked a security guard to let him into the Medical Library on the first floor since it was too early for the librarian. Ronnie Smithwick was an incredibly smart guy with a near-photographic memory, but Nick wanted to do some reading himself. He perused a dozen medical papers and also read newspaper and magazine articles. Unfortunately, everything that Ronnie had said was true, further reinforced by seeing it in print in respected publications.

The terror of smallpox was not just that it caused death but that it did so in such a horrifying and visible way. Sheets of vesicles covered every centimeter of a person's face, then often turned into pustules. The skin itself could be exquisitely tender, causing pain that equaled that in the abdomen. The individual eventually passed out from toxemia, but not always before convulsing. The uniformly fatal hemorrhagic form could be worse, causing the person to look alien, with swollen sausage-like limbs and bleeding from orifices.

Nick clicked the library door closed behind him and walked to his office in the attached Medical Arts Building. He sat at his desk and made several phone calls, then went to see his patient in the preoperative area. Today was one of his block days when a "block" of time was set aside for him to operate. If he did not schedule an operation or operations to fill that time within seventy-two hours beforehand, then the time would be given to another surgeon who had requested to be moved up on the schedule. Mrs. Pennington knew that this was one of her days to get Anna ready and drive her to Our Lady of Charity school.

Nick finished his operation, a straightforward right lower lobectomy on a fifty-four-year-old man with lung cancer, then dressed and went back to his office. He needed to make additional calls and then speak with his partner before the latter began his office hours. Dr. Kenneth Olson, a decade Nick's senior, was the only other Thoracic Surgeon in Glaston, was Nick's closest colleague and advisor, and would have to cover Nick's patients while Nick was away.

"I think that you're on a wild goose chase." Ken Olson leaned back in his leather desk chair, long legs propped on the uncluttered desk. He was so different from Nick physically—tall, sandy-haired, broad-shouldered—but they shared an abundance of compulsion. Nick could trust him to cover his patients while Nick was away. "Heaven knows you could use some time off, but why not the Cote d'Azur? Russia in January, give me a break."

"I can't let this drop, Ken," Nick said. "Someone in Russia, years ago, implanted a foreign object in my patient. No one can tell me why. The parents were told only that Alex needed a minor chest procedure, and the boy has three barely visible scars to show for it."

"So call the orphanage or the hospital or wherever he was."

Nick related what he had learned from the orphanage calls.

Ken took his wingtips off the desk. "Would they have done an actual chest operation in an orphanage? And who there would be sophisticated enough to do it?"

"There was a surgeon from Moscow who came to the orphanage every few months. He brought two suitcases of equipment with him and apparently a nurse or assistant."

"So the plastic object was probably placed through one of those three incisions," Ken said. "But what operation was the surgeon *supposed* to be doing? It had to be more than a chest tube. I mean, he had to do a full thoracoscopy in order to see what he was doing. This was fairly sophisticated work in a small child."

"What operation would one do on a four-year-old via left thoracoscopy?" Nick asked. "Obviously, resection of blebs like I did, except the lung itself showed little evidence of that."

"Cardiac surgeons ligate PDAs in infants, sometimes right in the ICU," Ken said. The ductus arteriosus was a short blood vessel that connected the aorta to the pulmonary artery in a fetus. Important for fetal life, it was supposed to close within days after a newborn took his or her first deep breath. Sometimes, it remained open, or patent, resulting in too much blood circulating back through the pulmonary artery to the lungs. Such a patent ductus arteriosus, a PDA, needed to be closed, and one way was to place a clip across it at surgery.

"Again, fairly sophisticated," Nick said. "We don't even do that here in Glaston. But the staff in Russia did relate something about a blood vessel in the record."

"All this is interesting speculation, but why not let it rest?" Ken asked. "The foreign object is gone, the boy's fine, and Russia is a long way away. You're not in medical school; no one's going to test you on this, Dr. Alpha Omega Alpha." He referred to the medical school honorary society to which Nick had been elected.

"Well, there is more to this than I was going to go into," said Nick. "But you might as well know." He gave Ken a summary of what he and Ronnie had discussed, from the dissolving plastic, to the possible smallpox within, to the potential viability of smallpox over years, to the known Russian stockpile.

Ken shook his head. "You realize how unbelievable this is? I mean, this type of thing just does not happen in a town like Glaston. It sounds like a bad conspiracy novel."

"I've been thinking about this a lot," Nick said. "It may *be* some sort of conspiracy. What motive would a surgeon have to do this? Is it some sort of personal vendetta, or does he need to prove that he can do it, or is he sociopathic or psychopathic? Or, and this is what worries me most, maybe he is just doing it for money. What if he was paid to do it by a larger organization?"

"You mean like the evil international organization in a James Bond movie?" Ken asked. "What was it called, SPECTRE?" He laughed.

"You laugh, but that may not be as far-fetched as it sounds," Nick said. "It would not have to be international, just Russian. How about a terrorist group within Russia? Or even a branch of the government or military?"

"Why would such a group want to give smallpox to a child?"

"First, even one case of smallpox can represent a national emergency," Nick said, "since no one has immunity now, it can spread like wildfire and there is no treatment. Dr. Henderson in his review made that point. But how do we know that it was only one child? This surgeon apparently traveled to more than one orphanage. And maybe there is more than one surgeon."

"So," Ken said, "let me play along. There is a nefarious organization that wanted to give a child, or children, smallpox. What purpose would this have? To terrorize the country? To prove the inadequacies of the public health system? To get back at the Russian government?"

"I've had time to think about this more than you have," Nick said. "If the organization and the surgeon are in Russia, they are more likely to want the infection in another country, particularly if they are actually working for the Russian government. And America would be their country of choice. And how better to get the infection into the United States than through innocent children about to be adopted? The orphanages are the source of essentially all children adopted from Russia into the United States. Coincidentally, they are places where a warped surgeon could get away with operations free of scrutiny."

"A Trojan Horse scenario," Ken said.

"I hadn't thought of that," Nick said, "but it's not a bad analogy. Do you know how many children are adopted from Russia each year by families in the United States?"

"No idea."

"I did some research this morning," Nick said. "It's probably over four thousand and rising each year. Lynn and I were well aware when we went this route that there were fewer and fewer domestic adoptions for many reasons. More access to contraception and legal abortion, decreases in teen birth rate, and decreased stigma around being a single parent. So, couples—in our case, infertile—turn to international adoption, and fully a quarter of all of these are from Russia. Now, four thousand is a large number, but my point is that it would not be difficult to target some small number of these."

"And the dissolvable plastic idea is a way to get them into the country first," said Ken, "and the infection would occur later. I suppose this would also throw off suspicion about the source of the infection."

"Correct," Nick said. "No one would imagine that the plastic object would be discovered. There was a one-in-a-million chance that a child would need a left chest operation before the plastic dissolved and a similar chance that the object would be found even if a boy needed an operation. And, not to be morbid, but it would not likely even be found at autopsy unless a Pathologist was specifically looking for it. And why would they even do an autopsy on a child who had just succumbed to smallpox?"

"So, let's say that this incredible theory is true," Ken said. "Why do you have to go to Russia yourself? Wouldn't this be something for the CIA or our State Department or somebody to handle?"

"Ken, we don't have much time. In fact, I do not even want to wait for the several days to a week for the CDC to confirm that this is smallpox. Everything adds up, as bizarre as it initially sounds, and there certainly was something in that plastic that was meant to be freed into a boy's body. The one area of plastic in the object I removed from Alex had been almost completely hydrolyzed; it apparently fell apart just from Ronnie moving it around under the dissecting microscope. Who knows what might have happened, maybe in hours or days, if I had not removed it? Talk about luck."

"So, there must be records somewhere," Ken said. "You could x-ray every child adopted from Russia to see if there was anything foreign."

"Who knows how long it would take even if such a list exists," Nick said. "But most of all, even a CT scan would not detect the tiny, radiolucent plastic that I removed. It might look like a slight bump in the pleura. Plus, what if some plastic objects were put in some kids that contained nothing, sort of a sham? Anyone diabolical enough to do this might have thought of this further complication."

"Okay," Ken said, "what if we wait until smallpox is confirmed by the CDC—and, by the way, I am less convinced by all of this than you are, it's so crazy—and then the CDC vaccinates all children adopted from Russia. Problem solved; epidemic contained. After all, vaccination used to be routine anyway."

Nick laid out the reasons why vaccination was impractical, likely ineffective, and potentially dangerous. "And we don't always know who is immunocompromised. I read a story about a military recruit with unrecognized AIDS who died after being vaccinated."

"Could we watch and wait until a child showed the earliest signs of smallpox and then treat them?" Ken asked.

"There is no treatment," said Nick. "Ronnie told me that, and I looked again through the medical literature this morning; I thought there might be something new. You can give the vaccine after infection, but at best, that just attenuates the effects of the infection some. There is variola immune globulin, which is given as many doses intramuscular, but this doesn't work very well either. Also, it cannot be given to immunocompromised patients or ones with eczema. And you don't usually even know who is infected until the rash appears, which is days after the infection begins."

"You could check all kids adopted from Russia to see whether they had scars on their chest," Ken said. "But you would need that list."

"Which probably doesn't exist or would take weeks to get ahold of if it does. And then what would you do? You can't do a thoracoscopy on all of them. It requires general anesthesia and how would we convince parents that this conspiracy could be serious? If you did operate on all of these kids, how many plastic objects might break while being removed? Alex's almost did. Plus, some of the operations could have been sham, with empty plastic objects or even just small cuts in the skin."

"So, what do you think is the best option?" Ken asked, leaning back into his chair.

"The best option is to learn which children are carrying a loaded object and offer the parents vaccination or thoracoscopy to remove it. It's not perfect, but it is a better plan than all of the others we have discussed."

"But you still need a list," said Ken. "In fact, you need a better list than even our government can produce. You need a list that has only the adopted kids with ticking time bombs in their chests, not every adopted kid. No one has that list."

"I would bet my life that the Russian surgeon does," said Nick. "From residency, every surgeon keeps lists of every operation. We need numbers and types of cases to pass our Boards and then to be re-certified every ten years. Now, this guy is not using these cases for his Boards or just out of habit. He has more than habit to drive him. He would have kept a list if he was getting paid by the procedure, or if this was some sick research experiment, or even out of compulsion or pride. I know that he has a list."

"Then let the CIA track him down," Ken said. "Do you know his name?"

"His name is Yatovsky, Nikolai Yatovsky. I even have an address in Moscow, probably his office."

"Then you're golden," Ken said.

"We already went over this," Nick said. "There is no time. It will be days or weeks before I convince somebody in our government that this is a priority if I even can. Who knows what political ramifications will then interfere? Maybe our foreign service cannot be seen as accusing Russia of this science fiction conspiracy; maybe there is all sorts of red tape and diplomatic maneuvering. In the meantime, some child or children are getting infected with one of mankind's most horrific diseases."

"What can you do by going to Russia yourself?" asked Ken. "Your superb training did not include courses in international espionage."

"I can find this surgeon and confront him," said Nick. "Or I can convince somebody in his office to give me his records, even if I have to bribe them. I don't have every detail worked out, but I do know at least two orphanages that he visited, and I know his office address."

"This is really a long shot," Ken said.

"Even if I can just visit Anna's old orphanage and look at their records or speak to more of the staff there, then I will have at least accomplished something."

"How is that going to help?" asked Ken.

"It may not help every adopted child, but it will help Anna and me," Nick said, staring at a gold paperweight of the letter O on Ken's desk. "Lynn and I never paid much attention to them, but when we got Anna back to the States, we noticed three tiny scars."

Ken sat forward. "On the left chest?"

Nick nodded his head. "It looks as if my daughter had the same operation."

CHAPTER 11

The wooden stairs to Nick and Anna's basement were narrow and the ceiling above low, so Nick descended slowly, bending his head forward, left hand grasping the cool railing. The gray Samsonite suitcase lay on a wooden shelf; it was the only suitcase that Nick had ever owned. Slimmer than a more modern one, the hard-sided case would nevertheless need to be checked at the airport. And it would need to hold clothes suitable for a Russian winter. Nick remembered the bitter cold of the December in Moscow when he and Lynn had traveled to adopt Anna.

He could wear some of the bulkier items, like his sweater and coat and boots, and he really would not need much for the few days that he intended to be there. He reconsidered, wondering if he could fit everything into his backpack instead. This could be carried on and also taken with him if circumstances in Russia required him to move around at all. The backpack was not huge but was larger than a daypack. He carried both the suitcase and his old blue backpack upstairs.

Nick placed his thin, white thermal underwear in the bottom of the backpack next to his toiletries kit. As a runner, he was accustomed to dressing in layers in cold weather, and the long-sleeved and full-legged underwear performed as well as the old-school thick, waffled "long underwear" that his father had worn walking on the Delaware beach in winter. The sweat pants and top that he had worn for sleeping the last time went in next, then a few pairs of thick socks. The traveler's checks that he would purchase at his bank the next morning would go into a money belt to be worn under his clothing.

Nick was not concerned about the cost of this sudden trip. His practice, though only eighteen months old, was growing well, and his base salary was guaranteed by the hospital for his first two years. He lived frugally, not because he was concerned about saving money, but because that was just the way that he was. Boring. At least, that was what he imagined most people thought, everyone but Lynn.

Lynn had not been concerned that he read Consumer Reports and purchased the highest-rated sedan, a Honda Accord. With cloth seats. Or that he always drove it under the speed limit. Well, that did bother her sometimes. She seemed to see something charming in his serious curiosity about arcane subjects, even when he went on and on, in pedagogic tones, about those subjects. He would indulge in alcohol sometimes, but rarely to excess and never if he had to drive. And marijuana was out of the question for fear of being arrested and kicked out of medical school or residency.

Nick did have a weakness for reading, if that was a weakness. It started with the dog stories of Jim Kjelgaard and Jack London when Nick was in junior high school, then rolled into science fiction and fantasy: Baum, Burroughs, Wells, Verne, Heinlein, E.E. Smith, Andre Norton, Asimov, Bradbury, Dick, Le Guin, Tolkien, Philip Jose Farmer, Harlan Ellison, Vance, Gibson, Gaiman. He read all of Arthur Conan Doyle, from *Lost World* to the complete Sherlock Holmes. All of Rudyard Kipling and Poe, poetry and prose. Tennyson, Eliot, and Larkin. Hemingway, Faulkner, Rushdie, Eco, Marquez, Updike, Styron. Biographies of Roosevelt, Peter the Great, Sir Richard Francis Burton, Wilde, and Franklin. Mystery and suspense of Christie, Highsmith, Hillerman, Parker, James Lee Burke, le Carre, Leonard, King, Gerritsen, Koontz, Orwell, Huxley, Rand, Vonnegut, Lewis, Ballard.

Musing about this now, Nick wondered if he was letting an over-active imagination, amplified by his love of science fiction and mystery, lead him down an unrealistic path. He went over the hard facts and again explored in his mind the few explanations for those facts. He could not get around the conclusion that Anna was in potential danger. She clearly had a left chest operation in an orphanage visited by a rogue surgeon. Her little body might actually be harboring smallpox within a disintegrating package, and there were risks to blind vaccination, even if he could convince the CDC to give her the vaccine. Nick also had not told Ken that Anna suffered from occasional flare-ups of eczema, which placed her at much greater risk for a reaction to either the vaccine or immune globulin, a reaction as severe as encephalitis. She might have to take this risk, but not without strong evidence that it was necessary. And there was little time to get that evidence.

Earlier that day Nick had signed out his patients to Ken. Sarah Burley was ready to go home and Nick had convinced a skeptical Bull Burley that Nick was not abandoning her and that he would be back from "vacation" to see her in his postoperative clinic the next week. Alex Corbett was fine, and Ken would discharge him the next day. Nick's right lower lobectomy patient had not really been walking much yet and would stay another day.

Nick had arranged his flight to Moscow through Anthracite Travel. This one-person agency was owned and operated by Sandra Rosenthal, whom Nick had gotten to know well through caring for her husband. Joel Rosenthal, at age sixty-five, a few years older than his wife, had suffered from a life of gastroesophageal reflux. This began as occasional heartburn, then progressed to daily heartburn, and then trouble swallowing solid food. Fortunately, this dysphagia was not due to cancer but rather a benign stricture or narrowing of the esophagus just superior to the stomach. He was initially treated with acid-suppressing medicine, and his esophagus was dilated (stretched) by a local gastroenterologist.

When the stricture recurred despite multiple dilatations, Dr. Lombardo dilated it again and at the same time did an anti-reflux operation, a Nissen fundoplication. This entailed wrapping the upper stomach around the lowest part of the esophagus, creating a type of one-way valve to prevent acid or bile from the stomach from going back up into the esophagus. Without the constant inflammation caused by the acid or bile, the esophagus would heal without the scar-like fibrosis and contraction that led to narrowing.

The operation was done properly, but the esophagus was too far gone by that time, and the tight stricture remained recalcitrant. That was when Dr. Lombardo retired, and Nick arrived. It was apparent to Nick that the severely diseased segment of the esophagus would need to be replaced. Unlike a narrow area of a blood vessel, which was never exposed to bacteria and could be replaced with material foreign to the body, any substitute for the esophagus had to come from the patient's own body. Since only a short segment of the esophagus had to be replaced, Nick used a segment of the small intestine, the jejunum, with its blood supply maintained.

The operation went very well, and the only complication was a prolonged ileus, basically an unpredictable temporary paralysis of the intestine. This was common after major surgery but usually resolved after a few days. Joel Rosenthal's ileus lasted over two weeks, mandating intravenous feeding, which could not be managed outside the hospital in Glaston. Nick felt bad about this and spent some time talking with Joel and Sandy every day when he made rounds. He later saw them frequently in the office until he was sure that all was well. Ultimately, Joel ate better than he had in fifteen years and was exceptionally grateful.

The Anthracite Travel office comprised one long room a block off Main Street in Glaston. Sandy rose from behind her desk when Nick walked in and she rushed to him, her short legs carrying her into a tight hug around his middle. She looked up at him through large glasses, her eyes distorted by the thick lenses, her face lit by a broad smile.

"Doctor, Doctor, so good to see you! Why do you visit my humble office today? Please, sit. May I offer you a cookie and some tea? My sister made some rugelach to die for."

Nick knew better than to refuse, as Sandy would just persist. "Tea would be wonderful. Thank you."

"And rugelach."

"Yes, please."

Sandy busied herself on a countertop behind her desk. "So, you are finally going to take a vacation?"

"No, not yet. Probably when Anna's school is out for the summer. A new doctor has to establish himself."

"You already have an excellent reputation, Doctor. People talk, I listen."

"Thank you, Sandy. Actually, I need a flight to Moscow as soon as possible, even tomorrow. I also need an interpreter or guide in Moscow." Nick and Lynn had been escorted by such a guide when they had gone to Russia before; that guide had been a sports physician seeking to supplement his income. They had seen again and again, while there, that the Russian people were very practical, opportunistic in a good way, and would readily take on additional work or barter for goods or services. Bribes were commonplace, say, to get some paperwork completed faster in a bureaucratic office. Bribes could be money or, just as often, a small gift or a cake.

"You won't get a flight tomorrow, but maybe Sunday. And you're going to pay through the tuchus," Sandy said. "Let me look." She set down a teacup and a small plate of filled pastry.

"We had better make it a round-trip ticket if you know what day you want to return. That will save you a lot of questions when you arrive, questions about what you are doing in

Russia. 'Business or pleasure, Doctor? Oh, not a medical conference? No family here? Why no return ticket?'"

"That's fine," Nick said. "Let's make it three days later. But be sure that I can change it if necessary. I don't think that my research will take too long."

"Research?"

"My daughter, Anna, was adopted from Russia. I need to look up some things at her orphanage, things that are difficult to describe over the phone."

Sandy looked at him a long moment, then gave a shrug and turned back to her screen.

"I hope someday to take Anna back," Nick said quickly. "But I can't take her out of school now and there won't be time for much sightseeing."

"Well, you came to the right agent if you want a guide," Sandy said. "Joel and I attend synagogue in Ashton, just up the Interstate—Joel says there aren't enough Jews in Glaston to share a good schvitz—and we sponsor Russian immigrants all the time. Some have even stayed with us for a while. There's a list of students living in Moscow who speak English well and are always looking to make a few rubles."

"That sounds great," Nick said.

"I assume that you have a passport, but you will need a tourist visa also. This is very short notice, but I happen to have connections. Ah, here is a flight from JFK. Now, will your cell phone work in Russia?"

"I don't have the slightest idea," said Nick. "I just got it last month at that store in the mall. It apparently is the very latest model, not even fully released to the general public yet. But it was time for me to finally get rid of my old brick of a phone. It cost me over three hundred dollars, so it had better do everything but mow my lawn." He pulled his flip phone out of its small holster on his belt and handed it to Sandy.

"Motorola T720, very nice," Sandy said, flipping open the silver phone. "I read about this, color screen, good battery,

GSM technology, actually tri-band. You need a phone that can do at least 900 MHz and 1900 MHz; that way, you can use it in both the U.S. and Russia. We will need to call AT&T right now and unlock it so that you can use it overseas. And don't forget to take adaptors for the electric outlets so that you can keep it charged."

"I still have all of our adaptors, but I'm glad that you reminded me."

The call to AT&T consumed the next half hour, Nick making the call with Sandy's guidance. He hung up, slipped the phone back into its holster, and turned to her. "What's next?"

"Look, you don't need to wait around. I will make some calls and get back to you real soon."

"Sandy, you're a lifesaver," Nick had said.

"No, Doctor, you are the lifesaver."

"Daddy!" Anna ran into Nick's arms just as he set the full backpack on the floor. "Take me with you. Mrs. Pennington says you are going to Russia!"

Nick got a scent of apple shampoo as he hugged Anna to him, her straight hair tickling his cheek. "I promise that we will go together sometime when you don't have school. Plus, I'm only going to be there a couple of days." He set her down. "I need to look up some things in Moscow and I can't do it over the phone."

Anna frowned and pushed her lips out in an exaggerated pout.

"I'll bring you back something," Nick said, and immediately felt guilty using such a boringly common parent's bribe.

"Sobaka!" Anna said, one of the few Russian words that she knew.

"I don't think they'd let me take a dog on the plane, honey," Nick said.

"Maybe a small one?"

"Not even a small one," Nick said. "Don't worry. I will find something nice." He changed the subject. "You're going to have to help Mrs. Pennington take care of the house. She'll be sleeping here while I'm gone. But we have all day tomorrow together. I don't leave until Sunday. How about a movie and pizza?"

"Yes, yes, yes," said Anna, spinning around, arms outstretched.

Nick opened the top drawer of the bedroom dresser and found his passport in the front corner, hidden under some folded white handkerchiefs. The only time that he had used it was on his and Lynn's original trip to Russia. He opened the blue cover and saw the smiling face of a Thoracic Surgery Fellow looking out, anticipating becoming a new father with his beautiful wife, returning to his clinical years at a great training program, his future bright.

"Let me see, Daddy," said Anna, reaching out.

Nick handed her the passport.

"You look a little thinner, and your hair was longer," Anna said.

"I was in my research year. I had time to run every day and your Mom and I were always doing something on the weekends."

"Like what?"

"Oh, Philadelphia and the area around it have lots to do. During the winter, there are museums like the Museum of Art and the Rodin and, not far away, the Brandywine River Museum. Longwood Gardens has the most incredible plants in the world all year round. And lights at Christmas. Winterthur is an estate with spectacular gardens and collections of American furniture. And during the summer, we could, as your Mom would say, 'go down the Shore' to Atlantic City or Ocean City or even Cape May."

"I wouldn't like to see furniture," Anna said, "but the shore sounds good."

"Yes," said Nick, "that's where I grew up, in Delaware. I miss the sound of the ocean sometimes, even the smell. But we'll get back there after I'm a little better established in Glaston. It's not a long drive."

Nick found that everything, with a little manipulation, fit into the backpack, and it would be far more manageable than the hard-sided old Samsonite. He snapped shut the metal latches on each side and set the empty suitcase aside against the wall of his bedroom.

"Tomorrow is our day together. I need to stop at the travel agency, but then we can see a movie and have pizza at Joey's. Sunday, I'll be able to eat breakfast with you in the morning before I drive to the airport. This is not the local airport, but JFK in New York. The flight does not leave until the afternoon and basically flies overnight."

And will I be able to sleep on the plane? Nick thought. *And what will I find out the next day about my daughter's life?*

CHAPTER 12

After lunch, Nick and Anna drove into town, parking directly in front of Anthracite Travel. Snow was falling, but few of the people on the sidewalk or roads seemed to notice, most were dressed in warm coats and boots, many of their vehicles four-wheel drive, all accustomed to winter in the mountains of Northeastern Pennsylvania. Downtown Glaston was not busy on a Saturday afternoon, though, affected as so many small towns by the allure of shopping malls around the periphery. Nick waited as two women, arm in arm, shuffled down the sidewalk, taking short steps so as not to slip.

Sandy jumped up as they entered the agency, her mouth widening into a broad smile, eyes twinkling behind her large glasses. "Doctor Turner! And who is this?" She looked down slightly. "This must be Anna. Aren't you beautiful?"

Anna smiled at the chubby woman grasping her cheeks.

"I have everything you need, Doctor. The tourist visa was driven up from Philly this morning. It cost me all the remaining rugelach, but it was worth it. Your tickets will be available when you check in at the counter at JFK. We have already unlocked your phone. I wish we could have gotten you in first class for your long legs, but the coach tickets were dear enough on such short notice."

"Sandy, I cannot thank you enough."

"Listen, Joel has to eat all of my cooking now, no excuses, no kvetching. That is thanks enough."

The movies playing at the mall Cineplex included *Catch Me if You Can*, the movie version of *Chicago*, and a Star Trek movie, but Anna wanted to see the animated film *Spirited Away*. Movies often came to Glaston a little later than the big cities, and by the time Nick and Anna had seen *Lilo & Stitch* a few weeks before, there had been a preview of *Spirited Away*. Nick thought that it looked a little strange, albeit beautiful, but Anna's likes and dislikes were sometimes unpredictable. He was happy enough to have this day with her before his trip into the unknown.

Nick had fallen asleep in movie theaters more than once, particularly during medical school and residency, Lynn waking him as the final credits rolled. This time, though, he watched the entire movie, sharing a small box of popcorn with Anna, not wanting to fill up before their early pizza dinner. Anna was rapt, and Nick had to admit that the images on screen were both imaginative and very different from the usual cartoon.

Every so often, Nick turned slightly to his right to look at Anna. She seemed perfect, her face a study in concentration, skin flawless in the hazy light from the screen, chewing popcorn. More than once, though, he could not stop himself from picturing the three scars on the side and back of her left chest, as they were just beneath the green sweater that she wore. Even now, sitting in this dark theater, there was probably a piece of plastic in her that was slowly, slowly dissolving, eventually—and unpredictably—to release a deadly virus. He forced himself to look back at the screen.

The movie ended and Anna leapt to her feet, clapping along with the other children and their parents and grandparents.

"Ready for Joey's?" Nick asked.

"Yes, Daddy, yes!"

*

Joey's Pizza was on Main Street but at the very end of the town proper. It filled the first floor of an old brick building, the two floors above containing apartments. Joey and his family had lived in one of these apartments, but the business was doing well, and they had recently moved to a small house not far from Nick and Anna's. His daughter Gia attended Our Lady of Charity with Anna, and they sometimes played together.

Joey had grown up in a small town south of Scranton, a town heavily influenced by the Italian heritage of most of its residents. His grandparents, who lived with them, spoke very little English, Joey's parents spoke both English and Italian well, and Joey spoke only a little Italian. The entire family worked in their restaurant, Joey clearing tables and dishwashing, then making pasta under the watchful eye of his grandmother, and then cooking the veal and chicken specialties. He was an altar boy and later joined five other young men in carrying a statue of a saint on their shoulders during the annual festival parade, the wooden poles that supported the platform bending under the statue's weight.

After marrying a Glaston girl, and entrepreneurial by nature anyway, he opened Joey's Pizza. The restaurant's name belied the breadth of its offerings, but people in Glaston soon learned that by word of mouth. Joey still made the pasta by hand and still cooked the veal saltimbocca and piccata and marsala, still served sambuca to the old neighborhood men near closing time, carefully floating three coffee beans in each small glass of the clear liqueur.

Nick loved the fact that various ethnic groups in this part of Pennsylvania had not totally assimilated into a perfectly homogeneous American culture but rather had maintained many of the customs and foods from their parents' and grandparents' and great-grandparents' native country. Many Polish, Welsh, Irish, and Germans had come over to work in the anthracite coal mines of Northeastern Pennsylvania; others had simply seen opportunity and familiar terrain. Some of Nick's older patients still dressed up to see him in the office, bringing along their daughters or sons to translate, humbly presenting him on their postoperative visit with homemade pierogi or strudel.

Nick and Anna sat down at a plain oak table just back from the large front window. It was early for dinner, but Joey's menu did not change, and the restaurant was continuously open from eleven in the morning until no one wanted to stay. There were already people at half a dozen of the small tables, and a multigenerational family occupied a long one in the back. Out the window headlights were coming on in the few cars driving through the darkening day, the road mushy with snow, streetlights painting the sidewalk snow. Joey had taken in the several tiny sidewalk tables popular with coffee drinkers in other months.

Anna ordered two slices of pizza with extra cheese, her movie popcorn having been apparently already digested. Nick went with the white pizza, something he had not seen or had not noticed until moving to Glaston. He did not remember ever seeing it on a menu in Delaware or Philadelphia, even on South Street, though it had probably existed. It was a known specialty of Joey's parents and Joey had popularized it in Glaston. Just homemade crust, terrific cheeses, herbs...wonderful. They both ordered cherry Cokes.

The food arrived quickly, and Anna lifted a steaming piece to her mouth, biting off the point and chewing. Nick cut off a piece of his with a knife and fork as Anna stared. "Daddy, you are such a surgeon," she said. "Always so neat and clean." She chewed vigorously behind her smile, then drew a long drink through her straw.

"Do you really have to go all the way to Russia?" she asked, now frowning theatrically. "I bet that they don't have pizza like this, and I'm going to miss you." It was true that he had not left town or been apart from Anna since they moved there.

Why *was* he going? He realized again how out of character this was for him, the impulsivity, the lack of a definite plan, the possible risks. But the stakes had never been this high either, with the very real threat to the one person most dear to him, his Anna. With Lynn there had been nothing that he could do; she had essentially been struck by a fatal thunderbolt, an act over which he had no control whatsoever, its outcome immutable by the time he even got that call in the OR. With Anna, there was something that he could do.

He thought over his options again and concluded that he must do this himself. He had gotten about as much information as he could by calling. The Russian surgeon certainly was not going to speak with him over the phone, and maybe not even if confronted. If he tried to involve the U.S. government, he would first have to convince them, presumably the FBI or CIA, that there was a threat. Then, there would be a lengthy process of diplomacy and bureaucracy, with the risk of driving any Russian bad guys underground. Even in the very best circumstances, it would take weeks, months, or years.

And all the while there might be a tiny piece of plastic in his daughter's chest, plastic which was dissolving to release a virus into her tissues, dissolving at an unknown and unpredictable rate.

"I would guess that there is pizza in Russia," he said, "but I agree that it would not be as good as this. Maybe I should take Joey with me."

"No, take me with you!"

"But you can't make pizza."

"I can learn real quick. Mr. Joey can teach me."

"That actually sounds like a good idea for a business: bring world-class pizza to Russia. Maybe we can do that if this Thoracic Surgery thing doesn't work out for me. For this trip, though, you have to stay here in school. I'll be back in no time, probably a few days."

To Nick's surprise, Anna finished her entire drink and all but one crust of her pizza. When she saw him looking, she said, "That would be for the dog. If we had a dog."

"I love dogs," said Nick. "I just want to fence in the backyard first." Nick did not want to lead her on, but he knew that she liked talking about dogs, so he went on. "What kind of dog would be good?"

"Any kind! Probably not too tiny or too huge. But any kind."

"Why don't we look at some pictures when I get back? That will be fun. Right now, do you want some dessert? Want to split a cannoli?"

"No, the white stuff in the middle is too cheesy. May I have some of Mr. Joey's ice cream?"

"Gelato. That does sound good. What flavor would you choose?"

"Strawberry!"

So, they shared strawberry.

When they got home Anna ran up the stairs to get ready for bed, and Nick checked that the doors were locked and the drapes drawn. Few people in Glaston ever locked their doors or cars, and Nick often did not either, but recent events had spooked him. There was indeed evil in the world, and it could be unpredictable and capricious. A few days ago, he would have been worried more about his Thoracic Surgery Oral Board Exam than a potentially fatal virus in his little girl. He had passed the written exam, and the Orals loomed, but the Boards were on the back burner now.

Compared to what faced him Nick would actually have enjoyed studying for the Boards. It would normally have seemed onerous, even daunting, as there was so much to know about Adult Cardiac Surgery, Thoracic Surgery, and Congenital Cardiac

Surgery. He did not practice heart surgery of any kind in adults or children, but the training and testing were the same for all Cardiothoracic Surgeons, at least in the United States. Even recertification every ten years included all of these areas, regardless of whether a surgeon had touched the heart in the last decade.

Studying would have been a delight, however, compared to his single-handed mission to a far country. He would be a naïf dabbling in spy craft, an amateur sleuth who did not speak the language, a natural compulsive who had only the bones of a plan. His only advantages were a certain amount of intelligence and a driving abundance of love for his daughter.

As if on cue, Anna called, "I'm ready, Daddy," and he started up the stairs.

The only nights that Nick had not read to Anna at bedtime had been those nights when he slept in the hospital during his fellowship. Although one could not predict, Nick hoped that Anna would have his love of reading or perhaps could absorb it during these times in her room. Typically, she would be in her pajamas and under the covers, and Nick would sit next to her outside the covers, both of their backs propped forward by pillows against the wooden headboard, a headboard cast off from Lynn's parents.

Recently Anna had been requesting some old favorites, such as *The Garden of Abdul Gasazi* by Chris Van Allsburg and *Free Fall* by David Weisner. Nick loved both of these authors/ illustrators' work, so he was always happy to return to these. The black and white images from the former reminded him of landscapes and cityscapes on a clear night with a full moon; the latter began and ended with colorful images of a bedspread similar to Anna's. Nick had a number of their other books, all wonderful. Anna had also had a run with *Owl Moon* by Jane Yolen and John Schoenherr, another work with peaceful, quiet night scenes in nature.

Tonight, she wanted *King Bidgood's in the Bathtub* by Audrey and Don Wood, a beautifully illustrated and comically written story. Nick opened to the first page and began reading, making sure that Anna could both see the theatrical pictures and follow the words. When he finished and closed the cover, Anna said, "Another, another!"

Probably influenced by his mind being on Russia, Nick selected Jan Brett's *The Mitten*. Another beautifully illustrated story with a light-hearted theme, the book was inspired by a Ukrainian folktale and the pictures definitely had that feel to them. Anna laughed at the expressive animals in the tale, occasionally looking up at Nick to gauge his reaction. It was hard for him to be light-hearted, thinking about his trip the next day, but he thought that he acted okay.

Nick pulled the covers under Anna's chin and kissed her on her forehead. "I love you, Anna."

She pulled him down into a hug, their cheeks touching, her arms tight around his neck as if never letting go. "I love you, Daddy."

Moonlight bathed Nick's bedroom, and he hesitated at the doorway, hand halfway to the light switch, deciding to leave the light off for a few minutes. The moonlight angled through the bedroom window, striking the mirror and the framed photographs on his dresser. He walked over and picked up the picture of Lynn at the shore.

It had been evening then, the sun just visible above the cottage roofs, but the beach and sky were still bright. Lynn was playful as they walked at the edge of the surf, throwing wilted seaweed at him and sprinting away, her slim legs dusted with sand. It was their first real vacation as a married couple, and after four days the burdens of medical school had finally left them.

Lynn had dashed to the empty lifeguard stand and climbed

up, swinging her body into the broad seat, laughing at her escape. She was leaning over the arm as Nick ran up, dark hair tumbling across her face. As he focused the camera, she brushed the hair behind her right ear and smiled, the slanting light from the west catching her laughing blue eyes, her white sweater aglow.

God, she had been beautiful. He carried the photo to the window for more light, Pennsylvania moonlight that a second later might be charming a carefree young couple at the Atlantic shore. She wore no makeup in the picture, and a few freckles touched her light tan. He smelled a hint of her perfume and turned, but of course, the room was empty, the shadows deepening. As he looked back at the picture, he could taste the salt air, then realized it was his tears.

CHAPTER 13

Nick awoke with a start, his head snapping up, the sound of his own snore fading. He was in the left aisle seat of the middle seating section of the plane, many rows back from the partition separating coach from first class. He must have dozed off just after the flight ascended.

It had been a long day already. He had breakfast with Anna and Mrs. Pennington, then left for John F. Kennedy Airport at around nine thirty. The January day was cold and wet, with rain but no snow or ice. It still was a gray, miserable drive east on Interstate 80 to New York. At the airport, Nick followed signs to the long-term parking lot, retrieved his backpack from the trunk of the Accord, then took the shuttle bus to the Delta terminal. After coffee and a bagel, he walked toward the gate, surrounded by conversations in several languages from international travelers.

Nick was one of the first to sit down in the lounge at the gate, but soon others arrived, mostly single or in pairs. He wondered whether the tall blond man wearing jeans and Western boots was American or Russian. Several men entered wearing traditional Russian fur hats, but Nick overheard them speaking English with New Jersey accents. An elderly man wore a white turban.

It appeared that one couple was traveling for purposes of adoption, carrying a folded empty stroller and a soft baby bag. They sat behind Nick, and their conversation with the large woman next to them was easily audible. They were from Springfield, Massachusetts, they said proudly, home of the Basketball Hall of Fame, Smith & Wesson gun manufacturer, the Big E State Fair, and neighbor to great colleges such as Smith and Mt. Holyoke. Logan Airport in Boston was closer to their home, but the timing of this flight worked out better. The woman set the pink baby bag down between their clean new boots and asked an Asian man to take their picture.

Nick did not welcome the bittersweet memories that washed in, and he stood up to get in line to board.

Now Nick was staring at a small screen in the back of the seat his knees were rubbing, a tiny airplane blinking at the end of a curving red line which crossed the outline of Greenland. The graphic told him that their altitude was thirty-five thousand feet, and they were traveling at the equivalent of six to seven hundred miles per hour ground speed. They were 2,830 miles from Moscow, the total 4,800 miles from JFK to the Sheremetyevo Airport to be covered in eight or nine hours.

Nick's messenger bag rested on his boots under the seat in front, and he pulled it into his lap. He pushed aside a paperback edition of *The Amazing Adventures of Kavalier & Clay* and pulled out a manila folder. Sandy Rosenthal had faxed him a little information about his Russian guide, including a black and white photo. The guide was a young woman known to a good friend of the Rosenthals, a student who needed some extra income to pay tuition.

Dina Chislova stared out at him from the photo. Round face, full lips, dark hair short in what Nick thought was described as a pixie style. Her dark eyes looked directly into the camera, her face unsmiling. *Cute but intense*, Nick thought. Sandy's handwritten note described Dina as being in her early thirties, a graduate student in English and Russian Literature at The Peoples University of Russia in Moscow. She had a car and would arrange for a room for Nick. Nick would pay her by the day, and she was free all of January, as her postgraduate program had some type of intercession, and classes did not resume until February.

Nick ate some of the chicken and rice dinner when it was offered by the steward. After his tray was taken, he leaned the seat back and closed his eyes to sleep. It would be eleven in the morning in Moscow when they arrived, but still early morning hours in Glaston time. He wanted to be as rested as possible for what lay ahead.

Nick woke with sore legs and no feeling in the last two fingers of his right hand. The feeling returned in time for him to wash his face and brush his teeth in the small bathroom in the rear. Usually clean-shaven, he wondered if the faint growth of beard made him look tougher than he felt.

The plane descended through a gunmetal Moscow sky and landed. It taxied to the gate, but the passengers were not allowed to disembark, as the ground crew failed to maneuver the boarding ramp close enough to the plane door. A Russian stewardess looking out a window simply said, "Snow." A tractor pushed the entire plane back several feet and this allowed the passengers to exit. Nick recalled that on his last visit to Moscow with Lynn there had been a similar delay, that time solved with much metallic hammering.

Inside the terminal, a stern man in a dark khaki uniform directed the crowd down a flight of stairs, a fellow traveler commenting to Nick that the escalator had not worked in the five years that he had been doing business in Moscow. The passport check area lay ahead, but they first merged with a plane-load of Mongolians, many wearing boots, round fur hats, and blooming trousers held up by wide sashes. Feeling as if he had entered an Indiana Jones movie, Nick was propelled with them toward the single gate, his eyes level with the tops of their hats. No one spoke.

The mob broke into five lines as it approached the passport check area. As many dour, uniformed young men sat behind glass windows in closet-sized booths. Some would not be old enough to vote in the United States, Nick mused, but here they were given the authority to potentially make life miserable for any selected traveler. Nick's official stared at his passport for thirty seconds, then at Nick, then back at the passport. Minutes later, Nick was waved through. He remembered this taste of paranoia that had been a constant companion of the Russian people for most of their long history despite the rise of capitalism and the supposed advent of democracy.

Some passengers rented luggage carts for three American dollars, but Nick had only the one backpack and his messenger bag, so he approached Customs. After another thirty-minute wait in line at Customs, his bags were x-rayed, and he was allowed to enter the main lobby of the Sheremetyevo Airport.

There was a bristling gauntlet of people holding signs with names on them, names in English and names in Cyrillic, but Nick did not see his name. The lobby was dark, bitter cold, and seemingly still under construction. Nick was approached by taxi drivers offering to drive, or to change money or just to help him use the phone, manifesting the familiar Russian entrepreneurship that Nick found both harassing and laudable. Nick said, "Nyet, spasibo," though most seemed to speak some English. Then he saw Dina Chislova.

She stood a little apart from the other signholders, breathing deeply as if she had just run, her placard held in two outstretched arms above her head. The sign, handwritten red letters on cardboard, said "Doctor Nicholas." There was not likely another Doctor Nicholas in the airport, plus it was definitely her. Even more attractive than her photo, Nick found himself staring, as she did not immediately see him. She wore a dark, double-breasted, medium-length coat, what Nick's mother would have called a Navy pea coat, her short hair sticking out in places beneath a gray wool cap. She was a head shorter than Nick and appeared to be of medium build beneath the thick coat.

"Ms. Chislova," Nick called as he walked briskly toward her. "I am Nicholas Turner." He held out his hand.

Dark, intelligent eyes looked up into his and she did not match his smile. "You are late. Let us go." She moved to take his backpack, but he managed to hold on to it. "And call me Dina."

"The flight was delayed, and then they couldn't..." he started to say, but she kept talking as she turned toward the doors to outside.

"I rush out to bribe guard not to tow car, so I hope it is still there."

They pushed through the crowd, everyone in a heavy coat, many men and women in the ubiquitous fur caps with fur ear flaps. Nick was shocked by the cold as they exited onto the sidewalk at the front of the terminal.

"Wait here," Dina said and disappeared down the sidewalk to their left.

Ten minutes later, a small car screeched to the curb, spraying ice. Dina appeared from the driver's door on the left, came around, and, opening the passenger door, pulled forward the seatback and effortlessly threw his backpack onto the back seat. "Boot door is broken," she said. "Get in."

The black car was about the size of a Volkswagen Golf but was not as stylish. It appeared to be at least twenty years old but acted sprightly enough as Dina blasted into a gap in traffic exiting the airport. They pulled onto a four-lane boulevard lined with faceless, block-like buildings.

"You are younger than I expected," Dina said, turning to look at Nick. "I was told that you were a prominent surgeon, but you look too young."

"I do not feel too young right now," Nick said, weary from his trip. "And I am a surgeon, just not a prominent one." He looked at her profile as she concentrated on the road ahead. "I understand that you are a student?"

"When I can afford to be, da. But I am almost done. One more semester." She turned and looked directly into Nick's eyes. "Do I look too old to still be a student?"

"You don't look old at all," Nick stammered. "I mean, I was a student until I was older than you."

"But you are a surgeon, Doctor Nicholas, and I will be a teacher of literature."

"Please call me Nick," he said.

"All right, Nick," she said. It sounded like *Neek*. "Since we are both young." Nick thought that she suppressed a smile.

The car entered a bridge, and through the frosted window, Nick saw a river below.

"Moskva River," Dina said. "We are now in Moscow."

They continued down the Leningradsky Prospect, Dina cutting around other cars with the skill and seeming abandon of a New York taxi driver. Traffic was heavy on this weekday, most of the cars small but aggressive. Nick did see a few larger Volvos, a Mercedes, a Mercury Marquis, and Russian cars that he could not name. The surrounding landscape was obscured by sooty snow, as if an artist had used a little too much charcoal and smeared it. There were people out, all wearing fur hats, never with the ear flaps down. Dogs were abundant.

They turned off onto a smaller road and the snow seemed deeper, the sidewalks narrower, the buildings older and less industrial in appearance. Dina pulled to the curb and parked. She threw forward her seat and hauled Nick's bag onto the sidewalk. He made it around the front of the car in time to take the pack, his messenger bag over his shoulder, his blue down coat unzipped. Nick followed Dina up three concrete front stairs and into the lobby of an older apartment building.

Paint was peeling on all walls of the dark space, a single bare bulb above making shadows on the floor. There was just enough room for the two of them and the bags, and Nick pressed against Dina briefly in order to close the door behind. She pulled open the accordion screen to a tiny elevator and they rose slowly to the eighth floor, Nick holding the backpack up to his chest. Did he even need a pack this big? This adventure could be over in a day or two, and he would not need many clothes.

The bulb on the eighth-floor landing was out. Dina used two different keys on two locks, then showed Nick in with the sweep of an arm. "My palace."

"This is your place?" Nick was confused. "Where will I be staying?"

"You will be staying here," Dina said. She pulled off her boots and cap.

"I'll be staying with you?" Nick asked. "I mean, in your apartment?"

"Yes."

"You know, you really don't know me. I'm harmless, but still..."

"I need the money," Dina said. "And I am tougher than I look. I will show you your room. Take your boots off."

Nick saw a kitchenette to his left past two other narrow doors but Dina led him forward through an opening into a small living/dining room, then through a doorway on the right into another room. There was a fold-out couch against the left side wall, a dirty window straight ahead above a radiator, and bookshelves across the right wall to the ceiling, their shelves bending with the weight of many books. The bottom shelf held extra quilts. She put down his bag.

"The loo is off the front hallway, next to the kitchen," Dina said. "Please take your time, and when you are ready, you can tell me your plans and how I may help." She unbuttoned her coat as she walked out of the room.

The apartment was warm despite the glacial air outside. Nick took off his coat and laid it over the backpack, deciding to keep his white cable-knit sweater on. He looked at his watch, which he had reset while the plane was taxiing to the gate: four p.m. Moscow time. He calculated that it would be about nine o'clock back home. Anna would be in school, but he could let Mrs. Pennington know that he had arrived. He flipped open his phone, hoping that it really had been 'turned on' for international calls.

Mrs. Pennington answered on the third ring.

"Hello, Mrs. Pennington. I've made it," Nick said.

"You sound a long way away, Doctor, but I can hear you. I'm so glad you are there. What's it like in Russia?"

"Right now, cold and dark. I will almost certainly crash into bed soon. But everything here is fine. Please tell Anna that I will try to call tomorrow when she is home."

"I will tell her. Oh, it might be easier for you, given the time difference, to call Wednesday. The Bishop is visiting the school, and there will be no classes, just an assembly at eleven. So Anna will be here until then. And we are fine also, so do what you need to do so that you can come back soon. Don't worry about anything here."

Nick retrieved his toiletries kit from the messenger bag and padded in his wool socks to the 'loo.' The first door was the toilet room, with a rough roll of paper, flushing toilet, and boughs of fresh branches above the toilet. The next small room contained a bathtub and sink, with one thin hand towel on a peg.

He did not know why exactly, but he wanted to wash his face and shave. He used the small rough bar of soap to wash, unable to generate any lather. Fortunately, he had a travel size can of Gillette Foamy and a razor, and he shaved quickly using the small mirror, doffing and donning the heavy sweater, then brushed his hair. The man facing him in the mirror did not look to Nick like a prominent surgeon. Would he look authoritative enough, or sympathetic enough, to get the information he needed at Anna's old orphanage?

CHAPTER 14

Special Agent Elizabeth Jankiewicz heard her pager buzzing, vibrating against the wooden bench of the natatorium, before she even left the pool. She had completed 126 of a planned 130 laps, almost two miles of freestyle, but she could not ignore that irritating sound, the sound of some enormous, angry insect. Who needed the FBI on a Sunday night in January? Why couldn't it wait until Monday? She pulled herself out and padded wetly to the bench near the wall, stretching off her goggles, water dripping from her dark green swimsuit.

As the newest Special Agent in the Philadelphia District Office, having just started in November, she was not surprised that she seemed to be assigned more weekend call duty, but it always bothered her to be disturbed mid-workout. Also, there was a rapidly closing window of time during which she had been given access to this pool at the Christian Street Y, evening time well outside of normal free swim times at the facility. Her friendship with one of the swim instructors, a neighbor in her building, offered this special dispensation, one which she would never abuse.

In fact, she had grown fond of this place, historically one of the first Black YMCAs in America, used by Wilt Chamberlain and Earl Monroe, visited by Joe Louis and Wilma Rudolph. Beth Jankiewicz, blond with blue eyes, was not remotely African American, but she liked the organization's warmth and inclusiveness.

She toweled off quickly and wrapped the towel around her waist. The pool area was always warm and humid and redolent of chlorine, so even though wet, she was warm enough. She picked up the pager. The number, of course, was that of her FBI District Office on Arch Street. She flipped open her phone and dialed.

"FBI." The voice was that of DeeDee Chambers, a voice that Beth, even with her short tenure in the office, associated with off-hours calls. Beth could picture DeeDee sitting at her desk in the narrow eighth-floor office, gray hair pulled tightly back in a bun, glasses on the tip of her nose, surrounded by pictures of her grandchildren. She was probably staring out the thin window at the snow falling onto wet city streets, an open crossword puzzle book in her lap.

"DeeDee, this is Beth. I mean, Special Agent Jankiewicz."

"Oh, hi, Beth. You'll get a kick out of this one. A microbiologist at the CDC needs to speak with somebody in our District Office."

"At the what?"

"The CDC, the Centers for Disease Control. They're in Atlanta."

"And he had to do this on Sunday night?" asked Beth.

"I posed the same question before I bothered you. He says that it is a requirement as well as his duty. He would only say that he discovered something that he is obligated to report to the FBI."

"Why the Philadelphia office if he is in Atlanta?" Beth asked.

"He probably wanted to speak to a woman. Just joking. You know the first female Special Agent was right here in Philadelphia, the only female hired by J. Edgar himself. And no, I was not working the switchboard in 1924 when Lenore Houston walked the halls."

"What's the real reason?"

"I didn't get that far. Or why he was working on a Sunday

night. Anyway, his name is Dr. Patel and I have his number when you are ready."

Beth believed that Dr. Patel could wait a half hour until she showered the chlorine off, got dressed, and returned to her apartment. She might need to take notes, and although she appeared to be alone, the locker room was hardly private. After showering, she rolled her damp swimsuit in her towel and tucked it into a side pocket of her backpack. The green swimsuit, the exact color of a Masters sportscoat in the world of professional golf, was one of several practice suits remaining from her days at Slippery Rock State College, the Western Pennsylvania school where she got her degree in Political Science, swam the eight-hundred-meter freestyle, and played water polo.

She took the GLOCK 22 from the locker and clipped it onto her waistband, covering it with her winter coat. Special Agents were required to be armed at all times, and Beth was pleased that her hands were large enough to handle the standard-issue handgun. Standing over 5′9″ tall, she had nevertheless been dwarfed by her football-playing brothers and football-coaching father. All had grown up in Butler, Pennsylvania, one brother going to Penn State on scholarship and the other to Pitt. Not quite good enough for the NFL, Bobbie had taken an insurance job in New York City, and Frank worked construction in Warren, Ohio.

It had been Bobbie's death in the World Trade Center in September 2001 that propelled Beth to the FBI Academy. After Slippery Rock, she had completed law school at Duquesne, then joined one of the big Pittsburgh firms, but the constant focus on billable hours was wearing, and she had considered the FBI off and on ever since they had come to Duquesne recruiting the year of her graduation. The application process had taken a while, but Beth had always excelled academically, and her law degree helped also. After five months at the Academy here she was, the most junior Special Agent in Philadelphia and probably in any of the country's fifty-six District Offices.

In her apartment, Beth hung her suit over the shower rod to dry, made a mug of strong hot tea, and sat down at her small desk. She dialed the number that DeeDee had given her.

When a man answered with hello, Beth said "Dr. Patel. This is Special Agent Elizabeth Jankiewicz with the Philadelphia Office of the FBI. I understand you wished to report something."

"Yes, yes. It may be nothing at all, it probably is nothing at all, it is all a little surprising. But I am required to report what I am seeing." He spoke rapidly in a high-pitched voice, his accent indicating his likely country of origin. "I reported it to my superior, and she said for me to call you directly and to document that I had called."

"What would the CDC be seeing on a Sunday night that requires reporting to the FBI?" Beth asked.

"Well, I normally would not even have looked at this sample until Monday or Tuesday, but I had already come in to the lab to catch up today and the electron microscope was already fired up, as it were, so I decided to get a jump on the week's work."

"What exactly are you reporting, Dr. Patel?" Beth tried to keep him on track so that she could get this over.

"I am seeing a select agent, in fact, a Tier One select agent. Of the sixty-some select agents and toxins, biological agents determined to pose a potentially severe threat to the public, only about a dozen are in Tier One. These typically have high communicability, low dose needed to infect, and even a history of weaponization. They can produce a mass casualty event. They must be reported, whatever the surprising circumstances of their discovery." Dr. Patel sounded as if he were reading from a manual, but he probably just had a good memory. And a pedantic manner.

Beth's memory was good, too, and she had just graduated from the Academy. It had been driven into her that the FBI's first priority, especially after 9/11, was protecting the United States from terrorism, and this included biological terrorism. Dr. Patel was referring to the list of bacteria, viruses, and toxins regulated by the Department of Health and Human Services, agents such as Ebola virus and ricin. She could not imagine what he had found, but she began to take notes.

"What did you find, Dr. Patel, and how did you find it?" Beth asked.

"Well, I was away last week at a Microbiology conference, an event held every January in Lake Tahoe. Not an easy place to get to from Atlanta, but the organizer works at Stanford and likes to ski. Anyway, when I returned, I knew that work would have piled up so I came in this weekend. On my desk was a tightly sealed cylinder with a warning tape on it and a note from my supervisor 'May need EM.'"

"EM?"

"Electron Microscopy. My specialty. There was an attached typewritten note which she had already opened, so I read this and then suited up in PPE, basically like a spacesuit, and went into the isolation area with the tube. And what I saw was surprising and not absolutely definitive but worrisome enough that I called my supervisor to let her know. I am well aware of the regulations."

"Dr. Patel, what did you find?"

"So, inside the tube was a small piece of plastic and in a small chamber in the plastic was some dried material, and when I looked at a sample of this, I saw it."

Beth's pen had been poised to write for minutes. "What did you see, Doctor?"

"I saw an Orthopoxvirus!"

"What is an Orthopoxvirus?" Beth asked.

"Smallpox, of course. Smallpox." He paused. "Well, it could also be cowpox or monkeypox or some other virus in that genus, but variola major, smallpox, is the concern."

"But smallpox was eradicated years ago."

"It was eradicated worldwide in one of the greatest feats of public health in history. But samples still exist in two places: the place where I work, the CDC, and the Russian State Research Center of Virology and Biotechnology, commonly known as VECTOR."

"VECTOR. It sounds like an evil organization from a James Bond novel."

"Maybe it is. And that is the problem. What if a specimen got out of the lab and into the populace, either accidentally or intentionally? Worse, what if that specimen were a variant of the original, a variant more transmissible, more contagious, more virulent? That could happen organically if research were still being carried out or intentionally, so-called weaponization."

"But what about vaccination?"

"I am vaccinated because of what I do, and I will bet that you have been also. But they stopped vaccinating the public decades ago and no one knows if even that immunity would last this long, or if it would work against a variant. That's why variola major is still a Tier One select agent and that is why I am calling you."

"Actually, why are you calling me? I work in the Philadelphia office," Beth said.

"The specimen was sent to us from a hospital in Eastern Pennsylvania, in your District. The note from the Pathologist who sent it said that the plastic object had been removed from a patient, and in examining it, he saw characteristics worrisome for possible smallpox. Sounds like a pretty smart guy for a small-town Pathologist. He also wrote that it was completely removed intact and appears to have been a single object, but he would personally like to know the results of our analysis as soon as they are available. The whole scenario is very unusual."

"But if he was a bad guy," said Beth, "why would he send it to the CDC? And where would he have gotten a smallpox culture? What's his name?"

"Hold on." She heard rustling papers. "Dr. Ronald Smithwick, Chief of Pathology, Glaston Memorial Hospital, Glaston, Pennsylvania. Here is his office number."

Beth was writing rapidly. "When will you know for sure that this is smallpox? I'm going to speak with Dr. Smithwick, but I don't want to grill him hard if this turns out to be something else."

"I am seeing the classic brick-shaped virion under EM, the surface a homogeneous guilloche appearance. But you are right; it could be any member of the Orthopoxvirus genus. It will take a PCR assay to distinguish among them."

"What is..." Beth began.

"Polymerase Chain Reaction," Patel said, "a DNA-based test." He went on to describe PCR and the research contributions of the Mayo Clinic and Fort Detrick to the technique.

"Fascinating," Beth said, "but when will you know if this is smallpox?"

"PCR assays are quite common and could theoretically be done anywhere. But if smallpox is even suspected then one must have a Level D lab, what some call Biosafety Level Four. Fortunately, that includes us and Fort Detrick. The real catch may be getting enough genome copies from this unusual dried sample. We need probably ten to twenty-five copies. That isn't my area of expertise, I am an EM guy, but that is what I have heard. I will speak with them first thing in the morning."

"Please make a note to call me, or have them call me the moment you know." She gave him her cell phone number.

"By the way," Patel added, "smallpox only lives in humans. So, if our specimen contains smallpox, then it came from a human. And if it is a weaponized variant, then it was developed in human subjects."

"Who could even think of doing human experimentation like this or using human subjects to develop a biological weapon?"

"Remember Nazi atrocities. And imagine if you had the only vaccine for a weaponized variant of smallpox? What would that be worth?"

"But who..." Beth paused.

"Only two places in the world have smallpox," Patel said. "And I can guarantee you that this did not come from my CDC."

CHAPTER 15

At 8:05 the next morning, Beth called Dr. Ronald Smithwick from her office in the William J. Green Building. The secretary who answered, pointing out that this was a good time, before the first frozen section request came in from the OR, put her through.

"Good morning. Dr. Smithwick." The voice sounded cheerful and perhaps British.

"Good morning, Doctor. My name is Special Agent Elizabeth Jankiewicz. I am with the Philadelphia District Office of the FBI."

"I thought that you might be calling. Rather, I am not surprised that you are calling."

"Oh, how so?" Beth asked.

"Since I have not committed a crime, and since I recently sent a specimen to the CDC, then even an amateur detective would conclude that the call is in reference to that specimen. My fellow countryman Sherlock Holmes would further surmise that someone at the CDC was on the ball and examined it expeditiously, that electron microscopy confirmed my own limited identification, that your office was notified equally expeditiously and according to protocol, and that now you are obligated to learn the circumstances of this unusual and likely trivial event so that you can get on to fighting real crime.

"Also," he went on, "the fact that you are calling me early

on a Monday morning suggests that either the CDC microbiologist or you or both were working on the weekend, so you both have a sense of duty and protocol and probably curiosity. Or you do more weekend duty because you are more junior and/or you were always an over-achiever."

Definitely British, Beth thought. *And talkative.*

"Would you like to hazard a guess at my shoe size, Sherlock?" she asked.

He paused. "I apologize, Special Agent. All doctors are detectives at heart, and Pathologists even more so than other specialties. And I love the works of Conan Doyle, even the Professor Challenger novels."

Should she impress him by letting him know that she had read *The Lost World* and the others also? Better to let him underestimate her.

"So, Dr. Smithwick, start at the beginning. Maybe there is a simple explanation for all this."

"I'm afraid that there is no simple explanation, but I will tell you what happened." He relayed the events of Nick's operation on Alex Corbett. "I mean, boys are not born with pieces of plastic in their chests."

"I want to know more about that boy," Beth said, "and more about the surgeon, but please go on." She still took notes by hand rather than typing contemporaneously, so in the upper right of her legal pad, she wrote 'Surgeon' and 'Boy' as a reminder.

"The surgeon was surprised at this finding as well," Smithwick said, "and he personally delivered the specimen to my laboratory."

"Did anyone else see him remove the plastic from the boy?" Beth asked.

"I never would have even considered the implication of your question," Smithwick said, "but yes, there would have been several people in the OR who watched the whole thing on the video monitor."

"The video monitor? Was the operation filmed?"

"It was a video-assisted operation. That is, it was done with thin instruments and a video camera introduced through punctures rather than a large incision. The surgeon watches what he is doing on a video monitor, like a television screen. So anyone in the room can watch what he is doing."

Beth wrote 'OR Staff' beneath 'Surgeon' and 'Boy.'

"Is there a recording of the operation?" she asked, poised to write.

"I doubt it since it was routine, but I really don't know. In the early days of laparoscopic surgery, maybe ten years ago, surgeons would record such procedures on VHS tapes and even give them to the patients. A lot of people have videos of their laparoscopic gallbladder procedures in a stack of their favorite movies next to the VHS machine. But I think that most surgeons gave that up."

Beth wrote 'Video Recording of Operation?'

"So, the surgeon brought this piece of plastic to you," said Beth. "Then what?"

Smithwick told her about looking at the plastic under a dissecting microscope and then getting busy with other work.

"Go on," said Beth.

"I am our only full-time Pathologist, and it was a busy day, so I did not get back to the plastic until after dark. Well, it's always dark in the basement where they jail Pathologists, but you understand; it was nighttime. I finished dictating a few final Path Reports then had a spot 'o tea, then put the plastic back under the dissecting microscope. I took a scalpel and gently pried apart the two halves of the sandwich..."

"The sandwich?" Beth asked.

"Sorry. The plastic appeared to be two small rectangular pieces sealed together, with a possible chamber in the center, like a little ravioli, as it were." He told her about the scablike material and signs of a possible virus. "And although viruses require a human or animal host for survival, one particular virus has been known to persist in human eschar, scabs, for many years."

"Smallpox," Beth said.

"Variola major indeed. Now, I had no proof that this was really smallpox."

"For that, you would need EM or PCR," Beth said.

"*Exactement, Madame,*" Smithwick said. "And how likely would it be, even if it were smallpox, that anything would be viable? But Pathologists always take precautions and now I took extra precautions, sealing the object and its contents in two containers. I then sent it by special courier to the CDC and Bob's your uncle. They have not called me yet, but they may do so today, or they may wait until final confirmation. Again, the object is gone and cannot infect or harm anyone in Glaston now."

"So, this sounds as if someone went to a great deal of effort to construct a tiny plastic ravioli or, as my mother might have said, a tiny plastic pierogi. And a potentially dangerous one."

"There is an additional feature of the object," said Smithwick, "which shows even greater intention." He told her about the thinner plastic over the chamber, likely dissolving.

"What purpose would that have?" asked Beth.

"It would expose the body to whatever was in the cavity," said Smithwick. "But not immediately, only after some time. Like a miniature biological time bomb."

"Well, that's fucking diabolical," Beth said. Then, "Please excuse the language."

"No fucking problem. You are fucking correct."

"So, you are surmising that the boy could have been exposed to smallpox some time in the future. And if he got it, he could infect others."

"And few in the United States, or anywhere else for that matter, have immunity now. And there is not much vaccine, if vaccine would even work against this particular virus."

"What do you mean, 'this particular virus'?" Beth asked.

"Someone who went to the trouble of building this tiny Trojan Horse," said Smithwick, "might also have gone to the trouble of improving the smallpox. That is, improving it as a pathogen. But now I am stepping into your territory."

"You are suggesting bioterrorism?"

"A so-called weaponized variant of an already lethal microbe," said Smithwick. "But remember, we do not know for certain that we are dealing with smallpox and if so, is it still viable?"

Beth was silent for thirty seconds, writing.

"Was there anything else about the plastic object?" she asked.

"The only other feature was a tiny Cyrillic 'yah', like a capital R facing backward, embossed in one corner."

"Cyrillic like Russian?"

"Yes."

She paused again. "Did you take a picture?"

"I regret that I did not," said Smithwick. "After seeing what I saw, my heart was racing, and I sealed the thing up tight as fast as I could."

"All right, so that's the object," Beth said. "How did it get in the boy?"

"The boy had been adopted from Russia several years ago. Sometime before adoption, he had undergone a chest operation at the orphanage. The object might have been placed then. At least, that is what we are speculating. And, I can think of no other explanation."

"The boy had a chest operation at an orphanage, not in a hospital?" Beth was incredulous.

"It was a video-assisted operation performed through small punctures. My surgeon friend says that it would take a surgeon with both excellent skills and abundant chutzpah, but it is theoretically possible."

"So now we have gone from a bizarre, serendipitous finding all the way to Russian bioterrorism," Beth said. "In one conversation."

"Someone once said 'I don't make the facts, ma'am, I just report 'em.' Pathologists are like Three Princes of Serendip who were 'always making discoveries, by accidents and sagacity, of things they were not in quest of.' Horace Walpole, 1754. We like to think that there is more sagacity than accident."

"And Pasteur said, 'Chance favors the prepared mind,' so maybe you are more sage than accident-prone."

Beth flipped to the next page of her legal pad and wrote 'Boy' at the top, circling the word. "Can you give me the boy's name and his parents' names, address, and phone number?" she asked.

"I will do so as soon as I can flip open his folder," Smithwick said. "But could I ask that you hold off questioning them until we know that it is necessary? After all, this may not be smallpox and the object has been removed. It would frighten them terribly to be called by an FBI agent and the boy has not even fully recovered from his recent operation. They know that there was an object removed but we were waiting for final results before telling them more."

"You are going to think that I am a terrible person, but we are trained to be pathologically suspicious. What if the boy was actually the Trojan Horse, and his parents knew it?"

"You're kidding? What parents would knowingly infect their child with smallpox?"

"Until they traveled to Russia, he was not really their child," Beth said. "And people do unbelievable things for huge amounts of money."

"I must tell you, that was never even on our list of possibilities. And we thought that we were speculating wildly. But will you consider holding off questioning them, at least until we receive final confirmation? The object is out and secure, and they are not going anywhere."

"No promises," Beth said, "but I will try." She put herself in the place of the boy's parents and imagined their emotions and how the questioning would go. She would have to discuss all of this with her superior, one of the Assistant Special

Agents in Charge, very soon. He might demand that she question the parents and might even suggest sending someone from the Scranton or Allentown Resident Agency to interview them in person. On the other hand, the story seemed so preposterous as she imagined relating it that he might not want much energy expended on it and might not want to risk the Bureau being embarrassed. What if it really was not smallpox but instead represented some type of Russian dirty trick or prank?

She flipped to a fresh page of her legal pad. "How about the surgeon? Can you give me his information? Or is he too sensitive for questioning, too?"

"He is more sensitive than the usual surgeon, though that's not saying much," Smithwick said. "There is a phrase that circulates through surgery training programs, which may or may not be apocryphal, that 'There is no crying in Surgery.' His name is Dr. Nicholas Turner, and he is one of our best. I will give you his address and phone number in a moment, but I doubt that you will be able to reach him."

"Why do you say that?"

"He just left on a well-deserved vacation, his first since he started his practice in Glaston over a year ago. I believe that he is out of the country possibly attending a medical meeting, and his mobile phone may or may not work. I believe that he was planning on using hotel phones and a calling card to reach his housekeeper and daughter."

"Well, isn't that convenient? He drops off a packet of smallpox in the lab and then leaves the country. And you think that I should not be as suspicious as I naturally am? I will need the names and contact information of the OR staff who may or may not have witnessed the discovery of the object."

"He will only be gone for a few days," said Smithwick. "His daughter—he is a single parent—is still here in school. He has almost never been apart from her, so I guarantee you that he will return soon. It will take me an hour or so to find out who was in the room that day, and then I can call you; is that acceptable?"

"Yes, but give me the boy's and Dr. Turner's information now."

So he did.

Nick's cell phone rang, startling him. He reached a damp hand into his pants pocket, brought out the silver phone, and flipped it open. With some trepidation, he said, "Hello."

"Cheers, my peripatetic professor. It's Ronnie, live from the dungeons of Glaston Memorial."

Relieved that it wasn't Mrs. Pennington, Nick said, "I am hardly a professor, Ronnie. You know they don't give academic appointments to small town private practice surgeons. What's up?"

"I trust that your flight was uneventful. Are you in a hotel somewhere in Moscow?"

"I am actually in the flat of my guide. I just shaved, and she is setting out some food for me."

"Well, that was quick work, Romeo," Smithwick said. "You must have made quite an initial impression at the airport."

"Settle down. She needs the money, so I will stay in an extra room. And she is not all that friendly, very business-like."

"I won't keep you from your borscht. You need to know that the FBI just called me, a Special Agent Elizabeth Jankiewicz. Also very business-like, one might say cynical even. At least suspicious. She was called by the CDC yesterday. EM is consistent with Variola major. I told her the story, and she was questioning why you brought the plastic object to the lab yourself and then left the country. I told her that the OR staff witnessed everything. So, I have to call her back with the staff names, which I can get. I convinced her to hold off questioning the Corbetts—for now. And, of course, she wants to speak with you. I gave her your mobile number but intimated that your phone might not work overseas, and I did not know where you were going. So, if you get a call from a 215 exchange, you may not want to answer."

"Wow, that was fast. And now there is even more pressure on me to get some answers. Our strange, unlikely scenario is becoming possible, even probable."

"The CDC still needs to do the PCR, and I will call you when I hear anything."

"Thanks, Ronnie. I hope that I am not getting you into trouble."

"Lying to the FBI? They can't deport me because I am a dual citizen. I will only get many years in jail. Where I am sure that the populace would love a pudgy and exceptionally attractive little Brit. But seriously, Nick, you be safe."

"I will, Ronnie, you know the steady, boring me." But Nick doubted that the coming days would be boring.

CHAPTER 16

As Nick stepped out of the bathroom, Dina called to him from the kitchenette. "Let us eat while we talk. You must be hungry—no, what is a stronger English word—ravenous after your long flight."

Nick actually had little appetite, but wanted to be courteous. "That would be very nice, Dina. Thank you."

Smells from the kitchen filled the small hallway; some sort of soup or stew with beef or lamb, it seemed. Nick could hear soft bubbling but could not see a stove, which must have been to the left of the kitchen doorway. He could see a small table with two chairs, its top red Formica, the near chair just past the door and the far chair against the outside wall of the apartment. Just then, Dina turned into view, setting bowls and cups on the table. "Come, eat."

Nick took his toiletry kit into his room and returned, noticing the fading daylight out the room's narrow window. There would be no time today to visit the orphanage. He hoped that they could drive there early in the morning.

"Sit here," Dina said, indicating the chair against the wall. She set down a salad that looked like coleslaw, two kinds of bread, butter, and two bowls of lamb and cabbage stew, one in front of each place. She sat down in the other chair, her back nearly at the doorway. "Would you like vodka?" she asked.

"Oh, no," Nick said. Then, so as not to appear as boring and straitlaced as he felt, "I like vodka, but not right now.

Thank you." He tried the stew, which, despite his lack of appetite, was hearty and very flavorful. Maybe he had been eating his own cooking for too long.

"Dina, this is delicious," he said. "How did you learn to cook?"

"I lived with Aunt Masha after my parents died. Momma and Poppa were intellectuals with little enough interest in eating, much less cooking. But Aunt Masha was opposite to them. Opposite to them in looks, too, soft and round as podushka. She would tear me away from my reading and make me stand beside her in the kitchen. I was the daughter that she never had. After a while, I began to enjoy it myself; perhaps as I got better, grew in confidence. By the time that she also died, I could certainly cook for myself."

"You have had tragedy in your life," Nick said.

She finished chewing a piece of dark bread but did not look up. "Aunt Masha suffered a heart attack, but my parents should never have died. They were intelligent, outspoken Jews at a time when it was best to be none of those things." Now, she looked directly into Nick's eyes. "What do you know about being a Jew in Russia?"

"I know nothing about being a Jew in Russia," said Nick, surprised. "I'm not even Jewish."

"And you are not eating. Please eat," she said, momentarily distracted. She dipped bread into her stew and seemed to organize her thoughts as she chewed.

"Throughout Russia's long history, there has been persecution, and much worse," Dina said. "Outright imprisonment, torture, pogroms. Our leaders have either been openly antisemitic or occultly so, even to the present. Stalin, while speaking against antisemitism, killed and tortured many. There is evidence that life would have been terrible for Jewish doctors if he had not died in March of 1953.

"My parents met at University right around the time of the Six-Day War. They were both doing postgraduate work in biochemistry and had no intention to emigrate themselves, but they were involved in organizations—peaceful organizations—that promoted the rights of Jews to leave Russia. After that War in the Middle East, many more Jews wanted to emigrate to Israel, and many were refused permission by the authorities. Have you heard the term 'refuseniks'? One excuse of the government was that these individuals had been given access to information vital to national security at some point in their education or work and, therefore, could not be allowed to leave Russia.

"Several years later, I believe in the early 1970s, the government imposed a 'diploma tax,' since a significant proportion of would-be emigrants were well-educated, often in mathematics or biology or medicine. This raised the fee to a number equal to ten annual salaries or more. No one could afford that.

"As I said, my parents did not want to leave. They were students immersed in their work, close to completing research for their doctoral theses. But they had very close friends who were desperate to make aliyah, and they joined those friends in meeting at night, talking and writing pamphlets."

"What is aliyah?" Nick asked.

"For many Jews, and certainly for those who felt the persecution, emigration to homeland Israel, aliyah, was more than a dream," said Dina. "Aliyah was a life goal, necessary for survival itself. The more persistent, vocal ones were put in prison for supposed crimes, prison terms of four or five years or more. The Prisoners of Zion they were called. This had been happening for decades."

It was already dark outside the kitchen window, not yet five; a January day in Moscow. Dina's face was lit from above by the dim ceiling bulb. She looked again directly into Nick's eyes.

"My parents were brave, idealistic, good people. They left me with Masha anyway when they were out at night, many nights at that time. One night, they did not return. I was six years old. Three years later, I was told that they died in prison, a prison far away. It was maybe from disease; I like to think it was from disease."

"I am so sorry, Dina," Nick said.

"It made me strong," Dina said, but she looked away. "Masha was called my aunt but she was not really even family. Just a very good friend of my mother. They both valued good friends since the government was such an enemy. Masha was not even a Jew, or she could not have inherited this apartment from her mother, and me from her."

Dina stood, took one step, and opened the small oven. "Let's stop talk about me. I want to hear about your mission in Moscow. I want to be a good guide." She set a plate of sausages and potatoes between them, aromatic steam rising toward Nick. He had eaten only a little of the stew, but his appetite had improved some so he took a sausage and two small pieces of potato.

As Nick was waiting for Dina to sit, his phone rang again. He flipped it open as it continued to ring, then immediately hit the red 'end call' button when he saw the 215 number indicating Philadelphia. He wanted it to appear as if the call did not even go through rather than receiving a voicemail.

Dina looked at him expectantly, but did not ask for details. She sat.

"My daughter, Anna, was adopted from an orphanage in Moscow," said Nick. "It is very important for me to look at her records there. It is information that I cannot get over the phone."

"It is a long way to travel for records," Dina said, "but I will help you get to the orphanage and will help translate as needed. I am guessing that you do not speak Russian?"

"I was here before, so I recognize a few words," Nick said. "And it is a beautiful language, and I would love to be able to speak with you...to be able to speak it well. But no, I do not speak Russian." Why had he almost blushed?

"And is your wife back in America with Anna?" Dina asked.

"Lynn died when Anna was four. That was three years ago."

"Now I am sorry, Neek," said Dina, putting her hand over his on the table.

"Thank you." Nick was accustomed to people's shock. "It was very sudden, a brain tumor which bled. She had never even had a headache."

Dina frowned but said nothing. She rose, opened a small box on the kitchen counter, and carefully arranged a plate of cookies. Resting on a white paper doily, the cookies appeared to be filled. She poured two small cups of coffee without asking and sat down. "Please," she said.

The steaming coffee smelled strong. Nick took a small bite of a cookie and was surprised by how good it tasted, like raisin-filled cookies back home but somehow richer in flavor. "Dina, these are wonderful," he said.

"Sliva, plum," she said. "One of Masha's specialties."

Nick chewed a larger bite, then carefully sipped the robust coffee.

Dina relieved the somewhat awkward silence. "Tell me about your daughter. Do you have a picture?"

Nick pulled a school photograph of Anna from his wallet. Her straight brown hair and brown eyes were more like his coloring than Lynn's jet-black hair and Irish blue eyes. Nick imagined Anna and her classmates lining up along the school gym's wall, waiting their turn in the photographer's chair, the girls forming one group, giggling at nothing or at the boys. Anna wore a white shirt and burgundy sweater, smiling broadly, seeming to look right at Nick. He swallowed, then handed the photo to Dina.

"Oh, Neek, she is beautiful!" said Dina with feeling. She continued to stare at the image. "I remember myself at that age. I had begun living with Masha full time and I changed schools. That is not common in Moscow, I mean changing schools, but it was good for me because my new school taught English every year. I missed my parents, but I loved the school. And they had many books, books by great Russians and books by English writers. I have been told that I escaped into books."

Dina handed the picture back, and Nick took another long look before slipping it back into his wallet. He was beginning to feel the effects of the long trip and time difference.

"Dina, I must thank you for this very pleasant and delicious dinner," Nick said. "I had no idea where or what I would be eating, but I could not have imagined a better meal."

"You are welcome," said Dina. "You must be tired. Just tell me what time that you would like to leave in the morning and I will be certain that you are awake and fed."

"Please let me help you clean up," Nick said.

"Oh no, you are a guest," said Dina. She stood.

Nick stood also and looked down at her across the small table. "But you must tell me what you are studying. And I, too, love to read."

Dina looked up at him, seeming to weigh her decision. Her full lips turned up in a smile. "You bring dishes and I will wash."

"I am very good at drying, also."

"In Russia, we air dry," Dina said, moving to the sink.

She lifted a wooden rack from beneath the sink and set it on the counter. Nick began carrying plates from the table, but slowly, as there was little room in the sink. Dina began washing with a thin cloth.

"I study English and Russian Literature," said Dina. "It is a three-year postgraduate program and after a lifetime of study, I am nearly done. I did take some time off to work to make money, but I should finish later this year."

"I know what a lifetime of schooling is like," said Nick. "I completed my training less than two years ago."

"I believe that our schooling is much like yours," said Dina, setting two clean plates on the rack. "At about age fourteen, after eight or nine years in school, we receive Attestat ob

Osnovam Obshchem Obrazovani, a Certificate of Basic General Education. After three or four more years, we attain the Attestat ob Sredem Obshchem Obrazovani, the Certificate of Secondary General Education, like your high school diploma. Then as many as six years at university and several postgraduate years." She brushed the hair back from her forehead with the thumb of a soapy right hand.

"And now you study literature," Nick said. "When you say English Literature, do you mean British Literature? That would be what we mean in the United States, as distinct from American Literature."

"Yes, I love so many of these writers. Shakespeare, of course, was a genius, but there are so many. And they are all so different, even those who are named together like The Lake District Poets. Jonathan Swift is so different from Tennyson, who is different from Wilde, Conrad, and Joyce. I lose myself in the unreliable narrator of Ishiguro and the magical realism of Rushdie and, oh my, the imagination of Tolkien." She turned to her right, looking up at Nick, her eyes shining.

Nick could not help smiling at her open joy. He almost reached to wipe off a clump of soap suds on her forehead, but caught himself. He had not been this close to an attractive woman in some time, a woman flushed with the heat of the kitchen and her passion for good books. For a moment, he could not think what to say, but he wanted her to continue.

"Have you read the poet T.S. Eliot?" he asked.

"Yes, yes," Dina said. "We studied 'The Waste Land' for days. But I like his other poems better, 'Prufrock' and 'Gerontion' and 'Hollow Men.' Especially 'Prufrock.' We would argue in class about what a line meant, but it was the feelings evoked that were more important to me. Some poems by Philip Larkin give me the same feeling, a little sad but showing the speaker's soul. A bit Russian in that way." She put the clean, wet coffee cups on the rack, hung the dish rag on the faucet, and turned to Nick. "Would you like vodka or brandy before you rest? I would like to hear what books you like."

It was early evening, but Nick was tired. "No, thank you very much. This was a wonderful dinner, and I could talk about books all night. We will talk more tomorrow. What time do you think that an orphanage would be open in the morning?"

"Probably eight or nine o'clock. I will wake you at seven, and even if it takes an hour to drive there, you will still have all day to see the records."

"That sounds fine," said Nick, taking a step to the kitchen doorway. "Thank you again and good night."

As he padded into the entry hall, Nick heard Dina say softly, "Spokoynoy nochi, Neek."

In his room, Nick opened the suitcase but decided to sleep in his long underwear, what he would have called his base layer if running in winter. As cold as it was outside, the apartment was almost excessively warm. Nick's room was in the back of the apartment building, and out the window, he could see the lighted windows of similar buildings lined up around a flat field. Nearly the size of a football gridiron, this appeared to be a common area shared by six identical, block-like structures. Two boys called to each other as they ran across the field below, immune to the bite of the evening chill. It would be very early morning at home, not a time to call Mrs. Pennington and Anna.

Dina must have made up the couch while Nick was shaving, for it had been folded out and covered with a thick comforter. He turned off the overhead light and lay down on his back, the thin curtains still allowing light from the other buildings to barely illuminate the bookshelf to his left. He would look at the book titles in the morning, although they were likely in Russian. His mind turned to Dina.

What an interesting woman. Self-reliant and obviously intelligent, she did not guard her emotions. She was very different from Lynn, not in a bad way, just different. A little softer in appearance, she seemed to be pretty tough at her core. The image of her flushed face turned up to his at the kitchen sink flashed into his thoughts.

"*Spokoynoy nochi, Dina,*" Nick thought.

CHAPTER 17

Nick woke with a start and then realized that there had been a light knock on the door. He did not know where he was; the room was still quite dark despite faint gray daylight attempting to penetrate the room's wispy curtains. After a second, he realized, and images flashed through his mind: saying goodbye to Anna, the airports, the apartment, Dina.

He had slept fitfully, getting up twice to briefly sit on the wide window ledge, seeing only dogs in the yard below, few lights in the buildings opposite. He pulled on pants, and, picking up his toiletries kit, crossed the small entry hall into the bathroom. He could hear sounds from the kitchenette and could smell coffee as he passed. He called out, "Good morning."

"Dobroye utro, Neek," said Dina, setting a plate on the table.

Nick never had much of a beard, but he quickly shaved again. After brushing his teeth with bottled water he returned to his room, dressing in a thin turtleneck garment covered by a thick wool cable-knit sweater, then pulled on wool socks and boots. He then remembered and took off his boots.

In the kitchen, the small red tabletop was paved with plates of food, vegetable salad, bread, butter, coffee, prune cookies, cheese, and some type of jam. Dina's back was to him as she stirred something on the stove. She wore black pants and a soft gray sweater, her short hair bobbing as she vigorously stirred. She turned with a pot in one hand, using a wooden spoon to push steaming rice cereal into two bowls, then looked up at him. "Kasha. Please sit, eat."

"Dina, any one of these dishes would be enough. Thank you," said Nick.

"In Russia, we eat. If you are still hungry after this, I will reheat the stew and the sausages."

Nick put jam on a piece of dark bread while he waited for the kasha to cool. The jam was apricot and was the best that Nick had ever eaten. He indulged in a prune cookie between sips of robust coffee, then started on the kasha. "I thought that Russians only drank tea," he said.

"And I thought that Americans only liked coffee, so you have coffee. We do love tea, but not always with meals. Sometimes after a meal, sometimes separate from meals. Good tea, chai, is very important."

"Everything is delicious," Nick said.

"Spasibo. You are kind." She had finished her kasha and some bread, *obviously unafraid to enjoy food*, Nick thought, though she appeared trim. "Where would you like me to take you today?" she asked.

"I'll get the address of the orphanage," Nick said. "I believe that it's on the northern edge of Moscow, though I really wasn't paying close attention when we were here before." He went to his room for the messenger bag and returned. "I thought that Anna might want to visit Russia someday, but that's still a long way in the future. And who's to say whether she would even care about the building where she lived as an infant."

Dina looked at the paper that Nick handed her, then went into the living room and returned with a folding map, holding it in two hands as she peered at the thin lines. Nick watched her concentrate, her eyes moving. *She appeared to Nick to wear no makeup, nor*, he thought, *did she need any.*

"We should be able to find this easily," she said. "The street is on the map, so we just find the facility. This area of Moscow is not the most beautiful; many apartment buildings and warehouses. There will be numbers. Would you like to go?"

They finished cleaning up and then put on boots and winter coats. Nick took his messenger bag and Dina her wool cap and scarf. She offered Nick a similar cap, one with the hint of a pleasant fragrance. So, she did use perfume.

They drove north on a four-lane road, making their way to the outer rim of Moscow proper. The opposite direction would have taken them to Red Square, the Bolshoi, couture shopping in Tretyakovsky Passage, and exclusive nightclubs such as Momo or Ministry. The morning was overcast, the street unplowed and slushy, the combination requiring Dina to reach out the window to splash water from a plastic bottle onto the windshield periodically. Each of these episodes allowed the interior's meager heat to dissipate. The car's suspension was less than compliant, but the potholes were apparently filled with hard ice or snow, so the ride was relatively smooth.

Looking out his window Nick saw colorful billboards advertising banks, cars, electronics, Coca-Cola, and Snickers candy bars, the words in both English and Cyrillic. Dina saw him occasionally bend his head down to look out a clear area of the windshield.

"The economy is a boom," she said. "For some. Muscovites have been starved for so long that they are gluttonous now, at least those with even a little money. They are living for the day, what Andrew Marvel would have called *carpe diem*. Tomorrow...who knows?"

She suddenly pulled the car to the curb and got out. "I will be right back," she said and disappeared into a small shop. Nick could not tell what type of store it was, as there was nothing in the window, but two women came out before Dina, each carrying string bags containing small boxes. Dina, too, had a string bag when she returned, setting it on the back seat before turning to face Nick.

"Cakes," she said, "for the orphanage staff. If you want their help, it is best to bring gifts."

"A bribe," said Nick.

"There is a saying, ne podmazhesh ne poyedesh. If you don't oil the machine, you cannot start your journey. Just think of it as a nice gift."

"I will pay you back for the cakes."

Dina looked straight ahead and smiled. "I will add it to your growing bill, Neek."

She pulled into traffic and they drove silently for several miles. There were fewer billboards now, fewer shops, more apartment buildings. The buildings were monolithic, each identical to its neighbor, each more than a dozen stories tall, each as boring as the next.

"I have been thinking that I should know more about your search," said Dina. "We will certainly be asked why you want to personally look at your daughter's records and I will probably be translating."

Nick had not considered this, but she was right. The story was so incredible that he had not intended to go into it with anyone in Russia, just that his daughter had an unusual but serious medical condition, and he needed to see her records. As a doctor himself, he could understand descriptions that might be poorly relayed over the phone. His weakness, though, was the language. If Dina knew more about what he was looking for, she might see something that he or the staff would miss.

Also, although he had only known her for a day, Nick trusted Dina. She clearly had no love of authority or of the government in particular; they had persecuted and probably killed her parents. She would have no motive whatsoever to undermine him in any way. She had opened painful parts of her life to him; heck, she was an orphan herself.

"I warn you that some of this will sound like science fiction or fantasy," Nick began, "but please believe me. I would not have come all this way if it were not true. I am not a person who imagines conspiracies around me, either, but I am very concerned about Anna. She is all that I have in life." He turned left in his seat to face Dina.

"It appears that Anna had an operation while she was at the orphanage, an operation on her chest that was relatively sophisticated and was done at the orphanage itself."

"Not in a hospital?" Dina asked.

"I do this type of surgery in a hospital now, and only in a hospital," Nick went on. "At the time this was performed on Anna it was an operation that was not done even in every hospital. It was fairly new, a minimally invasive operation done with a scope and small punctures between the ribs. There apparently was a surgeon who traveled to more than one orphanage and operated on children. This in itself would be very unusual, but even more questionable is the reason to do the operation. I mean, what condition in these children would require a chest operation and then, why not do it in a hospital?"

Dina was silent, listening.

"There are conditions that might require such surgery, but they are not very common. Patent ductus arteriosis is the persistence of a small blood vessel that should close right after an infant is born and can cause heart problems if it does not. But again, this is not exceptionally common. And why not treat the child in a hospital if there is such a need?

"And it gets worse. In at least one of these children, and probably more, this surgeon implanted a small hollow piece of plastic inside the chest cavity."

"What!" Dina exclaimed. "Why would he—or she—do that?"

"It is a male surgeon," Nick said. "And it seems that the intent was evil. I know about all of this because I removed one of those pieces of plastic from a boy who had been adopted from Russia from a different orphanage. When we analyzed what was inside the plastic, we found a deadly virus, smallpox. This could have killed the boy and is also highly infectious."

"Neek, this is unbelievable," said Dina. "Why would anyone do that, and to a child?"

"Probably a combination of ego and money," Nick said. "And maybe some reason that we cannot even imagine. What if he were kicked out of the surgical establishment and wanted to get even, to show what he could do? More likely, someone paid him a lot of money."

"Who would pay money to harm children?" Dina asked.

"Now, please do not take offense at this and, again, do not think that I am paranoid, but what about the Russian government or some secret branch of the government? If smallpox infected the United States, it could cause incredible devastation. We do not have enough vaccine to control it."

"You do not have to convince me about any motive of the Russian government, however terrible," said Dina. "History is clear and they are no better now, just maybe better hidden." Then Dina turned to Nick, her eyes large. "Does Anna have this plastic?"

"Anna has three scars on her left chest, similar to the boy's," Nick said. "Whether or not she has the plastic, that is what I intend to find out."

They pulled over into a warehouse parking lot, and Dina opened her map. "We are almost there," she said and pulled back onto the road.

Dina looked at cross street signs and building numbers, when they existed. She drove more slowly and Nick peered through the grimy windshield. Ahead on the left a building looked familiar to Nick.

"There it is," he said.

The four-story rectangle was nestled between two much larger warehouses or factories. It did have many more windows than its neighbors, its window sills and central front door painted with yellow paint, paint peeling in areas. Down a long, thin alley on one side, a tall chain-link fence was visible, protecting the concrete play area in the back. *No wonder that Anna reveled in running barefoot in their grassy yard at home,* Nick thought. He seemed to remember two narrow strips of grass in the front but there was only gravel now. The economic boom had not yet reached this part of Moscow.

Dina parked the car, and, after allowing three large trucks to pass, they crossed the street. Nick knocked on the door and waited. He looked at his watch—nearly ten o'clock—and knocked more loudly. He heard a metallic click, and the door swung inward.

The large woman in the doorway, backlit by a bare bulb in the ceiling, appeared to be in her fifties, with coarse features and a direct gaze. She wore a long white lab coat over a full skirt and sweater. Nick detected body odor, a reflection of the different cultural standards around bathing frequency. Frowning, she looked as if she were about to speak, but Dina began talking rapidly, occasionally gesturing toward Nick. He heard the word "doctor" more than once. The woman's face did not soften as she spoke back to Dina, her body planted in the doorway, feet as wide apart as her broad shoulders.

"She says that the Director would have to approve your inspection of the records and he does not come in until noon. She is the Assistant Director. I told her that you were a famous doctor in America and that you adopted Anna here."

"Ask her if she would just show me the orphanage," said Nick, "so that I can tell Anna about it. I really want to see the infirmary and its equipment. And I recall the Director being very stern, very rigid. There is no guarantee that he would be more receptive."

Dina reached into her string bag and withdrew one of the two boxes. An appealing scent of apples and cinnamon filled the doorway. She began speaking again, handing the box to the Assistant Director.

"Tell her that we will be gone long before the Director arrives," added Nick.

Dina spoke again. The woman appeared to consider her options. Her expression did not soften, but she stepped aside and said, "Voyti."

"Spasibo," said Dina and stepped in. Nick followed.

They entered a narrow hallway, the one lightbulb above just adequate to allow careful passage. The Assistant Director entered the first doorway on the right, placing the box of pastries behind the door of a small office and then she waved them to follow her down the hall. They passed another doorway on the left, and Nick saw a larger office with a heavy desk, a brass plate on the door, and a window onto the street in front, likely the Director's office. They came to a junction with the building's long central hall, a wider passage extending both right and left to each end of the orphanage.

In and out of doorways, women in white moved. Each wore a thin white garment over their clothes, what Nick's mother would have called a housecoat. On each head was a white cap, *something like nurses used to wear,* Nick thought, on their feet, socks and sandals. Nick could hear the children's voices but did not see the children themselves.

They walked to the right a short distance, then entered a room that was obviously the infirmary or nurse's room. Fluorescent lights in the ceiling made the room much brighter than the hall, and an additional directional lamp on a pole unneeded except for closer inspection of a patient and presently off. One of the women in white, her back to them, was placing small packages from a cart into one of the cabinets that occupied the room's circumference. The Assistant Director spoke to her, and she turned, looking surprised.

The woman was quite thin, half her superior's size and half her age. The white housecoat and the white cap on her straight brown hair were both a bit too large for her. She looked directly at Nick as the Assistant Director continued, using words that contained America and doctor and, Nick thought, *Marta*. Could this be the English-speaking woman that he spoke to on the phone? He was about to say something but then caught himself: he did not want to risk getting her into trouble if she had bent the rules in speaking with him that night. He turned to inspect the room, not knowing how long he would have.

In the direct center of the room was a single flat examination table. *That could serve as an operating table*, he thought, *the directional lamp on the pole potentially bright enough to serve as an OR light*. Against one wall was a cart with a glass bottle and tubing and a small motor, a basic suction apparatus. And next to this Nick was shocked, and also not shocked, to see a laparoscopy tower.

Out of place in an orphanage infirmary, the metal rectangle on wheels was as tall as Nick, its shelves holding a small television monitor at eye level and below it a light source and video box. Nick did not see the rigid telescope or flexible fiberoptic light cords, but a surgeon could bring these with him and take them away when he left, traveling to the next orphanage. He also experienced a jolt of fear since this made it possible for Anna to have undergone a thoracoscopic procedure at this facility, as bizarre as that would have seemed once.

Nick turned to Dina. "Tell them that I recognize the equipment, and I am curious if a surgeon did operations here." Dina spoke, looking back and forth to each woman.

The young woman started to speak but the Assistant Director cut in loudly; Dina translated. "The Director's friend is a surgeon who helps us care for our children. He does routine examinations and some procedures, but I am not at liberty to say more; the Director has made that clear."

"May I know the surgeon's name and how I may find him? Perhaps we could talk, one surgeon to another." Dina translated, and the older woman spoke.

"She says that you may return at noon and ask the Director himself. She can say nothing about the surgeon."

"Can I get a look at Anna's record?" Nick asked. "Her name here was Anastasia and she was adopted in December of 1998."

Dina took the remaining box of pastry from her bag and spoke to the Assistant Director. The black-haired woman looked at her watch, then turned and spoke to the younger one, who bent and opened one drawer of a file cabinet near the door. Her fingers skimmed the tops of a dozen manila folders, then she took one out and handed it to Nick. Dina looked over his arm as he opened the thin folder.

There was a photograph of an infant, almost certainly Anna, stapled to the inside of the front. The next few pages were an intake form of some type from 1995. Then, there were two pages of hand-written and dated notes. Dina read quickly.

"On July 21, 1998, there was an operation on the left chest for an abnormal blood vessel. Recovery was good. That is all that it says."

"Is there any mention of a chip or plastic inserted?" asked Nick. He spoke to Dina, but out of the corner of his eye, he noted the thin young woman turn away.

"No, there is nothing more," said Dina. "Just a final note about receiving immunizations just before adoption."

Nick frowned. There was nothing more that he could learn from them. "We will have to return this afternoon to speak with the Director." He turned to the Assistant Director and gave a slight bow. "Please thank her for her help and tell her that we will be returning this afternoon since the Director may know something that is not written in the record or at least can put me in touch with the surgeon."

Nick followed the Assistant Director to the front door,

zipped his coat, and stepped out, moving aside to let Dina exit. He turned back to the large woman in the doorway and said, "Spasibo." She still did not smile.

Back in the car Nick said to Dina, "Where do we go to kill a couple of hours?"

"What do you mean, 'kill hours?'" asked Dina.

"Sorry. Where do we go to spend some time, before we can go back and speak with the Director?"

"I know exactly where we should go," said Dina. "After you and the Assistant Director left the medical room, the young woman handed me a note." Dina opened a small folded paper and showed it to Nick. "Her name is Marta."

"What does it say?"

"Meet me at the café in the bus station at noon. Vazhnyy. Important."

CHAPTER 18

Beth's phone call to Dr. Nicholas Turner ended after four odd-sounding rings. Initially, it had sounded as if the call were being routed, as she had heard a number of clicks, then delays, then the ringing, more buzzing than ringing really, then disconnect. She would try again later. In the meantime, she did not think that it was wise to delay talking with her immediate superior.

Each of the Special Agents reported to one of the several Assistant Special Agents in Charge. Beth had been assigned to Special Agent Frederick Lippert, an assignment met with little enthusiasm on the part of the latter. Lippert had been with the Bureau long enough that he had nurtured a number of newborn Special Agents, and it always added minutes or hours to his day.

Lippert had grown up in Camden, across the river, but after the Academy, he had been assigned to the New York District Office. He had moved several times within that District and had only left when offered—more accurately, assigned—this promotion in Philadelphia four years ago. It actually was good, as he could now visit his mother and aunts for a bountiful noon meal on Sundays.

Beth knocked on Lippert's half-open door, then entered his small office. She found herself looking across the top of his near-bald scalp toward the window beyond, his back to her, wingtips up on the windowsill, the black hair on the sides of his head defining a landing strip pointing to the gray January sky outside. He slowly turned and looked up at her, his dark eyes hard to read, his mouth a horizontal line, the top of his white shirt open to reveal black hair, striped tie loosened.

Beth thought, not for the first time, that Lippert would have been cast by a Hollywood director as a New York detective, one with a slightly weary, seen-it-all attitude. He even somehow appeared to walk bow-legged, his thick, short muscular frame rolling a little from side to side. She quickly sat in the one hard chair so as not to loom over him in the tight office. Lippert remained silent, waiting.

"This is an interesting case that is going to sound like the plot of a James Bond movie," Beth said, "and I am just beginning to investigate. But I feel duty-bound to tell you about it."

"So that your ass is covered," Lippert said.

"Exactly."

"Then I have taught you well. Proceed."

Beth told him about the call from Dr. Patel, glancing occasionally at her notes to get the terminology correct, and then about her conversation with Smithwick. She also told him what she had learned about the surgeon from a computer search: white-bread upbringing, trained right here in Philadelphia, tragically lost his wife, bought a small house in Glaston where his daughter attended Catholic school.

When she was finished, Lippert leaned back, his hands behind his head. "First," he said, "there is probably some explanation for all of this that we are missing. The story is just too far-fetched. So, I wouldn't go to the Agent in Charge yet and later end up with eggs on our faces. We could become the butt of years of office jokes. But we also cannot totally ignore this, since if somehow true, there would be catastrophic consequences. So, here are my thoughts."

Beth remained silent as Lippert sat forward, tapping a pen against his desk blotter.

"I just don't see the surgeon as the bad guy here," he said.

"There is nothing whatsoever in his background and, presumably, he was observed by the OR staff when he discovered the plastic object. So, you need to confirm this with the OR staff."

"I should have names and contact information very soon," Beth said. "The Pathologist promised to call me back."

"And keep trying the surgeon. We need to be sure that the stories match. Now, the parents of the boy..."

"The Corbetts."

"Yes, the Corbetts. They need to be cleared."

"I've investigated them enough to know that there has been nothing suspicious about their finances," Beth said. "I was hoping to wait for PCR confirmation of smallpox before I spoke with them directly since if there is nothing there, then we will have hit them at a time when their son is still in the hospital recovering. And I don't see them as a flight risk. If they were truly part of a scheme, they would not have even allowed the surgery. Apparently, a bedside procedure, placement of a chest drain, was an alternative that would not have risked discovery of the object."

"When will you have confirmation?"

"It could be as early as later today, but they cannot be certain due to the unusual nature of the material that they have in the plastic."

"Okay," Lippert said. "Talk to the OR staff and the surgeon and wait for the confirmation. Keep me up to date. And I would suggest not talking about this around the water cooler lest they think that both of us have been sucked into some conspiracy maelstrom."

"Got it. And the maelstrom—nice image."

For one of the first times, he smiled.

Beth's phone rang just as she entered her office on the floor below Lippert's: a 570 exchange, likely the Pathologist. She sat at her small desk, moving a legal pad into place, answering, "Special Agent Jankiewicz."

"This is Ronnie Smithwick from Glaston Memorial. I have those names that you wanted."

"I'm ready to write."

"There were three people in the OR when Dr. Turner found the plastic object: the scrub tech, circulating nurse, and nurse-anesthetist. Each of them could see a monitor, that is, they could see exactly what Dr. Turner was seeing. They also saw the plastic when it was removed and they watched him take it out of the room to bring it down to me." He gave her three names, phone numbers, and addresses.

"Do they know that I will be calling?" Beth asked.

"Yes, I told them that the FBI just needed some information since the patient was originally from Russia and the circumstances of the case were so unusual. I mentioned nothing whatsoever about any infectious disease and told them nothing more about the object."

"Thank you for your discretion, Dr. Smithwick. Our speculation alone could frighten many people, and it may be unnecessary. I do plan to speak with the nurses, but I suspect that our conversations will be brief. By the way, if Dr. Turner calls, please give him my number and ask him to call, day or night."

"It sounds as if you both keep surgeon's hours, Special Agent."

"Bioterrorism never sleeps, Doctor," Beth said. "Thank you again for your help."

It was late afternoon before Beth completed the brief telephone interviews with the operating room staff. She got the nurse-anesthetist right away, as she was off duty and at home. The other two called back, but it was after their shift ended. All told the same story about the events in the OR, essentially eliminating the surgeon as a suspect in anything.

And how could he be a suspect anyway? If he were involved in some elaborate Russian conspiracy, he would not have wanted the object found at all. It was also ridiculous to think that he would know when the boy would have a spontaneous pneumothorax and that he would be the surgeon on call and more.

Nevertheless, she tried calling Dr. Turner again, not caring if she woke him, and again struck out. This time, there were different sounds on the phone, but the call still did not go through.

The CDC had not called, and who knew when they would? Beth decided to take the Metro West from the 8th Street station, then board the Broad Street Line south to Christian Street and go for a long swim at the Y.

This time, her pager buzzed near the end of a long hot shower in the Christian Street Y locker room. She had completed her two miles, mostly freestyle but with the other three strokes mixed in for variety. She toweled herself dry and dressed, then called the District Office number. DeeDee Chambers answered.

"DeeDee, I'm not on call tonight," Beth said.

"I know, but that Dr. Patel called from the CDC, and he did not want to speak with anybody else."

"But he has my mobile phone number. He could have just called me."

"Maybe he had both numbers written down and he just called our number again. I don't know. He seems a little tightly wound, if you ask me. Very talkative. Is this the number that you have?" The Atlanta number that DeeDee read off was the same as Beth had in her phone log.

"All right," Beth said. "I'll call him right now."

*

Dr. Patel answered on the second ring. "Ah, Special Agent. I felt obligated to report that it will take a little longer for the PCR results. The specimen is just so unusual that even our most experienced laboratory technicians are challenged. I am confident, however, that they will succeed."

"Thank you, Dr. Patel."

"I feel guilty in even mentioning this, Special Agent, but the mere thought that confirmation may be positive has distributed electricity through our scientists, most of whom thought that we would never mention smallpox again. I mean, the destruction of the twin stores in the United States and Russia comes up at an international meeting every couple of years, but that has not gone anywhere. Make no mistake, we all hope that confirmation is negative since Variola major is like the boogeyman. But it has sparked animated discussion here. Like discussing a good horror movie. But with greater implications, of course." He did speak rapidly.

"Yes," Beth said. "I have done some reading and have seen pictures. Even one case of smallpox is a horror movie." An image of a child with confluent vesicles or pustules flashed into her mind, a photo from one of the old newspapers. "A pandemic for which there is no vaccine or treatment is unthinkable. When might you have a result?"

"I doubt that it will be tomorrow," Patel said. "Maybe the next day."

"Well, I will wait to hear from you, Dr. Patel. Thank you for calling." She ended the call.

Beth dried her hair with a blow dryer, then spun the combination lock and retrieved her gun and her winter coat from the locker. She placed the lock in the side pocket of her gym bag and walked down the quiet hall and out of the Y.

*

The next morning, Beth worked on other cases, but the mysterious plastic object never completely left her thoughts. At noon she pulled on her heavy coat and left the building, turning west, heading toward Thomas Jefferson University Medical Library. Ostensibly for medical faculty, students, and hospital staff, the Scott Memorial Library would certainly open its doors to a badge-waving Special Agent.

A drop in temperature overnight had promoted a robust growth of icicles on gutters, light poles, and some trees, adding rare sparkle to the urban landscape. The day was clear and bright and Beth was not bothered by the temperature in the teens. She had grown up in Western Pennsylvania and, for much of her life, had been out of the house before the sun rose, heading to pre-school swim practice in some cavernous building then, hair damp and smelling of chlorine and tinted green, rushing to homeroom or class. The walk this day was brisk and pleasant.

What she read about smallpox in the medical library was markedly less pleasant. How had she been so unaware of the history of this dreadful disease, a history spanning not just centuries but millennia? She flipped through images of children and adults affected by the virus, their bodies carpeted by fluid-filled vesicles, no square centimeter of skin normal. Other patients manifested swollen limbs and torsos, the skin thin and appearing ready to burst. One boy had hemorrhaged into his eyes, the pupils indistinct, lost in the sea of dark blood.

An hour of this was too much. She thanked the librarian on the way past the desk, then exited onto Walnut Street. She had intended to get some takeout lunch on the way back to the office, but now she had no appetite. Having walked four blocks, on impulse she entered the lobby of the Curtis Publishing Company. Once one of the largest publishers in the country, responsible for the Saturday Evening Post and Ladies Home Journal, it still had one gem in its Beaux-Arts building: the fifteen by forty-nine-foot glass-mosaic *Dream Garden* mural designed by Maxfield Parrish and produced by Louis Tiffany, one hundred thousand pieces of colored glass placed by hand to replicate Parrish's painting.

Beth had grown tired of the artist's *Daybreak* painting after seeing a print of it in her aunt's dining room on every holiday visit, and she had always liked his illustrations best—those for *The Knave of Hearts* were marvelous—but the beauty and magnitude of *Dream Garden* could not be compared to anything else. As Beth gazed across the formal reflecting pool to the work, she felt lighter, as if she might at any moment levitate, the weighty horrors of smallpox images leaving her body like smoke. She had been here twice before in her brief time in Philadelphia since the Curtis Building was so near her office, but the visits had never been so therapeutic.

She turned up 6th street when she left the Curtis lobby, passing Independence Hall and then the Liberty Bell on her right. Even in this cold, there were groups of tourists dotting the green spaces of the mall, unwilling to miss the iconic physical representation of America's freedom. Benjamin Franklin was buried a block over and the National Constitution Center, a museum dedicated to the document, was just ahead.

Beth felt a warm wave of patriotism, enough to push aside the uninvited mental video clip of the Twin Towers going down in New York and the uninvited stills of children suffering horribly from smallpox. If smallpox were indeed confirmed, as bizarre as that would be, she would not let this terrorism succeed in her country.

CHAPTER 19

Nick looked around the bus station 'snack bar,' waiting for Marta, anxious to hear what she might say. There was obviously some secrecy involved, and the information was 'important.'

He and Dina sat at a small table near the front wall of dirty windows, one of a half-dozen similar tables. To his left and opposite the wall of windows was a twenty-foot-long counter, behind which stood a cook in a white apron. Half of the counter seats were occupied, filled principally by men in the basic dress of workmen, and half of the tables by women in pairs. Past the counter, Nick could see the station waiting room through the café doorway. At the other end of the counter, behind Nick on his left, was a door leading into the 'bar,' a bare room with a counter and several additional plain tables. A number of men in the bar were lifting drinks and laughing, the clicking of glasses on wood echoing against the unadorned walls.

The only visible food was kielbasa, filling two shelves of the glass enclosed display on the counter and being fried on the burners behind the cook. There was a large coffee urn visible, but Dina had ordered tea for them both. It arrived with a small bowl of dark red jam, a tiny spoonful of which she stirred into her hot tea. Nick tried this, too, and was pleasantly surprised at the taste.

Nick looked up in time to see Marta come through the

doorway. She had replaced the white housecoat with a long wool coat and her sandals with medium-height brown boots. Her straight brown hair was pressed down by a knit cap, which she kept on after sitting next to Dina, her back to the door. She glanced out the window, then back at Nick, her eyes direct and intelligent. He thought that he would try English.

"Thank you for meeting us, Marta. May we order you something to eat?"

"Da. Chai, tea is nice," she said. Her accent was thicker than Dina's.

Dina walked to the counter and returned with tea. They sat silently, waiting for Marta to start.

"Do not return to the orphanage," she said, looking intently at Nick across the table. "The surgeon is not a nice man and he and the Director are very good friends. They drink together when he visits us and I have seen the surgeon hand over envelopes when they are in the office, I think money. No one pays attention to me. I am small. The Director will tell you nothing, and he may even tell the surgeon that you are curious."

"Why would the surgeon pay the Director?" asked Nick. "If anything, it should be the other way around. The surgeon would get paid for his medical services."

"I think he does bad things. Maybe experiments on our children."

"What would make you think that?" asked Nick.

"Why would surgeon, one who brays about his training at big institutions, go to an orphanage to examine infants and children? This is a job for Pediatrician or General Practice doctor." She took a sip of tea and went on, more animated.

"He drives up in large black Mercedes, parks in back, and Tanya—she is his personal nurse...and was more than that in the past—Tanya carries his suitcases into the clinic room. He strides in like a bear, flashing his gold Rolex watch and rings, leering at women staff. And sometimes touching them.

Not me because I do not have big breasts and buttocks." She looked sideways at Dina, who said nothing.

"We would take the child into the clinic, and they would lock the door. Perhaps two or three hours later, he would carry the child into the room next door, a room with a bed and a small tank of oxygen if needed. Usually, the child had a drain hanging down to a glass bottle full of liquid. Tanya would stay with the child, sometimes all night. There is a cot in the room also. We would take her food. I spoke with her as often as I could, and we became friends."

"Would the surgeon leave?" asked Nick. He was picturing his daughter being carried by this surgeon into the make-shift recovery room, three punctures in her chest, three punctures that she almost certainly did not need. He felt his anger and his anxiety growing.

"Nyet, no. He would go out drinking with the Director. Sometimes he would then go to a room nearby, although his apartment is in Moscow. Often he would come back and go into the room with Tanya. We would hear many noises. Moans and cries, not from the child, who I hope was sleeping. Tanya told me that he has stopped that, though, because she has gotten older and her beauty has gone. He likes the young ones."

A glass broke in the bar, and Marta started.

"The next day, the child was taken back to his bedroom with the other children. They must have removed the drain first. The child would be in pain, and we would give medicine. But children recover quickly. The surgeon would make his stop in the Director's office, then he and Tanya would get back into the Mercedes and drive away, maybe to another orphanage, maybe into Moscow. They both live in the city. But not together. They never lived together. At one time Tanya maybe was hoping for that, but the surgeon is all for himself."

"Before the operation," Nick began, "did there appear to be anything wrong with the children? Did they get short of breath or appear to be in pain?"

"No, they were all fine. The surgeon would examine several children selected by the Director and then the next month would operate on one when he returned. Many of the children went on to be adopted."

"Do you think that the Director already knew that these children would be adopted, I mean, before he selected them?" Nick asked.

Marta was still. "I never thought about this, but I think that all of those children were adopted. It would have been some months after the operation, maybe even a year in some cases. But I think that all were adopted. We are always so happy when the children find a family to love them. We cry when they leave."

"Marta, I think that my daughter, Anna, had an operation here," Nick said. "And she may be in danger because of it. That is why I am here. Do you know anything about the operation? Did Tanya ever tell you anything?"

"Oh, no. She was very afraid. Not just afraid of the Doctor, who would slap her and squeeze her arm very hard sometimes, leaving purple marks. But there were other people who scared her more, who even the surgeon treated with care. He said that they carried knives and would cut her face."

Nick could see Dina's concern as she turned to Marta. "You have been very brave," Dina said. "We do not want you to have any trouble. Do you know where we can find Tanya or the surgeon? We will never tell them about you."

"Do not even try to talk to the surgeon. He is zver, a beast, a monster. He will tell you nothing, and he would put you in danger to protect himself. Tanya was with him constantly until last year, in the clinic, in his car, in his bed. She put the children to sleep and woke them up. She knows everything that he did operating, even his private habits. At one time, she would have told you nothing." She stirred her tea. "She may have even loved him in some way. But she is angry now."

"Did he replace her?" Dina asked.

"Basically, yes," said Marta. "He replaced her in his operating, his car, his bed...everything. His new nurse, Lena, is smart and blonde and beautiful and arrogant and she likes money. She does not notice me at all. I am nothing to her, though I bring her food and blankets and whatever else she asks. The Director makes it clear that the Doctor gets whatever he wants. I saw Tanya twice last year after the Doctor cast her out, not in the nightclub where she works—I cannot afford that—but in a bar nearby."

"She works in a nightclub?" Nick asked.

"Da. One of the Doctor's friends is bol'shaya shishka," said Marta.

"Big pine cone, a big shot," Dina interjected.

"Yes, a big shot," said Marta. "Tanya says the Doctor's friends are not nice, maybe Mafia, but she needed a job. She still has her apartment in town, but she drinks even more now, needs money for vodka. She always did like vodka, but not like now. The first time I saw her, she drank like my father. The second time, like my uncle, who turned yellow and died from vomiting blood. Her face looked swollen and sad, and she cried that night. She has dreams of the little children, bad dreams. She hates the Doctor, hates him for so many reasons. She might talk with you."

"How do we find her?" asked Nick.

"She works at a gentleman's club in the city, The Smiling Mink," Marta said. "Not as a dancer but as a greeter, a pregee strasa." She turned to Dina.

"A receptionist," Dina said.

"Da, a receptionist. She takes men to tables, will arrange for a private room or a special dance, you know." She looked at Dina, then Nick. "Some days, she works during the day, sometimes the nights."

"And you really think that she will talk to us?" Nick asked.

"I do not know. But she is very angry at the doctor and even more guilty about helping him with the children, what she calls experiments. She does not know why she did it. She wishes that she could go back, that she never met him. When she drinks her vodka, she weeps and says, 'Their small bodies, their small faces looking up at me.'"

"How do we find The Smiling Mink?" Dina asked.

"It is on Georgiyevskiy Pereulok, not far from the Bolshoi," Marta said. "You will see a large bright sign. A mink. I never went in."

"Marta, you have been very kind to help us," Nick said. "And very courageous. Can we drive you back to the orphanage?"

"Oh, no," Marta said. "I will walk. The Director may be in his office now, and I do not want him to see me with you." She stood and pulled on her wool coat, slinging a rough scarf around her neck. "If you see Tanya, please tell her that I would like to see her again. Dosvidaniya." She walked rapidly into the station waiting room, then outside, not looking up as she passed the window.

Dina looked across the table at Nick. "Do we go to the Mink?"

Nick said nothing, looking at the cook frying sausages, then out the window. "It is probably our best option. We could go back and speak with the Director, but it seems very unlikely that he would help at all. In fact, he may be involved himself, at least receiving bribes. I was hoping that the orphanage records might have some indication of what was done to Anna, but that was a pipe dream."

"What is 'pipe dream'?" Dina asked.

"A pipe dream is a fantasy, one imagined while smoking drugs such as opium."

"I get it," Dina said. "This reminds me of Samuel Taylor Coleridge. You know that he never even finished *Christabel* and *Kubla Khan*. But you must have hope, Neek, for the sake of your daughter." She laid her left hand on his right across the table. "We are not done yet. How do you say it, 'not at a dead end.'"

She looked at her hand, then moved it to sip more tea.

"Even if I knew the surgeon's name and address, it is doubtful that he would feel any obligation to tell me anything, leaving aside the fact that his behavior is almost certainly criminal. I am glad that we came here, though, because I am now even more certain that he did these operations in orphanages, as bizarre as that sounds. And Anna had such an operation here. I just need to know whether they all had the same plastic object placed, and even if so, did the object contain a pathogen."

He looked out the window again. "We could visit the other orphanage where my patient had his operation. But that is a long way away, and there is no reason to believe that it would be any different there. The Director is likely being bribed to find appropriate children and then to remain silent. It sounds as if these children are already on the path to being adopted. I wonder if they all went to America?"

"Why would they all go to America?" Dina asked.

"If the Russian government is behind this, or some group within the government, then targeting their long-time nemesis would make sense," Nick said. "Imagine what would happen if smallpox became widespread in the United States. There is no treatment, and even if we had a vaccine—and we don't, to my knowledge—it could never be produced and distributed in time."

"But the disease would spread to other countries," said Dina. "The United States is not an isolated island. It would even affect Russia."

"But Russia has had time to develop and stockpile enough vaccine." He looked at her, almost apologetic. "I know that this all sounds like a bad conspiracy theory or a far-fetched movie plot. But so does doing chest operations in an orphanage, and so does plastic built to slowly dissolve and release a deadly virus. And we know that those last items are real. It happened."

There was laughter again from the bar room. A large man staggered past Nick, brushing his arm, a scent of beer and road tar lingering.

"So, we talk with Tanya or I go home," said Nick. "And I can't just go home. I came a long way for Anna."

"So, we go to the Mink," said Dina. It sounded like *Meenk*.

Nick could not suppress a smile. "To the Mink."

CHAPTER 20

The twelve-foot-tall neon mink looked down on them, its broad smile full of even white human teeth, a smile which remained even as the body repeatedly blinked off and back on.

"Like the Cheshire Cat," said Dina. "Lewis Carroll, Charles Dodgson, is one of my favorites. Leave it to Russian oligarch to steal one of literature's great images for use in his strip club."

They had driven straight from the northern industrial suburb to central Moscow, hoping to see Tanya while she was on duty. It was 3:10 p.m. now, so if she was working days, she was likely there.

The Smiling Mink was on a side street just off Tverskaya, within easy walking distance of Revolution Square. Before Dina had located a place to park, a number of blocks to the north, they had driven past shops with window displays of Dior, Chanel, and Balenciaga. Men's stores showed Italian suits and shoes; patisseries broadcast colorful displays of marzipan and chocolates. Some blocks could have been in Paris' 6th Arrondissement except for the bobbing sea of fur hats moving, despite the cold, along the sidewalk. *Rent here must be astronomical*, Nick thought.

Across the two-lane street from them, the club disclosed nothing of its purpose, its giant mink sign flashing brightly above twin black doors, each door dressed with a face-level circular mirror, probably one-way windows for a doorman within. A narrow street ran down the left side of the windowless building. As they watched, a midnight blue Range Rover pulled to the curb in front of the club. A thick-set man climbed down from the back passenger seat, his black hair oiled, his gray suit and tie partially hidden beneath a beautiful tan cashmere topcoat. The twin doors of the club opened out as he approached, each powered by a dark-suited man inside, then closed behind him, the club swallowing him as the SUV pulled away.

Nick turned to Dina. She looked good in her soft sweater and pea coat, her face pink in the cold, but neither of them was dressed nearly to the level of the man who had just entered the Smiling Mink. "Do you think they will let us in like this?"

"I think that we are fine," said Dina. "Do you have American dollars?"

"Yes."

"Even better." She took his hand, and they jogged across the street.

The doors opened, and Nick and Dina stepped past the doormen and into a small lobby. The men were security guards more than doormen, each unsmiling, each in an identical black suit, white shirt, and thin black tie, each frightening in his own way. The man on Nick's side was about Nick's height but even thinner than Nick. His face was pock-marked, his eyes unblinking, the top of a blue/black tattoo just visible on his left neck above the collar. Dina was dwarfed by his colleague, two inches taller than Nick and twice as heavy, a combination of fat and muscle. His nose had been broken in the past and poorly set. Nick's man said something, and Dina put out her hand to stop Nick from walking forward.

With hands on the outside of Nick and Dina's shoulders, the men guided them to face the swinging doors on the other side of the eight-foot-long lobby, then efficiently patted them down, presumably for weapons, maybe for recording devices. Satisfied, they pushed open the padded doors, and Nick and Dina entered the club.

They stood on a semi-circular entryway about a dozen feet wide at its center, the area bordered by ornate gold railing, the main floor of the club six or eight steps below. To their right was a large open window through which Nick could see coat racks, mostly empty at this time of day. Music played loudly, a song that Nick had heard many times, a song with a beat; was it by the singer Pink?

"Your coat, please, Neek," said Dina, almost shouting over the music. "Russians always check their coats." She laid both coats on the counter and they promptly disappeared, replaced by two tickets dealt by the woman on the other side.

Nick could now take in the Smiling Mink. He had never been in a strip club, although he had seen them portrayed in movies. Directly opposite their entryway, elevated above the main floor but below their present level, was the main attraction, the stage on which dancers gyrated and danced. There was no stripping involved, as the two women wore nothing but thongs. One was upside down on a pole, the other squatting at the edge of the stage as a man stuffed rubles into her thong. Other men watched intently from their seats, rimming the stage. The women appeared young and were quite beautiful, likely reflecting the upscale nature of the Smiling Mink. Not surprisingly, they, too, were smiling.

To the left was an ornate bar, its crystal buckets of iced champagne reflecting rows of bottles on the wall. The club's floor contained a dozen tables, the right wall booths. At the bottom of the entry stairs was a podium adorned by the mink logo and behind the podium was a well-dressed woman.

From this distance she was attractive, if just a little overweight. Taller than Dina, she stood up straight, both hands on the stand, and she watched them as they descended. She appeared to be in her late thirties, well made up, hair professionally dyed red. Nick thought that her eyes looked a little bloodshot but the light was dim. Her face lit by a warm smile, she spoke a question and Dina responded. The woman spoke again.

"We need three hundred American dollars to enter," said Dina, "or more if we want a private room."

Hearing English spoken and seeing the expression on Nick's face, she said "It is double that at night. Our girls are the most beautiful in Moscow, the most accommodating, you will see."

Nick had cash in his money belt beneath the sweater, but they did not need to enter if this wasn't Tanya. He saw no alternative but to ask directly.

"Is your name Tanya?"

She appeared a little surprised but not necessarily displeased that this tall American knew her name.

"Da, I am Tanya. Why do you ask?"

Just at that moment, the doors behind them opened, and the thin security guard appeared at the top of the stairs. Looking up, Tanya saw him and spoke in a louder voice to Dina.

"She says again how much is the entrance fee," said Dina. "I think that we should pay and go in. It may be safer to talk."

Nick took six fifty-dollar bills from his money belt, lifting his sweater as little as necessary, and handed them to Tanya. She smiled broadly and led them to a booth near the stage. As they sat, she asked over the music, her smile fading, "Now, why did you ask my name?"

"I came to Moscow to learn more about my daughter," Nick began. "Anna lived at the Kryukovo orphanage before my wife and I adopted her several years ago. While she was there, she had an operation, and she may be in danger now because of this. My name is Nicholas Turner and I am a surgeon. I understand that you are a nurse."

It looked as if Tanya was trying to process this. Dina spoke to her rapidly in Russian and Nick heard the name Marta. Tanya replied in Russian and walked away.

"She says that she will return after the waitress serves us. I told her that Marta gave us her name and that she may have information that could help your little girl, maybe even save her life. No one needs to know."

"Do you think that she will help?" asked Nick.

"I do not know."

The waitress wore a bikini bottom trimmed with dark fur, presumably faux mink, and nothing else. Her makeup was heavy, but she was clearly quite young, perhaps eighteen. She asked a question pleasantly.

"What would you like, Neek?" asked Dina. "We will have to order something."

"Is Russian beer any good?" Nick asked.

"It is okay."

"Then I will have that, please," Nick said. Dina spoke to the waitress, who turned and walked to the bar.

On stage the girls had switched places. Nick watched as the previous pole dancer writhed on the floor, the music now Euro-pop, heavy on synthesizer but still with a strong beat.

He turned back to find Dina looking at him. "Russian girls receive excellent training in gymnastics," she said.

"Obviously," he said.

The waitress returned and set down their drinks, her breast brushing Nick's shoulder. Dina had ordered vodka, and it came in a small icy carafe on a rectangular wooden plate, the carafe bracketed by slices of pickle and small pieces of toast. She poured a little into an accompanying shot glass, condensation forming immediately on the glass as she finished.

"I will never drink all of this," she said, "but the smallest order was 100 ml." She touched her glass to Nick's, saying "Na zdorov'ye," and upended the entire shot glass in one easy motion. She saw Nick watching.

"Vodka is our national beverage, mother's milk. Also, our national liability. That is all that I will have for now."

As Dina had predicted, the beer was okay. They had not eaten since breakfast, so they shared the toast and pickle slices. Tanya had not returned.

"I wonder if she's getting cold feet," Nick said.

"What do you mean, 'cold feet'?"

"It means to lose one's courage or to become timid or fearful about going through with something. Even if she hates the surgeon and even if she feels bad about what they did, she may be fearful to speak about it. She did not want the security man to think that she was doing anything more than showing us to our table."

"The guards probably work for the doctor's friend," said Dina, "the one who gave her the job. He may own this club and more. He may be Mafia, or oligarch, or corrupt government official. We do not know who is paying the doctor."

"And apparently paying well," said Nick. "He drives a Mercedes and hands out bundles of money to the orphanage Director, puts Tanya up in an apartment, who knows what else."

As if reading their thoughts, Tanya arrived. She kept her broad smile as she glanced toward the front door, then spoke rapidly in a low voice to Dina. She left as quickly as she came, a hint of perfume lingering as she returned to her hostess podium near the stairs.

"She cannot stay at our table, but she will talk. When we see her go through the side door near the bar, we will leave and meet her in the alley next to the club. She takes a break to smoke cigarettes, and this is common."

Between their booth and the stage, a door opened and the man who had entered the club before them stepped out, straightening his tie, his face flushed. He strode toward Tanya, who rushed up the stairs to get his tan coat. When they met near the doors to the front lobby, he slipped bills into her hand and kissed her cheek, then rushed out. Tanya looked their way as she walked down the stairs, then she left through the side door.

"That's our cue," said Nick, beginning to rise. "How do we pay?"

"Just leave the money and a tip on the table. The drinks were eighty dollars, so you could leave one hundred. Maybe our waitress will be able to afford more clothes."

"Eighty dollars for two drinks!" Nick said. "I hope that you are not charging me that much at your place."

"No," said Dina. "But I am also not offering such sophisticated entertainment."

They tipped for their coats, squeezed past the non-smiling guards, and stepped out into light snow, the colors of the neon sign above them reflected in wet car windows across the street. They turned right and walked down the alley next to the club. There were no windows on this side of the building and only one visible door halfway down. A large green dumpster stood beyond the door. As they got closer, the red tip of a cigarette was visible beyond the dumpster.

Tanya, one arm holding a stylish dark green coat against her body, her red hair fanning over the collar, took a long pull on the cigarette before speaking. "I no longer hiding this," she said in English. "I did not become nurse to hurt small children." Outside the dim light of the club, her eyes looked puffy and mildly bloodshot. She looked directly at Nick. "Was your child one of them?"

"Yes," he said. "My daughter Anna. She's seven now."

"And you want to know about the operation?"

"Anything that you can tell me. I am a surgeon. I operated on a boy from a different orphanage and found a small piece of plastic in his chest. My daughter has the same scars and may be at great risk from a similar object. Your surgeon operated on both."

Tanya started to speak, and then her eyes widened. She was looking over Dina's shoulder in the direction of the main street. Nick turned and saw the thin security guard staring at them from the alley's entrance, arms crossed. Tanya stamped out her cigarette and spoke rapidly to Dina as she rushed to the door. The guard walked around the corner toward the front door of the Smiling Mink.

Nick took Dina's arm. "Let's go this way." They walked briskly down the alley in a direction away from the front of the club. "We can find our way to the car, but I do not want to encounter that guard." After they had turned the corner onto another street, he asked, "What did she say?"

"She gave me the address of her apartment. Her shift is nearly over, and she will speak with us there around six o'clock. I think that we should drive the car back to my street and take the Metro to her place. We have time, and I cannot leave my car parked in this area."

Nick felt a sudden chill and looked behind him, but there was no dark-suited man following. He was definitely out of his element, his comfort zone. In the operating room, he was confident; he had trained most of his life for surgery, and he felt that he could handle most situations, even critical emergencies. But here he was in a foreign country, snow falling and the light of day fading, entering strip clubs guarded by sinister men, possibly angering more powerful sinister men. But he had been so close to getting some answers to his many questions.

As if sensing his mood, Dina put her arm through his. They walked briskly down the slushy sidewalk, dodging early office workers leaving and late shoppers arriving, the time bomb in his daughter's chest briefly forgotten.

CHAPTER 21

Tanya's apartment building was relatively modern and in a nice area not far from the club in which she worked. There was no doorman, but all of the lights in the steel and glass structure worked, as did the clean elevator. Dina pushed the button for the tenth floor.

"The doctor is taking good care of her," said Dina.

"Yes," said Nick, "either out of loyalty or, more likely, for her silence."

Apartment 1004 was in the front of the building. Dina rapped on the door, waited a full minute, and rapped again. They heard a bolt move, and then the door opened. Tanya's voice sounded raspy, "Prikhodit." She slid the bolt after they entered, then turned to them.

Tanya looked as if she had been crying, her heavy eye makeup streaked. She walked slowly around them, sitting carefully in one of four chairs at a small dining table, a clear odor of alcohol trailing her. She raised her left arm and placed her hand on a bag of frozen corn on the table, covering the hand with a thin towel. Nick sat in the chair nearest her and gently peeled back the towel. They all looked at the hand, at the swollen blue fifth finger, the pinkie finger, the swelling extending onto the side of the hand itself, a slight tremor evident.

She looked into Nick's eyes, then poured clear liquid from an unlabeled bottle into a shot glass. To Dina, she said, "Get glasses there," and pointed to a kitchen cupboard. Dina set down two more shot glasses and they were promptly filled by Tanya. "Homemade vodka from inside the Arctic Circle, much smoother than Stoli." She threw down her drink.

Nick took a sip of his and found that it was surprisingly smooth. Hard liquor normally burned his throat, but this was actually cool. Tanya looked up from her hand.

"Maks, the big one, hold down my hand, and Viktor break the finger. After Maks did this." She lifted her blouse on the right side to show a six-inch purple bruise on her ribcage. "They said Yatovsky and club owner want to give me lesson about speaking with unusual guests, lesson that would not mark my face or stop me from work. This time."

"They were here?" Dina looked around quickly.

"No, they did this at the Mink," said Tanya. "There are private rooms for customers, rooms with soundproofing for... usmotreniye."

"Discretion," Dina translated. She reached over and took Tanya's good hand in both of hers.

Nick asked, "Do you have any gauze or bandages?" He wanted to splint her hand in the proper position, her wrist extended, and her fingers flexed at the MCP joints. Not only would it heal properly but the pain would diminish much faster with splinting. Tanya pointed to a bathroom door.

Nick used a roll of gauze and a thin spatula from the kitchen drawer to fashion a rudimentary splint, wrapping the entire hand and forearm and elevating it on a small pillow.

"Spasibo," Tanya said.

Nick sat facing a large window that framed the Moscow nightscape, the snow lightening, a river in the distance. Dina caught his eye, concern on her face. He looked at the half-empty bottle of vodka, then up at Tanya.

"I am done with Moscow and this life," said Tanya. "These, how you say, golden handcuffs. The nice apartment, nice clothes, the attention of wealthy men. I did not grow up like this. I will return to Severomorsk, be a good nurse again, help people instead of hurt them."

She poured more vodka and then looked out the window.

"I had good childhood in Murmansk Oblast. Father was demanding, 'specially after Momma died, but he always want more for me. He was Navy man, tough, few words. I was top student in school, learned English and science. He saved every ruble to send me to Moscow for best nursing school. I work in a best hospital, in intensive care, then surgical theater...or, you say operating room. And met Kolya, Nikolai Yatovsky, the best surgeon in the hospital." She laughed. "He would say the best in the world."

Nick looked across the table to Dina. "He is not the only surgeon who might say that," he said. "We do not lack ego."

"Oh," Tanya said. "He was very, very good. His family was well off and had connections, so Kolya went to best schools, had best surgical training. He did big lung cancer surgery, windpipe surgery, no fear. He was one of first in Russia to do thoracoscopy surgery, what is now called video-assisted thoracic surgery. He started this over ten years ago when equipment was poor, none made for the chest. But he said, 'I could do this operation with knife and spoon if necessary.' He looked down on other surgeons who needed special equipment."

Her hand had slipped off the pillow. She winced and readjusted it.

"Kolya went to United States, I think 1983 or so, right after his chest surgery training, to Boston, to do research on dogs. He was back in less than a year, kicked out. He says that he showed that chest surgery can be done without anesthesia, but the surgeons there accused him of cruelty to the dogs. He has hated America ever since. He goes to a big meeting there every year, but his mouth erupts with terrible words when America and its sophisticated surgery is mentioned. 'A baboon could operate with their expensive equipment,' he would say. Do not mention America around Kolya." She pointed to their shot glasses. "You do not drink."

Nick and Dina, wanting her to continue, each took another sip.

"Not that he only got into trouble in America," Tanya went on. "He was always pushing limits, doing operations not approved or outside his training. He was called into office of Surgery Chief many times. On those nights, he would drink and complain about 'small-minded apparatchik' and 'they envy my skill.' I was with him then. I heard it all."

She swept back her hair with her good hand. "I was his scrub nurse for most of his cases. I even stayed into the night, since he was tireless, doing any surgery that came to him. I was young and pretty and he was dynamic, ambitious. Outside the hospital he could be fun, work hard and play hard, you know.

"But patients died. He would take out any lung cancer, even if it grew into aorta or esophagus or heart. Patients would bleed or die later in ICU. Even family of medical leaders. Finally, he was told he must leave. That night was terrible, and following week also, since no other hospital in Moscow or major city would allow him to work there. Then he got a phone call and went away for two weeks. When he returned, he was old self, confident and loud. He took me to dinner in fancy hotel."

She suddenly looked up. "I am bad host. Are you hungry?" She slowly rose, right hand holding her side, and went to the kitchen, returning with bread and cheese. "Please, eat." She sat and upended another shot of vodka, but still spoke clearly.

"Kolya had been offered job by one of our new oligarchs, a millionaire, maybe a billionaire. I learned later that this man had ties to the Kremlin but these were hidden, never even acknowledged by Kolya. I never met this man, but I have my suspicions about him. I think one of our younger, very bright businessmen. Made his money in pharmaceutical industry then branched into many more businesses, homes in London and Paris and some island. Always a step ahead, smart. If there was a national shortage of a medicine, he would have already accumulated a stockpile, now could sell at exorbitant price. That kind of smart.

"Kolya did not talk much about this man. But Kolya was not shy about either drinking or boasting, and I was with him a lot, so I learned. This oligarch was called 'Ulgay.'" Tanya looked at Dina.

"Eel," Dina translated.

"Yes, eel," said Tanya. "Not his actual name, nickname. Eel is smooth and quick. My father would fish for them in river at night. Not bad eating. So, Eel said to Kolya, 'what if a terrible disease was spreading and I had the only cure or the only vaccine? People, and governments, would pay any price.' Kolya agreed, of course. I did not know what this had to do with Kolya at first, but I learned." She extracted another cigarette from the box on the table, and Nick lit it for her with the neighboring lighter.

"We started with orphanages in Murmansk Oblast, my girlhood region. The orphanage director would be bribed to select a child scheduled for future adoption to America. Kolya and I flew there by private plane, Eel's plane but no markings to indicate this. Kolya would bring his chest instruments, wrapped and sterilized. Also, a small metal box which was locked. Video tower and simple anesthesia machine had already been delivered to orphanage and would remain there.

"I would start IV on child, put to sleep with intravenous medicine, then intubate. I am very good at this, much experience. I would direct single-lumen tube into right mainstem bronchus so only right lung would be ventilated. I can estimate, but would confirm by listening to breath sounds in each lung with stethoscope. No breath sounds on left meant left lung quiet and would deflate, allowing doctor room to look into chest cavity with scope, no lung ballooning and blocking view."

Nick understood exactly what she was saying, though

he was appalled that they were doing this in a room in an orphanage and not a sterile, well-equipped operating room. The intubation of the right mainstem bronchus was a known technique for ventilating only the right lung, thereby allowing the left to collapse. The tube would frequently block the orifice to the right upper lobe, which branched off high on the right mainstem, but most people, especially healthy children, could tolerate the lack of air going to this lobe.

"We turn child left side up and wash chest with alcohol. Kolya make three tiny cuts, only millimeters, just big enough for scope and instruments. He looks into chest cavity, goes right to apex of chest and makes small cut into pleura, then creates small pocket beneath pleura, then inserts into pocket tiny piece of white plastic he takes from locked metal case. Then uses tissue glue to seal pocket. He removes scope and instruments and closes cuts with dissolving suture and bandage. Then writes in his log book name of child, date, then a red Yah or not based on nature of plastic placed."

"Your letter R is Yah," Dina said, "but backward."

"Did any of these children have patent ductus arteriosus?" Nick asked. "Do you understand?"

"Yes, I know what you mean. He tell others that this is the reason for operation, but he never even looks in that part of the chest cavity. And children did not have heart murmur, I listen." She rearranged her arm on the pillow, wincing.

"Child wakes up and I stay with them all night. Operation very quick, and children heal well, so never a problem. Also, remember, he is very good surgeon despite being bastard. Kolya go out eating and drinking with orphanage director, sometimes return if he wants sex, sometimes not. Sex right in room with child sleeping. Pig! We leave next day."

Tanya was confirming much of what Nick had surmised, as outlandish as this was. No one would believe this story normally, but Nick had seen and held a similar plastic object, one removed from an identical location within the pleural cavity of a child. He was getting close to the most crucial information.

"Tanya, why would anybody do this?" Nick asked.

"I did not know this at beginning, but on occasion, I hear Kolya talking and pilots and bodyguards on Eel's plane talking, and I learn. Then I ask Kolya after drinking, and he brags and boasts about what he is doing. You will not believe this, but inside the plastic object is smallpox, you know, very infectious and deadly virus. The plastic will dissolve over time, a few years, and virus will be released. Child will die, probably horrible death." She dabbed tears from her eyes with her good hand. Dina handed her tissues.

"By then children would be in America, adopted. They would infect many others."

"Why choose children going to America?" Nick asked.

"Kolya hated America for what happened in his past, but he would have done this anyway for the money. Eel paid much money, enough for cars and watches and dacha on lake. Also, for ego, to show he was better than other surgeons, could do new video surgery even in the bare room of an orphanage. Eel wanted America because they have money to pay and he would charge enormous money for vaccine. Also, he needed Kremlin help and they hate America."

"What do you mean, 'he needed Kremlin help'?" Nick asked.

"Russian government has only store of live smallpox outside of one place in the United States. No one had vaccine and no one being immunized for decades. Eel was given culture of the virus, which he took to special hidden facility in Siberia, and his scientists experimented. They developed special type of smallpox, even more deadly, took them years. Kolya called it..." She said a word that Nick missed.

"Weaponized," said Dina.

"Weaponized," said Tanya. Her tears had stopped. She poured more vodka, the bottle nearly empty now. "If virus got loose, nothing in the world could stop it. No old vaccine would work, even if any old vaccine was stored. Only the new vaccine developed by Eel's scientists would work. People, governments would pay anything."

Nick looked over Dina's shoulder, out the window, lights along the river like low stars in the distance. The magnitude of what he was hearing struck him, but he needed to help his daughter first.

"We have a sample of this smallpox in America now since I removed it from a boy. I would hope that our researchers can now develop a vaccine, if I can get back and convince someone that this story is true. But right now, I need to know if my daughter is at risk. It appears that she had the same operation. Did all of the plastic objects contain smallpox?"

"No, most did, but not all. Eel is slippery as his name, planned from very beginning to be crafty, to hold the knowledge of who was at risk and who not, possible additional leverage for negotiation. This is why Kolya never failed to write in log book right after surgery, Yah for those with smallpox and nothing for placebo."

"Then we need that log book," said Nick. He simply could not submit Anna, his one love, to an operation that she might not need. Also, what if the operating surgeon could not find a tiny plastic object where Nick told him it should be? Would he then prolong the operation, searching Anna's entire chest cavity?

"Oh," said Tanya, "he always keeps it with him. Eel would kill him if it was lost. He took it to all orphanages, those near Moscow, Murmansk, Black Sea, Siberia. Took it to his dacha on hunting vacation, locked in top desk drawer. He is there now, every January, right before he flies to Society of Thoracic Surgeons annual meeting in United States. He goes several days early to visit host city. Does this every year."

"He will never give it to us voluntarily," Nick said. "From what you say, even begging on behalf of my daughter will go nowhere. Does he ever leave the book in the dacha?"

"He has left it locked in his desk at times," said Tanya. "And he usually does return for more hunting. But almost always, it is with him in his leather briefcase."

Nick looked across to Dina. "I think that I have to try the dacha. The STS meeting is in San Diego and he probably has already flown there. You do not need to go with me, as I may need to break into the building and the desk, which is certainly illegal. No one in the U.S. government, even if I could convince them, can get that notebook."

"Of course, I will go, Neek," said Dina. She turned to Tanya and spoke rapidly in Russian. Tanya spoke back, her voice finally slurring some from the vodka, her eyes tearing again.

"We will fly north tomorrow," said Dina. "Tanya will have the orphanage driver meet us at the airport. He knows the area and the dacha well and drives a rugged vehicle, good for the snow. He, too, hates the surgeon, as one time he drove a little girl to the lake house on this property, and the little girl died a horrible death."

"The smallpox got out into her body," said Tanya, weeping. "She was one of the first before the plastic was perfected. Her eyes turned black."

"Can we really trust this driver?" asked Nick.

Tanya looked up at him, her eyes now red. "He is my father."

CHAPTER 22

Nick and Dina stepped out of Tanya's apartment building and into wet snow. The temperature had dropped, their breath now visible, and both pulled on wool caps. All of Moscow seemed anxious to get home, the sidewalks full of men and women, heads down, not making eye contact. Cigarettes glowed in the darkness of the January evening, reminding Nick of the fireflies of his childhood. A kiosk to their right sold drinks, candy, cassette tapes, and papers to lines of students, all smoking, all talking. ABBA sang from the window of one of the apartment buildings on the tree-lined street.

In her last few minutes awake Tanya had given Dina her father's phone number and description. Tanya had found the ex-Navy man a job as the orphanage's driver after he retired from the military. She also sketched on a napkin the layout of the surgeon's dacha, the second-floor study, and the side door with its hidden key. She would move in with a friend in the morning, a nurse unknown to Yatovsky or the doormen, and planned to leave Moscow and move back with her father as soon as possible.

Dina had guided her to bed, removing her shoes and elevating the left arm on pillows as Nick had instructed. All this had given Nick time to think, even as he busied himself clearing glasses and the nearly empty bottle. When Dina returned from the bedroom, he said, "It looks as if I fly north." Nick had never even experienced the threat of violence, but he could see no other choice than to personally get Yatovsky's notebook. No government agency could possibly do so, and certainly not in time. Nick was no action hero, but his daughter's life was truly at risk. The plastic in Alex Corbett's chest was already hydrolyzed, already thin, when Nick found it, and Anna could be in the same situation. He could not suppress the images of children infected with smallpox.

"Let us get back to my apartment, and we think this through," Dina said.

Outside Tanya's building, they turned right and headed toward the Metro stop several blocks away, walking around vendors as a stream of pedestrians, heads down, pushed past closer to the street. Suddenly, Dina stopped, grasping Nick's arm.

"Neek, look. In the park."

Across the street to their left was a small park, its trees dusted with snow, paths crossing diagonally out of sight. Leaning against a tree was a large dark form, the red of a cigarette marking its huge head. The man, bear-like in a long coat and fur hat, stepped forward, flicking away the cigarette, and stepped into the street.

"It is Maks, the big man," said Dina with a gasp.

"Let's go," said Nick, putting his arm around Dina's waist and propelling them both into the alley on their right. They could see the lights of the street at the other end, a long city block away, and they ran, dodging dumpsters on both sides, not looking back, feet splashing in the melted snow. At the end, they turned to their left, Dina hitting the shoulder of a small older woman, spinning her, saying, "Izvinyayus, sorry."

"If we can just get to the Metro, we can get on, and he will never know where we got off," said Nick. "Or you can get on, and I can outrun him. We certainly can't fight him, but I know how to run."

"We will stay together," Dina said, turning them into the next alley on their left, heading back toward the street from which they started, closer to the Metro. Nick stole a glance back over his shoulder but saw no one following. They did not slow until they reached the tree-lined street. They heard no steps behind them. On their right were several apartment buildings, some with shops on the ground floor, then a large church, then the Metro station in the distance.

"I think we lost him," Nick said close to Dina's ear. He took her arm and encouraged her forward. How had he gotten into this? He was a surgeon; his territory was the OR, the ICU, even the medical library—but not an unfamiliar foreign street. His problems were solved by intelligence and fine motor skills, not by eluding capture and likely violence. He looked back at the alleyway.

Maks was there! Just stepping out of the shadow of the passage, a hulking presence, he scanned the street with dark eyes. *He must be faster than he looked*, Nick thought. In the light of a kiosk his long leather coat glistened like oil, his fur hat ringed with a nearby student's smoke. Something glinted in his hand—a knife! He looked toward Nick and Dina and they started forward.

"Into the church," Dina said. Ahead, the building occupied much of the block, the entrance facing the point of a triangle where the street split. Slush filled Nick's shoes as he took Dina's hand and jogged across the street. They entered with a group of women, and Nick stared in awe. Most of the interior of the church was covered in ornate brass—or could it be gold—off which reflected hundreds, thousands of thin candles in red, shoulder-high stands. Paintings of Jesus, Mary, and religious scenes broke the auric splendor. Dina snatched off his wool cap.

They had entered a large room with many alcoves on each side; ahead was a short, wide hall and then the main chamber. They allowed themselves to be carried along by the crowd of women, bending their heads in an attempt to blend in. The main hall was even more spectacular, four stories of shining gold, a balcony halfway up on the left. A railing prevented the worshipers from approaching the altar area, but some went around either side to get closer. Women in black robes and babushkas kept all the candles lit. The room was constructed without seats.

Just as they entered, a deep-voiced priest appeared through enormous gold doors behind the altar, a painted room with icons visible beyond. His sing-song words were answered by a ten-person choir in the balcony loft. Incense was waved, the spicy smell intoxicating. Worshippers stood and crossed themselves vigorously and repeatedly, bowing as their right hands crossed to the left. Some women knelt on the stone floor, and some stood. Most were elderly, all wearing babushkas, their stance wide and fixed, stockings rolled down around their thick ankles.

"What are they saying?" Nick whispered.

"Some say, 'God help Russia, God help us, God help me.'" Dina looked into his eyes, then over his shoulder. "Neek!" she cried.

Maks moved through the front doors behind them, oblivious to the women half his size as he pushed through. He did not remove his hat. He strode toward the short hallway and the main altar chamber.

Nick made a decision. He lifted Dina and stepped over the railing, rushing past the startled priest and through the tall golden doors to the protection of the icons beyond. He set Dina down and turned to the doors. He was thrilled to see a hinged brass bar for securing the doors closed, and he quickly dropped it into place. The priest would be angry, but almost certainly, he knew an alternative way into the room.

Nick and Dina could faintly hear but could not see the crowd of congregants in the altar chamber, women who moved as one to block the second and larger, sacrilegious man from defiling the ceremony. By the time Maks reached the barred doors Nick and Dina had rushed from the back room into a narrow hallway, then out a back door into the night. There was the Metro station, just across a square from the back of the church, and they ran for it like rabbits to a burrow.

Nick had no time to take in the splendor of the underground hall itself, characteristic of many Moscow Metro stations, as they just had time for Dina to pay and for them to rush between the closing doors of a car, enveloped and saved from near-certain violent harm.

They stepped into Dina's apartment and locked the door. Before Nick could speak Dina threw herself against him, hugging him tightly, her head against his chest. She was not crying, but Nick could feel her heart beating rapidly even through their coats. Not knowing what to say, Nick just held her. They were a physician and a graduate student, not soldiers or spies.

They had changed trains twice at different stations on the way back to the apartment but never saw Maks or any other suspicious person. Of course, neither Nick nor Dina was a professional at evading surveillance. In their favor, though, no one knew where Nick was staying, even if they knew his identity, and they did not know Dina at all.

After a minute, Dina pulled away. They both looked at each other, momentarily embarrassed by the contact, and then Dina said, "Take off wet shoes and socks." She disappeared into her bedroom, returning with thick woolen socks for both. "Please sit." She pointed into the small living room. "I will get food. And vodka."

Nick sat down on the small, firm couch and leaned back. His heart rate had slowed, but his racing thoughts had not. Even if Maks had not proven his proclivity for violence—what he and his partner had done to Tanya was evidence enough—his appearance itself was frightening. As tall as Nick, he outweighed him by a hundred pounds, his hands huge, his nose broken at least once. Nick had never even been in a schoolyard fight. The big man could have knocked him out with one blow or, worse, brushed him aside to get to Dina. Nick could have done little to protect her. A good surgeon but not much of a man.

Dina returned from the kitchen, setting a tray on the low table and pulling up a padded chair across the table from Nick. On several small plates were slices of sausage, cheese, and pickle. Half a round loaf of dark bread sat atop two shot glasses, an ice-cold bottle of vodka glistening with condensation in the warm room. Dina poured them each a full glass and, indicating to Nick to take a slice of pickle, held her glass in the air. "Na zdorov'ye." She ate the pickle and, bringing the glass to her lips and throwing her head back, drank the clear liquid in one swallow. "Your turn for a toast."

"To unbroken body parts," Nick said with a wry smile, bringing his glass to his lips.

"No, Neek, pickle first," said Dina. "Or cheese or meat, something first, then vodka." She ate another pickle slice, then tossed down the second shot. Nick followed. The drink was cold and surprisingly smooth. Back home a shot of liquor would have made his eyes water, but this vodka was somehow different.

"Do you think that Maks just wanted to scare us?" he asked.

"The doctor knows by now that we ask about him. And he has much to hide. He may have even heard from the orphanage that someone was there."

"He probably only wanted to scare us, and he did that," said Nick. "I doubt that he would have tried to grab us and take us somewhere, although he might have had others nearby to help him. Maybe I have read too many thrillers." He did not tell Dina that he might have seen a glint of metal in Maks' hand when the thug stood in the light of the kiosk, not a gun but maybe a knife. He shuddered.

Dina extended the plate of meat, and Nick took a slice. It tasted like the kielbasa, which was so ubiquitous in

Northeastern Pennsylvania. He thought of Anna back home, but it was too late to call now. The thought did remind him, however, of his mission.

"Can you help me schedule a flight north tomorrow?" he asked. "There is a good chance that Yatovsky is already in America ahead of the Society of Thoracic Surgeons annual congress and his dacha will be empty. Tanya spent a lot of time with him and knows his habits. If she is correct, his notebook with all of the children's names may be in his desk there. It could be my last chance to find out if my daughter is at risk or if we have to put her at risk to search in her chest for a plastic foreign body."

"We go together, Neek. I will get us a flight in the morning."

Nick started to object but she put her finger to her lips. She handed him another shot of vodka and the plate of pickle slices. "To good fortune in the land where the sun does not rise," she said, tossing back the drink.

Nick followed; pickle, then shot. He looked across the small table to Dina just as she reached up with both hands and pulled her hair behind her ears. She saw him looking and smiled. She really was a lovely woman, the low light from the doorway accentuating her cheekbones and her eyes. His face felt flushed from the vodka and the warmth of the apartment. "To Anna," Nick said, and they both drank again.

"You really do not have to go, Dina. We have done nothing illegal yet, but entering someone else's lake house is clearly against the law. And that may be the lesser risk. Yatovsky and his powerful partners have a great deal to lose if their scheme is exposed. These are crimes against children, against humanity itself. I cannot believe that I am planning to do this. I mean, I have never broken the law at all, well maybe a speeding ticket rushing to the hospital. I cannot return home knowing that I did not do everything that I could, but I do not like putting you at any risk at all. You have been great." He seemed to be talking rapidly, running on.

Nick watched, as if in a dream, as Dina came around the table and knelt on the couch, straddling him, one knee on either side of his thighs. She took his face gently in both hands and said, "You are a good man, Neek," and kissed him full on his mouth, pushing him back with the pressure of her lips on his, not stopping. He felt her breasts pushing against him through their sweaters, and he circled her waist and back with his arms and pulled her tightly to him. She kissed his cheeks and his neck and he could smell her hair, still a little damp from the snow.

Then she was off him briefly, and he did not remember how their clothes got removed, but she was back straddling him, and he was inside her, so warm and so wet. It had been such a long time since he...and she was rotating her hips as she kissed him again, and he lost all control and exploded into her, throbbing and throbbing and throbbing as she pressed against him and moaned.

Now he reached up and pushed her hair behind her ears and drew her head down for another long kiss, his hands moving down her back to cup her thighs. Both of them were naked, but the room was warm, and he stayed inside her until she started to move her hips again, now getting hard and thrusting himself, his hands moving to her breasts as she arched her back. He came again as she wrapped her arms around his neck, pressing her cheek against his, and was still.

"Oh, Neek," she said softly, "you beautiful man."

CHAPTER 23

Nick awoke disoriented. The headache did not help, but he was momentarily confused, thinking that he was in his bed in Pennsylvania. Sunlight from the window to the right of the bed hit him at an angle similar to that of his bedroom at home. Then he remembered that he was in Moscow, and then memories of the day and night before came rushing back...and then memories of Dina. He lay back and let those memories linger.

An image of Lynn flashed into Nick's memory, her head thrown back and laughing as they walked near their apartment in Philadelphia. Lynn and Dina were different in so many ways but both were remarkable in so many ways. Lynn would not have wanted him to remain celibate and alone for the rest of his life, and Nick felt okay with what had happened.

After their lovemaking, Dina must have retrieved a blanket from her bedroom because he remembered both of them wrapped inside it on the small couch, kissing and caressing and saying little. It had been so long since he had done anything like this with a woman that, at times, it had seemed like he never would. He had been so busy with his move and his new practice and with Anna, and he was not the most outgoing person to begin with. But here he was in a foreign country with a stunning, intelligent, and kind woman, one who also seemed to like him, one who was also smooth and warm and naked.

They must have gone into Dina's bedroom because he

remembered waking once to find her sleeping tightly against him, her head on his chest, one leg thrown over his thigh. He was alone in her narrow bed now, and he could hear sounds from the kitchen. Before he could get up, Dina came through the doorway with a small tray, bringing with her a big smile and the smell of strong coffee. She was already dressed in dark pants and a thick white sweater, her hair brushed and glistening. She sat on the side of the bed as Nick moved over to make room.

Nick could smell soap as she leaned down and gave him a long kiss, her hand cupping his unshaven jaw.

"I let you sleep," she said. "You must have been worn out from eluding bad guys last night."

He smiled, and their eyes met. "That is not why I was worn out last night." He pulled her down for another kiss. "It is fortunate that I am an endurance athlete."

"Certainly, fortunate for me," said Dina, smiling back. She poured dark coffee into a small cup and handed it to Nick. She offered bread and jam and leftover meat and cheese from the night before. "Eat quickly and dress. We have a flight this afternoon and must drive to the airport."

"You arranged the flight already?" Nick sat up, regretting the move as his head throbbed suddenly. He sipped the coffee but was not hungry.

"We fly north from one of the smallest of Moscow's five main airports, not Sheremetyevo. The airplane will be propeller, not jet, but will be fine. We must drive to airport." Dina reached down and pulled a small soft suitcase from under the bed. "Please go, pack."

Nick slipped out of bed and walked quickly, naked, into his room, scooping up his clothes from the living room as he passed through. He shaved and quickly showered in the bathroom, ducking under the spray of the handheld bathtub hose, then dried himself with the thin towel. He took three ibuprofen tablets. Back in his room, he pulled on a snug long-sleeved winter running garment, covering this with a black wool sweater. Moscow was already cold and the Arctic Circle must be frigid. He packed everything he had brought back into the backpack.

It took a while for the interior of Dina's car to warm as they drove through city streets toward the small town on the Moscow periphery. Although daytime, the light seemed weak, as if the sun had simply given up. The slush-covered streets looked dirty, as did all of the cars. Nick saw a number of people working on their cars along the side of the road, hoods up, tools scattered. Dina told him that many Russians repaired their own cars to keep them running.

They passed through a 'bedroom community' of Moscow, an American idiom that amused Dina as she said it, with hundreds of stark apartment buildings, nothing distinguishing one from its neighbor, nothing decorative whatsoever. Then there was a little countryside, then the small town clustered around the airport, this facility obviously the town's *raison d'etre*. They passed a few individual private homes, most dilapidated but more spacious than a flat.

Dina pointed out an area of larger homes. "The Mafia," she said. "Not Mafia like *The Godfather* movie. When a Russian speaks of those who have money it is always 'The Mafia.' Sometimes a bank president or businessman is killed and who is responsible? The Mafia."

Although larger than the others, these homes would sell poorly in any upper middle-class suburb in the United States, Nick thought. It appeared that he and Anna lived better than the vast majority of Russians.

Unlike Moscow, in this smaller town, there were few cars. People walked to bus stops, pausing to buy items from kiosks, all bundled in layers against the chill air. Nick saw the airport gate ahead, its Aeroflot logo prominent: a winged hammer and scythe. Dina drove through the gate and then toward the terminal building, two stories tall and fifty yards long, an imposing block of paneled metal and, like nearly all buildings that Nick had seen today, dirty. The single parking lot was not far from the building. They parked, took their bags, and Dina locked the car, leaning in to push down the passenger lock, then using her key on the driver's door.

Inside the terminal doorway, Dina said, "Wait here, Neek" She walked to a small ticket window on their right. Nick set down his bag and looked around. The lobby was filthy and cold. Ahead were windows bordered by greasy curtains, the runway visible beyond. A stray dog searched for promising trash near Nick's feet. Dina returned with tickets to Aeroflot Flight 2369, service to the frozen north. There were no such things as seat assignments and no need to check luggage, as they would carry their own on board.

Nick looked up to see a black cat on a shelf, a lurking panther watching the airport dog. The cat leapt from the shelf and walked past them, causing Nick to think, *a black cat crossing my path is just what I need when we are about to board a small plane to fly across a thousand miles of arctic tundra.* He did not recall seeing dogs or cats in the Delta terminal at JFK.

The snack bar around the corner from the ticket window proved to be a forty-foot counter with glass-enclosed shelves and burners behind. Only the last five or six feet were being used, the remainder empty. The only food appeared to be kielbasa and a large coffee urn. Their fellow travelers, apparently manifesting sound judgment born of experience, had only the coffee.

Dina followed Nick down a flight of stairs to the toilets. This was fortunate, as it cost Russian rubles to use the room. Two large women sat behind a desk, guarding both restrooms. Dina paid, and Nick peed. It was obvious to him that the money collected did not go toward disinfectant. Before going back upstairs, they saw another doorway, an entrance to the bar, a bare room with a counter and several plain tables, décor unimportant to the number of men drinking.

Back on the main floor, they carried their bags out the back door of the terminal and into a low corrugated metal building, passing through a metal detector and traversing a hallway to their boarding area. A matron checked their tickets and weighed their luggage, making sure that neither was over the twenty-kilogram limit. They were waved into another bare room, and after twenty minutes of standing, a transport vehicle arrived, a large rectangular bus with holding straps but no seats. It carried them across the snow-covered runway to their plane.

At least the sun was shining now. Their luggage was taken from them, and they boarded via a back door. A tall stewardess said something, and they sat down, leaving their coats and hats on. All of the forty people in the nearly full plane kept their coats and fur hats on, though the cabin would warm once they were underway. The seats were thin but acceptable, and Nick saw that the carpet was in pieces and loose in areas. Above each two seats was a bell and tiny green light to call the stewardess, a superfluous accessory as the stewardess promptly fell asleep in a back seat. Nick correctly anticipated no beverages or snacks.

Most of the passengers also fell asleep as the plane ascended. They passed over the suburbs of Moscow, apartment buildings below like rows of Legos when seen from the air, all identical. There was no landscaping and no redeeming feature to any building. They left the huge city behind, and, eventually even the flat, snowy countryside disappeared beneath the clouds. Their flight would take two hours to a first stop, then an additional hour after a thirty-minute layover.

Nick turned to Dina, who sat nearer the window in the two-person row. "What happened last night, Dina? I mean, I know what happened, but how did it happen?"

She looked up at him, her eyes large in the dim cabin light. "There was an escape from danger, there was vodka, there was a man and a woman. You are a handsome man who is intelligent and kind and..." He turned her chin up and kissed her on the lips, a long kiss, neither wanting to stop. He said nothing but took her right hand in his left as she put her head against his shoulder, and they slept.

Nick and Dina woke as the plane descended through dense clouds. Suddenly the air was clear, and they saw that they flew over vast forests, woods interspersed with tracts of white fields and an occasional serpentine frozen river. The landscape was mostly flat. The airplane landed with several bumps and the stewardess, now just awake herself, indicated that all aboard must disembark at this penultimate stop.

The runway was like an icy lake, forcing the passengers to take small steps as they walked in a line toward the terminal. The word 'terminal' would have glorified the two low wooden buildings, each the size of a small house, each puffing smoke from a stone chimney. A few cars waited to pick up arriving relatives. The air was dry and exceptionally cold, the smell of wood fires familiar and comforting. The airfield was completely surrounded by forest, huge pines dusted with snow, soundless, a little ominous.

The main building that they entered was one square room with a snack area through another door; no restroom was evident. A dog near the far wall licked itself, otherwise unmoving and unconcerned despite the foot traffic. No one removed his coat or fur hat. Nick and Dina waited twenty minutes, then again passed through a checkpoint, then reboarded the plane. They were told that because of strong winds, the remaining flight would take two hours instead of one.

Shortly after takeoff, Nick rose to use the bathroom, passing the somnolent stewardess in her back row. There was water on the floor of the tiny space, more than in the container of water for washing that rested in the sink. One would never sit on the toilet or even hover too close. There was no soap and a single thin towel was shared by all on the flight. Back in his seat Nick joined Dina in promptly falling asleep.

When the plane descended again, they were over islands and frozen water, likely one of the many lakes in the Murmansk Oblast. Although lacking amenities, the flight was smooth overall. Nick pointed this out to Dina.

"I did not want to tell you," said Dina, "but Aeroflot has appalling record for flight maintenance and safety. Two planes identical to this one crashed just last week." She smiled up at Nick, her eyes shining, and he could not resist kissing her again.

They landed and the plane taxied to the relatively new terminal, a mostly stone structure as the surrounding area was known for its quarries. They were near the small city of Apatity, two hundred kilometers south of Murmansk and its naval yards on the Barents Sea. The lobby of the building was spacious and surprisingly clean. In the restroom, Nick saw urinals on one wall and stalls with holes in the floor along another wall. *Better to squat over a hole*, he thought, *than try to hover over a dirty toilet seat*. As he exited the restroom, he almost hit the airport dog as it searched for trash. Dina pointed at the dog as she came up to Nick, saying "sobaka, dog." The dogs' ears perked at the words, but it moved on when nothing more was forthcoming.

Dina moved to a bank of pay phones on a wall. "We must call Tanya's father, Vasily. He will pick us up in car." She pulled a card from her bag and punched in numbers, then more numbers. Nick heard her speak rapidly, then listen, then speak. She put the receiver in its cradle and turned. "Probably thirty to forty minutes. He has been waiting in Apatity, not town where he lives and not town of orphanage, but close. He has orphanage Jeep."

"Great. This will give me time to call Anna back home."

Mrs. Pennington answered, and then Nick heard a chair

scrape as Anna rushed to the phone. She must have been at the kitchen table eating breakfast.

"Daddy! I miss you. When are you coming home?"

"I miss you too, honey," Nick said. "It's only been two days but it seems like forever."

"It snowed here, Daddy, and everything is white. After the assembly today, Mrs. Pennington and I are going to make a snowman. She has some leftover coal for eyes from when she and her husband had a coal stove in the family room, and we have a huge carrot for a nose. She says it is a wet snow, so we should be able to roll up the snow."

Nick felt an even greater longing to be with her, to make the snowman together. "It is snowy here, too. But we don't plan to make a snowman. We are going to visit a doctor's cabin in the woods, on a lake. Kind of like the deer hunting cabins outside Glaston."

"Who is with you?" Anna asked.

"There is a woman named Dina who translates and is my guide."

"Is she pretty?"

Nick looked across the terminal lobby where Dina sat at a small table, drinking tea, waiting for Nick before eating a pastry. "Yes, she is very pretty."

"And nice?"

"Yes," Nick said, "she is very nice."

"When can I meet her?" Anna asked.

"That will not be easy, munchkin, since she is a long way from Pennsylvania. But we will see. I told her all about you."

"Does she have a dog? A sobaka?" asked Anna, proud to know the word.

"No sobaka," Nick said. "She lives in a tiny apartment in a big city. But she has a kind heart and I think that she would like dogs. I will ask her. Now, you listen to Mrs. Pennington and have fun building the snowman. I hope to get the information I need and come home soon."

"I love you, Daddy."

"I love you, too, Anna."

Nick walked across the polished stone lobby and sat across from Dina at the small table. Through a large window he could see a few cars pulling to the curb to pick up passengers, but nothing that looked like a Jeep.

"Anna wants to know if you like dogs," he said. He took a sip of sweet, warm tea.

"You told her about me?" Dina asked, smiling.

"And she wanted to know if you were pretty."

"And what did you tell her?" Dina raised her eyebrows.

"I told her that you were very pretty." Nick took her right hand in his left across the table. "And very nice."

Dina blushed. "Please eat some pastry. Vasily will be here soon."

They finished the tea and pastry, then Dina waved and pointed out the window. "That must be him. He looks just as Tanya described."

The vehicle that had pulled to the curb looked to be a rugged, Jeep-like one, possibly even sold or donated to the orphanage by the military. It rode somewhat high on large tires with deep treads. The man who had stepped from its driver's door was not tall, but he had a presence, with a trim build, straight back, and controlled movements. His gray hair was short and in a type of crew cut, his eyes light blue and unwavering as he approached them.

"Ya Vasily, k vashim uslugam." He took Nick's hand in a strong grip, repeating the process with Dina and adding a subtle bow. He opened the back of the Jeep and loaded their bags into a short but deep space, and then he moved to open the passenger door for Dina. Nick climbed into the flat back seat. A bright dome light lit the interior, but Vasily extinguished it as he drove out of the airport, his right arm working the long floor shifter with practiced precision.

The snow here was two feet deep, the roads pure ice. Despite this Vasily drove quite fast, a lifetime of driving on these roads evident. The Jeep was endowed with an excellent heater as well, a welcome feature. Nick asked and learned, through Dina, that the vehicle was a Russian UAZ, used by the military for decades.

The road straightened, and Vasily turned to Dina, speaking in short sentences with emphasis, like some military briefing. At one point he gripped the wheel tightly with both hands and paused, then continued. After nearly five minutes, he stopped, and Dina turned back to look at Nick, her face a mask of concern.

"Tanya called her father late last night when she woke to go to the bathroom. She told him enough about Dr. Yatovsky to show how evil he is, although this did not surprise her father who has seen the way the surgeon treats everyone. She emphasized that your daughter may be at risk, as a girl from our homeland, and that you need records that may be at the dacha. Vasily has driven there many times, once even transporting a sick young girl and two nurses from the orphanage, a girl whose suffering he will never forget, worse suffering than he has seen during war." Vasily nodded his head when he recognized his name and a few of the words.

"But there is more," Dina went on. "Tanya called again not long ago. She thought that she would be safe in her apartment today with the door locked until she could move in with her friend and disappear from sight. But Maks and his partner somehow got in."

Nick unconsciously took in a breath. His heart started beating faster.

"They beat her, but it did not take much for her to talk since any movement of her finger caused excruciating pain. She had to tell them of our plan to get into the lake house. They apparently do not know much about us specifically because Tanya did not know much, but Dr. Yatovsky is very angry. He is already traveling to San Diego, but he is angry."

"How is Tanya now?" Nick asked.

"She is at her friend's apartment, and no one can find her now. She is in pain, bruised, but nothing else broken it seems."

Vasily turned his head and spoke again.

"He says we must get into the dacha tonight. We have a head start, but Tanya thinks that they are on their way."

CHAPTER 24

Night fell abruptly. It had been twilight at three p.m. when they landed, and in January, there was a little sun evident at midday, but most days inside the Arctic Circle in winter were like dawn or dusk elsewhere. During the summer, the sun never set, and people went to bed strictly by the clock. The powerful headlights of the UAZ, however, cut through the darkness, showing only forest and fields on either side of the road, no houses, no people.

"We will drive through Apatity," said Nina after speaking with Vasily, "but only to get on the road north. Vasily thinks that we should go straight to the dacha without wasting time. His flat is in a smaller town along the way, but we can go there when we are done. He does not want to delay since Viktor and Maks may have access to the private plane that the surgeon always came in. It is fast."

Apatity, a small city of about one hundred thousand, had a more comfortable feel to Nick than Moscow. Some of this may have been due to Nick's small-town upbringing, but the deep snow also tended to make each scene look cleaner than anything in Moscow. Buildings were lower and somewhat newer; there were more trees and seemingly more children and dogs. There were powdery walkways, crystalline snow twinkling from the many lights. Some of the children carried small metal sleds, which Nick pointed out to Dina.

"Vasily says that in the winter, the snow, often two meters

deep, buries any car parked on the street. Only Jeeps and trucks are of any use. As many people do not drive in the winter anyway, they just leave the cars buried all winter—the cars are like bears hibernating." She smiled. "The children carry their sleds up and slide down the frozen mounds. They also ski to school."

"The children are all colorfully dressed," said Nick, watching them skate or ski, pulling the ubiquitous sleds, dogs scampering around their legs.

"Oh, no one in Russia would dress a child in black," said Dina.

They drove down the main street, passing a sports facility, theater, museum, town hall, dentist's office, women's clinic, medical clinic, stores, and daycare. Near the end was a building dedicated to geology, an important subject in the area because of the quarries, and low apartment buildings. The town was doing relatively well economically, chiefly due to a large phosphorus mining facility nearby, a plant which attracted workers from nearby Finland and even Sweden and Norway.

"We are supposed to register with the local police, but it is best that we do not," Dina said. "We have no idea how connected the surgeon is to the government, and it is better to fly under the radar, as you say."

As they left the city proper Nick saw one leftover Christmas tree next to an apartment doorway. On the other side of the walk was a Santa Claus decoration (Dina called him Def Moros), a little taller and sterner than Santa in America. Vasily turned right, then left, then right again, the road now narrower, the UAZ bumping vigorously. He said something to Dina.

"We must go around the police checkpoint at the edge of town. Most cars go through slowly, but if the officer holds up his hand, then we must stop. We cannot risk this, and Vasily knows these roads well."

Ten minutes later, after many turns and much bouncing, they turned back onto a larger, smoother road, a surface smooth chiefly because it was frozen. They came to a fork in the road, where one way led to Murmansk and the other to St. Petersburg, a sign indicating that the latter was sixteen hundred kilometers away. They drove north toward Murmansk. Finland was about 550 kilometers to their left, or west, a land that Nick pictured as Lapland, a land of reindeer and Northern Lights.

"We will not go all the way to Murmansk," said Dina. "The lake house is to the west of this road, down a smaller road through the forest. Vasily says such a road would be nearly impassable in the winter, but the doctor has it plowed as he likes to travel here to hunt before going to America. It may still be challenging, but Vasily knows the road well, and this Jeep is good."

Nick's phone rang, and he started. At home, he was accustomed to getting calls any time of day or night, always acting as if he were already awake, perfectly alert and composed and able to answer any question from an ER physician or floor nurse. Somehow, he was not prepared for this interruption when he was inside the Arctic Circle in a foreign country. He saw that it was from Smithwick.

"Hello, Ronnie," Nick said.

"Good morning, Nick—er, good afternoon," Smithwick said. "The CDC called. PCR has confirmed that there is Variola major in the specimen, and there is nothing to indicate that it is not viable."

Nick was quiet, staring through a side window at the white landscape.

"They are sending a bit of the specimen to Fort Detrick for a second assay, since this is all so unusual," Smithwick said. "Then both labs will try to culture the virus. That will be the true test."

"Every day is bringing an even stronger reason for me to press ahead," said Nick.

"Are you still in Moscow?" Smithwick asked.

"No, I am almost two thousand kilometers north of Moscow, nearer Murmansk, being carried down an icy road in a Russian Jeep," Nick said. "I cannot even begin to tell you everything that has happened since we last spoke, and I don't have time now. I really appreciate all of your help, Ronnie. I look forward to telling you the story when I get back."

"I will greatly look forward to it," Smithwick said. "And be safe, Nick. You are obviously not dealing with normal people with normal human morals. If they are willing to infect young children with smallpox, they will do anything. You decide whether to answer calls from the FBI. I am certain that they already know what the CDC knows, and they will be increasingly anxious to speak with you."

Nick thought again about the FBI. He would love to pass this burden to them, to those accustomed to dealing with bad guys. But what could they do? If Nick had the notebook in hand, then they could arrest or detain Yatovsky. Without the notebook, however, Nick would never know if Anna or any other children needed exploratory surgery, surgery which would be like looking for a needle in a haystack unless one knew that the plastic was there. What would he tell the FBI if he answered a call? That he was in Russia about to break into a lodge?

"Thank you again, Ronnie. I may have the Russian surgeon's notebook in hand soon, and then I can come home." He disconnected and slipped the phone back into his pocket.

The road north was a serpentine trail of ice, its two lanes of width glistening in the moonlight and defined only by the forest and fields on either side. Vasily handled the UAZ with confidence, using the snow at the sides of the road for traction and shifting the transfer case for additional stability when they passed a slow-moving truck. They entered and eventually exited a game preserve but saw no game.

"They have moose, brown bear, fox, winter hare, marten, ermine. I would love to see an owl," said Dina.

They drove for several miles through an area devoid of trees, very different from the pine and spruce forest that had tightly bordered the road. In the distance to their right was a plethora of twinkling lights, a sight both beautiful and surprising in the clear night. Vasily turned to Dina and spoke for some time.

"In the distance is one of the world's largest nickel plants and the town that grew up around it," Dina translated. "The pay is good, but the conditions are terrible for the environment and for the workers, who must wear special breathing apparatus when working and often have many ailments until they retire at a young age. The ailments do not retire. Almost all lose the sense of smell, and some develop holes in the wall between the nostrils."

"The nasal septum," said Nick.

"Yes. There are many specialized mines and factories in this area, all powered by a nearby atomic facility. One town with a specialty steel plant is named Oleingorsky, which means 'Town of Reindeer.' There are also many military sites because of the proximity to NATO forces in Finland and Norway. Murmansk itself houses an atomic submarine port, and in the past, special permission was required even for simple travel to this area."

Nick was physically comfortable, as the vehicle's heater was powerful, and the back seat, flat and lightly padded, was fine. His thoughts, however, were unsettled. He had never broken into a building in his life, had never even considered it, and they were about to enter someone's private lodge. He told himself that this 'someone' was hardly a normal person, was a monster willing to sacrifice children for his personal gain, for wealth, for ego. He certainly did not deserve Nick's discomfort at breaking the law.

The entire process should be quick: retrieving the key

and entering the lower side door, rushing to the upstairs office, going through the desk drawers, and leaving with the green leather-bound notebook. Tanya said that Yatovsky had stopped turning on the security system years before, as there had been too many false alarms, each alarm compelling him to let the local police wander through his well-appointed dacha. The thought of them running their hands over his soft leather armchairs, tracking mud onto the Persian carpets, and relieving themselves in his marble bathroom was too much for him to bear.

Vasily was speaking to Dina again. After several minutes, she turned back to Nick.

"Murmansk is larger than Apatity, but we will not need to go there. It is right on the Barents Sea north of us. The city was bombed into dust by German airplanes during the Great Patriotic War when British and American troops nevertheless kept the port open in order to supply much of Russia. The town was rebuilt and, therefore, is newer than many Russian cities. There is a monument or cemetery dedicated to the Americans who helped during the war, and some British men return to Murmansk every year for a reunion. Fewer and fewer men each year, of course. The sign outside the town is in both Russian and English."

Vasily slowed the UAZ, barely creeping forward. There was little danger of slowing on the highway, as they had not seen another vehicle for over twenty minutes. He turned the wheel slightly to the left, the powerful headlights thrown against the unbroken pine forest bordering the road. He rolled forward a little more, then turned harder to the left and entered a narrow trail. Little more than one lane wide, its entrance was hardly evident from the highway, but Vasily had obviously been here before.

The trail had been plowed, probably before Yatovsky arrived for his pre-conference hunting, but snow had fallen since then. The several inches of snow on the trail, though, was nothing compared to the two-foot walls of it on either side. The crystalline snow on the trail was marked only by the linear hoofmarks of reindeer or elk. No person had been there since this snow fell.

"When did it last snow?" asked Nick, Dina translating.

"Vasily says yesterday."

"Then Yatovsky is on his way to San Diego for the STS," said Nick. "It starts soon. And, there should be nobody at the dacha if Tanya is correct."

They drove between the walls of snow and pines, the nearly full moon bright in the clear night when glimpsed between gaps in the canopy of boughs. It was a dreamlike tunnel, a carnival ride through a penumbral landscape. The UAZ rocked and bumped but never lost traction. Nick saw its deep-treaded tracks when he looked back once.

"Vasily says that the lake is ahead and on our right, but we cannot see it because of the forest. The surgeon owns much land. His dacha is near the lake."

Indeed, they already had driven six or seven miles down the single-lane trail. Nick began to get anxious, leaning forward to peer through the flat windshield. What if there was someone at the lodge? They could simply turn around and get out, he supposed. But what if it was a guard or a tough guy like Maks? What if he followed them? He remembered the glint of metal in Maks' hand.

There appeared to be a lighter opening in the distance; then, suddenly, they were out of the forest. Vasily stopped the Jeep so that they could scan the area ahead.

The lodge lay directly ahead of them, a hundred yards in the distance. The headlights did not reach that far, and there were no lights in or around the house, but the moon was nearly full and the night clear, the few tall pines leading up to the dacha casting knife-sharp shadows on the glistening snow. The driveway led to a courtyard in the rear of the house, and there appeared to be a separate, smaller, one-story structure on the other side of the courtyard, tight against the forest and upsloping hill behind. Halfway to the house, another driveway branched to the right, leading down the long hillside to the lake.

Vasily drove forward slowly, leaving the dense forest behind and moving into an open landscape with a clear view of the lake. They could now see that the right-hand driveway led downhill to a small boathouse at the lake's edge, about two hundred yards away. The two-story structure might have contained one or two small rooms on each floor, and there was a narrow balcony on the lake side of the second floor. The lake itself was impressive, an immense sheet of unbroken ice and deep snow extending at least a mile in width to the forest on the other side. There appeared to be a few openings in the sheet of pines for lodges or boathouses, none with visible lights.

They drove past this turnoff and headed for the lodge. Although both driveways had been plowed Nick was pleased to see that there were no treads in the snow that had fallen since. Of course, someone could have been left behind in the dacha or boathouse, but there were no bootprints either. They were alone in the moonlit landscape, one which was beautiful despite their anticipation of committing a crime. The entire lawn or field from the lodge down to the lake was free of trees, no doubt providing an unobstructed view of the lake from each of the front-facing rooms.

The drive that they were on entered the courtyard at the rear of the lodge, but this was actually on level with the second floor of the structure. The house itself was partially built into the hill, with the top floor completely above ground at courtyard level and the bottom floor backed into the hillside, three sides free as any other house but its back wall against the stone of this hill. The dacha was built to look like a large hunting cabin, its sides and peaked roof constructed of logs, its front facing the lake despite the entrance on the second level at the rear. Nick also knew from Tanya's description that there was a side door that they could not see yet, the door through which they would enter. *This hunting cabin would have held four homes like his in Pennsylvania,* Nick thought.

As they drove into the courtyard, they could see that the other small building was a garage, one large enough for two garage doors, each bisected and constructed to open outward. It, too, was built into the hillside behind it. There were no windows. On the other side of the flat courtyard was another narrow driveway leading down and around the far side of the lodge to provide access to the first floor. Vasily eased the UAZ down this drive, passing the side door and stopping in front of a broad patio. He turned off the vehicle and climbed out, walking around to open the deep cargo area. Nick and Dina exited and looked around.

The house had much glass on the lake-facing side, a feature that was discordant to the hunting lodge theme but that provided beautiful views of the lake. Above them were second floor balconies, empty of furniture now. A large stone chimney flanked each side of the central peak of the roof, indicating two fireplaces inside. Although there was a hint of burned wood in the air, the chimneys emitted no smoke. There was a broad central front door of rough wood, in the center of which was a brass boar's head door knocker.

Nick turned and looked down across the broad lawn to the lake. The moonlit scene, almost as bright as the dusky daylight inside the Arctic Circle, reminded him of illustrated books that he had read Anna when she was younger, books drawn by Chris Van Allsburg. There was something about the black and white and gray dreamlike vista, the distinct shadows. He turned back as Vasily handed them each a sturdy metal flashlight and kept one for himself. He spoke to Dina.

"Vasily says if we see him flash the light on the window while we are in the house, we are to run back to the Jeep, no matter what we are doing. He will keep watch here. We cannot take long. He is worried about the doctor's men."

"Let's find the key," said Nick. He took Dina's arm, guiding her around the side of the house they had just passed in the Jeep. There was a single door in the center of the wall, the remainder of the wall on both sides of the door covered to Nick's height by iron racks of firewood. Nick bent to the rack on the left side and reached behind it at knee height. He lifted a thick silver key as he rose and he smiled down at Dina.

"Are you sure that you want to become a criminal? You can wait with Vasily."

"We are in this together," Dina said. She stood on her toes and kissed him.

Nick held Dina tightly to him, her head against his chest, and then he turned to enter the lodge.

CHAPTER 25

The heavy door opened soundlessly into a hallway the width of Nick's outstretched arms. Nick considered taking off his snow-wet boots before stepping onto the flagstone floor, but he thought that he and Dina might have to leave quickly, so he kept them on, vigorously brushing the soles and sides on a dense woven mat just inside the doorway. Dina followed. The hallway extended twenty feet before them with one door on either side but no door at the end, where it appeared to open into a larger space.

Nick knew from what Tanya had told them that there was a Great Room that occupied almost the entire first floor, but she had said nothing about possible rooms along this hall. There was just enough moonlight from the glass in the door behind them and from the Great Room that they did not need flashlights yet. Nick cautiously opened the door on the left, needing to be certain that the dacha was unoccupied; a tiny part of him imagining a large man sitting just inside the doorway, smiling and pointing a pistol.

There was no man. The room was a bedroom, perhaps a guest room, carpeted in a plush wall to wall carpet of white, a double bed made up and ready for someone, a wide upholstered chair facing the full wall of windows. Nick could see the tracks of their UAZ where it had come around the house, but the vehicle itself was ahead, outside the Great Room. The door on the right also opened into a bedroom but there was little light as this was the back of the lodge, the part which was built into the hill. A narrow window on the side wall, next to the outside door that they had entered, cast light onto another bed, this one with heavy wood headboard and footboard. A long wood chest of drawers and a small table and lamp were the only other furnishings. No man, no gun. Nick closed both doors as Dina walked ahead.

Nick heard Dina suddenly cry out, and he ran to her, but she began to laugh. She had stepped into the Great Room, and just to her left was a huge stuffed bear, rearing up on its back legs, mouth open in a roar, giant claws glistening. It was a beautiful work of taxidermy, matched only by the many others around the room.

The Great Room lived up to its name. Forty feet long and two stories tall, its front wall was entirely glass broken by wooden columns. Through the glass, Nick could see Vasily outside the UAZ, hands in pockets, his attention on the driveway entrance from the forest. Across the room from where they stood, a massive fireplace filled half the wall, a wall otherwise heavy with the heads of trophy animals, elk and moose and mountain goat but also Cape buffalo and leopard. Next to a zebra head were several antelope-like creatures, one with large twisted horns and another whose horns were like enormous spikes. A warthog grimaced next to a black-eyed polar bear.

The floor of the room was entirely composed of flagstones, smooth and varying shades of gray, but much of it was covered in Persian rugs, the deep reds of the fabric and the sharp patterns splendid even in moonlight. Three overstuffed sofas circled the hearth on three sides, and various other sofas and chairs, some in leather, clustered in seating areas back nearly to the rearing bear. Past the bear to their left, and along the glass front wall, was a long dining table, rustic, its top thick wood, its legs stout. To their right was a fifteen-foot square kitchen, completely open to the Great Room, with the stove and ventilator hood against the windowless back wall, an island of polished wood in the room's center. An ornate samovar sat on a rear countertop.

Nick put a hand on Dina's back and guided her with him along the rear wall of the room and toward the staircase leading to the second floor. Above their heads now was the undersurface of a long balcony, essentially an open hall above them, a rail on the front side, which connected one end of the second floor to the other, traveling the entire length of the Great Room. They passed a powder room door on their right, a room that extended into the hillside, then came to the stairs just before the fireplace wall. They went quickly up a dozen steps away from the Great Room, then turned on a landing and went up a dozen more to the balcony. When Nick looked back, he saw a window above the landing and, through it, the empty courtyard at the rear of the second level.

Tanya had told them that the doctor's study was to the right. They passed through an archway into an entrance hall, the rear door to the courtyard now evident, then through a similar arched doorway on the other side and into the study. In this room the stone wall and fireplace were on their immediate left, then the entire front wall of glass again. The unimpeded view of the frozen lake was spectacular in the light of the moon and must have been panoramic in daylight. Half of the far wall was comprised of glass-walled gun safes, one for rifles and one for shotguns, the rear wall all bookshelves.

The room was dominated by the doctor's massive desk. Centered toward the rear wall, with a tall leather chair behind, the desk afforded a clear view of the grounds and lake house and lake, its green leather top free of a computer terminal or anything else that would block the view. On the left side of the desktop was a short reading lamp, on the right a two-volume *Atlas of Thoracic Surgery*, the title in English, by Academician Boris Petrovsky; its green cover and red accents, elegant compared to a smaller book, *Surgery of the Trachea*, by M.I. Perelman.

Nick lifted the lid of a beautiful square wooden box in the center of the desk, furthest from the chair, and found that it was a cigar humidor, the smell of tobacco wafting toward him, the labels of the cigars aligned, Cohiba and Montecristo, Partagas and Romeo y Julieta. Next to the box was a heavy glass ashtray and a cigar cutter attached to an eight-inch antler.

Nick sat down in the desk chair and pulled the center drawer. "Damn!" escaped him as the drawer remained closed. He directed his flashlight down and saw a small brass circle and keyhole in the drawer's front panel. He tried the three deeper drawers on the left and the three on the right but all were apparently locked by the same mechanism. Tanya had said that the doctor always kept his leather-bound notebook, his log of patient names and procedures, in the top center drawer, at least when he planned to leave the country. Nick had not come halfway across the world to be stopped by a locked drawer, but no matter how hard he pulled, it would not move. The book that would tell Nick if there was a time bomb in his daughter's chest was on the other side of a piece of wood.

They had no tools with them to pry open the drawer and no time to go back to the Jeep. Why hadn't he thought of bringing tools? *What kind of burglar was he*, Nick thought ironically. They had not prepared him for breaking and entering in medical school, though surgery residency had taught him to be inventive and resilient. He looked around the room.

There was nothing useable on the bookshelves. Under other circumstances both Nick and Dina would have loved perusing the books, many of which were beautifully bound. Where there were gaps in the books, Yatorsky had placed various objects, some artful and some rustic: a foot-tall bronze stag, a balalaika, chess sets of wood and marble, matryoska nesting dolls. Nick wondered if the desk key was somewhere in the room, maybe in the nesting dolls, maybe beneath the ornate gold mantle clock, but there was no time to search.

The shelves also contained many framed photographs of the Russian surgeon, most taken at the beginning or end of hunts, the large man surrounded by other large men—not a single woman—all dressed in bulky furs, all proudly brandishing guns. In some, the surgeon's booted foot was pressed against the neck of a dead animal, his long rifle raised, a broad smile evident within the salt-and-pepper beard, dark eyes glistening in the light of a flash. This man could not hide in a crowd and probably would never want to, his ego likely searing those in the hunting party one step behind.

But Nick needed a key or a tool.

He moved to the gun cases and pulled at the doors. One was locked but the one containing shotguns opened. There were drawers beneath the eight or ten racked guns, and Nick pulled open the top one. In the drawer were ear protectors and thin leather gloves, shell holders on belts, and plastic eyeglasses with ear loops. The second drawer held more promise, as it was full of knives, folding knives and double-bladed ones, bayonets, and several large tactical or military knives in metal sheaths. Nick drew one of the larger ones from its sheath and moved back to the desk.

He tried slipping the blade into the crack around the center drawer and, eventually, he was able to get it in just beneath the desktop. He was cutting into the wood and chipping the drawer badly, but he was able to torque the blade, and the drawer moved out a little. He pushed against the knife's handle, and the tempered steel blade, still unbent and unbroken, the end of an eighteen-inch lever, forced the drawer open with the sound of splintering wood, Nick falling forward onto the desktop, the blade just missing his groin. He slowly stood.

"That could have been bad," he said, the tip of the knife an inch from his pants zipper.

"For both of us," Dina said as their eyes met.

Nick sat down and Dina came to stand behind his left shoulder, both staring into the drawer as Nick pulled it fully out. Dina directed the beam of her flashlight into the space. No leather notebook was obvious. Just inside the front of the drawer on the left were colorful brochures and Nick scooped these up, spreading them on the desktop. They were all tourist pamphlets about San Diego and Southern California, probably requested by Yatovsky when he registered for the STS Annual Conference there. On the top was one titled La Jolla, with a backdrop of a rocky cove and many sea lions. The Gaslamp Quarter showed older shops and restaurants with outdoor seating, and Seaport Village newer shops in low buildings as in an outdoor mall. There was Whale Watching and The Famous San Diego Zoo. The Zoo brochure was folded open.

Beneath the multi-colored booklets were some papers with hand-written Russian script. One looked to be an itinerary with dates and short notations. Nick held it in front of the flashlight so that Dina could see.

"He was intending to fly out two days ago," said Dina, "so he is probably there now. His hotel is the Marriott Marquis on the marina, apparently very near the Convention Center and the conference. Is there a large boat that can be toured?"

"The USS Midway is an aircraft carrier, I believe," said Nick. "I have never been to San Diego, but it is a popular place for medical meetings due to the beautiful weather in the winter."

"On his last day he has written 'Zoo.' I would think that he has enough animals looking at him here, and not in a nice way. But maybe he is scouting for his next prize."

Nick folded the itinerary and pocketed it, then swept his hand to the back of the drawer. On the right side, he encountered metal and then carefully withdrew a large black handgun. There was a round logo on the checkered grip and the name Beretta etched into the barrel. He put it back; he was not here to steal, just to learn. The only other contents of the drawer were some pens, a pair of scissors, two additional cigar cutters, and matches.

It suddenly struck Nick that he probably should be wearing surgical gloves. Again, he was not thinking like a thief. On the other hand, he had never been fingerprinted, so there was no record with which to match fingerprints if it ever came to that. He doubted that Yatovsky would involve police anyway, although he may have government connections. Dina probably had never been fingerprinted either, but she had touched nothing anyway.

Tanya had said that Yatovsky always left the notebook in the top center drawer when he left the country, but on a rare occasion, he took it with him. Nick reached to his right and pulled at the top drawer there, but it did not move. He ran his fingers under the desktop where the center drawer lock had been engaged, and he felt two thin metal bars, one going to the right and one to the left, attached by a small metal wheel in the center. He pulled the right-hand bar toward the center, and it moved, the wheel turning and withdrawing the left-hand bar towards the center also.

Nick pulled open all six drawers in turn. He found files of papers in both large bottom drawers, a middle drawer with various surgical instruments—Kelly clamps, needle holders, fine hemostats, a rongeur, a periosteal elevator—the top drawer with typical writing supplies. The top drawer on the left contained binoculars, and the middle additional surgical instruments, including a large Bethune rib cutter. There simply was no leather notebook.

"He must have taken it with him," said Nick, not even attempting to hide his disappointment. "All of this for nothing." He looked over his shoulder at Dina.

Dina was staring straight ahead, out the windows, a look of shock on her face. Nick turned to look and saw the sweep of Vitaly's flashlight beam cut across the window, casting shadows on the study's ceiling as it crossed vertical beams between the huge panels of glass.

"Let's go!" Nick did not even attempt to close the desk drawers. He sprang up from the chair, grasping his flashlight from the desktop, pushing Dina toward the arched doorway into the back entrance hall, then through the second arch and to their left down the stairs. They raced through the Great Room, Nick waving to Vitaly as the man moved his beam across all of the front windows. They burst out the side door, and Nick slammed it closed, relocking it not a consideration as they ran to the Jeep, trying to keep their footing in the snow. They turned the corner and saw Vitaly getting into the UAZ, apparently having seen Nick waving. He had opened both back doors, and Nick and Dina leapt from each side onto the flat back seat as Vitaly ignited the engine. He pointed ahead.

A black Range Rover had exited the forest on the entrance road and was now moving rapidly toward the back courtyard on the driveway.

CHAPTER 26

As the Range Rover passed behind the corner of the dacha to enter the rear courtyard Vasily accelerated forward, driving across the lawn parallel to the driveway, heading to intersect the drive to the boathouse. He stared forward, concentrating, frequently turning the steering wheel as the UAZ lost traction, slid, and then regained traction. He spoke rapidly.

"Vasily says that we cannot outrun the Range Rover, even on snowy roads. But he knows the lake, and they do not. He grew up on these lakes, swimming and boating in the summer and ice fishing in the winter. They will have to turn around in the courtyard, so we will have a lead."

Although the snow was deep a layer of ice had formed during some earlier thaw, allowing the deeply treaded tires to catch. They barreled forward, the Jeep throwing Nick and Dina back and forth and even up off the firm seat at times, their hands holding the backs of the seats in front. They made it to the narrow, plowed drive and turned abruptly left as they slid onto it, now driving directly down the hill toward the lake and boathouse. Vasily had not turned on the headlights, nor were they needed in the moonlight. Nick looked back and, through the narrow back window, saw the headlights of the Range Rover just leaving the courtyard up the hill.

What would happen if they were caught? The stakes for Yatovsky and whoever was backing him, at a minimum, an unscrupulous oligarch and probably some hidden part of the

Russian government itself, were high. They were carrying out dangerous and highly unethical medical experimentation, procedures which were calculated to kill children and even start a pandemic. Governments could be held hostage for trillions of dollars and could be left begging for the only vaccine that would work against a weaponized variant of smallpox. These people would not hesitate to kill or, worse, torture to find out how much was known. And Nick had exposed the beautiful, kind woman next to him to this risk.

They were next to the boathouse now. The narrow two-story structure was built to mimic the lodge, with rough timber and a peaked roof, a balcony on the second floor facing the lake. Apparently, there was a dock extending thirty feet into the lake since, although snow buried the dock itself, the vertical round posts that anchored it to the bottom of the lake were visible, their round snowy tops looking like two parallel rows of snow cones, glistening in the subzero air.

Vasily came to the end of the plowed drive and continued forward, Dina gasping, the Jeep bumping down the lawn and directly onto the ice of the lake, the posts of the dock now on their right. He drove a little further onto the lake, then abruptly turned right, accelerating parallel to the lakeshore about fifty yards from the edge itself. Nick saw only forest hugging the shore here. Vasily then turned left, driving deeper onto the lake itself, then left again, heading back the way that they had come but five hundred yards onto the lake, heading towards its center.

"We're going back in their direction," Nick said. "They will catch us."

Hearing Nick's questioning tone, Vasily spoke rapidly, continuing to accelerate.

"He says that even on the lake, we cannot outrun the Range Rover. It is a very good vehicle. But Vasily wants them to think that they can catch us and to drive straight towards us. This part of the lake is shallow, perhaps twenty meters deep, and there is a warm thermal spring beneath the surface, not too far out from the surgeon's dock. With just a little more time, this area of thin ice will be between us and the boathouse. We just drove around it, but they will see us and drive straight towards us. With the snow, the area of thin ice looks no different from the rest. But Vasily knows the lake. And a Range Rover is very heavy."

They looked to their left and saw the lights of the black SUV just passing the lake house, then bumping down onto the ice. For a moment there was a flash of interior light and they glimpsed two men, one large and one thin, then the light was extinguished. It struck Nick that they might have guns, but they would not have fired at this distance anyway.

Vasily kept the same course but slowed a little, wanting them to believe that they would intersect their prey if they accelerated directly forward. They did this, picking up speed on the flat white surface and turning on their high beams to keep the UAZ in sight. Vasily angled slightly right, heading now towards a distant open area on the far shore, possibly another estate, wanting to keep the larger SUV traveling directly towards the thin ice.

Suddenly, they heard a loud crack, like a gunshot, and then another, each followed by an echo. Nick and Dina looked back and saw that the front windows of the Range Rover were down and extended arms held handguns, but the distance was still too great to shoot. The cracking sounds had come from the ice onto which the SUV had driven. The vehicle slowed, the driver likely braking hard as he realized what was happening, but it was too late.

The next instant, the front edge of the Range Rover angled down sharply as if pushed by a giant hand, the icy water covering the hood and then the roof, the car filling. A second later, Nick could see only the glow of taillights as the entire vehicle disappeared, and then those, too, were gone.

Vasily looked in the rearview mirror, his expression grim,

but he kept driving. He turned his head to the side and spoke.

"We will continue across the lake and go to Vasily's flat by a different route," Dina said. "There could be more men coming, who knows? Vasily knows many ways back."

"Can the men survive?" Nick asked Vasily, and Dina translated. Vasily spoke for several minutes.

"If they can get out of the car and then out of the lake onto the ice and then run back to the dacha, they might have a chance. But water this cold causes the muscles to stop working almost immediately, so they will have no time to tread water or swim. And waterlogged winter clothes are heavy. If the ice holds around the edge of the hole, then they might be able to climb out. But hypothermia will come quickly in the air. Also, they are probably city men, so they may not know how to swim. Do you care so much about men who were about to shoot you? And did not care about your daughter or other children?"

He turned to look at her. "It's not in my nature to kill people, no matter what they have done. I guess I would kill to save Anna or you, but I hope it never gets to that. I just want her to be safe and live a normal life. That's why I am in the middle of a frozen lake in Russia instead of in a small, warm house in Pennsylvania. But then, I would never have met you."

Dina lifted herself and kissed him, a long kiss, as Vasily stared ahead and drove, clouds and thick snowflakes starting to hide the moon.

It took over an hour to drive to the apartment, Vasily taking mostly smaller roads, their surfaces often unplowed, forest on either side. Nick had looked back once when they were still on the lake, but the new snowfall was becoming heavy, and he could see only a few yards behind the Jeep. He might never know the fate of the men in the Range Rover, men who, in one brief glimpse, had looked a lot like Maks and Viktor. Nick had little sympathy for the men who had tortured Tanya and might have killed Dina and him, but he had never knowingly hurt anyone, and his feelings were conflicted.

They had left the frozen lake on the side opposite Yatovsky's dacha, Vitaly able to find a familiar access road even in the white curtain of falling snow. Dina had slept off and on during the drive, her head on Nick's shoulder, but the bumping of the UAZ prevented any reasonable rest, and they were both tired by the time they pulled behind a small house. Vitaly collected their bags, led them up a flight of outdoor stairs, and unlocked the door to his apartment. They stepped in, brushing the wet snow from their clothes and hair.

The apartment comprised the top, second floor of the house, its separate entrance in the back entering directly into a kitchen. They left their boots on a rough rug just inside the door and their coats on pegs extending from the wall. The kitchen was larger than Dina's, with a table suitable for four. A door at the rear appeared to lead into a hallway.

Vasily gestured for them to sit, then took vodka from a small freezer atop the refrigerator and three shot glasses from a shelf. He spoke with a question.

"Would you like food?" said Dina.

"No, thank you, maybe in the morning," said Nick. "Well, it is already morning, but I mean after a little sleep."

Vasily poured vodka into each glass, but before he could speak, Nick stood.

"It is my turn to toast. To Vasily, a brave friend who saved our lives."

Dina translated, and they each upended his glass. "Vasily says they hurt his girl, and he has hurt them. He is not a mean man, but family is family."

Vasily began to refill their glasses, but Nick held out his hand.

"Remember, Neek, Russian custom says no less than three toasts."

"I must break with custom tonight, with apologies. Let us get some rest and when we wake, I will tell you my plan."

Vasily downed his second shot anyway, then led them down the hall, pointing out the small bathroom as they passed.

"We will share the bedroom, and Vasily will sleep in the living room." When Nick objected, Dina said, "In Russia, we use the main room for everything: dinner, sleep, entertainment. It is not worth arguing with him. And I suspect that he can be stubborn. Or, were you going to object to sharing the bedroom with me?" She smiled.

"Spasibo, Vasily," Nick said, following Dina into the bedroom.

They made love spoon fashion this time, on their sides, Dina's back against Nick's front, her face turned back for kisses, his hand cupping one breast. She guided him inside her, and they moved slowly, Nick realizing that this might be the last time he and Dina could share this, at least for a while. When she came, she pressed her buttocks back against him, her shuddering and soft moan causing him to lose control.

Nick turned onto his back, weariness sweeping over him. He reached to the small bedside table for his sports watch, holding it up before his eyes and setting an alarm for three hours. It was not much time, but he could always sleep on the long flight to San Diego.

Nick woke to the vibrating of his watch. He turned his head to see Dina looking at him, her eyes large and brown in the darkness of the room, her right arm over his chest, her head on his right shoulder. How had fortune led him to this beautiful, intelligent, brave woman? After Lynn had died Nick thought that he could never love a woman the way that he had loved Lynn, and he guessed that was still true. But it seemed more and more possible that he could love a different woman in a different way, a profound but different way. He kissed her, the thought of leaving her soon almost physically painful.

"I must fly to San Diego," he said softly. "There is nothing more that I can learn in Russia. After all that we have been through, I still do not know if Anna is at risk, or whether she needs an exploratory chest operation, or whether other children do."

"But how will you get the notebook?" Dina asked. "He is not going to just hand it to you."

"I may be able to convince him to let me look at it or just the page with Anna's name on it. A quick look will allow me to see whether there is a red backward R, a red Yah, next to her name. Tanya said that is how he marked those with the virus inside."

"Why would he cooperate in any way? He could just walk away."

"I could promise not to call the FBI until he was out of the country," said Nick. "Everything that he does seems to be for self-interest, so you are probably right. He will not give me anything unless threatened. But that is a very real threat."

"I don't know how to say this, Neek, but even if you learn about Anna, all of the other children may be at risk if you let him leave with the notebook."

Nick said nothing as he thought.

"I may need to grab the notebook, or even his briefcase, and run. It would not be the first crime that I have committed in order to save these children."

They were silent for several minutes, Dina stroking his chest.

"Can you help me book a flight to San Diego as soon as possible?"

*

They had breakfast with Vasily at the kitchen table, Dina and Vasily talking while Nick got through to the Marriott hotel in San Diego. Dina had already booked Nick's flights and the tickets could be picked up at the airport, flights to Moscow, then London, then Los Angeles, then San Diego. He would have abundant time to sleep and to read.

The bread and jam were delicious, the jam homemade from local mountain berries by one of Vasily's neighbors. The tea was strong and served sweetened.

Vasily drove them to the airport in a car borrowed from another neighbor. None of them believed that the UAZ would be recognized, and it was very unlikely that the doctor's henchmen had time to make a call from the lake property—they had barely arrived when they began chasing the Jeep onto the lake—but Vasily thought it best to be safe. He also drove to a small side entrance to the terminal rather than the central front doors.

Just inside the door, Nick set down his bag and Dina rushed into his arms, each not letting go, eyes closed, heartbeats palpable even through the thick clothes. She would take a later flight to the Moscow airport, where her car was parked while he was going to Sheremetyevo. This would be the last time they were together until some unknown day in the future. Her eyes were wet when she looked up to kiss Nick.

"Nothing will keep me from seeing you when this is over," Nick said, surprised at this rare intensity of his own emotions, "whether that is in Russia, America, or in between. You are very special, Dina. You must keep yourself safe." He looked down into her eyes, brushed hair from her forehead, and smiled. "I know how much you want to go back to the Smiling Mink, but you must lead a quiet life for a while." She laughed and kissed him again.

Nick turned and waved as he walked to the gate.

CHAPTER 27

It was Thursday afternoon when Beth received a call from the CDC. She was at her desk in the small office that she shared with two other junior Special Agents, neither of whom were in the office. She was not surprised that it was again Dr. Patel who called.

"Oh, Special Agent, I have news for you," Patel said. Beth could picture him physically shivering in anticipation. "It is Variola, it is Variola major!"

"Are you sure?" Beth asked. *Stupid question*, she thought, but she was not really anticipating this result.

"Oh, yes. That's why it took so long. Something like this cannot be taken lightly. We did a PCR, and so did Ft. Detrick. Not easy testing dried-out samples like this, but the boys in the lab—and girls, of course—are the best anywhere."

"So, if that material had gotten into someone's body, he or she would have come down with smallpox?" Beth asked. She was picturing a child's face from one of the library books, the skin a cobblestone street of vesicles.

"We cannot say that with 100 percent scientific certainty," he said. "But I believe that it would be likely."

"And that person would be contagious?"

"If someone came down with clinical smallpox, then they would definitely be contagious. In fact, there are now meetings scheduled at high levels of our organization to talk about responses to this finding. For instance, the drive to destroy the

Variola major cultures here and in Russia may now be moot, as the cow has already left the barn, as it were. And I do not mean cowpox by that." Patel chuckled at his joke. "Developing a vaccine may now be a priority."

"But is this some different variant of smallpox?" Beth asked, the specter of weaponization and bioterrorism becoming more real.

"We do not know yet. But in the U.S., or anywhere for that matter, we are not even prepared for the so-called routine variety. Let's hope that this was some pathetic joke or a one-off experiment by some sick individual."

Outside Beth's narrow window, the day appeared to have darkened. "Thank you, Dr. Patel. And please thank your colleagues for their amazing work."

She would need to speak with the Corbetts after all.

Fred Lippert was in the break room on his floor, pouring coffee from the round glass pot into a cup emblazoned with Rodin's *The Thinker* sculpture. He saw Beth staring at the cup.

"A great museum, if you haven't been there. Right on the Franklin Parkway, on your right as you head towards the Museum of Art. Small but terrific sculptures: *Bacchus, The Gates of Hell, Burghers of Calais*, this guy." He held up his cup. "Outside of Paris, the best."

"I guess I didn't take you for a museum guy," Beth said.

"What kind of guy did you take me for?" He was not smiling as he raised the cup to his lips, dark eyes looking directly at hers through steam rising from the mug.

"Oh, maybe a Flyers or Phantoms guy, a gun range guy, a gym guy."

"Well, I am familiar with gun ranges and gyms, and I have attended a few Phantoms matches, the Flyers tickets being a little expensive for FBI wages. But none of that precludes a love of good art." He rotated the image on his cup towards Beth.

"Point taken," Beth said.

Lippert continued to look at her, silent, waiting.

"The CDC called to confirm that there was a smallpox virus in our plastic object. They cannot say yet that it would have caused infection, but why else would someone put it there? So, I need to speak with the Corbetts. It was their adopted son who carried the object into the United States from Russia. And I want to speak with them in person to assure myself that they are truly innocent in all this."

"How about sending a Special Agent from one of our satellite offices?" Lippert asked. "They are closer."

"By the time that I explain this bizarre story and its microbiology, I can be there myself. Glaston is just up the Northeast Extension of the Turnpike. Will you approve me checking out a car?"

"Absolutely. And in the meantime, I need to bring Garrett up to speed on this. Whatever the actual threat, this case represents the very definition of bioterrorism. Now that we know that it was not some prank, the Special Agent in Charge must know. I have a meeting with him right after lunch, and I will tell him then. Keep me apprised of anything that you learn so that I can appear less unsettled than I am about this. What happened to the good old days of gangsters and drugs?"

"There still seems to be plenty of that, too," Beth said.

"What about the surgeon?" Lippert asked.

"I've called his mobile phone twice with no success. He is out of the country at a conference, and he may not have configured his phone for international use. Also, he just seems to have operated on a particular patient with a very unusual finding, an innocent bystander, as it were. Plus, if he was actually involved in some way, why would he have brought the plastic object to the Pathologist"

"Okay. Maybe ask the Corbetts about him anyway. Did they

know him beforehand? What did he tell them? You know."

"Yes, I know."

Lippert saw her look. "Sorry if I am patronizing," he said. "And take your fist out from under your chin, Ms. Thinker."

As Beth exited the Lehigh Tunnel on the Northeast Extension of the Pennsylvania Turnpike, I-495, she noticed a clear change in both terrain and weather. The only tunnel on this highway was not even a mile long, but she was now surrounded by mountains and overcast skies, a dusting of snow on the roadsides, and more cars with skis lashed to rooftop rails. Unlike most people, she had also noticed that the entrance to the Northbound tunnel had been rectangular while that from the Southbound to her left was round, but she would have to ask someone about that later.

She would also have to ask why a town up ahead was named Jim Thorpe, as the green road signs proclaimed. She knew a little about the legendary Olympian but not why anyone would christen an entire town after him. Further north was Wilkes-Barre, obviously named after Wilkes and Barre, whomever they were, but how did one pronounce it: Wilkes-Barr, or Wilkes-Bare, or Wilkes-Berry? She probably would never know since she would not be going that far.

The Patriot Blue Ford Taurus already had over eighty thousand miles on the odometer, but the V6 engine was fine, the heater powerful, and the car had been equipped with snow tires in the rear. She nevertheless was careful on the two-lane road leading to Glaston as it wound up and down hills, for she could only guess what eighteen-wheeler was around the next bend in the road. The leafless trees on her right allowed a view of the small river a thousand feet below road level, the water moving briskly over rocks, white caps visible even from this distance. *That must be cold*, Beth thought.

She coasted down a long, winding hill, then the road leveled, and she was on the outskirts of Glaston, some older houses near the road and a few small strip malls. She glimpsed the town square one block over, but she needed to pass the college and then the hospital before she could look for the Corbett's neighborhood. She passed a few large, old, well-maintained houses near the hospital, probably built by physicians when the hospital was young, then three miles further on, crossed the small river and found Deer Trail Drive.

Although not exactly a development, the neighborhood was a line of similar upper-middle-class houses built around the same time, possibly when a large farm was sold. The properties were generous by Beth's standards, three to five acres, the lawns sloping up to a plateau on which the homes were built, all of the two-story houses in a curving line, backyards continuing the upward slope to the wall of woods. A few had separate garages and many had lawn sheds, likely for riding mowers or small tractors. Swing sets were visible wherever the back yards were flat enough to allow them, some the fancy wooden sets that Beth had seen in catalogs.

She drove slowly along the line of mailboxes on her left. On her right were only more woods, so the houses could have been numbered sequentially, but someone had decided to make them all even numbers, presumably to keep with U.S. convention. For some reason, they also began with 302.

Beth turned left before the 310 mailbox and drove up a thin driveway, rear tires occasionally spinning on the icy asphalt. The house up the hill on her right was a rectangle of brick, its windows trimmed in white and bracketed by white shutters. The maturity of trees in the landscaped yard suggested that the house was thirty or forty years old, but it was well maintained. She parked near the double garage door, got out, and stepped carefully along the walk to the front door.

The Westminster chime of the doorbell had not even finished when Megan Corbett answered the door. She wore an apron and was drying her hands on a towel; a questioning look on her face. During the drive up the turnpike, Beth had practiced what she would say, knowing that anyone would be frightened to have an FBI agent appear at her door.

"Mrs. Corbett, I am FBI Special Agent Elizabeth Jankiewicz." Beth held up her badge so that Megan could see it through the glass storm door. "You've done nothing wrong and are not in any trouble. I would just like to ask you a few questions."

"About what?" Megan was clearly flustered, and she had not unlocked the storm door.

"We were contacted about the small object that Dr. Turner removed from your son, and we know that Alexander was adopted from Russia. I just need to ask you about your time in Russia during the adoption."

"Why does the FBI want to know about our son?" Megan's voice had risen.

"May I come in, Mrs. Corbett? This will not take long, and there is nothing for you to worry about."

"Of course. Where are my manners?" She opened the glass door, and Beth stepped inside, wiping her shoes on a small mat near the door. The house smelled of something baking.

"Do you think that your husband could come home from work so that we can all talk together?" Beth asked. "It shouldn't take more than thirty minutes."

"I'll call him right now," Megan said. "I would like to have him here too. He just works in town at the hardware store, and I'm sure that his father can cover for an hour. Sam took over the business from his dad, but Mike still comes in most days. May I offer you a cookie while you wait? I just baked Alex's favorite, Toll House chocolate chip cookies, just out of the oven."

Beth had eaten two wonderful cookies by the time that Sam appeared. They all sat together in a small living room to the right of the entrance hall, the furniture conservative and appearing to have never been used. Sam and Megan sat together on a small couch, holding hands and both looking at Beth, who sat in a wing chair near the window. They had calmed down a little, but both had seen Beth's gun when she unzipped her coat.

"We learned about the small object that Dr. Turner removed from Alex when he did the chest surgery, and anything unusual with any connection to Russia must be investigated. So, that's why I'm here," Beth began. "Why don't you begin by telling me a little about yourselves? How did you meet?" She wanted them to relax even more.

"Oh, we've known each other practically our entire lives," Sam said, sitting forward. "It wasn't until high school that we began dating, of course."

"Sam was a guard on the Glaston High football team, and I was a pom-pom girl," Megan said. "It was in the stars."

Beth was not sure that these high school activities always led to marriage, but she let it stand.

"We saw each other mostly on weekends and during the summer for a few years," Sam said, "since I went to Albright for my business degree and Megan went to Penn State, Wilkes-Barre, and then University Park."

So, it is pronounced 'Wilkes-Berry' Beth thought.

"I always knew that I would take over Corbett's, but Dad wanted me to have a degree. So, we waited until we both graduated before tying the knot. Then Megan taught junior high, and we tried to get pregnant. And then we tried IVF, and then tried local adoption, and finally accepted international adoption. And it couldn't have worked out better, could it honey?" Sam looked sideways at Megan. "Alex is great."

"Was the adoption expensive?" Beth asked. She wanted to be sure that there was no financial incentive for allowing one's son to have a procedure in Russia. Yet she was increasingly doubtful that this guileless couple had any knowledge of what their son had carried.

"Oh, it was expensive," Sam said. "But the business is doing well, and this was the most important thing in our lives."

"So, what do you know about your son's operation in Russia?"

"Only that it was a minor chest procedure done right at the orphanage. All of their records are terrible."

"And did they know before the operation that you and Megan would be adopting Alex," Beth asked. "I mean, what was the timing?"

"I don't know about that," Sam said, "but the orphanage director did say at one point that they earmarked certain children for American adoption, ones that seemed outgoing and pleasant. So, Alex was destined for America."

"And we are blessed that he found us," Megan said, squeezing Sam's hand.

"By the way," Beth said, "did you know Dr. Turner before this recent operation?"

"Oh no," Sam said. "He was just on-call the day that we went to the ER. And what a wonderful, caring man. But Officer—oh, I'm not sure what to call you—what is the plastic object? Is Alex in any danger at all?"

"We are still studying the object," Beth said, "but it is no longer in Alex, regardless." She was wondering to herself how many days or weeks that it might have been before the plastic dissolved, releasing smallpox into the joy of their life.

CHAPTER 28

Megan Corbett had given Beth two cookies for the drive back to Philadelphia, a gift that Beth eagerly accepted. "Alex is still napping upstairs," Megan had said, "and he won't miss them."

In retrospect, it probably had not been necessary for Beth to interview the Corbetts in person, but she could not have been sure of that earlier. They comprised one of only two leads in this case and she had learned that it was much more difficult for an individual to hide anything during a face-to-face interview than one carried out over the phone.

Their son had experienced a normal childhood with no additional operations, no unusual illnesses, and no unusual visitors or phone calls. Until his spontaneous pneumothorax, he was just like any other healthy boy. He had some minor problems right after adoption, such as not knowing how to use stairs, hoarding food in his room, and being shy. But all of that had passed, too.

They truly appeared to be passive players in this science fiction drama.

The late afternoon light was receding as Beth merged onto the Turnpike South. Her cell phone service was terrible, and she hoped that it would improve south of the tunnel. She wanted to call the office and get to work on learning more about Dr. Nicholas Turner. It was still far-fetched to think that a small-town surgeon was anything more than a victim of fate in this story. But the story itself was far-fetched and the Corbetts were completely innocent.

A larger question was, "Who made the plastic object, and why?" It appeared to be the work of someone in Russia, someone with incredibly diverse talents or, more likely, someone with extensive resources and access to such talents. And access to one of only two sources of smallpox in the world. It had to be the Russian government. But why?

An outbreak of smallpox in the United States would be catastrophic, as there was no treatment and a scant chance of containment. Our country would need to turn away from everything else in the world and make this disease its single priority, which would help Russia. However, Russia would be at risk also, since a virus ignores international boundaries, unless they had an effective vaccine in large quantities. Could any government be that evil?

There were obvious examples in history of evil governments, but nothing on this scale. They would become a pariah among countries, except that the pandemic would have originated in the United States. Russia would simply appear prescient in stocking effective vaccines. And they could sell vaccines to other countries at any price.

This opportunity to make enormous amounts of money raised another possibility: could one person or one company, apparently in Russia, have the resources—and lack of conscience—to start a pandemic? An effective vaccine, particularly against a weaponized smallpox variant, would be the most precious of all commodities since none would exist anywhere else, and this individual or corporation would control it all.

So, as far-fetched as it seemed, either a government or a corporation or an individual could, theoretically, be behind this. Someone knew how to make the plastic, someone had the smallpox, someone could enlist a surgeon or surgeons, someone could make a specific vaccine. A big, wealthy someone, whether government or oligarch or corporation, could put it all together. With an ocean of money and a teardrop of conscience.

No, it was too much. Who could be so evil as to consciously start a pandemic? The suffering would be on a scale that would dwarf that of World Wars or famine. Just for world dominance or just for unprecedented wealth? Beth's thoughts were spinning.

South of the tunnel there was better cell phone service and she pulled over, dialing her office the moment that she stopped. It was Friday afternoon and she wanted to get the secretary that she shared with the other junior Special Agents before Olivia left for a drink with friends or whatever she did on Friday evenings. Namely, what Beth never did.

"Olivia," she said when the secretary answered, "can you query the State Department? I need to know where, if anywhere, Dr. Nicholas Turner has traveled outside the country. He lives in Glaston, PA, but lived in Philadelphia before that. Anything else that you can learn about him before you leave would be wonderful. And please let the switchboard know to call me, even this weekend if the State Department sends anything or calls."

"Got it," Olivia said.

"And can you transfer me to Fred Lippert's office? I want to bring him up to date before he signs out for the weekend."

"Special Agent Lippert," Fred answered himself, his secretary likely off early this Friday afternoon.

"Fred, this is Beth Jankiewicz. I just left the Corbetts a little while ago, and I'm still on the Turnpike Extension. I wanted you to know that they are innocent bystanders in this saga. Literally high school sweethearts, solid Glaston citizens, infertility treatments, then adoption. I already checked their finances, and there is nothing amiss and no financial motive to participate in anything whatsoever illegal. And Megan makes a damn good Toll House cookie."

"I'm glad to hear that, and not surprised, but don't tell

Garrett the cookie part. I just left him and he ran up one side of me and down the other about this case, asking me question after question as I answered 'We don't know' or 'We can only speculate.' Terrorism is the Bureau's number one focus these days and, unless it is a sick prank, the Glaston case meets the definition."

There was a pause, and Beth waited. "Our only other lead is the surgeon," Fred said. "He may or may not be a terrorist, but he might know something that we don't. And what other choice do we have? We can't visit Russian orphanages looking for clues, we can't investigate every child adopted from Russia, and who knows if adopted children are the only vehicle? Adults could just as easily bring a piece of embedded plastic into the U.S. Like Trojan Horses, but human."

"I'm on it," Beth said. "I'm going to find out if he has ever left the country in the past and where exactly he is now. If necessary, I will call his babysitter or even drive back to Glaston. I still cannot see him having an active role, but I agree that he is our only other lead. I mean, he appears to be a solid, over-achieving American doctor. And he is the one who brought the object to the Pathologist's attention. I mean, he walked the thing down to Pathology personally."

"Please keep me apprised of anything that you learn. Garrett wants to think about the case over the weekend, but it sounds as if he is prepared to throw some resources at this. He is also going to have to report it up soon. As embarrassing as it is to know so little, once anyone mentions the words 'smallpox' or 'bioterrorism' then the temperature gets turned up."

"I may have something later today or tomorrow."

"Call me whatever day or time. You have my cell phone number."

It was late afternoon on Saturday when the switchboard called Beth. The pager went home with whoever was on call that weekend, but the operator had all of the home and cell phone numbers anyway.

Beth had considered spending the day digging into Dr. Nicholas Turner's Philadelphia background after again getting no response from his cell phone, but one good conversation with him would probably obviate the need to do so. Also, she simply had to have some personal time to shop and do laundry. She was in Blockbuster, picking out a couple of VCR movies, when her cell phone vibrated. It was DeeDee again.

"Do you work every weekend, DeeDee?" Beth asked.

"Yes, I do, Special Agent. That way, I can watch the grandkids during the week. Child care is so expensive, and they seem to like my cooking anyway."

"Your daughter is a lucky woman. And the grandkids, too." Beth felt an unexpected pang of nostalgia for the simple domestic life of her childhood, being driven to swim practice, home-cooked dinners together most nights, crowding around the one television. She would be alone again this night, a success in the eyes of her family and former classmates, but at a price.

"Thank you," DeeDee said. "I saw a note that you wanted to be called if anything came in from the State Department. We just received a fax. Would you like me to leave it on your desk?"

"No," Beth said, stepping into a quiet area of the store. "Can you read it to me now?"

"Well, it is titled 'Nicholas Turner, M.D., International Travel,'" DeeDee said. "The first trip was in 1998 from PHL to SVO and back again, round trip. That was the only trip until..."

"Wait a minute, DeeDee. What is SVO?"

"It says in small print on the next line, Philadelphia to Sher-e-met-yevo, if I am pronouncing that right."

"Sheremetyevo in Russia?" Beth asked, her heart rate accelerating. "His first trip out of the country was to Russia?"

"And his last trip, too," DeeDee said. "He was there last week."

"What did you just say?" Beth asked.

"His only other international trip was JFK to SVO last week, returning from KVK to SVO to LHR to LAX to SAN."

"Is SAN San Diego?" Beth asked. The Blockbuster store was beginning to get warm, and she slipped out of her coat, letting it fall to the floor, without taking the phone from her ear.

"Uh, yes, yes, it is," DeeDee said. "Dr. Turner arrived there very late Thursday night."

"He is in San Diego!" Beth exclaimed. "And he still will not answer my calls. And he has a Russian connection." Beth realized that she was thinking out loud, but she was realizing that fucking Dr. Turner might not be so sweet and innocent after all. In fact, he was obstructing an FBI investigation at a minimum.

"DeeDee, I will call you right back. I need to speak with Special Agent Lippert about this." She ended the call and immediately dialed Fred Lippert. He was out of breath when he answered.

"Lippert," he said.

"This is Beth. Should I give you a minute?"

"Heavy bag. No, go ahead. I should recover quickly."

"Dr. Nicholas Turner has only been out of the country twice. Both times were to Russia." She let that linger, picturing Fred at some gym, sweat dripping, chest heaving, thoughts racing.

"You wouldn't have called me late Saturday afternoon to joke about this," he said.

"It gets better," Beth said. "One time was in 1998, and the second time was last week. He arrived back in the U.S. late Thursday night, landing in San Diego. So, the fucker...excuse me, the doctor could have answered my calls, at least the last two days."

"This is way too coincidental," said Lippert. "I still can't put together any motive, or why he would call attention to the plastic object, or why the hell he is in San Diego. I suggest that you call our office there and ask them to help find him. They will be able to do that much faster than we can from the East Coast. If you need Garrett to call their Special Agent in Charge to apply some pressure, just let me know. I will be calling him about this."

Beth hesitated a moment, then leaned in. "Fred, I would like to fly out there. Nobody knows this case like I do, and it is too complicated to educate another Special Agent over the phone." She went on rapidly before he could answer. "You said yourself that the Special Agent in Charge was prepared to devote some resources to this, it is a bioterrorism case, and it is our bioterrorism case." She had almost said, '*My* bioterrorism case.'

"I think that we can swing that. As strange as the case is, it could be big, and Garrett will want to keep it. You can ask DeeDee to find someone in the San Diego office for you to speak with right away. Then, you need to put out the doctor's picture and passport information so that he doesn't leave the country." Fred had indeed recovered quickly, his breathing normal, his manner business-like. "And call me with what you learn. I'm having a hard time putting this all together, but Dr. Turner has suddenly turned into a major lead."

"You got it," Beth said. "Thank you."

She closed her phone and bent to pick up her coat. No movies tonight. She was considering whether it would be better to be at home or the office when she spoke with San Diego. There was other work that she needed to do while she waited for the call, chiefly to make sure that Dr. Turner, whether or not he was a terrorist, did not elude them.

Beth felt newly energized, planning the next steps. This was at least solid investigative work, what she had been trained to do. She could track down this young surgeon regardless of where he was in San Diego and could get some answers. No more speculation about dissolving plastic and weaponized viruses and Russian motives. She left the Romantic Comedy aisle and exited the store onto the sidewalk, flipping open her phone to call DeeDee, wondering how fast she could fly to California that night.

CHAPTER 29

The San Diego International Airport was closer to the city itself, Nick thought, *than any other major city airport.* As his plane banked and descended, Nick saw the dark water of San Diego Bay and the lights on Coronado Island and then the hotels on the water near the Convention Center and then the office buildings of San Diego, not the height of those in New York or Chicago but tall enough. It was nearly midnight, but the night was clear and the town well-lit. Weary from his flights, he tried to stretch in his seat. He would be off the plane soon.

The Aeroflot flights to Moscow and then to London Heathrow were uneventful. He had entered the gate at Apatity with some trepidation, and they had asked him something about a local stamp or paper, but he acted ignorant and apparently looked innocent enough, so they passed him through. He slept for the entire two-hour flight and then again for much of the four-hour leg to England, waking frequently in the cramped seat. He read a little of the *Kavalier & Clay* novel, but his mind kept wandering, first to Dina and then to Anna.

Would Dina get back with Vasily to the airport for her later flight to Moscow? Would she then get to her apartment safely? Nick had retraced the events of the last two days in his mind, and he did not believe that they had been identified, or at least Dina had not. If Yatovsky had pushed hard enough he might have learned something about Nick from the orphanage they had visited, but he would need deep government connections and time to track Nick now. Nick felt that once Dina was in her apartment, she would be safe, for no one knew her name or location. She could stay inside until Nick dealt with Yatovsky. But how was he going to do that?

Nick had eleven hours on the flight to Los Angeles to think about this, but he still was not convinced that his plan would work. He felt certain that he could find Yatovsky at the conference since he had the surgeon's itinerary that Dina had translated, but could he convince Yatovsky that it was in his best interest to show Nick the notebook? Could Nick really make him believe that he might be arrested by the FBI if he did not?

An alternative was to play the role of a young Thoracic Surgeon who had heard rumors of Yatovsky's accomplishments with a thoracoscope and would love to hear about them. This would play into the older surgeon's immense ego and his desire to show up American Surgery, but Nick was not much of an actor, and he did not think that he could pull this off. Also, it would require not only ego but also very bad judgment for Yatovsky to relate the details of his crimes to a stranger.

No, Nick would have to show that he already knew the details of the scheme and would bring it down unless his daughter could be helped. In reality, he would also have to help all of the children whose names were in the notebook, and that would require him to take the book rather than just look at it. If he could get his hands on it, even as part of a lie, he knew that he could outrun the older, heavier surgeon, who could hardly then go to the police. Nick could even photocopy the book in a hotel business center and return the book via the front desk clerk. Nick had never stolen anything, at least not before this whole escapade began, but children's lives and possibly a larger population of people were at risk from the weaponized virus. And he had already crossed that threshold into criminal behavior at the lake house.

Nick even wondered if he could get the notebook, even the whole briefcase, if necessary, without confronting Yatovsky directly. What if the surgeon set it down during one of the lectures or at lunch? What if Nick got into the Russian's room at the hotel, maybe by fooling a maid to let him in when he feigned being locked out? But Tanya had said that Yatovsky never left the notebook unless operating or hunting or sleeping, not even while getting a massage at the Smiling Mink. No wonder Nick had slept fitfully on the plane.

It took very little time for the cab to reach the Marriott, as the streets had few cars. At one o'clock in the morning, the lobby was nearly empty also, thoracic surgeons not being in the habit of late-night partying. The hotel had a Bayview Room at $226 per night, and Nick used his credit card to reserve it for three nights. Once in his room on the eleventh floor Nick pushed open the curtains and looked out at the dark water of San Diego Bay, the lights of Coronado Island across the water, a large Navy vessel moving slowly towards its base to the left. This would be a beautiful city to visit under other circumstances, such as just attending the conference.

Nick had attended one Society of Thoracic Surgeons Annual Meeting, while he was a Thoracic Surgery Fellow in Philadelphia. His institution would pay for the Fellows to attend one meeting each year, more generous than his General Surgery Residency, which would cover the cost of one such meeting during the entire five years, usually scheduled by a Resident during one of the last years so that he or she could put out feelers for a fellowship or a job. Nick had flown to Ft. Lauderdale for the 36th Annual Meeting, leaving Lynn and Anna behind in the bitter Pennsylvania winter.

Ft. Lauderdale in January had been glorious, as had been the chance to sleep later than four in the morning. Nick had gotten up early enough anyway to run. His hotel, another Marriott he remembered, was on the water, and Nick recalled a beautiful run north along a promenade, the ocean to his right the entire way up, other hotels and condominium buildings on his left. At one point, he passed the International Swimming Hall of Fame, but it was not open that early; he was more of a runner than a swimmer anyway. He had plenty of time to shower, put on a sports coat and tie, and take a shuttle bus to the Convention Center near the cruise ship port.

This annual conference typically ran Monday through Wednesday. Nick had attended nearly every minute, from early morning breakfast sessions with experts, to the Presidential Address, through sessions in which six to ten research studies were presented related to Cardiac Surgery or Thoracic Surgery, even to movies of operations in the evenings. On breaks and at lunch, he walked the huge exhibit hall, stopping at booths showing new instruments and scopes or new textbooks. He had flown home late Wednesday night and was back in his hospital on rounds the next morning.

Nick pulled the curtains closed. He would try to sleep for a few hours, blissfully supine and stretched out, in the inviting bed.

Nick would have liked to run in one or both of the green Embarcadero parks visible out his window the next morning. He had no running clothes with him—in fact, his few items of clothing were more appropriate for a Russian winter—and he had far more important things to do. But he still pictured himself jogging past the docked boats in the marina and onto a park path, early morning sunlight glinting off the blue waters of the Bay, the fifty to sixty-degree temperature perfect. Maybe another time in the future, maybe with Anna, maybe (could he let his thoughts reach that far?) with Dina.

He called down to the desk and learned of a large used clothing store in the Gaslamp Quarter, a store that opened early and closed late, one within easy walking distance. Nick did not need the full dark suit and tie, *de rigueur* for surgeons at these conferences, but he needed something other than his heavy sweater. He wanted to blend in while he stalked Yatovsky. He might get by wearing his pants and even his boots but a thick winter sweater would look very odd here.

He cashed a traveler's check and set out. The Gaslamp Quarter proved to be a charming area of small shops and restaurants just across Harbor Drive and the train tracks from the hotel. Few of the shops were open but a number of the proprietors of small ethnic restaurants were setting tables outside next to the sidewalk, calling in various languages through open doors to the inside, wiping tabletops vigorously. A few people sat on the tiny balconies of five-story apartment buildings, sipping coffee, still in pajamas and robes. Nick bought a cinnamon and raisin bagel and coffee from one shop, eating the bagel hungrily as he walked. Nick saw the clothing store before he got to it, for there were racks of shirts and dresses on the sidewalk next to the wall of the store.

The bushy-haired shopkeeper had a similarly gray walrus mustache and a pleasant manner. He found Nick a button-collared white long-sleeved shirt and a size forty dark blue sportscoat, both a little large on Nick's slim frame but okay under the circumstances. A tie with alternating stripes of cardinal red and gold had probably been discarded by a University of Southern California alumnus, but the other ties were all dark, so Nick took that one. The shopkeeper's black cat seemed to like it. He left the clothes on and tucked his sweater into a bag.

Nick walked straight back to the hotel to drop the sweater in his room so that he could get to the Convention Center before it got much later in the morning. The breakfast sessions were over by now, but the main events had not started. He still needed to register since he had not even planned to attend this meeting and had not pre-registered, but that would not take long. As he crossed back over the train tracks, first northbound, then a sidewalk, then southbound, then Harbor Drive, he saw a number of dark-suited men and women walking down the sidewalk to his left, towards the Annual Meeting, some singly and some in pairs, the most prescient wearing sunglasses for the outdoor walk. Most would be surgeons, some Residents or Fellows; the industry representatives, dressed as well or better than the doctors, would already be in the Exhibit Hall preparing their displays.

For some reason this year's Annual Meeting was on a Friday, Saturday, Sunday rather than the usual Monday, Tuesday, Wednesday. It probably had something to do with a hotel or Convention Center conflict with another meeting. In any case, it benefited Nick since the meeting was just beginning that day. Yatovsky may have attended the Tech-Con, additional sessions less research-oriented and more practical, on Thursday, but he was unlikely to miss the main Meeting.

The San Diego Convention Center was an attractive structure, or at least one with a certain style, unlike the usual rectangular behemoths in other cities. It was long and relatively low, basically two tall stories, with a flying buttress theme facing the street and large circular windows on the ends. Connecting the windows on the second story was a wide corridor roofed by some semi-circular clear glass or plastic.

Nick pushed open the glass doors of the Convention Center and saw the large Registration area on the main floor to his left. The Center was enormous, the lobby at least two stories tall with long escalators at each end. People walked briskly, sometimes in groups, sometimes alone, eyes intent on the red program booklet as they sought the correct room and location for the session they desired. There was a coffee kiosk and a few benches, but most people seemed to be in purposeful motion, typical of thoracic surgeons, polished black shoes clicking on the tile floor.

Nick passed the doors to the main Exhibit Hall filling the wall to his right, but the doors were closed at this hour, typically opening at nine or ten o'clock. He came to the Registration area, one forty-foot-long counter divided by signs into designated desktops: Advanced Registration, A-K; Advanced Registration L-Z; On-Site Registration, Members; On-Site Registration, Guests; Exhibitors. Nick walked up to the On-Site Registration, Guest. He was not yet a member of the Society of Thoracic Surgeons, although he intended to apply for membership sometime. He paid the $250 fee with his credit card. This would have been $100 if he were a Member and had registered ahead, or $90 if a nurse or Physician Assistant, or free if a Resident of Fellow with a letter from his or her Chief.

He was handed a badge, his name and town printed by the computer on a three-inch-square piece of thick white paper and slipped into a clear plastic holder. He clipped this onto the sports coat pocket over his left breast. The faux leather bag that came with registration was surprisingly nice, although emblazoned with the name of the medical equipment company which had underwritten the cost. Inside was the program book, a San Diego tourism guidebook, a lanyard as an alternative for holding one's badge, and a Society of Thoracic Surgeons ballpoint pen. Nick moved to a bench near the front window to peruse the program.

The front of the booklet, bordered in red, showed images of a stethoscope and bound volumes of *The Annals of Thoracic Surgery*, in addition to shadow images of a man and woman looking intently forward and up, likely toward their bright future in Thoracic Surgery. The words "39th Annual Meeting" and the dates and location were in the lower right. Inside was a Welcome note from the President of the organization, Dr. William Baumgartner, then the Program-at-a-Glance page, then pages of more detailed schedules of sessions and their room locations. There was a page of How I Do It seminars (Advanced Techniques in Aortic Root Reconstruction, Repair of Tetralogy of Fallot with Atrioventricular Septal Defect, and others) and Meet the Experts sessions (VATS Lobectomy,

Endovascular Stenting, and others).

Nick would have enjoyed hearing the Ethics Debate listed on the Clinical Workshops page: "Surgeons are Ethically Obligated to Refer Patients to Other Surgeons Who Achieve Better Results." Surgical Motion Pictures on Saturday night included several using the relatively new surgical robot, including Total Robotic Esophagectomy and Total Endoscopic Robotic Thymectomy. Social Events at the back of the booklet included events at Sea World and the San Diego Zoo, as well as a Cooking School class and La Jolla Shopping and Sightseeing.

Nick reached into his pants pocket and pulled out the folded paper on which Dina had written Yatovsky's itinerary. The first Scientific Session of research papers was already underway, but at eleven a.m. there was the Presidential Address in the main hall. Nick saw from a sign overhead that this hall was on the second floor, so he refolded the paper and headed towards the escalator. It was early, but at least he might be able to see the Russian surgeon in person by waiting near one of the hall's entrance doors. Nick still was not sure exactly when he would confront the man, but it would have to be a time when they were alone or nearly so, certainly not in a crowd.

He stepped onto the bottom step of the two-story escalator and looked up. Dozens of men and women of all ages traveled up and down, every step occupied, dark suits and dresses indicating oneness with the herd. Midway up the down escalator to his left, Nick saw a large man in a blue pin-striped suit, his white dress shirt straining against a barrel chest and large abdomen. The suit had wider stripes than most, formal but missing the fashion mark, the red tie similarly garish. He carried a worn brown leather briefcase in his right hand, his large left hand gripping the moving railing. The man turned to look at Nick as they passed, his eyes dark above a full salt-and-pepper beard.

It was Yatovsky.

CHAPTER 30

Yatovsky looked away, no recognition in his manner; Nick was just another faceless young surgeon in the crowd. The Russian's broad back descended rapidly as Nick, looking back, ascended. There was no way Nick could have leapt across the wide metal expanse separating the moving stairways in order to follow him, and the older man was gone into the crowd by the time Nick reached the top. He would wait for him outside the lecture hall as he had planned, since Yatovsky would still keep to his itinerary.

Now that he had seen Yatovsky, Nick was not likely to miss him. As tall as Nick, the man was much heavier, not exactly fat but large, a man who ate well but could also hunt outdoors within the Arctic Circle. He also stood out among the dark blue blazers and black suits, his suit a twelve on a conservative scale ending at ten. Yatovsky's eyes were frightening: small, dark, and intelligent, like those of some predator bear or feral hog. Nick moved back into the broad concourse outside the hall, a position that allowed him to see all of the several double doors into the cavernous room.

At 10:50 Yatovsky appeared from Nick's left and entered the hall, Nick following. The Russian moved to a section of chairs about twenty rows from the stage, near the center of the room. Since all aisle seats were taken, he brushed past several seated surgeons and sat down, putting his briefcase halfway under the seat with the back of his right foot pressing it against the chair leg. There was a seat in the row behind, two chairs further in, and Nick took it.

He could easily see Yatovsky and, if Nick bent down, the briefcase. The case itself had a flat bottom on which it sat and soft brown leather sides that tapered toward the top, each side topped by a round handle. It appeared that the top opened like a large doctor's bag to either side on hinges, allowing a broader opening. Nick pictured himself pulling the briefcase out from behind the chair and running for the door as the Russian bellowed, unable to miss the theft due to his foot pressing against the leather case. One of the many surgeons between Nick and the door would certainly stop him, as he would if he thought someone was stealing another man's luggage.

There were a number of people already on the stage, as there had been several awards presented. Although he had never met him, Nick recognized the President, Dr. Baumgartner, from pictures that he had seen. The Johns Hopkins Cardiac Surgeon was reputed to be a genuinely nice, humble man, a rarity in a field that demanded perfectionism and intensity and which was often nourished by ego. Nick listened attentively to his excellent lecture, as did Yatovsky, and then everyone rose to leave.

Nick followed Yatovsky out of the hall, keeping about six to eight feet back, his eyes on the briefcase swinging with the man's right arm. Inside was the notebook that could tell Nick whether his daughter was at risk, whether she needed an operation right away. Nick was certain that Anna's chest contained a tiny plastic chip, even now dissolving; the only question was whether that pellet contained a virulent, mutant strain of smallpox or was just a dummy, part of this surgeon's sick—and evidently enormously profitable—game.

Yatovsky went down the same escalator, then waited in line at the coffee kiosk to buy and rapidly consume a large iced donut. It was noon, but Nick had eaten the bagel for breakfast and was not hungry. He followed the striped blue suit through wide doors to their right and into the Exhibit Hall. There might be an opportunity to get the man alone in some quiet part of the hall, maybe among the partitioned walls of research posters on the right side. It would not be in the main part of the hall, already packed with surgeons and broadcasting a carnival atmosphere.

The Exhibit Hall was the size of two football fields side by side, its metal rafters three stories above the carpeted floor. It was roughly divided into a half-dozen wide paths with slightly narrower paths crossing every twenty yards at right angles, a small city within the Convention Center. Vendors had booths of equal depth but various widths along a pathway, some as small as ten to fifteen feet wide and some three to four times that. Most impressive were the major surgical equipment companies, who had set up displays the size of small single-story houses, their floorplans divided into open rooms devoted to different technologies or products.

Yatovsky started down the left aisle, stopping at a publisher of surgical textbooks to flip through a two-volume set of *Shield's General Thoracic Surgery* and a few smaller texts. He walked past a few booths set up by hospital systems to recruit Cardiothoracic Surgeons, including one from the National Health Service in England, and then picked up some long, thin laparoscopic instruments at another wide display. Across the aisle, he carefully handled some very old medical books, their covers of tan leather cracked with age beneath protective clear plastic. A young woman at the next booth modeled venous compression stockings.

The largest, house-size displays were more towards the center of the hall. Ethicon-made surgical staplers and other instruments. There were video screens showing their instruments in use and a dozen company representatives, clean-cut and well-dressed young men and women whose eyes scanned the badges of those walking by, particularly seeking the red-badged STS members who were more likely to have purchasing authority or at least clout in their hospital. Olympus, maker of scopes and video equipment crucial for minimally-invasive endoscopic surgery, was next door and equally large.

Yatovsky seemed fascinated by the DaVinci surgical robot at the Intuitive company area. He stood still, watching a surgeon speak to a small group of seated attendees, the surgeon describing what was happening on the video behind him. The tips of robotic instruments were shown in close-up on the screen, placing fine stitches in what appeared to Nick to be a heart mitral valve. The person manipulating the instruments was not even at the operating table during this surgery; rather, in a corner of the operating room sitting at the robotic console, his forehead pressed against the 3D eyepiece, fingers of both hands through circular loops in the handpieces.

Around a partition was a large space containing two robots, each comprised of a console and a unit with four robotic arms. Each of the units with the articulating robot arms sat to the side of an operating table on which was a two-foot square tray holding colorful plastic pieces of various shapes: half-inch yellow blocks, pea-sized green balls, one-inch red circular loops, open cylinders, and upright pegs. At one console sat a middle-aged woman in a black pantsuit; at the other, a large teen-aged boy with close-cropped red hair, their foreheads pressed against soft bars beneath which were the goggle-like eyepieces.

These units were set up to allow surgeons to actually get the feel of what performing robotic surgery might be like. Each operator could grasp one of the tiny plastic objects with the fine pincher grasper at the tip of a robotic arm and move it to another spot, or place it in a cylinder, or drop a loop over a peg, rudimentary exercises but enough for a novice. A video screen above each console displayed what the operator was seeing: the plastic objects magnified to the size of bricks and soccer balls, the relatively clumsy movements of the novice woman and boy evident to all.

Actually, the boy, perhaps fifteen years old, possibly the son of one of the surgeons, appeared more facile than the older woman. Although she was likely an experienced surgeon, he had grown up playing video games every day. Yatovsky was clearly fascinated by this new technology. He had been forward-thinking enough to embrace video-assisted thoracic surgery before most other surgeons, and he might see this as the next advance. Nick doubted that this existed in Russia. Yatovsky spoke to one of the Intuitive representatives who indicated that he should wait until the boy was done.

Ten minutes later, neither operator had moved, each immersed in manipulating the small objects. Yatovsky, his anger finally boiling over, said to the worker, "He is boy who will never do surgery; I am visiting Russian Professor. Tell him to get up." His voice was deep and accented, his arms both pointing to the adolescent.

The representative touched the boy's shoulder and bending, said something into his ear. The teenager rose, and Yatovsky brushed him back impatiently as he sat down on a metal stool in front of the console. He had been observing well, for he immediately put the thumb and middle finger of each hand into the small white canvas loops of each handpiece, leaving each index finger free to pull the clutch button and, having thereby disconnected the robotic arms from the handpieces, could adjust the latter to a comfortable position. His forearms rested on a padded horizontal bar as he leaned into the eyepiece. Nick saw him press his left foot onto a pedal and, by moving his arms forward simultaneously, could zoom in the camera. The Russian began grasping the plastic pieces.

The briefcase was now between Yatovsky's feet, but the surgeon would occasionally move his left foot to the side to press the floor pedal so that he could zoom the telescopic camera in and out. Nick thought that it might be possible for him to slide the briefcase backward quickly and disappear into the crowd at one of these times, and he moved closer to the seated man as if he were waiting his turn at the console.

"Nick!" said a voice just behind him.

Nick turned around to see a beaming young man who immediately stepped forward and enveloped Nick in a hug.

"Scottie, what a pleasant surprise," said Nick, smiling. Scottie Chang was Nick's Co-Chief Resident during General Surgery and both had gone into Cardiothoracic Surgery. Scottie had gone back to California for his fellowship and had stayed on as an academic Cardiac Surgeon in his home state. He looked about the same as always: straight black hair perfectly in place, wearing a blue blazer and light blue bow tie.

"So, how's practice in the woods of Pennsylvania?" Scottie asked. Nick caught Scottie glancing at Nick's boots.

"I'm not exactly in the woods," Nick said. "I'm doing just about everything I was trained to do, except no transplants. It's been really good so far. How about you?"

"It's been busy, with trying to get a lab going while still taking care of patients. A lot of CABGs, some valves. As the young guy I get some of the middle of the night stuff, a couple of dissections, one post-infarction VSD."

"Wow. That brings back memories. By the way, are you and Grace married yet?"

"Just last summer," Scottie said. "We wanted to wait until I was done with all my training." He paused. "I was sorry to hear about Lynn."

"Thank you," said Nick.

"Hey, do you want to get together while you're here?"

"Oh, it was really a spur of the moment decision for me to come," said Nick. Scottie could not know how truly spur of the moment it was. "And I haven't figured out what I am doing each day. Can I give you a call?"

Scottie wrote down his number and waved as he walked away. Nick turned back to the robot console.

Yatovsky was gone! Another man was in his place on the metal stool, leaning into the console. The Russian had either gotten frustrated or been tapped out.

Nick looked at his watch: nearly one-thirty. He unfolded Yatovsky's itinerary, then opened the Program Book. Dina had written down a session on 'The Geriatric Patient' beginning at 1:30 p.m. This seemed like an odd choice for Yatovsky, but Nick saw in the Program that there was no competing session, so he left the Exhibit Hall and headed for the second floor.

By the time Nick found the assigned hall, the first speaker was sitting down, and the second was walking to the stage. Nick remained standing at the back and scanned the seated surgeons. Yatovsky was there, again in the center and about twenty rows back. Nick found an empty seat two rows behind. He would follow the Russian when he left and would approach him if any opportunity presented.

Nick was surprised to see the red-headed teenager who had angered Yatovsky at the robot stand up from the front row and snap several pictures of the speaker with a small silver camera. It must have been the man's son. Nick saw from the program that the speaker was a name he recognized since they both practiced General Thoracic Surgery in Pennsylvania. The talk was on 'Principles of Cardiothoracic Surgery in the Elderly.' This was likely to be boring.

It was as tedious as predicted, and the less-patient Russian rose first to leave. Nick followed him out and continued a reasonable distance behind as the surgeon turned away from the escalator to the main lobby and walked in the direction of the back of the Convention Center. They ended at a long-windowed hallway through which one could see the glistening blue water of the Bay. There were several double doors that led out to a large open concrete deck. Nick could see a few surgeons walk across the wide deck and disappear through an opening in the four-foot-high concrete wall, their heads descending as they apparently went downstairs towards the marina and Embarcadero.

Yatovsky pushed a door open and went out into the sunshine, walking to the wall but not down the stairs. Instead, he moved next to a large round planter containing a low cactus-like tree, set down the briefcase, and extracted a leather cigar case from the inner right-hand pocket of his suit coat. He took out a long cigar, licked it, and then clipped a small wedge from the end with a gold cigar cutter. From his pants pocket, he took a gold butane lighter and, flicking it with a lateral motion of his thumb, generated a compact blue flame. He drew in on the cigar, holding the tip near the flame until the end glowed red; he lifted his head and blew smoke towards the Bay. He leaned his forearms on the wall, just as he had on the robot console earlier.

The Russian would never be more alone than this. Nick pushed through the door and walked briskly across the deck.

CHAPTER 31

"Professor Yatovsky," Nick said when he was next to the other man, "I am Dr. Nicholas Turner, a General Thoracic Surgeon like you."

Yatovsky turned, his dark eyes steady on Nick's as he stared for a long moment. He turned his head slightly and blew out a concentrated column of gray smoke, not caring that most of it enveloped Nick. "Oh, I doubt, young man, that you are like me." There was a faint smile on his lips, his voice deep, accented, haughty. "Few, if any, Americans are. But I forget my manners. How may I help you?"

This close, the Russian was even more like a bear, large, powerful, cunning, confident that nothing in the forest could threaten him, exuding brawn as strong as his musky cologne. Nick had no plan but to be direct.

"As a Thoracic Surgeon I can understand exactly what you did to children in the orphanages."

Nick detected only the slightest pause as Yatovsky drew on his cigar. "I do not know what you talk about," Yatovsky said. "Children, orphanage, what do these have to do with me?" His eyes were just as piercing but they appeared narrower now as he contemplated Nick. *How much could this young man know? More important, how much could he prove? What did he want?*

"I recently discovered a foreign object in the left pleural cavity of a boy," Nick said. "Why should a child have a piece of plastic in him, I thought? He certainly wasn't born with it.

So I did a little research and found that you had operated on him before he was adopted by an American couple."

The Russian did not look at Nick. He drew on his cigar, looking across the concrete walks and green grass of the small park to the waters of the Bay. "Surgeons are always leaving foreign material behind. We leave stainless steel staples and polypropylene mesh. What is so unusual about that?" The Russian's English was accented but excellent.

"This piece of plastic was intentionally buried beneath the pleura at the apex of the left chest cavity. It had no purpose and was intended to remain undiscovered, as it is radiolucent and small."

Yatovsky took the cigar from his mouth. "So, in hypothetical case that you present, what would be the harm in an inert piece of sterile plastic?" He contemplated the paper band that he had left on the cigar, the end nearer his mouth, half the band orange, the other half black studded with tiny white dots. Past the large man's left shoulder, Nick could see a cargo dock, a Dole ship being unloaded, and the Coronado Bridge in the distance.

"The plastic itself was sterile and inert, but what was inside was decidedly not. In fact, it was potentially highly infectious." Nick stopped short of saying that it was smallpox inside, then reconsidered. The more specific he was, the more likely Yatovsky was to believe that Nick knew the whole scheme. "It contained smallpox," he said and watched the large man for a reaction.

Yatovsky maintained his composure but he stopped smoking, turning to look at Nick now. "Your story is getting more and more absurd. What would be the purpose of such a thing?"

"It could be money," said Nick. "You have expensive cars, dacha, jewelry." Nick pointed to the large gold watch on Yatovsky's left wrist. "Especially for a surgeon who was fired by his hospital, one not working."

"Was not fired," Yatovsky said loudly, his dark eyes holding Nick's. "I left due to jealousy of superiors. I am the master surgeon, the one advancing the field; all knew it. In any field, there will be casualties for the ultimate benefit of many, a few deaths in order to save many. The narrow thinkers could not see this."

"And I suppose the American thinkers could not see your brilliance, either, when they kicked you out," Nick said, stifling the urge to move back as the Russian leaned forward. *Steady,* Nick told himself, *you've faced life-threatening bleeding in the OR and, recently, threats to life itself in Russia. You can't let this bully shake you.*

"Americans are worst of all!" Yatovsky shouted. "Conceited pricks who think they know it all, think that they invented surgery. Halsted himself learned from the Germans, Austrians, and Swiss. Russia invented surgical staplers which were then smuggled into the United States in a suitcase and became the basis for huge American companies, growing billionaires. Minimally invasive surgery started in Europe also, but Americans give no credit. If I can do sophisticated chest surgery in an orphanage, think what I could do in wealthy American hospital."

"So, you admit to doing operations on children in orphanages?"

"I admit to nothing! But if I did sophisticated video-assisted chest surgery in such a place, it would show superior skill, would it not?"

"Yes, it would require skill," said Nick, "and would also require a complete lack of ethics, of human decency. None of those children needed an operation, and if they did, why not do it in a hospital?"

Yatovsky did not answer. He looked away and drew deeply on his cigar.

Nick felt more and more frustrated. He had worked under many surgeons with huge egos, so he knew Yatovsky's type, but Nick also was no detective. Maybe he really was out of his league. Was it time to give up and call the FBI? No. They might arrest or detain the Russian but the notebook would be gone, hidden or destroyed.

"And do you hate America so much that you targeted children destined to live here?" Nick asked.

"Americans look down on everyone," Yatovsky said, looking back at Nick. "They humiliated me when I was in Boston but they do the same to many. It would be wonderful for all of you to learn lesson, to realize that you do not have the cure for every disease." He paused. "Diseases such as smallpox, for example—since you mentioned this." For the first time, Nick noticed the hint of a smile.

"Whether you have done this for money or ego or out of bitterness, I cannot allow innocent children to remain at risk," Nick said. "It was bad enough that you put them through the risk and pain of an operation they did not need and probably killed at least one, but many of them carry a ticking time bomb. I need to know which ones. I need your notebook."

"My notebook?" Yatovsky raised his eyebrows. "How do you know about...ah, Tanya. You have talked with the bitch Tanya." Now, he actually smiled. "How is the ungrateful cunt doing? Still sucking off men in the strip club?"

"I need your notebook, or we can go and make a copy of it," Nick said. He wanted to leave the subject of Tanya. She was probably safe at her friend's place or might be on her way home to her father, but Yatovsky had already shown a propensity for vengeance and for long memory.

"You need my notebook!" Yatovsky said loudly. "The American boy surgeon with a science fiction story about orphans and plastic and smallpox wants the notebook of the accomplished scientist. What if I do have a notebook? What if it contains confidential results of my research? Why would I give it to anybody, most of all you?"

"Because if you don't, I will call the FBI," said Nick, holding up a piece of paper on which he had written an invented Philadelphia phone number. "Do you know about our FBI?"

Nick noted a little moisture on Yatovsky's forehead. The large man drew on his cigar, now half its original length, the tip glowing red. "Why would FBI care about a Russian surgeon attending a medical convention?"

"They know the whole story," Nick said. "They just do not know that we are in the United States at this meeting. Originally, I did not plan to be here. If I call them, I believe that they will detain you in the United States."

Nick had to give Yatovsky credit: he was not easily shaken. Most Cardiothoracic Surgeons could handle unforeseen circumstances, even life-threatening emergencies, in and out of the operating room. Events happened all the time. And the Russian had ego on top of this. He felt that he could get out of this, as he had always found a way to land on his feet. Nick would have to be careful, as all that he had right now was this bluff.

"And if I give you this notebook, then you will not call? How do I know?"

"I frankly don't care what happens to you," Nick said. "I just want to save the children."

"So, you will operate to remove this supposed piece of plastic in all of them?"

"Just the ones marked with the red symbol in your book. The others are dummies."

"You seem to know a lot," Yatovsky said. "Fucking Tanya." He waited for a group of surgeons to walk past them towards the stairs. "Were you also the man in Moscow that Viktor told me about, or do you have friends there?"

Nick did not want the man to think that he had any help at all, particularly help from Dina, Tanya's father, or Marta at the orphanage. "That was me."

"You have been exceptionally persistent and have traveled long way," Yatovsky said. "Why such effort for a story that may or may not be true?"

Nick paused before speaking, but he wanted Yatovsky to

understand that he would not back down, that this was deeply personal. "My daughter was adopted from a Russian orphanage. She has three small left chest scars."

Yatovsky studied the inch of fine gray ash at the end of his cigar, then flicked the body of the cigar with the middle finger of the hand holding it, sending the ash to the concrete deck near his polished brown Italian shoes. "Now I see your interest in my affairs beyond your naive, self-serving American altruism. Perhaps we can both get what we want. You want to know if your daughter's small body carries a genetically modified, highly virulent virus, one, by the way, for which no vaccine or treatment exists in the United States." He was enjoying this provocation of the slim American surgeon.

"I need to know about all of the children," Nick said, trying not to show the effect of Yatovsky's words.

The Russian went on as if he had not heard. "Whereas I want to enjoy remaining time in San Diego and then return to lifestyle in Russia. Which I can do, having been compensated richly for certain technical jobs on behalf of those wealthier and better connected than I. In fact, my work for them is nearly complete anyway." He leaned close enough to Nick to broadcast the smell of wet tobacco. "But how can I trust you not to call your FBI anyway?"

Nick was happy to hear that his FBI bluff seemed to be working. "Remember, I am naïve and altruistic. You should be able to trust me."

Yatovsky looked out to the Bay as he drew again on the remains of his cigar. He turned back to Nick and said, "I will give you a copy, but not the book itself. The list that you want is only a small part of it and the rest contains my notes and observations about what is, you must admit, a remarkable achievement. It may even have historic value."

"Don't flatter yourself, Professor," said Nick. "What you did could not be called achievement. There are other words that could be assigned. But let us both go to the Business

Center here and copy the list, then you may enjoy the rest of your sunny stay in California."

"Ah, but I do not have the notebook with me."

"I learned that you always had it with you," Nick said, "that you never went anywhere, except perhaps hunting, without it. I suspect that it is in the briefcase at your feet."

"So, you know of my love for hunting also?" asked Yatovsky, skewing the direction of the conversation. "You should see my dacha." He paused. "But maybe you have. Viktor called me to say that he and Maks were flying there to prevent a break-in, then I heard nothing more from him." He seemed to look at Nick with new respect. Perhaps the young American was tougher than he seemed.

"Where is the notebook?" Nick pressed.

"In Russia, hotel rooms do not have safes. After all, we are not supposed to have anything to hide from each other. But here, in my suite, nice safe in wall of closet. So, I lock up notebook. Just close door of safe, put in four-digit number, do not even need a key." He seemed to brighten. "Here is what we do. I make copy of list tonight when I return to room and I meet you tomorrow."

"How do I know that you will not fly back to Russia tonight?" Nick asked. He thought about suggesting that they go to Yatovsky's room together, but the picture of being alone in a room with this amoral bear of a man caused a chill. Nick would have no chance in a physical encounter, and he doubted that the Russian would hesitate to use some weapon.

Yatovsky was speaking. "It looks as if we must trust each other, does it not? Although it might represent only a temporary inconvenience, I would prefer that your wild speculative story be kept with you alone. Or do others already know?"

"One FBI agent knows enough to have you detained in the United States for questioning. Other than that, no one else knows anything." Nick would give any lie to keep Dina out of the conversation.

"Fine. You will make no call and I will give you copy tomorrow. I have trip planned to San Diego Zoo, so I will meet you there. I visited when STS Meeting was here in 1997 and it was wonderful. And, of course, I like animals."

"What are you talking about," asked Nick. "We can just meet in the hotel lobby, then go our separate ways." He did not add that Yatovsky liked animals enough to shoot many of them and display their mounted heads.

"No, I do not want other surgeons to see us together, and I do not want you to play any tricks. We will meet in an open public area, many children around..."

"Yes, since you love children so much," Nick said.

"...then you can tour the Zoo," Yatovsky continued, "or fly home to take care of your daughter before she is covered in vesicles and bleeds from eyes and rectum." He dropped his cigar butt and ground it under his shoe.

"Bastard!" Nick shouted. "You had better be there." He did not like this at all but he did not think that he could push his bluff much further.

"I will be there, near the polar bears at say, ten o'clock. This list has little importance to me now. Perhaps more importance to others in Moscow, but they need not know any of what happens here, and I can get on with my next venture. I may even be the first to bring surgical robots into Russia."

"The polar bears at ten," Nick repeated.

"Majestic creatures," Yatovsky said as he walked towards the stairs. "I have several on my wall."

CHAPTER 32

Nick walked through the front gate of the San Diego Zoo at 9:05 a.m. On this warm, sunny Saturday he did not want to risk a long line of families or anything else that would delay him getting to the polar bear area by ten. He still did not trust Yatovsky and he had been unable to shake the fear that the Russian was up to something. Yatovsky had appeared pleased when he learned that the only people who knew about his deeds were Nick and one distant FBI agent. Fortunately, the zoo was an open public space with many witnesses, but the Russian had been there before, and he seemed familiar with it.

After their encounter the day before, Nick had walked down a flight of concrete stairs on the marina side of the Convention Center, the south tower of the Marriott visible to his right, semi-circular, smooth, the tall windows shining silver in the late afternoon sun. He saw before him a twenty-foot-tall sculpture on a ten-foot pedestal, a free-form twisting mass of steel; a sign on the pedestal said it was a gift from the people of Mexico in the year 2000, a work called "The Flame of Friendship." He took another flight of stairs down to the marina level and walked to his nearby hotel.

Joggers passed him on the wide concourse, as did people on bikes. The marina seemed to have hundreds of boats, a few more motorboats than sailboats, some huge and obviously expensive. Seagulls flew overhead, occasionally landing for some scrap of dropped food. At one point, three Navy helicopters flew from behind Nick and north over the bay. There were many dogs and many families, distracted children dripping ice cream from slanting cones as they watched the helicopters above.

Nick had experienced a pang of longing and had called Anna as soon as he got back to his room.

Still fatigued from his adventures inside the Arctic Circle and his subsequent travel, Nick had gone to bed early, but he had slept fitfully, at one point even stepping out onto the small balcony. The moon, nearly full, cast a golden path across the Bay, and, under other circumstances, would have been beautiful, but Nick's mind churned with memories of his conversation that afternoon and with anticipation of getting the list of names. This led to thoughts of Anna sleeping under the same moon in a much colder Pennsylvania. He would see her soon.

The cab to the northern part of Balboa Park and the Zoo had covered the three and a half miles in fifteen or twenty minutes, so Nick had waited outside the entrance until the grounds opened at nine. Just inside the front gate now he unfolded the large map that he had been given. The dominant color of the map was green, with globular representations of treetops as if seen from a hot air balloon looking down onto the zoo landscape. A tan path went around the circumference, and another essentially bisected the greenery, and others branched off into blind circles or shortcuts between the main thoroughfares.

The many buildings, varying in size and shape, were uniformly roofed in orange on the map, some with small numbers corresponding to a key in the map's upper right corner: Kid's Store, Treehouse Trader, Panda Shop, Ituri Forest Outpost, and more. The animals in a given location were each represented by a small black square containing a white silhouette of the animal: the zebras and tigers also with stripes, the panda with black eyeshadow, the giraffe with broad spots. There were two up escalators called Speedramps connecting the canyons to the upper mesas, for visitors who did not wish to walk up a long incline. Nick was reminded of the Chutes and Ladders game that he played with Anna.

Nick was intrigued to see two parallel lines extending obliquely from the west of the park to the southeast corner, lines from which hung tiny gondola cabs. It was an aerial tram called Skyfari. He looked up from the map, and to his left, he could see the tan cabs suspended from a taut thick cable, probably a hundred feet in the air above the trees. He would love to return here someday, as Anna would be thrilled to soar above all of the animals and plants.

The Polar Bear Plunge was at the very western end of the Zoo, at the farthest point from where Nick stood. He thought about riding the Skyfari since its East terminal was a short distance to his left. It would take him right over the roof of the Reptile House, over the Scripps Aviary and Gorilla Tropics, to the West terminal next to the polar bears. It was only 9:10, however, so he had plenty of time to walk. He turned right and headed towards the koalas.

Nick was wearing the same long pants, boots, and long-sleeved shirt while all around him were kids in shorts and tee-shirts. He stayed in the shade as much as possible, and the day was not too hot yet. At the koala exhibit he took out the map again, then turned sharply left onto a path named Bear Canyon. This seemed to be a little more in the woods, and he thought that he would rather see lions and bears than the hoofed animals and dry mesas further along and up the hill. The path sloped down the entire way, leading toward the bottom of a canyon.

Nick passed various types of bears, including sloth bears

and sun bears, the latter being the smallest of bears and the most arboreal, named for the cream-colored patch on their chest. There were Grizzly Bears and Andean Bears, a monkey called Francois' Langur and a cute Red Panda. In the distance, there seemed to be an aviary, but this could not be the large Scripps Aviary beneath the aerial tram ride. He opened the map and read 'Owens Rain Forest Aviary.' He wondered how much money one would need to donate in order to name an aviary.

Nick liked seeing different kinds of animals but had mixed feelings about seeing them confined. He knew that they were well cared for, often better than they would be in their native habitat, but he valued his own independence so much that the thought of confinement was disturbing. He had a sense of wonder about the incredible variety of evolved animals, however, and doubted that he could ever afford a safari to see them in the wild. He had even enjoyed the birds and aquatic life of the Atlantic coast and Chesapeake Bay when he was growing up in Delaware.

He came to a crossing path, and on the other side, directly ahead, was one of the Speedramp escalators. He glanced at the map and decided to take this up to the Horn and Hoof Mesa. This would then lead him to the polar bears after a short walk. He might be a few minutes early, but not much. At the top of the escalator, he turned left. His eyes were drawn up by movement, and he saw the gondola cars of the Skyfari ahead and above him, some coming and some going, as the West terminal was just ahead on his right. Every ten to fifteen seconds, a car entered beneath the roof, and a different car emerged heading east towards the Scripps Aviary, the Reptile House, and the main entrance to the Zoo. Each gondola car held one, two, up to four people, many pointing excitedly, others with cameras, all looking over the waist-high rim. A flat roof held up by four thin poles prevented the adults from fully standing, but many of the children could.

Nick passed the Skyfari West terminal and continued steeply down to his left, past some small gazelles and a family of sizeable peccaries, towards the Polar Bear Plunge. Nick could see the sign to the Plunge area, and standing in front, unable to be missed, was Yatovsky. He wore the same blue suit, broad red tie, and polished brown shoes, and he must have been warm. There was a brief flash of reflected sunlight as he raised his large gold watch to face level, his hands free of the leather briefcase at his feet. Nick heard him say something in Russian as four small children rushing to see the polar bears got too close. He turned just as Nick approached.

"Ah, the maichick, the boy who thinks he knows much," Yatovsky said, smiling. "You look surprised to see me here. Did you think that I would run back to Mother Russia just because you threaten me?"

"Just give me the copies and I will turn and never see you again," Nick said. He would have to get the list translated, and soon, but that was not a major problem, particularly given what he had already been through.

"I hope that you have had the opportunity to see many wonderful animals here," Yatovsky said. "I plan to spend the entire day. I have been looking forward to it. Right behind me, there are Siberian reindeer, caribou, raccoons, arctic fox, and, of course, bears. Do you know how magnificent is a bear? They run faster than you, swim faster than you, climb faster than you, and are a hundred times stronger. Do not let one catch you; kill yourself first. They hold you down and begin eating the muscle and soft tissue of your limbs while you still live, the pain incredible and never-ending. See what can happen if you provoke something, or someone, stronger than you?" He smiled at Nick, enjoying this. "First, let us finish our business high above the treetops, in total privacy." His large arm indicated the Skyfari building that Nick had just passed, and he started walking towards it, powerful legs acting as pistons against the steep slope of the path.

"There is no need for this drama," Nick said, catching up. "No one is watching us." *Although*, Nick thought, *the Russian certainly stood out from the surrounding visitors.*

"It is a beautiful three-and-a-half minute ride, private, the next car tens of meters away. It will end near the Main Entrance and you can rush away to save your little girl from the deadly pathogen that she may or may not carry."

They came to the ramp leading up to the loading platform of the aerial tram. As this would be over in four to five minutes, Nick would go along. They waited behind a young couple, arms around each others' waist, probably high school age. Nick doubted that they would be looking down at the animals from the way they were acting. Rushing into place behind Nick and Yatovsky was a Japanese family of four, the man with a video camera already filming, his two children pointing excitedly.

Nick watched to their right as a car came in under the high roof of the concrete loading platform, discharged two older couples, and then came toward them around a huge turnstile, now empty. As there was no motor visible to drive the thick cables, Nick presumed that it was at the East terminal. The high school pair took a few steps across the platform and climbed into the car, sitting together facing forward. The car could accommodate two more people on the other side, facing backward, and the tram attendant, looking towards Nick and Yatovsky, raised his eyebrows and gestured at the empty seat. Yatovsky waved him off, the car door was closed, and the cab jerked forward along the overhead cable. The next car would be theirs.

Yatovsky took the back, forward-facing seat, his large body covering the thin wood slats of the seat, his legs splayed apart. He set the briefcase on the floor between his feet. Nick had no choice but to take the bench opposite, although he would not have sat next to the large man anyway. The car jerked forward, and within seconds, they were out from under the terminal roof and back in bright sunshine, the inside of the car shaded by the flat square roof on its four thin poles. The wide-open area between the top of the tub-like car, with its thin aluminum railing six inches above the tub, and the flat roof over their heads allowed a 360-degree view and, if one leaned over the edge a little, a view below also.

On the horizon, over Nick's left shoulder, rose an architecturally interesting tower based in a different part of Balboa Park to the south of the Zoo. Below their Skyfari cab, there appeared to be a forest, the panda enclosure just coming into view in the direction they were heading. Behind Nick in the distance was the large aviary. He turned back.

Yatovsky had opened the top of the briefcase and was bent over, reaching in, presumably to bring out the paper copies that he had promised. "How could you ever believe," he said in an amused tone, "that I could turn over a list so valuable to an American boy surgeon, a list that my oligarch superior could sell for billions to the American government or more billions to a government that hates America, a list that makes the only vaccine that will work priceless? Boy, you are a rabbit in a car with a bear."

Yatovsky rose up from his seat, something glistening in his left hand, and sprang at Nick. Nick reacted instinctively, reaching up to grasp one of the larger man's outstretched wrists in each hand, the Russian's weight propelling him forward and off balance, driving Nick back against the seat, his own torso arching backward. Nick's neck was now against the back of the tub, his arms extended. In Yatovsky's left hand was a small syringe and needle, something that a diabetic might easily carry through customs. "Neurotoxin," Yatovsky growled. "One prick and no one will ever suspect. Instant death. I will be gone."

Nick could smell the dark cigar on the man's breath and the body odor on the unwashed shirt and suit as the Russian's weight pushed him harder against the wooden slats of the seat.

The man was indeed a bear, heavier and stronger than Nick, and Nick would lose this fight. Yatovsky even stepped up onto the seat now with both feet, straddling Nick's legs, bringing even more weight to bear on Nick's weakening arms. Nick pictured the thin needle pricking his exposed neck or even driving through his clothing. No injection would be needed, just a pinprick into any part of his skin. Nick had heard of Russian poisons through newspaper stories of street assassinations, one even involving the sharp tip of an umbrella on a British sidewalk, and he knew that a microscopic amount could kill. Nick had definitely been naïve, and he was about to die for his naivete.

At a near standstill for over a minute, the Russian's additional leverage from squatting on the bench was having an effect. Nick could not hold out much longer. Although his arms were weak, Nick's legs were strong and limber. He had been a runner all his life and had been particularly good on hills. He began to roll up his legs, tight against his abdomen and under the larger man's hips and lower abdomen. It was like doing a "crunch" in gym class. He got his shoes against Yatovsky and pushed up hard, extending his arms over his head and sliding his body further down into the seat.

The Russian's entire upper body was now over the edge of the tub and falling forward. his eyes widening, his hand releasing the syringe. Both arms began to flail as his entire body left the car, continuing to arc into a forward somersault with a twist at the end as he plummeted, now feet-first, toward the building below. Nick rose to look over the edge and back as the car continued inexorably forward on its cable. They were directly over the Reptile House near the end of the ride. Nick saw the wide eyes and wide-open mouth as Yatovsky crashed feet-first through a skylight and into one of the exhibits below.

CHAPTER 33

Nick heard three loud screams from the Russian, screams audible through the broken skylight, the screams of a man still alive and terrified, the last cry fading as the car moved on. Then there were other people screaming, men and women and children, and Nick could see people running out of the Reptile House as his car went under the roof of the Skyfari East Terminal. When the car stopped, he grabbed the briefcase and ran down the ramp toward the Reptile House next door.

People were running from an entrance on the right-hand side of the building, so Nick entered there. The Reptile House apparently had a central core of offices and labs and working space, hidden from the public and inaccessible to anyone but the zookeepers, a core concentrically surrounded on all four sides by the glass-enclosed exhibits of snakes and other lizards that the public saw, then the public corridor, then the outer wall open to the outside through large apertures crisscrossed by iron lattices. The skylight through which Yatovsky had fallen was in the most distant corner from Nick, so Nick turned right, passing large timber rattlesnakes and green mambas and king cobras behind glass on his left, and then at the corner, he turned left.

The frightened people had already run from the Reptile House, and the remaining curious ones stood at the end of the corridor, staring horrified into the corner exhibit. Nick ran, the brown briefcase swinging, pushing through the cluster of a dozen gawkers to the front of the group. His eyes caught the banner above the glass window into the six-foot square space: "Ethiopian Mountain Adder," with a colorful picture of a muscular green snake, its body sharply marked with diamond patches of black, its head large and wedge-like, its eyes shiny obsidian.

This corner exhibit was special in that it had glass on two sides and was larger than most of the others. Yatovsky sat facing Nick, his back against the right-side back wall, his legs splayed. He might have broken his back, but much of the force of the twenty-five-foot fall had been absorbed by the glass of the skylight, the bar of lights and heating lamps below that, and the thinly-spaced wire of the enclosure's roof below those. He had landed buttocks-first on a pile of wood branches, through which now writhed at least a dozen eighteen-inch snakes, offspring of the large mother adder which emitted a hissing sound from its rock perch next to Yatovsky's face. The floor of the enclosure was littered with shattered glass and the wire roof and light bar hung down against the other wall.

The Russian was still alive, his chest drawing in deep, slow breaths as he stared through the glass at Nick. There was a developing bruise with puncture marks and swelling on the right side of his neck and small puncture marks on his hands and exposed ankles. He raised his left hand slightly toward the on-lookers and immediately cried out as two of the baby vipers struck with blinding speed, sinking fangs into the flesh of his hand and then releasing.

Yatovsky could not stop himself from moaning and turning his head. This was unfortunate, as it frightened the thick four-foot adult snake near his face, a snake already agitated and hissing. The muscular adder launched itself with speed and force into the cheek below Yatovsky's right eye, Nick and the other spectators gasping and involuntarily stepping back as the viper chewed once on the cheek and released, Yatovsky's hoarse cry now high-pitched and whimpering. Two other baby snakes slithered from Yatovsky's left pants leg as the limb twitched, but the Russian appeared not to notice, his eyes now closed. Nick could see no motion of the chest.

A security guard had arrived with a young male zookeeper, and another white-haired member of the Reptile House staff was cautiously opening a small door in the free back wall of the exhibit, a wall free of Yatovsky but partially blocked by the downed lightbar and wire. He pushed the wire to the side with a long wooden stick ending in a metal hook as Nick turned to the guard.

"I know who this man is, and I can tell you what happened," he said. "And we will need to call the FBI. I have an agent's number. And it is very important that I photocopy a few pages of a notebook. Can we go to an office and talk?"

"We can go to the Curator's office," said the zookeeper. "The police are on their way." He was short and thin, with black hair and an attempt at a black mustache. His eyes were wide and his speech rapid, but he seemed more excited by something unusual happening on his watch than by the actual horrid death. There was a round San Diego Zoo patch on the breast of his short-sleeved tan uniform shirt, a brass rectangular name badge 'Sean' on the other breast. A walkie-talkie on his belt crackled, but he ignored it.

"And one other thing," Nick said, turning to the guard. "This is very important. There may be a syringe and needle, possibly broken, on the roof of this building or in with the Ethiopian Mountain Adders. The man we just saw was holding it when he fell. It must be handled with great care, with gloves, as it contains poison." He saw the guard nod.

The guard stayed behind as Sean led Nick halfway back down the hall through which Nick had run. He stepped into a gap between glass enclosures containing on their left a green tree python, reminding Nick of the Kaa character in *The Jungle Book* movie, and on their right a pure white snake.

"A monocellate cobra," Sean said, seeing Nick looking, as

he inserted a key into an unmarked door. "Leucistic or albino snakes are beautiful and prized by collectors but they often die young in the wild, unable to easily hide from predators."

They entered a room that had none of the attractive features of the public-facing displays. Larger than a four-to-six-car garage, the windowless room had walls of cinderblock painted white on three sides and one of black concrete or stucco towards the public displays, this wall marked by a row of small hinged doors into the reptile enclosures. To Nick's immediate right was a pegboard on the wall, and from this, neatly hung snake hooks on poles of various lengths, the reptile house equivalent of a gardener's tool rack. The room's ceiling was about fifteen feet above the concrete floor, crossed at all angles by white pipes of varying diameters, and from which hung long fluorescent lights.

"We can use the Curator's office," Sean said, turning to their left. "He's delivering a Santa Catalina Island Rattlesnake to the Columbus Zoo. Rattlesnakes are our *forte*, you know. One of our early Consultant Curators and Board members was Laurence Klauber, who literally wrote the book on rattlesnakes, two volumes actually, *Rattlesnakes: Their Habits, Life Histories and Influence on Mankind.* The Catalina rattlesnake is really cool since it has no rattle; no reason to have it since it lives on an island without large mammals to step on it—except people now, of course. But it did evolve that way. Beautiful snake, sort of pale tan color most of the time."

This guy must be starved for an audience interested in snakes, thought Nick, *since he already seems to have forgotten the violent death of one of his zoo's visitors.*

Then something struck the young curator, and he turned back to Nick.

"You know, I didn't get your name."

"Dr. Nicholas Turner. I'm just visiting from Pennsylvania, attending a convention."

"What kind of doctor are you?" Sean asked.

"Chest surgeon."

"Wow."

They walked between tall wire shelving units, each three-foot wide unit moveable on lockable wheels, most of the half-dozen shelves on each holding some reptile in a cage. Some of the cages were glass or clear plastic with a wire roof, and some were solid with a clear glass-hinged door, latches on three sides, and snakes within. Turtles crawled or swam in open-topped cases. Most contained some type of plant. Some had lamps above, and some had bowls of water. Sean glanced back again.

"Some snakes will drink standing water, and some won't," he said. "Imagine if you are a snake in a forest and you are accustomed to drinking drops of water that fall from leaves when it rains, your head up, your mouth open. Well, then we would have to give you water from an eyedropper. And even if you are a viper, you won't strike because you're getting a nice drink."

Nick shuddered, images of the thick green vipers that Yatovsky had angered flashing in his mind. He changed the subject. "What are the yellow squares with TX on some cages?"

"Oh, those are animals under treatment."

Sean preceded Nick through a doorway into a small meeting or break room, empty of people but containing a rectangular table and eight chairs, some framed diplomas or certificates on the wall, a coffee machine and a refrigerator in a corner. He went through another doorway and into an office. There were two desks with chairs behind them and two freestanding chairs. The walls were lined by waist-high cabinets topped by countertops, above which were books behind glass doors. Several metal file cabinets crowded the desk chairs. Nick was pleased to see a copy machine on one counter, right next to a series of snake skeletons and turtle shells.

Sean took a seat behind the smaller desk and motioned for Nick to sit in one of the freestanding chairs. "That is the

Curator's desk, but this is Malcolm's, and he won't mind. He's out there trying to wrangle those pissed-off snakes out of the display. The mother won't be a problem after she settles down; hell, Malcolm's been around a long time and dealt with a lot of angry snakes. The babies are another matter, small, fast, not used to a hook. Plus, they may be hiding in the unlucky guy's clothes. It could take a while."

He stroked his wisp of a mustache and looked across the desk into Nick's eyes. "You can't take the little ones for granted. Most vipers, like the Ethiopian Mountain Adder, are viviparous, and the live babies—could be a dozen or twenty or more—are ready at birth."

"Could their venom work that fast?" asked Nick. "I think that we watched the man die."

"I doubt that the venom alone killed him," said Sean thoughtfully. "It was just too fast. Not impossible, of course, but even if they did not kill him, the bites are incredibly painful. He may have had a heart attack. He looked like a big guy. But you're the doctor. Do you know anything about snake venom?"

"Very little," said Nick, "and I hope that you will tell me more." It was almost too easy to keep Sean talking while Nick finished his final, crucial task. "Do you mind if I use the copier while we talk?"

"Be my guest," Sean said. "I doubt that it gets much use."

Nick pulled open the top of the briefcase at his feet and immediately saw the notebook that Tanya had described. About eight by six inches in size and a half-inch thick, it was bound in soft green leather, unmarked and unadorned. Nick opened it and flipped quickly through pages of Russian handwritten script, long paragraphs separated by underlined titles. He could make nothing of this but about twenty pages in there began several pages of a list, what looked like first and last names and dates, probably a column of orphanage names since many words were repeated, and a short phrase. And in the left-most column, next to more than half of the names, was a red Cyrillic Я. The pages following the list were blank.

Nick rose and opened the cover of the copy machine. He pressed the first page of the list onto the glass and hit the copy button, then the next and the next, one copy per page.

Sean was saying something but in his excitement at finding the notebook at last Nick had not been listening. "Can you repeat that, Sean?" Nick asked.

"Snake venom can be cytotoxic, neurotoxic, hemotoxic, maybe cardiotoxic, and often more than one of these. Cytotoxic causes tissue damage and can be extremely painful; hemotoxic can prevent blood from clotting, leading to bleeding, and neurotoxic can cause drowsiness, blurred vision, and even paralysis. Some of the deadliest snakes, the sea snakes and cobras, are neurotoxic. The Ethiopian Mountain Adder's is mostly hemorrhagic and cytotoxic. But the effects can also be proportional to how much venom is injected. Are you familiar with elapids versus vipers?" Sean was relishing his lecture.

Nick was on the next to last page of the list. "Please tell me."

"Elapids, such as cobras and mambas, have fixed fangs; they strike and hold. Vipers like our *Bitis parviocula* and rattlesnakes have retracted fangs. Although they rarely hold, the vipers can inject a large volume of venom, and they strike with speed and force. The Ethiopian Mountain Adder is a truly beautiful snake, and we were the first to legally import them to the United States. They live in the Bale Mountains of Ethiopia and hold a certain reputation among the locals. We were also the first to breed them, and that display was the first to show this to the public. We had special wire on the roof of the cage with very tiny holes so the babies could not get through. After this, we may not do it again. But this is hardly the snakes' fault." He shook his head as the walkie-talkie on his belt buzzed.

Sean held it to his ear, then spoke into it, "In the Curator's office."

Nick folded the copies twice and slipped them into his pants pocket. He sat down and dropped the notebook back into the briefcase. There were several fountain pens on the flat floor of the briefcase, sunglasses, and a thin, hard-sided eyeglass case that may have held the poison syringe—a syringe likely now on the roof of the Reptile House or in the display. Nick closed the briefcase just as two men entered the office, the security guard whom he had seen earlier waiting just outside the door in the break room.

One of the men wore the blue uniform of a San Diego policeman, the second a brown sports coat and khaki pants, apparently a detective. He was short and balding, and his eyes were bright. He flipped open a black badge holder.

"I am Detective Cruz, and this is Corporal Tiegen. May I ask your name?"

"Dr. Nicholas Turner," Nick said, sitting up straighter and holding out his hand. They shook.

"Dr. Turner," Cruz said, "I hear that you may have information about this rather dramatic death?"

"So he is dead?" Nick asked.

"They haven't been able to get him out yet, and it's not safe for the EMTs to go in, so he's not been pronounced. But he's dead. Terrible way to go, alive after the fall according to the witnesses and quite able to experience, well..."

"I can tell you all that you will need, but first, I think that you should call the FBI," Nick said.

Cruz frowned. "This is our jurisdiction, Doctor."

"The dead man is a Russian national and a terrorist. This agent at the Philadelphia office knows about him." Nick handed Cruz a note with Special Agent Jankiewicz's name and phone number.

Cruz looked at the paper and frowned more. He looked up at Nick. "I will call him, then we can talk."

"Her," said Nick. "The Special Agent is a 'her,' Elizabeth."

Cruz stepped into the break room to make the call and

Sean took the opportunity to educate more about snakes.

"If the enclosure were not so large and the roof wide open, we could have used 5 percent isoflurane gas. Probably the safest way to deal with a group of angry vipers, though we don't need to use it very often. Mostly for one snake in a shift box. I don't envy Malcolm right now."

Cruz returned. "She was not as surprised as I would have thought that you are in San Diego with a dead Russian. She says that she is quite anxious to speak with you. She is going to get on the next flight but will also send someone from the San Diego office right now." Cruz pulled a chair closer, drawing a small blue ring-bound notebook and pen from the inner pocket of his coat. "Why don't you tell me the story?"

So, Nick began.

CHAPTER 34

Nick had just finished telling his story to Detective Cruz when FBI Special Agent Calvin Rugsteller entered the Reptile House office. Nick repeated the entire story for the lanky Special Agent while Cruz left to speak with witnesses. Nick had reiterated to Cruz the need for great care around the syringe, which was probably somewhere on the roof. Nick also recognized that the syringe and a possible additional one or two in Yatovsky's briefcase were the best evidence that Nick's life had been threatened on the Skyfari. This and witnesses.

Nick was still answering Rugsteller's questions when the uniformed San Diego policeman appeared in the doorway. Nick was escorted to the main office of the Zoo, passing Cruz speaking to an Asian-American family near the Reptile House entrance, notebook and pen in hand. Rugsteller stayed behind with Yatovsky's briefcase. Nick was guided into a windowless meeting room and was asked to hand over his phone, passport, and wallet. He considered objecting but chose not to, as he was confident that his story would be supported by witnesses and by Special Agent Jankiewicz. The policeman stood outside the door.

Two hours passed, Nick putting his chin to his chest and closing his eyes and dozing, a talent developed from years as a surgical resident. At one point a thick green snake appeared in a dream and he woke with a start, but he drifted off again. The room was warm and he had no idea how long he would be made to wait.

Nick looked at his watch when Cruz and the Special Agent rapped on the door jamb: four p.m.

"The witnesses corroborated your story, Dr. Turner, particularly the family in the Skyfari car behind yours. They saw the large man in a suit leap onto the thinner man, the struggle, the plunge. We also found the syringe on the roof of the Reptile House, broken but still wet inside. There was a second syringe in a case in the briefcase, so these will be analyzed."

"You must have found the notebook in the briefcase, too," Nick said. "After my story, you understand its importance."

"Yes, we have it," Rugsteller said. "Now, you are not under arrest, but I am going to ask you to stay in San Diego tonight and to drive with me to our Field Office tomorrow to meet with Special Agent Jankiewicz. She also asked that we keep your passport and driver's license—with your permission—as she does not seem to trust you as much as we do."

"I can't understand why not," Nick said without any facial expression.

"You may keep your wallet and phone. Short of arresting you, we can't keep you from calling anyone," said Rugsteller. "I'll drive you to your hotel."

Cruz did not look happy, but he said nothing as Nick and Rugsteller left the room and walked towards the front gate of the Zoo. The detective still had a body to deal with.

At the Marriott Nick went straight to the Business Center. He made another copy of the list from Yatovsky's notebook, wrote a cover letter, and sealed both in a large envelope. Then he flipped open his phone and called Ronnie Smithwick. Nick was alone in the Business Center, though he looked out through the glass walls, half expecting to see Rugsteller. Or worse, Cruz.

"Hello, Smithwick here," came the cheery voice.

"Ronnie, this is Nick Turner."

"Holy shit, Nick, where are you?"

"I'm in San Diego, of course. And I just left a dead Russian at the San Diego Zoo." Nick smiled, imagining Ronnie's face as he digested these words.

"San Diego Zoo, dead Russian! Bloody hell, Nick. It's Saturday evening, but Edward and I have only had one drink, so I can't be imagining this."

"I will tell you the whole story in detail when I get back," Nick said, "but for now, please allow me to give you the high points. I need you to do something tomorrow."

"Okay, okay, are you all right?"

"I'm fine. But I still can't rest until I am sure that Anna is safe. Here are the basics. We learned that the Russian surgeon kept a list of all of the orphanage children and he marked those in whom he had implanted a plastic chip with a red backward R; you know, the Cyrillic backward R letter."

"Who is 'we,'" Smithwick asked.

"Dina and I. I will tell you about her later, too. So, we went to his hunting lodge inside the Arctic Circle and were chased by some thugs onto a frozen lake, but he had already left for the Society of Thoracic Surgeons annual conference in San Diego, and he always keeps the notebook with him. So, I flew to San Diego and confronted him."

"Wait, wait, wait," Smithwick said. "Hunting lodge, frozen lake, thugs?"

"I didn't even tell you about the Smiling Mink strip club and Tanya getting tortured and escaping through a Russian church and more. But listen, he agreed to meet me at the Zoo, but then he tried to kill me, but, instead, he was killed by poisonous snakes, and I got the notebook."

"Poisonous fucking snakes!" Smithwick said. "Nick, do you realize what you are saying? This is not like you; you don't make things up. Some think that you have little imagination, if you must know."

"I copied the list of children's names, but, of course, they are all in Russian, and I cannot be sure about the dates. But many of them have the red R next to them and one of those might be Anna. I have to stay here to meet with the FBI tomorrow so I am mailing a copy to you overnight. I also included the name, address, and phone number of Sandra Rosenthal, a former patient's wife who can get them translated for you. That way, we will not waste time. Can you give me your home address? Tomorrow is Sunday, so they have to deliver to your home."

"It's 204 South Aspen Street," Smithwick said. "It's one of those small but elegant houses in town. Like me, small but elegant."

"Thank you, Ronnie," Nick said. "You are a great friend. I promise I will tell you all of the details soon. And you know, I am finding that we all have powers within us that only come out when we are forced to protect a loved one."

Nick wrote Smithwick's home address on the envelope, then went to the front desk and paid for overnight Federal Express delivery. He was tempted to get something to eat but he wanted more to speak with Anna and Dina. He took the elevator to his room, took off his shoes, and stretched out on the bed. It seemed like days since he had been in the room, though it had only been that morning.

Anna herself answered on the second ring. "Daddy! Are you coming home?"

"Almost certainly, I will be home late tomorrow. I am in San Diego at a surgical convention and I have one more thing that I must do in the morning. Then I should be able to fly home. But it will probably be very late by the time I get home, so don't wait up." Nick had realized that his car was at JFK, so he would have to fly there and then drive home to Glaston. Given the time difference, it could be after midnight when he got home.

"Only if you promise to wake me when you come in," Anna said.

"Absolutely. I miss you so much, Anna," Nick said. This entire adventure had been for Anna, and it was almost over. Even if she needed an operation, she should be fine, and Nick would know that it was an operation that had to be done, not a blind exploration on a supposition. "I will wake you and give you a giant hug."

"Mrs. Pennington and I just watched 'Touched by an Angel' on TV. The episode was called 'A Time for Every Purpose,' which is from the Bible. It was a good one. I already had my pajamas on, and it is very cold outside, but we sat under a blanket on the couch and ate popcorn, and it was fun."

"I can hardly wait to do that with you," Nick said. He really, really meant it.

Dina answered on the second ring, too, a little breathless, "Da?" and before Nick's response came over the line, "Slushaya vas."

"Dina, this is Nick."

"Neek, Neek, are you all right? I am so worried."

"I am fine. I am in San Diego. I got the notebook, and Yatovsky is dead."

"Neek, what did you do?" Nina asked, her voice rising. Nick had a vision of her beautiful face animated by this shock.

"I did not kill him," Nick said. "In fact, he tried to kill me. Please sit down, and I will tell you the unbelievable story. But before I do that, I want you to know that I miss you very much. I have not been able to stop thinking about you. Are you safe?"

"I have not gone out, and they do not know where I live, so I am fine. But I worry so much about you."

"I am fine, and I hope to be able to fly home tomorrow," Nick said. "I also miss Anna very much. But let me tell you what happened." He told Dina about confronting Yatovsky at the Convention Center and reluctantly agreeing to meet at the Zoo the next day. "He loves animals, of course."

"Yes," Dina said. "He loves to shoot them and stuff them."

Nick told her about meeting the Russian and getting on the Skyfari ride.

"Then he jumped at me with a syringe in his hand, intending to inject me with some poison or nerve agent. It would appear to others that I had just passed out in the car, and he would get away. Apparently, he has access to such substances, and they would not be detected by airport security."

"My God," Dina gasped.

"Well," Nick said, "I grappled with him, and he was much stronger, but I got my runner's legs under him and pushed him into a somersault over the edge of the car. Do you understand 'somersault'?"

"Yes, sy-ta," Dina said. "Did he fall?"

"We were just above the Reptile House, nearing the end of the ride, and he fell through the roof of the building, actually through a glass skylight, directly into a cage full of poisonous snakes."

"Snakes!" Dina exclaimed.

"I told you this would be unbelievable, but it is true," Nick said. "The snakes bit him, and he died. His briefcase was still in the cab, and I was able to find the notebook and copy the list of children."

"Snakes is a terrible way to die," Dina said. "But what he did to children was terrible also. Was Anna on the list?"

"I mailed a copy of the list home to be translated by someone I know there. I could not tell for sure about Anna. But there were a number of names with a red 'Yah' next to them, just as Tanya said."

"Oh, Neek, I am so glad that you are okay. I am in pain to

not be with you. Where are you now?"

"Police came, of course, but after a lot of talking and speaking with witnesses, they let me go back to my hotel," Nick said. "But I must meet with the FBI in the morning. The Special Agent from Philadelphia is flying here, the one who knows about the plastic chips and smallpox. She has been leaving messages on my phone. I could not speak to her then for fear of the FBI scaring Yatovsky and his colleagues and driving them into hiding. I would never have gotten the notebook and the list."

"Oh, my Neek, what you have been through," Dina said.

"What we both have been through. Did you already forget being chased through the streets of Moscow and then over a frozen lake? You have been a brave partner, Dina. You did not ask for any of this. We are almost done. I just have to meet with the FBI, then confirm that Anna is safe."

"Do you think that I can leave my flat now?" Dina asked. "I am getting restless."

"With Yatovsky dead and the FBI getting involved, it should be safe. Even if Maks and Viktor are still alive, they will be getting no orders from the surgeon. Maybe do not venture far for a little longer."

"Please call me when you get home, Neek. I miss you."

"I miss you, Dina. Spokoynoy nochi."

"It is daytime here, Neek. Dasvidaniya to me, and to you spokoynoy nochi."

He fell asleep later thinking of that first night in her kitchen, when Dina looked up at him, eyes bright, her lovely face flushed with the heat.

CHAPTER 35

Nick arrived first at the FBI San Diego Field Office, driven from his hotel by Special Agent Calvin Rugsteller. Nick was anxious to get home to Anna, but he understood the need to explain what he knew and to suggest what needed to be done for all the children whose names in Yatovsky's ledger followed the red Я. He had been thinking a lot about the latter topic.

He also hoped that he would be debriefed rather than interrogated. After all, they were all on the same side in this, all had a common goal. True, he had not answered calls from Special Agent Jankiewicz. But could that really be construed as withholding information or impeding an investigation? Nick had no idea.

Nick had packed and checked out of the Marriott before Rugsteller arrived, trusting that he could find a flight home after the morning meeting. He was waiting outside the hotel doors when the FBI sedan pulled up. Nick tossed his bag onto the back seat and climbed into the passenger seat, happy to see that the tall Rugsteller already had the seat pushed back. They drove down the curving driveway, then north in the direction of the airport, then onto Interstate 5 North.

Nick turned towards Rugsteller. "I assumed that the FBI Office would be in the city," Nick said.

"It was near Balboa Park, where we were yesterday until the mid-seventies," Rugsteller said, mirrored sunglasses hiding his eyes as he looked to his right at Nick. "Then we moved to the Sorrento Valley. The old site was popular with J. Edgar Hoover himself. He came to this area every year, sometimes for an entire month. He would have his annual physical exam in La Jolla and would often stay there. He loved the horses, and the Hotel Del Charro was close to the Del Mar Racetrack. It was also discreet, with some free-standing cabins. Hoover and Clyde Tolson always stayed in Bungalow A."

"Is the hotel still there?" Nick asked.

"No, it closed in the early seventies also. Now, there are condos. But J. Edgar didn't care since he had a heart attack and died in 1972." Nick had misjudged Rugsteller; the Special Agent was quite garrulous.

"Hoover was a dog-lover," Rugsteller continued. "Cairn Terriers and Beagles, I'm told. Most years, they came with him."

Nick saw signs to La Jolla and the University of California San Diego, then they were off the Interstate and soon pulling into the Field Office parking lot. Nick took his bag with him as he followed Rugsteller into the building, the bag then run through a metal detector. They entered a stairwell and climbed one flight, then down a long hall and into a simple small meeting room. Nick looked around as the Special Agent went to get each of them coffee and a bagel.

A rectangular table filled the bare-walled room, a table which could accommodate only six people comfortably. The room did have large windows looking onto the front of the Field Office site. Nick tossed his bag into a corner, then sat on one long side of the table nearest the windows as Rugsteller set down their coffee cups. Nick eagerly bit into his cinnamon-raisin bagel and wondered what Special Agent Jankiewicz would be like.

It took Beth Jankiewicz less than ten minutes to travel from the Holiday Inn Sorrento Valley to the FBI Field Office by taxi.

It had taken longer for the desk clerk to find a cab on Sunday morning, and Beth had even considered walking the short distance. With flight delays, she had gotten to the hotel late the night before, but after a morning shower, she felt ready for the day.

Dr. Nicholas Turner had arrived before her, and he rose from his seat as she entered the meeting room, extending his hand to shake, smiling, brown eyes direct. "Special Agent Jankiewicz, I'm Dr. Nick Turner. I'm so pleased to meet you." He was tall and slim, his grip surprisingly strong. Not bull-strong like her brothers, but strong enough for a thin guy.

"Dr. Turner, Rugsteller," Beth said, shaking the latter's hand as he finished chewing something. She did not smile. She wanted Dr. Nicholas Turner to understand how pissed she was that he had ignored her calls. Until she was satisfied otherwise, anyway, it appeared that he had consciously ignored them. She would get to that. "Please, sit."

Beth sat with her back to the door, opposite Nick, taking a pad and pen out of her valise. Nick silently watched her purposeful movements, and her blonde head bowed over her preparations. She was tall, trim, athletic, her shoulders relatively broad—maybe a pole vaulter in college, maybe a swimmer. She wrote something at the top of the pad, probably a title on one side and the date opposite. She then looked up, all business, her eyes focused on Nick's.

"Dr. Turner," she said, "had you ever met the Corbetts before January 21, 2003?"

"No," Nick said. "I may have purchased something from their hardware store when I first bought our house, but I don't remember ever seeing Sam there."

"But you seem to be on a first-name basis," Beth said.

"I only call a patient or family member by their first name if they ask me to. Or if they are a child." Nick was not surprised that Special Agent Jankiewicz was a little argumentative. But equanimity was one of Nick's strengths.

"So, you met them at the hospital and took their son to the operating room. Did he definitely need the operation?"

"There were other options, which I discussed with them," Nick said, "but we mutually agreed that operation was best."

"And if you hadn't operated, their son might have died of smallpox," Beth said.

"That's not why I operated, of course," Nick said, "but knowing what I know now, that would have been a possibility."

"What did you think the plastic object was when you found it?"

"I had no idea," Nick said. "It took a very bright Pathologist to figure it out."

"Yes, I have spoken with Dr. Smithwick," Beth said. "So, let me save some time, Doctor, and ask why you immediately flew to Russia after learning this information?"

"Alexander Corbett had three small scars on his chest indicating probable prior surgery, and the plastic had to get inside him somehow. When I asked the Corbetts about this, I learned that Alex had been adopted from Russia and that he had undergone some chest procedure before he was adopted, possibly due to a congenital abnormality. The fact that this surgery had been performed in the orphanage itself was a surprise, but it seemed likely that the plastic had been introduced then. When I learned that it might contain smallpox, it drove me to Russia."

"Wait a minute," Beth said. "Why did that information compel you to drop everything and fly overseas?" Her gaze was fixed on Nick's eyes.

"Because my daughter, Anna, was also adopted from Russia. And she has the same three scars."

Beth just stared, trying to keep her face neutral.

"So," she said, "you thought that your daughter might have such a plastic object, and maybe even smallpox, inside her."

"A time bomb." Nick looked just as intently across the table. "And she is my life."

"Why didn't you contact some government agency that deals with bioterrorism, say, for example, the FBI?" Beth asked.

"It was obvious that the people who did this, whether some rouge surgeon or an organization, were unethical, criminal, and frankly, evil," Nick said. "Any hint that they were being investigated would spook them. Records would be destroyed, and the people would hide somewhere. I would never know whether Anna was at risk, and putting her through an unnecessary exploratory operation had little appeal. Also, I would have had to first convince the FBI that this incredible scenario was true and then wait for the wheels of government to start turning. I pictured a tiny plastic box dissolving more each day that I waited."

Beth remained silent, so Nick went on. "I tried calling the orphanages, but adoptees' medical records are sketchy at best, and I wasn't getting anywhere. I had to go myself."

"What was your plan," Beth asked. "You are only one person."

"That was my advantage. I could stay under the radar. I could ask innocent questions, find records, find the surgeon." Nick put his forearms on the table and leaned forward as he told the story he had told several times. He would just hit the highlights.

"I visited Anna's old orphanage and learned that the surgeon, Yatovsky, had operated there also. A person there directed us..."

"Us?" Beth broke in.

"A Russian woman, Dina, was my guide," Nick said, an image of Dina from their first meeting in the airport flashing in his mind. "So, we were directed to Yatovsky's former nurse and lover, Tanya, who told us about Yatovsky's notebook. The man was obsessive about his list of operations, and he placed a red 'yah,' a backward capital R, next to those kids with the smallpox implant. That sent us north to his hunting lodge, but the notebook was not there, so I flew to San Diego and the STS Conference he always attends. I confronted him at the conference and met him yesterday at the zoo, where he tried to kill me but fell to his death instead. And we have the notebook, or rather, you have the notebook." Nick sat back.

"Have you ever considered a career in the FBI?" Beth said, shaking her head. "And do you expect me to believe all of that? By the way, did you consciously ignore my calls?"

"Yes, I did." Nick had never been able to lie. "Until I learned all that I could to save Anna and the other kids I couldn't risk the government driving Yatovsky into hiding."

"And Dr. Smithwick knew where you were and didn't tell me," Beth said. "I believe that could be construed as impeding an investigation."

"Ronnie only did that upon my begging him for the sake of my daughter," Nick said.

"Another thing," said Beth, "was the surgeon working alone?" This clearly was bioterrorism, possibly on a large scale.

"Tanya, his former nurse, was convinced there was a wealthy oligarch; she referred to him as The Eel," Nick said. "That would make sense since Yatovsky had no other job and he lived lavishly. His hunting lodge was world-class, and he had Mercedes cars and Range Rovers, bodyguards, and access to private planes. But Yatovsky was motivated by more than money. He has a pathologic ego; he felt mistreated by the medical establishment, and he felt that his intellect and surgical talent had never been appreciated. In fact, his ability to perform video-assisted thoracic surgery years ago, in an orphanage room, is pretty impressive."

"The FBI has a lot of work to do," Beth said, writing quickly, wondering how much of a role she would have in this work. "In the meantime, what is your recommendation, as a chest surgeon, with respect to the children?"

"I have thought a lot about this," Nick said. "We cannot

waste any time in removing the plastic objects from children whose names are marked with a yah in Yatovsky's notebook. Alex Corbett's plastic was almost completely hydrolyzed on one side and some of the children may have had the object implanted before his was. Even garden variety smallpox has no treatment or vaccine and this smallpox may have been modified, what you would call weaponized."

"Who would do these operations?" Beth asked.

"Any competent Thoracic Surgeon in the child's town can do it after they understand where to find the object and what to do with it. I can make a video of a case—Anna's will be one of the first such cases if it is necessary—and I can make myself available to speak with any surgeon. I am about 95 percent sure that the object will be in the same location in each child, beneath the pleura of the apex of the left chest cavity; there may even be adhesions of the lung to this spot, pointing the way. In the end, the surgery will be the least difficult aspect of this."

"What do you mean?" Beth asked.

"Your job, I mean the FBI's job, will be to convince parents that their perfectly healthy child needs an operation. If you point out that their child was adopted from Russia and has three small left chest scars, it will buy you some credibility. Again, I will be happy to speak with anyone. But your real problem will be keeping a lid on this story and preventing panic. The surgeons will be good about confidentiality since that is ingrained, but when the parents hear 'smallpox,' there could be problems. And if the press hears..."

"You really have thought about this," Beth said.

"Finally, the government should cover all of the medical expenses for these children."

"Of course," Beth said. "You know, another thought just popped into my thoughts: what if parents refuse the operation?"

"I told you that your job is harder," Nick said. "If we truly believe that a child harbors smallpox waiting to infect, then that child is a huge public health risk. I don't know what the laws are now, but years ago, a person could be incarcerated or quarantined if they were such a risk and knowingly refused treatment. Remember the story of Typhoid Mary."

"I doubt that that would be practical, especially for a child. Plus, parents would indeed go to the press," Beth said.

"There will probably be very few children in that category, that is, having had the implant and refusing removal," Nick said. "Maybe they could be compulsively monitored and then isolated if any symptom appears. Plus, the CDC and other labs can get to work on a vaccine against this particular variant."

Beth found herself unable to be angry at this dedicated father. Everything that he did was for his daughter, with no hint of artifice or personal gain in his story. She would be making phone calls to superiors all day, to the highest levels of the Bureau, as this would probably be the biggest case of her career, a career just beginning.

Nick pushed his chair back and asked, "May I go now? I need to get back to Anna." He looked over at Rugsteller. "I would be grateful for a ride or a taxi to the airport." He stood and looked across to Special Agent Jankiewicz. "Plus, as you know, I am only a phone call away."

Beth could not suppress a smile.

CHAPTER 36

Two weeks after returning from San Diego Nick walked into the Pathology Lab in the basement of Glaston Memorial Hospital, startling Smithwick leaning over his microscope. The small man looked up, his face breaking into a huge smile. "Nick! How is Anna doing?"

"She's great, Ronnie," Nick said. "Not back at school yet but she probably could be. Just a little sore, of course."

The list from Yatovsky's notebook, when translated, had clearly shown a red Я next to Anna's name. Nick sat with her and explained that a small piece of plastic had been left inside her when she had undergone an operation in Russia, and it needed to be removed. His partner, Dr. Olson, would do it, and she would stay one night in the hospital.

"Why don't you do it, Daddy? Isn't this what you do?" she had asked.

"It is what I do, but it is not a good idea for surgeons to operate on their own family members. You tend to treat them differently, which is not good. You know Dr. Olson, though, and I will be just outside the OR the whole time."

The case had gone fine, and Ken had recorded the whole thing. Anna stayed one night in the hospital and had been home for nearly a week, anxious to get back to her classmates.

"You know, Nick," Smithwick said, "I indulged myself with a quick look under the dissecting microscope, wearing my full protective gear, when Ken personally delivered the plastic object. The one side was definitely hydrolyzing, so it is really, really good that it is out. I packed it up tight and sent it to the CDC right away."

"And I sent the video of the case to Special Agent Jankiewicz," Nick said, "so that she can send copies to any surgeon who ends up doing one of these cases. The operation is perfectly straightforward; one just needs to know where to look for the object. And, one must be extremely careful in handling it, of course. Ken's voice-over recommends not grasping the object with any force, and trying to get it into an endoscopic bag with minimal trauma."

"Are you aware of other operations being performed?" Smithwick asked. "I glanced at the list that you sent me from the notebook and there appeared to be quite a few names with red backward R's next to them."

"There were four main sections, corresponding to the four orphanages to which Yatovsky traveled," Nick said. "Each orphanage had one to three pages and there were about eight names on every page, everything written in precise small script. So, sixty names in all, in chronological order under each orphanage heading, starting in 1996 and continuing to the present. Both Anna and Alex Corbett had procedures in the first year, so they have had the plastic longer than anyone else."

"All the more reason to get it out now," Smithwick said.

"In fact, there was one child who died that same year, 1996, from Alex's orphanage. Tanya's father knew about this since he had driven the child and two nurses to Yatovsky's boathouse. He said that it was a horrible death, and he did not want to talk about it anymore. He crossed himself about six times."

"So how many total children had an R next to their names?" Smithwick asked.

"I counted forty-one," Nick said. "I'm still not sure why he did sham operations on the other nineteen. We don't know if they have an object without smallpox or no object at all.

Maybe it was just to keep us guessing in the case that one was discovered since, without the notebook key, all would need to be removed. These cases were scattered among the others with no evident pattern. Even these kids will need to be monitored closely."

"So why isn't the FBI scrambling to get all of the other objects removed?" Smithwick asked.

"It took them several days to get the notebook translated," Nick said. "They translated the whole thing, whereas we just concentrated on the list of children's names. Apparently, there is a lot of writing about Yatovsky's brilliance and the many slights against him and more. Special Agent Jankiewicz is still handling the domestic part of the case, and others will be doing the overseas work. She sounded pumped to even be leading the USA work since it turns out that she is quite junior in the ranks."

"I spoke with her on the phone a couple of times," Smithwick said, "and I later learned that she even visited Glaston one day, speaking with the Corbetts but no one else. She always sounded very business-like, little humor."

"I think that she has a sense of humor," Nick said, remembering their parting words, "but as I said, she has just begun her FBI career, so she is still a little by the book. I really haven't spoken with her much. I get the impression that her superiors want to get the messaging right so that they can control any reaction if word leaks out. I have warned Dina that she will almost certainly be interviewed at some point, and she has warned Tanya. Tanya, by the way, the former nurse who helped us and got hurt in the process, has moved back with her father up north."

"And how is your Russian princess, Miss Dina?"

"She is very special, Ronnie. Don't tell anyone, but we speak almost every night. She is hard at work so that she can graduate this spring."

"I will look forward to meeting her," Smithwick said.

"We will see," Nick said. "By the way, I also learned from Special Agent Jankiewicz that Yatovsky tried to kill me with a very sophisticated neurotoxin. This is more evidence, in my mind, and I am sure in hers, that there is an organization with significant resources behind all of this, maybe even the Russian government. Whoever has a vaccine against this variant would have the world at their feet if smallpox broke out."

"It's ironic, don't you think," Smithwick said, "that the Russian got injected with poison just after he tried to inject you with poison? Divine justice."

"I can still picture him in the cage with those snakes," Nick said, shivering involuntarily. "A horrible death deserved or not."

"I looked up Ethiopian Mountain Adder," Smithwick said. "Beautiful snake, really. Cleopatra should have chosen such a beautiful snake."

"I think that the beauty was lost on Yatovsky," Nick said.

"So, what are you going to do for your next adventure?" Smithwick asked. "It will be hard to top Russian strip clubs, thugs with knives, beautiful accomplices, cars plunging into frozen lakes, and death by snakes. Just routine life for the typical community hospital Thoracic Surgeon."

"I am looking forward to pizza and movies with Anna, and helping the people of Glaston by curing cancer when I can and relieving suffering when I can, and sleeping in my own bed, and running in the park. You know, I feel like Bilbo returning to the Shire after his great adventure, looking forward to his house in the hill and his pipe and good food."

"I am more hobbit-like than you are, my friend, and not just in stature," Smithwick said. "Have you ever seen my feet?"

"No," said Nick, "and I don't want to."

This day in mid-February was bright and clear and bitter cold. As he left the hospital and headed toward Ballenger Park,

Nick was happy that he had stored his running jacket, gloves, and wool cap in his OR locker, ready to put on today before he went down the back stairs and out. He started out slowly, his breath visible, then falling into his old confident stride. He had not run for a number of days, but then, he had been busy with other activities: breaking and entering, sending an occupied Range Rover to the bottom of a lake, narrowly escaping death at the hands of a maniac, things like that.

Tanya had told Dina that there had been no mention in the Murmansk Oblast of a Range Rover or bodies. Of course, the lake was still frozen, the ice still thick enough to drive on. Nor had Tanya's old friends at the Smiling Mink seen Maks or Viktor. Almost certainly, they were at the bottom of the lake with the car.

Whatever organization they had worked for had likely gone to ground, remaining out of sight and quiet. At a minimum, they realized that neither the surgeon nor the thugs had resurfaced, and the organization might have learned that the surgeon was dead. The Russian government, particularly, had discreet sources in the United States. This organization would have to be stopped since nothing would prevent them from doing something like this again, working against a different country, further modifying the virus, who knows. Fortunately for Nick, this was not his problem. Anna was safe, and that was everything for Nick.

Nick had been so focused on Anna that until now, running past the lake in Ballenger Park, he had not considered that he might have saved dozens of children, maybe thousands of people those children would have infected, maybe millions of people in a world pandemic of weaponized smallpox. No one in the FBI had called to thank him; no one had offered a reward or a medal.

Nor did he care about any of that and he certainly did not want money or a medal. His daughter was safe, and that was all that mattered. Nick was ready to get back into his routine in his small city. One patient at a time.

His thoughts may have been prophetic, as his pager went off as he was running up toward the bandstand. It was the ER number, of course. Welcome back. He stopped at the bandstand and let his breathing slow, flipped open his phone, and dialed the number. "Dr. Turner, answering your page."

"Let me get the doctor," said a female voice.

"Nick, this is Carolyn. I have a seventy-two-year-old man with an empyema, fever to 102, white count 17,000, blood pressure soft, tachycardiac, chest full of fluid. We're giving him fluids and antibiotics, but he is going to need it drained. On CT scan it appears to be loculated. It seems that he has been trying to ignore pneumonia for some time."

One patient at a time. Nick could handle this.

"I'll be right there."

EPILOGUE

The interior of her Dad's Accord was getting very hot, parked along the driveway leading to the International Terminal at JFK Airport. He would have to turn on the car soon simply to run the air conditioning. What a difference this July day was compared to the last time that he had driven to JFK, in January, the start of what he sometimes called his Great Adventure.

Anna had chosen to sit in the back seat with Maggie the dog. Actually, Maggie the black Labrador puppy, as she was only five months old. Housebroken, fortunately, but still a puppy, tail wagging vigorously every time that her Dad looked into the back. He clearly loved Maggie, although it was true that Anna had used her recovery from surgery to her advantage, as any child innately would, to press for a dog.

Anna herself was a bundle of energy today, barely able to contain herself while waiting for Dina to arrive. She had bathed that morning, this timing unusual for her, and had brushed her straight hair again and again during breakfast. She had eaten little and had pushed to leave early for JFK, although the plane from Sheremetyevo International did not arrive until one p.m.

Anna and Dina had spoken on the phone many times and a photo had arrived in the mail last month but that could not compare to seeing her Daddy's "girlfriend" with her own eyes. This was a big event in Anna's life and, although Dina would only stay for two weeks, there were sightseeing trips planned to New York City, the Delaware shore where her Dad grew up, and more.

Her Dad's phone buzzed, and he flipped it open and said a few words. He turned around and looked at Anna after closing the phone. "She's here." He was smiling broadly. He turned on the car and they drove up the driveway and parked near the terminal's main doors, in shade now and much cooler. They got out and stood on the broad concrete sidewalk, Maggie on a leash but pressed against Anna's leg, panting a little.

And then Dina appeared at the door, then running toward her Dad, suitcase abandoned halfway there, tears in her eyes, calling "Neek." She leapt into her Dad's arms, and they kissed and kissed some more. Anna had never seen her Dad kiss a woman like this. Then they just hugged, Dina's head on her Dad's chest, her eyes closed.

Anna looked down at Maggie, then up at her father, hugging Dina, and she just smiled and smiled.

Acknowledgments

The first chapters of *Thorax* were written as preparatory exercises for a seminar, Medical Fiction Writing for Physicians. Held on a brisk September weekend in Cape Cod twenty years ago, the course was led by best-selling medical thriller authors Tess Gerritsen and the late Michael Palmer. Tess has continued to write terrific novels and has remained supportive of new authors, including me.

The professionals at Atmosphere Press have been a delight, supportive but not overbearing or proscriptive. Their *raison d'etre* has been to publish author-centric books, leaving the writer firmly in charge of his or her work; they have succeeded in this. Although I have written and rewritten *Thorax* over two decades, Developmental Editor Jonathan Smith still found ways to make it better. Cover artist Ronaldo Alves worked closely with me on our bold and somewhat ominous design, writing coach Tammy Letherer helped polish the back cover preview text, proofreader Chris Knight proved to be more fastidious than a surgeon, and Managing Editor Alex Kale coordinated the entire process. Although the industry has recently touted author-centric publishing, Atmosphere Press has been doing this for a long time.

I grew up in a family of readers, exemplified by my father, a West Virginia coal miner and later coal industry leader, who kept a stack of books next to his chair, often reading one per night, my mother checking them in and out of the library a dozen at a time. My four siblings and I always had books within reach.

Thorax is dedicated to our daughter, Katherine, whom I call Katya. Adopted from a Russian orphanage inside the Arctic Circle, she never looked back, a model of unfailing kindness and generosity of spirit that, throughout her life, has had people shaking their heads in wonder.

And most of all, deep gratitude to my wife of fifty years, Diane, who understands why it took me twenty years to finish this work (patients always came before writing and often before family events), who shared me with the dawn operating room and the midnight desk.

About Atmosphere Press

Founded in 2015, Atmosphere Press was built on the principles of Honesty, Transparency, Professionalism, Kindness, and Making Your Book Awesome. As an ethical and author-friendly hybrid press, we stay true to that founding mission today.

If you're a reader, enter our giveaway for a free book here:

SCAN TO ENTER
BOOK GIVEAWAY

If you're a writer, submit your manuscript for consideration here:

SCAN TO SUBMIT
MANUSCRIPT

And always feel free to visit Atmosphere Press and our authors online at atmospherepress.com. See you there soon!

About the Author

Mark Katlic, M.D., is a Phi Beta Kappa graduate of Washington & Jefferson College and an Alpha Omega Alpha graduate of the Johns Hopkins University School of Medicine. He completed residencies in Surgery and Cardiothoracic Surgery at the Massachusetts General Hospital, then practiced Thoracic Surgery for forty years, first in Northeastern Pennsylvania and then in Baltimore. He was Chair of Surgery for LifeBridge Health System in Baltimore until his retirement in 2024. Mark lives on a farm north of the city with his wife of fifty years, Diane, Tux the dog, four cats, two horses, and the photogenic fauna of field and forest.

Milton Keynes UK
Ingram Content Group UK Ltd.
UKHW011822140624
444031UK00010B/145/J

9 798891 323322